# Money Game

Smoove Dolla

**Lock Down Publications and Ca$h Presents**

# Money Game

**A Novel by *Smoove Dolla***

Smoove Dolla

**Lock Down Publications**
P.O. Box 944
Stockbridge, Ga 30281
www.lockdownpublications.com

**Lock Down Publications**
**Like our page on Facebook: Lock Down Publications @**
**www.facebook.com/lockdownpublications.ldp**
Book interior design by: **Shawn Walker**
Edited by: **Tamira Butler**

# Stay Connected with Us!

Text **LOCKDOWN** to 22828 to stay up-to-date with new releases, sneak peaks, contests and more...
Thank you!

Smoove Dolla

# Submission Guideline.

Submit the first three chapters of your completed manuscript to ldpsubmissions@gmail.com, subject line: Your book's title. The manuscript must be in a .doc file and sent as an attachment. Document should be in Times New Roman, double spaced and in size 12 font. Also, provide your synopsis and full contact information. If sending multiple submissions, they must each be in a separate email.

Have a story but no way to send it electronically? You can still submit to LDP/Ca$h Presents. Send in the first three chapters, written or typed, of your completed manuscript to:

LDP: Submissions Dept
P.O. Box 944
Stockbridge, Ga 30281

*DO NOT send original manuscript. Must be a duplicate.*

Provide your synopsis and a cover letter containing your full contact information.

Thanks for considering LDP and Ca$h Presents.

6

Money Game

## Acknowledgements

First and foremost, I want to thank the Supreme Architect of the Universe, Allah. I am so grateful that you created me. Thanks for my many talents and gifts that you have blessed me with. Thanks to CA$H for giving me a chance to be a part of the Lock Down family. The game is ours. Thanks to the two gorgeous women, my daughter, Anajhia, and my mother, Ebony, who have helped me in every way they possibly could. I love you both more than I can express. I apologize for all the wrongdoing I've done that has caused you to hurt in any way.

Thanks to Steve Harvey for inspiring me to follow the right path and pursue my dreams.

Oh man, let me tell you, I've had to write this same novel from scratch three times. The first time, the detectives confiscated it during a search warrant, and tried to use it as evidence on my case but couldn't. It was a hassle trying to get it back, so I gave up on it. The second time I wrote it, I trusted a so-called friend to hold it for me because I couldn't take it to prison with me. She ended up falling off on me after a couple months of me being in prison. It took me four months to get the courage to pick up a pen to start writing again for the third time. Without me having perseverance, you wouldn't be reading this novel right now.

I want to give a special shout out to everyone who has helped in any way, who has read the manuscript, for the feedback and encouraging me to continue to write. Shout out to Slim, Sky, True, Jabbar, Tre, Koolaid, DC, Flex, Big J out of South Law, Crystal, Erika, my daughter's mother Aviance, Brent, Fish, Bobby, Jonathan, Mikki, Cat Man, Aunt Grace, Aunt Kim, GG, Monique, Biscuit, Lashunda, Kee-Kee, marquis, Bird, Jackie, my father Marcus, Net, Baby Boy, Maya, Valirie, Tony Staxx aka Bruce Leroy, Mondo Money, Quicck, Antue, J, Trice, Bre'Anna, Taz, Money,

Frankie, Micheal Stanton, Mickey Royal, Grimy, Polo, Big Hen, JB, LP, Forever, AD, Los, Waco, Steve O, G-Raf, Compton, Cabagge, Rosewood, Black from 5th Ward, you next homie, Southwest, Bobo, Will, G-town and Fam, Magic, Kenny Red, Pimpin' Ken, Good game, Rosebudd, OG Slim, Know Love, Macknificent, Governor, OG Big L, Solo, 8 Ball, Me Me, Quicy, Keith, Young Lace, Candy Man.

Shout out to my homegirl Nitty out of Arlington, Texas, thanks for the support, love, and game you've given me. Shout out to QC. Thanks for everything. You are an amazing woman. I wish the best for you and yours.

Stay on the lookout for more work from me. I also write stage plays and movie scripts. Be on the lookout!

# Money Game

I learned in life that you have to play for keeps. Some niggas didn't realize until it was too late that this game was no joke. People who thought that way were either killed, or became drug addicts. Because of its addictive nature, the game turns you out to its lifestyle.

—Excerpt from:
*Rose Budd Bitter Dose*
*American Pimp*

Smoove Dolla

## Prologue

"Bobby, when I kick this do'e in, go in ready to bust. I'll be right behind you," Tunke repeated himself for the third time tonight, making sure his first cousin had the plan down pat.

"I got it man. I got it," Bobby responded, a bit annoyed by Tunke pressing him.

"Alright. You know what they did to the last niggas that tried to jack them. I know you don't wanna end up like them."

Bobby looked at Tunke like he was crazy. "I be damn if I get cut up and thrown in the dumpster. I do this shit, Tunke, man. Let's get this shit over with, bro," Bobby said while wrapping a black bandana around half of his face.

Once they stepped onto the porch of their target's apartment door, they got into position. Bobby stood with his pistol in both hands pointed at the door, with Tunke standing with his back against the door. Tunke knew once this door was kicked open, there was no turning back the hands of time, so they had to succeed in this. Plus, this was their only option at the moment to get some big money that would put them on their feet. In their minds, this was better than sticking up Mexican and white men for their wallets.

Tunke gave the door the kick of his life. Bobby walked in the doorway, after Tunke side stepped to the left. Bobby spotted Lil' Chris on the couch reaching for his automatic 12-gauge sawed-off shotgun, but before Lil' Chris could get a perfect aim, Bobby squeezed off two shots, missing him by a couple of inches, putting two holes into the old black leather couch.

Tunke went right behind Bobby, standing in the doorway, and started letting off a couple shots. He missed also. Tunke moved swiftly outside on the porch again before Lil' Chris dove to the floor and squeezed four shots towards the door. Bobby stuck his pistol inside the apartment and fired three shots in Lil' Chris' direction without looking. He hit nothing but the wall and couch again.

Black was in the kitchen whipping up crack when the door got kicked open and the shots started ringing, making him duck down on the side of the counter. Scooter was upstairs in the bathroom taking a shit when he heard the gunfire. With almost $65,000, about $13,000 worth of drugs in the apartment, and two of his closest homeboys all in jeopardy, he half-ass wiped himself to see what was going on downstairs. He flushed the toilet, rushed to pull up his pants, and then started creeping out the bathroom with his pistol in his hand. When he noticed he was clear, he walked towards the top of the stairs.

Tunke noticed someone raising a gun at them at the top of the stairs. He pushed Bobby out the doorway before he got shot, making him fall to the ground. Tunke rushed to the other side of the door just in time. Bullets flew an inch away from his head. Unable to handle the heat that was coming their way, Tunke couldn't think of anything else to do but run. "Run, nigga, run!" Tunke yelled at Bobby.

They both took off running as fast as they could from the porch in opposite directions. There was no way they could go in the same direction, with bullets coming out the door, and avoid being shot.

Seconds later, Lil' Chris and Scooter started running after Tunke because he was the only one they saw running. Once Tunke got around the building, he saw Bobby some yards ahead, so he followed behind him.

Lil' Chris and Scooter stopped at times to shoot at Tunke as he ran across the street, between cars and project buildings. Tunke stopped also and got three shots off to keep them at a distance, not hitting anyone but the wall, causing the bullets to ricochet to the ground.

There were a few people here and there outside in small crowds on this summer night. As soon as they heard gunfire, they did their best to avoid the bullets and scattered to safety. Bullets hit parked automobiles, a dumpster, and project buildings. Bobby was faster than Tunke and hit a corner thirteen seconds before he did. Once Tunke went around the corner, he didn't see Bobby anywhere. After running for 41 seconds as fast as he could, he stopped to catch his breath. While bent over, he looked around. There wasn't anyone's apartment around here that Tunke knew Bobby had gone in. Tunke thought he must have ran so fast down to the other end of the building and cut the corner.

When Tunke heard men talking, he started running again while looking back and ran right into a man named Tight game, who had just stepped off the porch of his younger brother's apartment, causing him to drop his lit Newport cigarette.

"Damn, youngin', watch where you going." After he made sure none of the ashes fell on his red tailor-made suit, he asked Tunke, "Why you running anyway? All them gunshots because of you?"

Tunke was speechless. He was shaken up from getting shot at, getting chased by some killers, and on top of that, he was worried about getting shot and killed.

"Calm down and catch yo' breath. Tell me what happened. Who you shooting at?" he asked Tunke.

"I gotta ge-get out of he-here. They tryna kill me."

They heard walking footsteps approaching them from behind. Tunke turned around quick and took two steps back. Tight Game noticed Scooter and Lil' Chris coming towards them, aiming their guns at Tunke. "Whoa, whoa, whoa, put them guns down. What's going on here?"

"This bitch-ass nigga tried to rob us, Tight game, man," Scooter said, heated.

"I understand y'all mad, but let him make it, y'all."

"Fuck naw! What I look like letting him make it when he tried to rob us? No, I can't do it, he good as smoke," he said, then pointed his gun at Tunke's head, making him more terrified than he already was.

"Now, Scooter, I don't mean to throw shit in your face. I must ask, though, tell me if I told you no or even hesitated when you wanted my bitch to drop that dope charge you caught two years ago?"

"No, you didn't."

"And Lil' Chris, I'm still getting your murder charge handled as well, where it will be dismissed. Just give me some more time. Chris, I didn't even trip on you not paying your bond payment in full on a charge like yours. I let you make it on the strength of I know you and we're from the same hood." Tight Game wasn't the type to do things for people then throw it in their faces. He reminded them of the favor that he had given them so he could get one out of them.

Tight Game was a known cross-country pimp with a lot of resources and the baddest hoes, who was the man in South Dallas, and one of the hottest, paid niggas in the city. He looked out for and supported hustlers and youngsters from Bunton, his hood where he grew up.

"Tight game, we appreciate that and all, but them two niggas would have robbed and killed us minutes ago if we didn't bust back. And you just want us to fo'get about it like it never happened."

"Not exactly. All I want is my favor in return. I helped y'all out for free. So, help me out and let him make it. He's only doing what he knows best to be his hustle. He getting money, just like y'all, but in a different way. Let him make it this time on the strength of me. If he tries it again, then kill him. It's as simple as that. But let me take care of him this time, y'all."

"Who gonna pay for the dope they fucked up? Black was whipping up $10,000 worth of crack when they came in. Somebody gonna have to pay, or I'ma lay him down right now for fucking off my money, Tight game," Lil' Chris declared angrily.

Tight Game pulled out a big stack and peeled off 100 hundred-dollar bills. "There, that should take care of the dope. Preciate it."

"Aight, aight, Tight game," he said, nodding his head while flipping through the bills. "This time, he good, but try that shit again, nigga, and I'ma have anotha body on my rap sheet. Come on, Scoota, let's shake the spot. I hope Black got all the shit out the spot by now."

"I hope so too, bro," Scooter said while turning around with Lil' Chris and running off in the opposite direction from Tunke and Tight game.

"Give me the gun, youngin'." Tunke looked in the direction they had gone. He couldn't see them anymore, but he could see their shadows getting smaller on the project's red brick wall. As he watched, his anxiety calmed inside of him, and he slowly released the grip on his .45.

# Money Game

Tunke was barely seventeen years old. He had never been shot at like that before. As far as getting shot at, the only bullets that came close to him were when he was with a group of Bonton Piru niggas beefing with some other gang or hood at a party or school game. So, of course, all this tonight made him very terrified. He released the gun into Tight Game's hand.

They both looked to their right, because they heard a door open. Bobby was walking out a door. "That's where you went to? Who stay there?" Tunke asked once Bobby walked up on them.

"It's a vacant," Bobby said.

Tunke got mad. "What! Why the fuck you didn't tell me to come in there with you, nigga? I coulda got killed a while ago."

"Shit, me too. I was scared, mane."

"But you do this shit tho. You outta there, bro," Tunke told Bobby.

"Whatever, Tunke. I'm gone. I'm goin' home," he said, then turned around and started running.

Tunke shook his head because of how his first cousin abandoned him. *Niggas will always let you down*, he said in his head as he watched Bobby run away.

"Don't worry about it, youngin'. Everything's goin' to be just fine. Come take a ride with me, I got something for you. I'ma 'bout to put you on some real game. A hustle I know that's fit for you."

Once they arrived at Tight Game's cocaine-white 1978 Cadillac, he examined it to see if it was damaged in any way. He was relieved when he saw it wasn't. They got into the 'Lac and then drove off.

As he made a right on Bexar Street, Tight game told Tunke, "I knew your moms and ol' man. Ol' Coach used to be one of my road dogs back in the day when he moved to Dallas from Memphis. This was before you were born. Yo' pops was one hellava player. He could have been a pimp himself, but it wasn't his destiny. The legal life pulled him in, and it has been quite successful for him. He's now a teacher and a coach of three different sports of a high school. He's doin' what he loves to do. I haven't talked to him in about two years now. How's he been?"

"I talked to him three weeks ago. He's doing good. I don't really talk to him much unless I gotta holla at my brother. He just won the 2004 basketball championship last year. He's happy about that."

Tight Game just nodded his head in a smooth manner while grinning, and said, "That's good for him. I've been around long enough to know who you're kin to. I've seen you in the projects and around the South a few times also. You didn't take the education and legal route yo' pops and moms did. I guess it was because you didn't grow up around the same things he did, and he didn't raise you. And your moms didn't have control over you once you hopped off the porch. You were doin' your thang as a young nigga on the jackin' blast and stealing ATM machines. You always had a clique of niggas following behind you. And I've seen you with the hottest honeys your age and older," he said while making a right on Hatcher. "Then I saw you when the jacking went downhill. You lost your car and everything when you went to juvenile. I know all this because I kept my eyes on you because you were a jackboy. I had to stay on my toes and watch you. I didn't want you to get hurt by me or anyone else because of the strength of your pops."

They pulled up on the left side of the famous Little World corner store in its small parking lot on Hatcher Street that only had ten parking spaces.

"You probably never knew it, but this is me and bottom bitch bonds company. So, if you or your hoes ever need help bonding out for anything, I got you right here. You see the white blonde in the blue jeans?" he said, as he pointed to a woman who was talking to three other beautiful white girls. The woman he pointed to had all six ears and eyes of all three women at attention, like everything she was saying was very important. She stood at 5'7, weighing 135 pounds, her breasts popping out for air in her white Louis Vuitton hamilton top. Long blonde hair stopped at the middle of her back. She had a small waist and flat stomach. Her light faded blue jeans were skin tight and fit perfectly on her fit legs. The bottom of her plump ass cheeks sat on the desk top.

"Yeah, I see her. What about her?"

"Can you believe she's a lawyer?"

16

Tight Game had mean game. He was one of the top pimps in Dallas. He had 43 women doing something to elevate himself and their lives. He was a true player indeed. Tunke wanted to know more about this lawyer. "You serious? How you end up getting a lawyer on your team?"

"I built her. I been having Christie since she was eighteen, fresh out of high school. She's 39 now. At the beginning, she was willing to do whatever for me, as long as I was caring for her like she wanted to be cared for. That's because of the situation she had with her father. Shit like, him not being there for her, gone all the time. He's a businessman with a bunch of businesses in Texas and other states. He got long bread. I ended up getting in his pockets as well after a while, through his daughter. It took him a while to like me though. He invited me to his mansion in Lewisville after he found out I was a Mason, a businessman like himself, and helping his daughter through college to become a lawyer.

"But before all that happened, I worked her for like two weeks, until I asked her more questions about herself that I had thought of. I found out she wanted to be a lawyer. Immediately, after she told me that, a light bulb came on inside my head. It took me three days to come up with the perfect plan. I took her out the streets, paid her college funds, and put her through school. I had her join a sorority. After some time, I had her become an Eastern Star just for networking and good connections. That's the main reason why I became a Mason myself back in the day.

"Anyway, after she graduated and started working as a criminal attorney, I knew everybody would want her because she's a top notch queen. So, I had her fucking with state and federal judges, DAs, and detectives for free for better connections and better deals, but not enough where it would ruin her career and value, but where she would gain power inside the courts. Some of the married ones we took pictures of and recorded for bribes, if we ever had to go that route.

"From all that, I built a million-dollar queen. She loved me for making her dreams come true, and she never left me. I gained a lot of respect in the game and received Pimp of the Year twice because of that. I've had a bunch of P's play dirty and tried to throw dirt all over my name, making attempts to snatch my ho up. They never were successful and didn't come close, because either they didn't have game or theirs wasn't as long as mine. I don't think she'll ever leave me because of the tight hold I have on her, but only time will tell. I think the only one that can make that happen is God. She's passed many of my tests. That's how I know she's loyal to me. You don't get too many bitches like her in your career. I'm a multi-millionaire. I own four tax offices, two loan companies, a bond company, and an escort service. And I'm about to open up a couple of franchises and a firm for Christie. It's all about elevation in this game, youngin'. Turning a good idea into a great thing."

Back a few weeks ago, Tunke had run across a prostitute. It didn't go right for him. He ended up losing her the second day of having her on the track. That's because he was unexperienced in the game and never was taught the Proper Rules of the game. And now, listening to Tight Game made Tunke want to know more about the game. "Give me the game, man."

"If you really want it, I'll give it to you, youngin'. Do you really want it tho, is the question."

"Yeah, I really want it."

"Well, looka here, youngin', at all times, the game is sold not told. But I still owe a couple of favors to your pops. He helped me out about, uhhh, 25 years ago, to be exact. I had knocked for a bitch from Park Row. The bitch's uncles and oldest brother tripped out when they found out she was getting pimped on. Even when they found out she was breaking her motherfuckin' self, they still was tripping hard on a pimp. See, I've never beaten a ho to make her ho for me. Never had that gorilla shit on my name unless it was a nigga throwing salt in my soup. But I have put my hands on a bitch to check her when she tested me.

"Anyway, I had gotten a few thousand out of her after I was told by my OG partna to get rid of the ho before she became a big problem, so I did. Her people were still fucked up after the fact. Word was out they were gonna kill me if they saw me in the streets. I didn't pay it any mind. So, one day, I got caught slipping. Coach and I were at a hangout spot named Top and Bottom, across the street here, when two of her uncles came up behind me while I was shooting pool, putting a blade to my neck. I didn't know Coach was cool with them until then, because I would have told him to talk to them prior to that day. But your pops saved me from getting my throat cut. I owe your pops big for that."

Even though Coach was just saving his friend's life back then, Tight game felt like he owed Coach a whole lot for what he did. He would have never attained anything he had today if it wasn't for him. On the other hand, deep down inside, Tunke was proud of what his pops did and glad someone like Tight Game spoke highly of his father. Plus, if Tight Game had died that day, he would have never been there to save his own life.

"This is what I'ma do for you. Pick one of the hoes you see in there, except for my bottom. They're all top notch queens with the best breasts money can buy, all money makers. Now, choose wisely. Don't think with your dick. When you see a ho, think about how much money she can make you, not how she can make you feel sexually. So, think about it for a minute."

Tunke examined all three white girls while they stood in the office space and talked amongst themselves. They were all curvaceous, unique, and buxom, but the first one he laid eyes on was a tall, long-haired blonde. Her curvy body fit perfectly in a magnetic dress that cost a few hundred dollars. It was a two-tone, glittery blue with white and grey on it. When light hit the dress, it sparkled. She had $8000 worth of jewelry on her wrist, ears, and fingers. She was a lovely sight to see.

Next to her was a white girl with long jet-black hair. She was on the borderline of being chubby, but she was very pretty and had an attractive, thick body. Her big breasts were spilling out her tight white dress. She would have been the first girl Tunke would have fucked on out the three women.

Last but not least, there was another pretty, tall, skinny red head. The first thing he noticed on her were her high-dollar tattoos. The colorful tattoos were worth thousands of dollars. She had her whole back and right arm tatted, both legs done up to her thighs in her red mini skirt, and both feet were hit up that sat in red, three-inch high heels.

It took Tunke close to two minutes to decide who he wanted. He picked the one with the expensive dress and jewelry on. She looked like money to him. He told Tight Game his choice.

"Good choice. Her name is Fancy. She's a good stepping queen with three years in the game. She loves and respects the game to the fullest. She's made me 39 Gs in one month this year. Fancy has the drive and the potential to be a bottom bitch, who will teach you the game and put you on top, in the circle of real certified players like myself. But before we get any deeper, let's see if she wants to separate from my pimpin' and into the midst of yours." He pulled off his phone from a white clip on his waistband, called and told her to step outside to talk to him.

While Fancy was on her way outside, Christie had a huge grin on her face. She was happy to see Tight Game. She hadn't seen him all day, since this morning. They were so deep into conversation about Christie winning her client's murder trial today that they hadn't noticed he had pulled up until now. Christie waved at Tight Game. Tunke could see she loved Tight Game dearly.

Once Tight Game and Fancy reached the trunk of the Cadillac, he asked, "How's your day goin'?"

"It went fine, Daddy. How about yours?"

"It's going great. Can't complain at all. Well, Fancy, I gave pimp in the car there, the chance to pick him a ho out of you, Sarah, and Taylor. He picked you. You have the choice to stay with me or you can choose him. I remember you mentioned that you want to be bottom bitch. Here is the opportunity to be that bottom you want to be. The young nigga is family. He's a boss player that's 'bout his paper. A hustler. You'll like him. So, what are you going to do?"

She thought hard about her next move. She looked down for a few seconds then raised her head back up. After looking at Tight Game in his light-brown eyes, she looked at her wife-in-laws and then at Tunke in the car. "I'ma choose him."

"That's good. You're a real ho, Fancy. Continue to love and respect this game. Do you wish to say anything before we part?"

"No, I have nothing else to say now," she said, a little hurt because Tight game just gave her up to another pimp. She would definitely miss him and some of her wife-in-laws. She only chose Tunke because Tight game confirmed him and he was a younger pimp. She trusted Tight Game's judgement. She had in her head that if she didn't like the way he pimped, she would run back to Tight game with $10,000 in her hand to give to him just to show him she really wanted to come back and that she isn't playing with his pimpin'.

"Wait here while I go get him for you."

Tight Game went to the driver's side window and told Tunke, "She said she'll choose up with you." That made Tunke smile. "I'm about to call one of my black hoes at my tax office on 2nd. She has my Caprice up there, and I'm giving it to you. When she comes and gets out, tell Fancy to get in so you and I can sit down and kick game. Get out and talk to her, pimp."

Tunke got out the 'Lac, walked up on her with a smile on his face and no fear in his body. After they introduced themselves to one another, Tunke got straight to business. "Look, ho, I must say that the game you've been accustomed to this far from Tight game is something I know you've grown used to, but now I'm your pimp. If you are not feeling me so far, you are free to leave now, just let me know in what direction you would like to go."

She just stood there looking into his eyes, asking herself was this what she really wanted and to see what else he would say next.

When he saw that she wasn't responding to what he just said, he switched gears in his game. "I chose you because I saw something in you I didn't see in those two hoes. Do you know what that was?"

"No, I don't. What did you see?" she asked out of curiosity.

"I see something unique in you. I see someone that I'd like to build alongside of me. And, of course, I saw big money and a beautiful future."

Tight Game's ho parked a space away from his Lac. The fine ho got out the Caprice, leaving the door open and the keys in the ignition. "Now what I want you to do is get in that Caprice, and wait for me. When I get to you, we'll get better acquainted with one another." He didn't know where the shit he was saying had come from. He was always good at macking and had good conversation when it came to dealing with females. Tunke only knew a tad bit about pimpin' from the pimps he'd heard pimpin' on the track in South Dallas and watching movies like *The Mack, Superfly, Pimpin' Ain't Easy, Willie Dynamite, Pimpin' Ken's Pimps up Hoes Down, Really Really Pimpin' in Da South*, and a documentary by Pimp Snooky. He had watched those movies after he had gotten knocked, and they shaped the little game he did have.

"Okay," she said, obeying his demand.

Once Tunke got back in the Cadillac, Tight game asked, "Is everything good?"

Tunke started smiling and said, "Yeah, man, everything good."

Tight Game handed him twenty-one hundred-dollar bills.

"Thanks, I promise I'll pay you back for everything," he said while putting the money in his pocket.

"You don't have to. Like I said before, it's a favor I'm paying you that I never got to pay your pops. He might not approve of me doing this, but he'll understand. But if you feel you still owe me, repay me in mastering the art of this game. Love, respect, and treat this game well, and it'll do the same for you. I must ask you what motivated you to try your hand at pimpin' anyway when I seen you on MLK three months ago?" Tight Game asked.

"I had came across this ho. She said she'd help me get some money. The second day of having her, I get knocked for her."

"What made you go to jacking after you lost her? Why didn't you cop another ho?

"I couldn't find one. To tell the truth, I didn't know how to get a bitch down. I stumbled upon the first one. I'd made attempts since then, but none of them bitches went for it. I needed money, so I went back to what I knew best."

"I understand. Did that pimp serve you, call you up letting you know he had her?"

"Naw."

"I see you wasn't properly blessed with the rules of the game.

That ho wasn't no good. She was supposed to lace you up with game, knowing you didn't know nothing. She was using you, for what I don't know. That was all your fault, tho'. You can't depend on a ho to give you game. You have to already have it. This is what you will have to do, these are the rules. When you knock for a ho, you make sure she breaks herself. For everything. All or nothing. Then you got to tell her about getting knocked. If she separates from your pimpin', she has to tell that other P to inform you that she's no longer yours. If she leaves you, don't trip. The game is cop and blow.

"Losing a ho should motivate you to pimp even harder with the next ho. Hoes will come and hoes will go. If you have one ho and you end up losing her, don't be afraid to be hoeless. That's the main reason why you should know how to manage money and save it. Put yourself on a budget for six months to a year. I know some Ps that's hoeless right now, but you'll never know it because they had money stashed, now they're campaigning and shining even harder than when they had a ho. Keep your game tight and sharp. Also, tell your ho not to recklessly eyeball another pimp, and don't look at any men if it ain't about no dough. You know where Harry Hines is at in the nawf, don't you?"

"Yeah, why, wuz up?"

"That's where you should take Fancy. She's known for busting that track open. It's Friday night, so she'll break big. Go past Denton Lane, it's a Super 8 on the right of Harry Hines and Mockingbird. How old are you?"

"Seventeen."

"Ok. Tell Fancy to check in for a night. She's 22. Here's a little history about her. She was raised by her foster family in Dallas because her mom swallowed half a bottle of pills when Fancy was eleven, and killed herself. It was over depression. CPS took her and her two little brothers. She lived with her foster parents until she graduated high school. I met her four months later, working the blade. She wasn't paying a pimp until she met me. Been with me for four years now. She's the type of ho who wants to be a part of something, a cause, really like every ho that fucks with a pimp. She can make anywhere from $800 to $1,500 a day, throughout the week on the blade. Also, she has a few high-dollar johns that call her every week. You got any questions you want to ask me about the game?"

It took Tunke about eight seconds to say, "Nall, I can't think of nothing right now."

"Well, if you think of anything, just ask me when you see me later on the track. If you run into a problem before you see me, just call me," he said, and then wrote his number down on a white napkin.

"Alright. Thanks, Tight Game."

"It's cool, Tunke. I didn't have anybody teaching me the game. I had to learn through experience in this game, but look where it got me. I'ma quick thinker and I'm sharp. That's how I made it without getting locked up or killed. You have to be if you truly serious about pimpin', Tunke. And another reason why I'm helping you out is because if you continue robbing and jacking, you'll be a dead man sooner or later, or in prison. That shit never lasts unless you hit a big lick, quit jacking, lay low, sit on it for a while, and then invest in something. I had to look out for my homie's son. I see you are a young player. You have potential to be somebody big. Just remember this, Tunke, this ain't forever. This game is about elevating. Always remember that. Well, I'ma let you get on your way. I'll meet up with you later. I'll bring Fancy's things by your room along with the papers to the car. Oh yea, don't go by your real name. Find you a pimping name to go by from now on."

"Aight, man, I'ma get at you," Tunke said while they were giving each other pimp handshakes.

"Do your thang, pimp," Tight game told him. "And stay down."

"I will." While Tunke was stepping out the Cadillac, a name came to him that he had been thinking about for the last past month now. He looked at Tight Game and asked him, "How 'bout my name being Monopoly?"

Tight Game smiled. "That's perfect, pimp. I like that, for real. Yeah, run with that name, pimp, and represent that," he said while nodding his head in approval.

"Alright, Tight game."

Tunke smiled all the way to his Chevy Caprice until he opened the driver's door. He put on a blank face because he needed to hide his happiness.

As Tunke pulled out the parking lot, he thought about what to say to Fancy. He remembered what an older pimp had told him on the track the night he knocked for his first ho. "Never run out of things to say to a woman, because when you do you run out of game, then the ho will choose a pimp who has game."

Tunke went for what he knew and everything Tight Game taught him. "First and foremost, I want you to understand something. I don't want you holding a penny of my money. After you break a trick, you break yourself." Then he went on to tell her about other rules.

She could tell he had little experience in the game because the pimpin' lingo didn't flow out fluently. She liked his style, though, and knew he had potential to be a good pimp, but she still tested him to see what he would say by asking, "Are you really a pimp?"

Tunke thought of something slick to say to her. "Am I really a pimp? I can't believe you asked a nigga something like that. Bitch, you must be blind." He pulled out the stack that Tight Game had given him along with $285, which was in ones, fives, twenties, and one fifty-dollar bill he won from a small dice game in the projects earlier today. "I know you saw this knot in my pocket. This came out a ho's ass. Bitch, you better wake up and smell this pimpin'," he said, repeating that last line he heard a pimp say to a ho on the track.

"How deep are you in hoes?" Fancy asked.

"You the only one for right now."

"So am I gonna be your bottom or what?" Fancy asked, testing him again to see where his head was at.

"You'll have to prove yourself to get in that spot. Stay down and we'll see."

She started telling herself in her head, *Oh yeah. I will show him. I'll make more money for him than I ever made for Tight game to be his bottom. I'm gonna make him brag about me being a down ho.*

*I'm gonna make my new daddy one of the richest and flyest pimps in Dallas.* Fancy was angry and hurt at the same time because of the fact that Tight game had given her up after paying him for over four years. She would put her pain into her work tonight on the track and do her best to release it.

Tunke pulled up in Super 8 hotel parking lot sixteen minutes later. He peeled off a hundred-dollar bill and handed it to her. "Go pay for a night."

As Fancy walked towards the entrance, he thought about what the pimp game would do for him. Ever since he was 11 years old, stealing and jacking were the only ways he knew how to get paid, something that became a thrill to him more than a hustle. He felt pimpin' would be more prosperous than jacking. Statistically, there were more successful pimps than successful jackers. Plus, he loved fucking with lots of women at one time. Monopoly would commit his heart to this game and learn everything he had to know to make him one of the best that ever pimped out of Dallas.


I ain't looking for no black bitch. I ain't looking for no white bitch. I'm looking for the right bitch. It ain't in their beauty, it's in their duty.
—Macknificent

# Chapter 1
7 years later

Cops and blows. Gains and losses. Ups and downs. Success and failures. That's exactly what I'd been enduring since I been in the game. A little over a year after I got in the game, things were starting to go good for me. Just when I was getting my game up and getting a name in the game, two out of four of my hoes got busted for prostitution in California. They snitched on me, and I got sent to federal prison for a year and a half for pimpin' across state lines.

Fancy quit hoing due to me getting locked up, claiming that she was tired of the game and wanted to pursue other avenues in life. She was my bottom bitch until months into my incarceration. She stayed in touch with me, though, and held me down here and there. She went to college and later became a therapist.

For the last four and half years that I'd been out of prison, I'd made some major moves for myself. I became a Mason. I currently co-own a successful online clothing business with my square baby mother. I took on being a song writer and R&B singer since I had the skills to do so. Even though I ate from all that as well worked a job, I still pimped. Pimpin' stuck with me like a mole on a human body.

I only had two queens for the time being. That was the only reason why I was on my way to the east side of Fort Worth to see if I could add another ho to the two.

While I rode down a multi-million-dollar street, I looked left and right for a decent ho on the track. Lancaster was one of the known tracks in Fort Worth. This street was infamous for prostitution, drugs, and the homeless.

There were people posted up in the hood on corners, and people mobbing and walking alone up and down Lancaster on this cool late evening in March. I saw a few prostitutes but none that I wanted. Some were doped up, and a couple looked burned out. I drove right past them.

As I drove further crossing Oakland St. on Lancaster, I saw a woman walking across the street to the right side. Her phat ass went jiggling like Jell-O in black tights as she started jogging to avoid getting hit by an oncoming car. I saw money. I had to get at her. I had already passed up the turn to get to her, so at the next turn, I made a right into a shopping center, passing up a McDonald's, 24 Fitness gym, Dollar General, and other businesses. I didn't want to lose track of her, so I gave the accelerator a little more gas to where I went five miles per hour over the parking lot speed limit through the thin traffic. I slowed down a little when crossing over Oakland again to the other side she was on. I parked in front of an open beauty supply store and hopped out, fast walking my way to this fine stallion.

"Look out, Night Star, slow down so I can talk to you," I told her.

Her fast pace came to a halt, and then she turned around to see me ten feet away from her. I closed the gap to where three feet were between us. She checked me out and then asked, "You a pimp, ain't you?"

"Only a ho would know something like that." My $30,000 worth of jewelry and fresh clothes spoke volumes. I had a light-brown, Versace, casual, button-down dress shirt, brown slacks, and brown alligator dress shoes on. "Why you walking so fast? Where you headed?" I asked out of curiosity.

"Meadow Brook."

I repeated her answer as a question to be sure I heard her correctly, because Meadow Brook was about eight to ten minutes away driving distance from where we stood. It was at least thirty minutes away walking distance. "Where at in Meadow Brook?"

"By the neighborhood Wal-Mart," she said.

"So you about to walk all the way over there instead of catching the bus?"

"Yeah, but I wanted to make some money on the way. I know I'll get stopped on the way," she said, letting me know she was indeed a ho. Her statement was true. I could understand why she said someone would stop. I was a living example. I had stopped to see if I could knock her. Her look were money makers. High-yellow skin. Long, highlighted blonde hair mixed with brown hair hung down her shoulders, bringing out her beautiful face. She was short, standing up to my shoulders. I was 6'2, so she had to be about 5'1. She had small, perky tits. Her stomach was flat and her waist length had to be between 24 to 26. Big hips, phat ass, thick thighs, and a fat pussy print flaunted in black tights.

I pointed to my new, fully loaded, grey Range Rover. "That's my Rover over there. Come on, I'll take yo' fine ass to Meadow Brook." If she accepted the ride, I'd continue to soft mack her on the way to her destination.

"You not gonna hurt me, are you?" she said, looking me in the eyes.

"No, why would I do that? I'm not tryna create a scar, I wanna make a star," I said, smiling, showing her my platinum diamond grill.

That made her smile also, and then she said, "Okay, you can drop me off."

On our way to the Rover, she asked, "They call me Pinky, what's your name?"

"Monopoly," I said while pushing the alarm to unlock the doors, and then we got inside.

"You don't act like you from around this way. Where you from?"

"I'm from sunny South Dallas."

"That's why I never seen you around here."

"I be all over Fort Worth. We just missed each other. Where you from out here?"

"From the Southside, Hemphill area."

When I stopped at the red light on Meadow Brook Drive, I hooked up my main phone to the AUX cable and put on "I Choose You" by UGK. I set the volume low, just enough where I knew she could hear every word, the beat, and my words as well. "Oh, you from where the Mexicans from. You must be mixed?"

"Yea, I'm mixed with white, Black, and Mexican. My mom's white. My dad's Black and Mexican."

I was about four minutes away from Wal-Mart, so I got straight to the point. "That's what's up. Anyway, I see you not paying a pimp or you just out here being a faggot ho. Which one is it? In the pimp game, a faggot is a prostitute with a pimp that doesn't follow the pimp's rules when he's not in her presence."

"I don't have a pimp."

"You should get down with me. I know you want a nigga that's compatible to you in this game."

"I don't know. I been out here making it on my own without a nigga." Every so often, I would look at her. She had her eyes on me as well. When she wasn't looking at me, I could tell she was in thought about something. And just maybe she was interested in fucking with my pimpin'.

"Fuck being on your own. I understand what you're saying, tho'. And I don't blame you for being on your own. That's because you haven't came across the right motherfucka to be compatible to you. We both know you need better instructions and guidance on how to better deal with this game we're both in. All I want is you to choose this opportunity to let me help you better your life and correct your direction so you can get what you striving for." I didn't have to say much after that. It was enough for affect. When I crossed 820 freeway, I asked, "Where you wanna get dropped off at?"

"I'm going to the Regency Oaks behind Auto Zone. But you can drop me off in the Auto Zone parking lot. I'll walk over there. Them niggas ruthless over there. They might try to rob you or something."

"I feel you. But it really don't matter. I know a few known niggas from around this way. Plus, I wouldn't be out here like this if I didn't have protection." I had to let her know it was with me in so many words. I had a burner on me. I knew I probably looked like I wasn't a street nigga because of what I had on. I got that a lot from hood bitches upon the first time we met each other.

One thing for sure, I wasn't a duck or lame to this street shit. I got the vibe that she was trying to cover up something. I wasn't sure, but whatever it was, if the bitch choose up, I'd end up finding out what it was, sooner or later. Hopefully, before any problems came into the picture.

Before getting out the SUV, she asked me for my number,

which I gave her. "I'll give you a call soon."

"Only call me if you want some of this million-dollar game I have and want to go somewhere on this Monopoly board," I said, letting her know I was serious about this pimpin'.

"I gotta go. I'll call you," she said then shut the passenger door.

After I left Fort Worth, I went back to the McConnell Lodge Hotel in Arlington and chilled with my bottom bitch, Shae. She'd been my bottom for five years now, ever since my incarceration. She was the only ho out of my hoes that held me down for my whole sentence with ho dough, visits, and whatever else I had wanted. I only had two queens at this time, which were Shae and my Mexican queen, Selena. Selena had a three-year-old daughter and a four-year-old son, so I let her spend time with them. Since I hadn't let her see them in two weeks, I gave her some time off to bond with them for a couple of days. I understood and supported her role as a mother.

Since Shae was hungry, we went to eat at Razzoo's at 6:13 P.M., until I got a call from Pinky at 7:09 P.M., which was a little over an hour after Pinky and I parted. "Hey, Monopoly, you busy?"

"Not really, just out and about. What's goin' on with you?"

"Just calling to tell you, I'ma choose up with you."

"Ok. Where are you? I asked her.

"In the same place. You can come pick me up if you want to."

"Alright. I'll be there in about 30 to 40 minutes."

"Okay. I have a friend too. She's at the room."

"That's cool. I'ma have to sit you both down and talk before you two come into what I have goin' on. Hold tight, I'm on my way."

It took us about eighteen minutes to finish the rest of our food. I left a $20 tip on the table for the waiter, then went to pay the bill.

While we were getting in the Range Rover, Shae asked, "Daddy, what's the plan?"

"I just met this bitch a couple of hours ago. Before I let her in our family, I want to do a good screening on her and her friend. In due time, as soon as possible, I want to know everything about these hoes. That means I want you to be in their ear and ask a lot of question after I accept them. I probably have to do a couple of tests on 'em. I'll let you know if I do."

"Okay, Daddy."

After we made it to Meadow Brook, I parked before calling Pinky. It rang three times then I got hit with the voicemail. Right after I hung up, I received a text saying she was busy and that she'd call me right back.

I thought to myself, *this bitch is playing games.* I decided that I'd give her some time to call back before jumping to any other conclusion. If I didn't hear anything within ten minutes, I'd leave. And if she called back later after I left Fort Worth, she was going to have to pay me extra for wasting a pimp's time.

Three minutes had passed when I saw her getting out a white Ford F150 truck by a laundry mat across the street. "There she go," I told Shae while pointing to her as she adjusted her tights while pulling them up. At the same time the truck drove away from her, she pulled her phone out her small purse.

Seconds later, my phone started ringing. It was Pinky. "Monopoly, one of my regulars pulled up on me. I had to make that money. You still here?"

"I thought you were bullshitting a pimp, I was about to go. But that's wuz up. Yea, I'm still here. Look to your right, over by the Auto Zone."

She looked in my direction until she spotted me. "Okay, I see you. I'm on my way."

When she got close enough to where we could see her good, Shae said, "Damn, Daddy, she is fine. Where you find her at?"

"Walking down the street by Lancaster. I'm 'bout to get this money up out this ho."

"I know you is," she agreed.

After I introduced Shae and Pinky to each other, I started asking questions while we still sat in the Range Rover in the Auto Zone parking lot. "I'm curious, why did you come all the way over here from where you were?" I really wanted to know. Her motives were strong. I knew it either had to be money, a boyfriend, or drugs to make a person walk from where she was to Meadow Brook. Even though Meadow Brook Drive wasn't a money spot for prostitution, I hoped money was the force that brought her here. That would prove that she loved money. If it was true, I needed a ho like that in my stable.

Her silence made me do a 180-degree turn towards the back seat. I turned the overhead light on to see a disappointed and embarrassed look on her pretty face. It was the same look of a child that got caught doin' something bad and was ashamed of it. I knew it had to be drugs. I didn't want to run this fine ho off without getting paid, so I told her, "Look, I'm not here to hurt you. I want to help you in every aspect of your life. By you choosin' me, you told me you want and need proper guidance and help to better your life. Because you want a man to handle things. If you really choose me, let me know now what drugs you're on."

"I snort boy," she said while searching my eyes for acceptance. In my mind, I thought she probably thought I looked like I don't do any drugs, or it looked like I wouldn't accept her using heroin, and that's why she didn't tell me in the first place.

"How long have you been using?"

"For 'bout six months now."

There were a couple of spots in Fort Worth that people were known for using heroin. I hate she got caught up in that crowd. She looked like she didn't do any drugs. Normally, I didn't deal with females on drugs, but I would change that depending on the drug and who it was. The only ones that I pimped on were hoes that weren't using at all, smoked weed, or either casually drank. I'd never been around a heroin user that long enough to know how they really acted while on it. My only knowledge came from word of mouth, and what I heard wasn't good at all.

I gave Pinky the benefit of the doubt. For one, she was a beautiful woman. Two, I knew she needed guidance from a man that had a sense of direction. I knew a lot of women would make small changes and make choices if they had the right man leading them. Three, I knew she was a money maker, so I accepted her with open arms. But I made a mental note that if she fucked up in a big way, it would be best to get rid of her. I wasn't putting up with no bullshit bitch. I didn't care how big she paid a pimp.

Shae turned around in her seat and asked Pinky, "Is your friend on boy too?"

"No. She smoke loud tho'." I was glad to hear that. I made a mental note whenever I sat them down one on one with me to ask them questions about themselves as well as one another so I could get some knowledge and understanding on them.

"Daddy, can I suggest something?"

"Yes, what is it?"

"If her friend looks the part to ho, I think you should give them a chance." She was right, I should give them a chance. I knew she'd let me know if I needed to get rid of them, not out of jealousy but because she cared about me succeeding in the game. What she did not know was I was planning on getting some money out of them for sure until they gave me a reason to blow them. And, too, she made it seem like Pinky had to be qualified for this opportunity to fuck with my pimpin'.

"Aight. I'll give y'all a chance."

They lived in a run-down, cheap motel in the hood on Lancaster, in an area infested with drugs, drug addicts, burned-out prostitutes, and the homeless. I didn't know how long they had been staying here, but it said a lot about them. Pinky didn't appear to be a hoodrat or a dingy bitch, but looks could be deceiving. Either they had the state of mind where they were afraid of getting out that shell, where they couldn't progress, or they were living here temporarily until they saved up enough money to move to something better. Either way, if they didn't get out this hell hole soon, they'd decay just like the rest of the people around here.

When her friend opened the door, she looked past Pinky right into my eyes for a couple of seconds, then checked me out from my bald fade down to my brown Ferragamo alligator dress shoes.

"Wuz up?" she asked me as Pinky walked past her.

"What's up?" I asked back after I stepped inside the motel. She closed the door behind me.

"I'm Monopoly. What's yo' name?"

"CeCe."

She wasn't as beautiful as Pinky, but she was a cutie with a big wide booty. She was short and thick, standing up to my chest. She was a dark chocolate-brown complexion. I could tell she had just dashed makeup on her face before we got here because of how fresh it was on her face. She probably did it to impress and look good for me. She had a baby face with pretty white teeth, and a few tattoos of names and other artwork on her small breasts, upper thigh, and upper arm.

She had a little fat on her stomach and two small grips of love handles on each side of her waist, but not too much where she was bad built and unattractive. She actually was a fine woman, a ho I could get some money out of. The only thing I didn't like about her was her hair. It was in a gelled ponytail that went a little past her shoulders. Shae was a gifted licensed hairstylist, so I'd have her do something to her hair before she did any calls.

"Let me get something clear. Are both of you choosing up with me?"

They both said, "Yeah."

"Now that we got that out the way, I need y'all to respect the pimp in front of you and drop out all you got and pay a pimp's fee."

"Hold on," Pinky said, then walked into the bathroom. I heard sticky tape being ripped off.

She returned in seconds with a brown paper bag in her hand.

"That's $1200." She went into her big purse and pulled out a few more bills. "And, that's two hundred and somethin'."

"What about you?" I asked CeCe.

She giggled and said, "That's both of our savings. I don't have nothing on me but eight dollars and some change. You want that too?"

"Yea, I want that too." I stuck my hand out towards her.

She went to get it off the television and gave it to me. "This pimp shit serious, ain't it?"

"Making easy money pimpin' hoes is serious," I said, using Memphis, Tennessee pimps' lingo. "I shouldn't accept this, but it's something. My fee is a $1000 apiece. I'ma get the rest and a lot more by the morning and some, so it's okay." I put all of the money inside the paper bag. I folded the bag tight then put it in my front pocket.

I must admit, I was surprised about how much money Pinky had given me. That made me look at her a little different. You had hoes that didn't do hard drugs that didn't have that much money saved up. That told me she knew how to control her drug habit. That meant it shouldn't be that hard for her to stop snorting. I hoped by Shae and me being drug and alcohol free it would rub off on Pinky. Eventually it would, if she stayed around us long enough.

"Let me get y'all IDs," I told them.

Pinky went into her Chanel purse, got hers, and gave it to me. At the same time, CeCe walked to the dresser and got hers out her purse. Then they both sat back on the bed looking at me. I examined the IDs. Their appearance and friendship reminded me of the gymnastic performers Simone Biles and Laurie Hernandez, but Pinky was 24 and CeCe was 20. I made a mental note to do a background check on them.

"Look y'all, since you both chose me as your pimp, now until you decide to leave my pimpin', I'm your instructor, teacher, professor, your God, your Daddy, your leader, and your guiding light to achieve greatness in this here game. From here on out, I want and need you both to give me the best of you, all of you, and everything you breathe and shit out, this sweet game. I'ma do the same in return, as well as appreciate your mind, your being around, and everything that you do for me. I will be your provider in this game, teaching you how to do your best, how to strengthen your weaknesses, and how to use your strengths and best skills to milk these tricks so we can succeed.

"Now, what I'm about to tell you is important to us all. I don't want y'all doin' anything that's uncomfortable. Hoing is what y'all been doin', so I don't think y'all are uncomfortable with that. By you choosing a pimp, it tells me you respect the game we're in. You have to like and love what you do to get what you want out this game and to be successful. You have to become addicted to the thrill of the hustle. To win the race, you have to ho with grace. Now, this game, it ain't all about selling pussy, even though it's a big part of it. What's so good about game is as long as you have it, you're good. You can use game and get paid instead of having sex. Over the course of these next three weeks, we're going to be chopping up a lot of game so you can break as many tricks as possible. Anyway, Pinky, can you dance?" I asked her that because she was bad enough to get into a high-dollar strip club.

CeCe looked at her and bust out laughing. "What's funny, CeCe?" I asked her.

"She couldn't dance if her life depended on it. She dance like a white girl with no rhythm. She can fuck, tho'. Fuck real good. But can't dance a lick."

"Uh, uh, shut up, CeCe," Pinky said, embarrassed but in a playful way.

"Bitch, you know it's true," CeCe said, laughing.

"It's alright, Pinky. What about you, CeCe, can you dance?"

"Yea, I can dance, but I don't wanna work in no strip club. I'd rather sell pussy."

"Okay. Now that we got that clear, let's get to my rules." It took me about twenty-five minutes to break down my rules and regulations, making sure they didn't have a problem and understood every word I spoke. For example, I told them they were always to give me the money they'd made when I commanded them to and every time I came around. To never look or talk to another pimp. If they chose another pimp, have him serve me, letting me know their separation from my pimpin'. I let them know how I wanted and needed things done and what order so the family could succeed. If they got arrested, know that I would bond them out, and to keep their mouths closed when they got interrogated, no matter what the detectives said. Also, what I wanted to be called. And to respect and honor me as their pimp, and if they didn't follow my rules, there would be consequences. There were other things that they needed to know that I would lace them up on during the course of weeks to come. I let Shae break down the shit I didn't want to teach them. Like my rates for everything, how to use a condom correctly when fucking with a customer. How to talk to and treat certain tricks. How to screen for undercovers, etc.

I thought of my homeboy, Cedric. He did most of my hoes' photos to make them look more professional. He's a professional photographer for a growing minor hood magazine, a rapper, a producer, and a DJ. I gave him a call.

"What's up, Tunke, bro?"

"Making money, bro. Tryna get my hoes prepped up so we can come up. How about you?"

"Fucking with this song, bro. I wrote two hooks already and I don't like no'un one of them. What you trying to get into?"

"I was calling to see if you were not busy so I could get some pictures taken for my hoes."

"Hell yeah, just come on over, I got you. I want you to check out this instrumental. Maybe you can help me. I know you'll like it. It's hot."

"Aight, cool. I'm in Fort Worth right now. I'ma run to the mall before it closes, then I'll head that way," I told him.

"Good. I'll have everything set up by time you get here."

After I had Pinky take a shower, we packed their things in my Range Rover, and headed to the beauty supply store for CeCe to get some hair. Then we went to the mall off Interstate 35 and Simaniar in Fort Worth. I wanted to go to The Parks in Arlington, but it would have been closed by the time we got there. I bought all three of them a bunch of Victoria's Secret lingerie, four Louis Vuitton outfits, cosmetics, and two pairs of high heels apiece.

It took me 40 minutes to drive to Cedric's house in Mesquite. My hoes were already getting themselves together on the way but had to finish inside his big studio room. A wall was knocked down between two big rooms that were joined together. He had four flat screens on the red-painted walls around the room. Two were computers, one was a 50 inch that displayed music videos, and another 50 inch that monitored the six cameras around the outside of the two-story house. He had a lot of recording equipment on one side of the room. Cedric and I sat in the office chairs in front of the computers while my hoes sat on the couches. I was surprised to see an empty studio. It was usually a bunch of people here.

He pushed a key on the keyboard, making the instrumental

come on. He turned it up on four small speakers and two big speakers, to where we all could hear him sing to the down-tempo instrumental. He couldn't sing a lick, but I liked the melody. The hook he wrote could be a whole lot better, but the beat was fire. "You wasn't lying, the instrumental's hot. I like the melody, but I don't like the hook, tho'. You can do better than that, bro. Let me listen to it for a minute, and I'll write it for you while you take the photos."

"Do yo' thang, bro. You should get on there with me. Write you a verse too."

Fourteen minutes later, my hoes were ready. Cedric left me alone to write while he took their photos.

It took me about thirty-two minutes to finish writing my verse, the hook, and to perfect everything. I didn't know how to fuck with the recording part on the computer, and I didn't want to bother him while he was in his zone, so I went over my verse and hook a little bit more. Then after I was done, I went to guide them on taking certain poses that excited and aroused tricks.

The pictures came out flawless. Most of the photos had my hoes in lingerie and two fully clothed. The pictures looked like they could be in Straight Stuntin', Smooth, and Phat Puffs. I knew these photos would attract tricks.

We downloaded all the photos to my laptop and their phones. I didn't post any pictures on the escort sites yet, until after I finished laying down the chorus and verse.

I ran down to my homie and my hoes what I wrote to the song called "Slow Down."

VERSE 1— From your feet all the way to your head
My kissing n lickin' got your eyes up in your head
Count how many licks it takes to get you there
Got your legs up in the air while you grasping for air
Hold on and please don't move
Just relax and let me do what I, I, I do
I got all night to prove to you
that he can't do what I, I, I, do
So we're just gonna

Smoove Dolla

HOOK—Slow down, tonight we're gonna take our time
No need to rush, because I'm about to put it down
When we recorded the song, I would sing my verse first then
the hook twice. His verse would come after that then the hook again
twice. Cedric's second verse would come in, after that a bridge, and
then I would end it with the hook.

My new hoes were surprised that I sang, and they liked the song.
I saw sparks in their eyes and aroused them when I sang. I knew
that added to the attraction and them wanting to fuck with me even
more in the game.

Cedric wrote his verse while I went in the booth to record the
chorus and my verse, then he recorded his verse last. After we were
done recording, everyone in the room including me agreed that it
was a good pantydropper song. As soon as it was mix and mastered,
it would sound even better. Other than a nigga pimpin', one of my
greatest joys and passions was music. I was in love with music in
general. I loved listening to music, writing music, and recording
music. To be able to express myself in my own words, in a melody
I came up with, and sing them myself or have someone I'm writing
for sing it was amazing. The feeling was incredible. To me, there
wasn't a higher feeling.

"How much you want for the pictures?" I asked Cedric.

"Bro, I don't want nothing. You already helped me out making
this track hotter than what it already was. When I DJ on the radio,
I'ma slide it in the mix. Don't be surprised when I call you to
perform this muthafucker and all the others we recorded together."

"Shit, I hope so. Do that, Ced Bro."

"I'ma do my best. We can do a video soon, too. I'ma make
arrangements for next month. I'll let you know when I'm ready.
When did you get that yellow ho?" he asked, talking about Pinky,
who sat on the other sofa across the room.

"I came up on the ho a couple of hours ago. You like?"

"Hell yeah. She bad than a bitch, bro. You gonna let yo' boy
fuck or what?" he said, throwing his hands up to the side.

"Yea, you know I got you. That ain't no problem." My hoes
were on the sofa talking amongst themselves. I interrupted them and

called Pinky over to us. She walked over and stood right in front of me. I reached under her black skirt, put her thong to the side, then I started rubbing two fingers on her pearl tongue in a circular motion. "My bro here wants some of this pussy here. Grab some protection and hook him up, baby."

"Okay, Daddy," she said, slightly moaning, getting turned on by my fingers. "You gon' join us?"

I smiled. "Naw, baby, I'm good. Not until you make me about $20,000." I couldn't lie, I really did want to fuck this fine, beautiful ho, but I had to control myself. She had to earn my dick, it wasn't free.

While they did their thang, I washed my hands and then helped Shae post their pictures on two different escort sites. A little after we left Cedric's house, their phones started ringing. I stayed at the hotel with them until 2 A.M., just to see how CeCe and Pinky would do on their first time out working the internet since they were both track hoes. Between the two, they had made me a little over a thousand dollars by 2 A.M.

Pinky took first place over my Mexican ho, Selena, being my top money maker. I wondered how Selena would feel about that when she came back tomorrow, and if that would make her compete with Pinky, making her work harder than she had before. I forget to tell her that when I talked to her a couple minutes ago. I would have to set that up to see what happened, see them battle it out to see who made the most bread.

I left them at the room and went to Shae's house in Arlington to go to sleep. I had to wake up early, around 6 A.M. for work. At 7 A.M. I worked as a forklift operator at Ashley Warehouse. I was so tired from the lack of sleep that as soon as I hit my bed, I passed out.

# Smoove Dolla

Clockin' doe, playin' bozoes
Setting trends N knockin' hoes
By day I'm the sun at night
I'm the moon, a real pimp
Knows how to be the center
of attention N the room, church!
—MOE REALLA


Real hoes don't play this game for money. They play it in hopes of receiving the love and affection from a pimp that all women desire. A hoe don't want a million dollars, she wants a man that makes her feel worth a million dollars.
— TRUE PIMPIN'

## Chapter 2

The next morning, when my phone alarm woke me, I didn't feel like getting out of bed. It wasn't because I didn't want to go to work. My job was fun and easy. It's just I was still tired. I laid there replaying in my head what my pimp partna, Serious Jones, said to me months ago. I remember him telling me, "You either gonna work for another man's business or pimp your own business. You can't do both, P. Yo' hoes gonna start feeling like you not really pimpin' because you working a 9 to 5." It was true, to a certain extent. But truth be told, a bitch of mine knew I was pimpin' in every sense of the word.

The only reason why I got a regular job was to cover my ass. If I got caught pimpin' again, they couldn't strip everything from me like they did the first time I got arrested in a sting operation with my hoes in California five years ago. That couldn't happen again. I wasn't on the Human Trafficking Watch, but I still wanted to be on the safe side. If I got caught up again, I'd say I was a working man. Plus, I owned a 35% share of my son's mama Tiffany's clothing business, and I received two royalty checks every year from songs I'd written and sold to major labels, as well as checks from my record label from album sales. I knew that would help to keep all I had in the bank and everything I owned.

This job also had a bunch of benefits other than the benefits of the company I worked for. Working there provided a steady flow of tricks for my hoes and a bunch of females that worked with me that I could turn out. I'd worked there for only seven months when I got out of prison, and then I quit. I got rehired five months ago just to keep the heat off my back. So, it all worked out in my favor in a bunch of ways.

I put on Yung Thug from the playlist on my phone while I took a quick shower, did my hygiene, and put on my work clothes.

Shortly after, I called Shae. "Top of the morning to you, my queen."

"Good morning, Daddy," she said sleepily.

"I know you sleep. I'm just calling to tell you my plans for today. When we get off the phone, I'ma text you a to-do list to take care of this morning. I'm setting up a private party for tonight. Y'all go shopping for things you all need and lingerie after my break. Pickup Selena before y'all go to the mall. Make sure you ask Pinky and CeCe their strengths and weaknesses, then tell them everything they need to know for the party so they'll know what to do."

"Okay. Do you want me to get up right now?"

"Nah, it's 6:40. You can sleep for about two hours if you want."

"Nah, I'll go ahead and get on it. I'll just take a good nap later. What do you want me to bring you to eat, Daddy?"

"Just bring me eight tacos from Dairy Queen and bring me a bottle of lemonade."

"K, Daddy," she said, yawning. "I'm 'bout to get up and get on it."

"I hear you yawning. You sure you don't wanna try to go back to sleep? You only had three hours of sleep, if that."

"Yeah, I'm sure, Daddy. Thanks for caring tho'."

"You welcome. You know I gotta make sure my queen good."

"Yeah, I know. Is there anything else you want me to do?"

"Uhh, oh yea, come up here by yourself. I don't want my hoes knowing I got a job and where I work."

"I got you, Daddy. Have a great day, and I love you, Daddy."

"Love you too. See you soon."

"Okay. See you at 12."

\*\*\*

My hoes' pictures got the reaction I expected from my co-workers, but only nine of them said they would show up. Plus, I had four other dudes I knew who said they were going to come too. But that wasn't enough. I thought at least 10 to 15 people would want to come from my job. A lot of them said they would be busy tonight, and some mentioned that if I did it tomorrow they would come. I hated that it was the last minute, but I tended to do that every now and then when things came to me out the blue. Anyway, word would get around about how they had a good time for the action themselves.

A lot of us were certified forklift operators, that got paid $18 and up an hour. So, I knew they could afford paying $100 to get in. It was going to be worth it. My hoes would be dancing, freakin' each other, and performing little short acts. What made private parties so live was the way the hoes got loose. They weren't like some of the girls in the strip club that didn't do certain things because of their morals or whatever the fuck the reason was. The girls that performed in the private parties knew what the niggas came to see, a freak show. Anyway, if the tricks wanted any sexual favors while there, that would be more money. Nothing less than $100. I had a hookup on half off on all the liquor and beer I wanted from some Asians I knew in Dallas. I put that on my to-do list, too, for Shae to get for me. And when Shae got here on our break, I'd show my co-workers the $3,000 worth of alcohol I had for them. I would be giving cups and beers away for free at the private party. All you could drink for free. Hopefully, that would tempt the rest to come.

On the small break that we got for 15 minutes, I thought of having some white hoes at the party. It'd been almost two months since I'd had a white ho in my stable. I knew some of them wanted white girls. Since I didn't have any, I thought about one of my good pimp partnas, Luxury P. Bunnies were all he pimped on, except when he was pimpin' on his blood sister, who was a prostitute, but they were both mixed with black and white. Their mom was a prostitute decades ago. Being that her kids were in the same game as she was, the apples didn't fall far away from the tree.

I quickly did the math in my head before calling him. I knew in his head he'd be missing money if he had his hoes at the party, so I knew he'd want to make a profit. I didn't blame him. I'd want the same thing.

I called him. "Woo, P, what's up?"

"You in Arlington?"

"Naw, P, I'm in DC, getting my bands up. Why, what's up?"

"I'm calling to see if you wanna make some money."

"Yea. What is it tho'? What's the play, P?"

After I told him what I had going on, he said, "Cool, P. What color are the tricks?"

"Majority of them are Mexicans. Some white. Two blacks."

"Ok. How much am I making off the door?"

"I'll give you $400 off every G. And plus, all the money they make off their performance. Take it or leave it, P."

"Look, I got some hoes still in Dallas. I'm sending two of my white hoes. Just send me the address and pictures of yo' hoes and all the other info. I'ma get some more tricks to come too. And we gonna do it like that. I'll call you later and let you know what's up."

"Bet. Send me some pictures of the two hoes. I'ma try to get some mo' people to come too," I told him.

* * *

Twenty-seven men had attended the party. Majority of them were working men, and there were a few dope boys. They sat on my two sofas, that I had covered with plastic, and a bunch of metal foldable chairs I had around the living room in my luxurious penthouse suite.

Even though I knew it wasn't going to get out of hand or have someone causing a disturbance, I still had four of my trusted armed homeboys working security. Keith was my door man. My young nigga, Poppa, was watching everything that went on, ready to put a nigga back in his place if he got out of line. B-Ray sold the drugs to the men who wanted them and kept an eye on everything, along with Poppa. And Lil' Ricky held $10,000 in ones to exchange them for bigger bills when the tricks wanted them. I was even gonna use Shae's Square Up account for the men who ran out of money by the time the fucking started. That way, they could use their credit cards to transfer money out of their accounts into Shae's hair business account.

Shae opened up the first show with a pole dance to "Can You Handle It" by Usher, in the center of the living room. She started off by grabbing the pole while throwing her ass in a circle. A few minutes later, she moved her long Brazilian sew-in from out the front to the back of her and then looked back at everyone seductively, making eye contact with the ones that had made it rain down on her while clapping her ass to the beat. After a while of dancing, she jumped up high on the pole and did a spin move to the middle of the pole. She had the strength to lock both hands and legs around the pole. She then popped her right cheek towards the crowd about fifteen times.

Then she unlocked her legs and grabbed the pole. She then put her legs into the air and slid her pussy up and down against the pole. You could see that her pussy was moist because of the thong being wet. Shae had almost every man in here eyes on her. You even had a couple dudes with their phones out recording it.

Two songs later, all the hoes except for Pinky started dancing and giving lap dances. Since Pinky couldn't dance, she DJ'd on my surround sound system, and while songs played, she served drinks in sexy lingerie.

After almost two hours of slow jams, rap, and a couple of pop songs, they began the balloon show. Only CeCe and Selena performed that act while the other hoes took a quick shower. They poured oil over each other's bodies in a sexy way and then used it to pop balloons. They put a balloon on a wooden chair and sat down on it. There were times they would try to sit down but then slip and fall down to the floor. They would get right up, laughing, and try to do it again. They had a bunch of fun playing around like that until every ho had a shower.

Luxury P's hoes raised the temperature when Carrie got on top of Ashley in a 69 position and they started eating each other out. The music was cut down low to where you could hear them moan and hear the sexual music, "Storm" by Jamie Foxx. I could tell they got down like that a lot with each other, because they knew each other's hot spots and knew how to entertain the audience without losing themselves in the moment at the same time. They were putting on a good show.

Shortly after, at the same time, Pinky heightened the excitement when she started eating Shae from the back. Shae had her back arched while clapping her phat ass cheeks in Pinky's face.

# Smoove Dolla

Her head went up and down through her ass. Cum glistened all over her pretty face. Pinky and Shae were the baddest here, so the sight of Pinky pleasing Shae in that manner and Shae loving the pleasure was beautiful to the eyes and aroused every man in here. I knew that made damn near every man in here want to fuck them, if not all of them. I sure did.

Carrie and Ashley stole the show when Carrie grabbed a thick, brown, 15-inch, two-way head rubber dildo, and put it deep inside Ashley's pink, fat pussy. Carrie was on top of Ashley, who had her legs folded back. She long dicked her for a minute, putting about ten inches in her, and slapped herself with the other side of it hard five times, turning her cheek red. Carrie spit on the dildo, went down on it a few times, then pulled the other end out of Ashley, and spat right on Ashley's wrinkled, pink asshole. She eased the big dildo into Ashley's ass slowly. When she got it in halfway, she deep throated it until her mouth touched around Ashley's butt hole. Carrie sucked it a few times while Ashley ate her out. Carrie then bit down on the rubber dick and guided it in and out of Ashley with her teeth.

Everyone except for Poppa and I went bananas. Most of the men stood up out of their seats and started jumping, yelling, applauding them, and cheering the hoes on while they rained money on them.

As I leaned up against the wall in the dimmed hallway, Shae looked at me with a seductive stare on her pretty face like she wanted to fuck me, and then she blew me a kiss. I smiled and blew her one back.

Shae couldn't handle what Pinky was doing to her pussy and butthole. Shae gasped, and her whole face beamed with satisfaction. At any moment, she would be squirting. She got up quick, and Pinky stood on her knees and got in between her legs and started sucking hard on Shae's pearl tongue. Seconds later, Pinky laid down on her back while Shae started squirting onto her body. She rubbed it all over her neck, tits, stomach, and pussy like she was being turned on by Shae's cum.

The men started making it rain on Pinky and Shae until Carrie and Ashley stole the attention again, three minutes later. Carrie gave

Ashley's mouth and face a cum shower while she just laid there.

Eighteen men left, leaving nine of them there, five Mexicans, three whites, and one Black. Some of the ones that left, walked out with one of the ho's numbers so they could meet up with them later on tonight or set something up for another day. One of the big-time dope dealers from North Dallas paid Shae $8000 to leave with him, so I let him have her for the night.

When time came to fuck the hoes, two Mexicans wanted Ashley and Pinky badly without them taking a shower. I made them pay $200 apiece for thirty minutes. It was like a big orgy all over the living room. Each ho was sucking and fucking someone or doing two men at the same time. A couple of the men waited to get their turn after a ho got out the shower. I had bought a 50-pack of condoms for this purpose.

At a time like this, I wished I had more queens in my stable so I could make more money than I did tonight. I made $6,200 tonight, plus the $8,000 that Shae made. All that was after I took out the $8,000 for Luxury P. The next time I had a party like this one in the future, I'ma have eight to ten hoes here, even if they weren't mine. By the end of the night, they might choose up with a pimp, liking what I had going. And the reason why I didn't try to knock Luxury P for his hoes was because there was a time when he could have knocked me for mine but didn't. I had to respect that. And, plus, he was my pimp partna. If his hoes didn't choose me verbally, I let them be.

After the tricks, my security, and Luxury P's hoes left, and mine took a shower, I had them sit down on the sofa in front of me. I stood up. "Night Stars, I am proud of y'all. Y'all did wonderful tonight. I appreciate you all for doing y'all's best, working as a team for it all to come out successful, and milking the shit out those tricks. For that reason, we're going big shopping tomorrow when you all wake up. I want this apartment spotless within an hour. So you all work together like y'all just did to get it done. Now excuse me while I retreat to my room. I'll tell you the next plan once this place is clean."

After they were finished cleaning up, I sent Pinky, CeCe, and

Selena to The W Hotel down the street in Downtown Dallas to work the internet. I kept them close so I wouldn't have to drive to break them if I wanted to. I went to sleep for three hours. When 5 A.M. came around, I called my hoes to get some rest for what we had planned later on today.

## Chapter 3

Yesterday, while ridin', my queens and I heard an advertisement on the radio that Baby Face, Marsha Ambrosius, and Tank had a concert coming up together next month at the Verizon Center in Grand Prairie. Shae reacted first in excitement, because Tank was one of her favorite R&B singers. Then CeCe, Pinky, and Selena joined in the conversation on how it was going to be a good concert.

Since my hoes did an awesome job for the last three weeks without any problems and did their best smashing for my ration, I wanted to do something for them, anyway, to show my appreciation better than I had been doing. I just didn't know what to do for them as a group, other than shopping, until now. I always let my hoes go shopping at least once a week. By them reacting to the advertisement, I knew they would like the concert. It was defined as fun for them, so I bought five tickets online.

Since my baby momma, Tiffany, had established one of the hottest female clothing lines in urban fashion, I wanted my hoes to advertise her designs. I gave her a call. "Hey, baby, what chu got goin' on?"

"Nuttin' much. Getting these packages ready to ship out in the morning. I'm surprised you called. You haven't called in four days. What's going on with you?"

"You wanna go to Speed's tonight? I need to talk some business with you."

"That's alright with me. I want to present something to you, too. What time you want to meet?"

"Meet me up there at 8. That's good with you?"

"Yeah, that's fine. I'll be up there," she told me.

After I got my hoes situated, I went to Speed's. Saturdays were the bar's busiest days. It was when they turned it into a club at night. There were a variety of races of both genders mingling in crowds and couples. The dance floor was full, and most of the pool tables were occupied. There were a few empty stools at the bar where Tiffany sat. There were a lot of sexy and fine young women here tonight. I swear, if Tiffany wasn't here, I would've done some macking to some of these females here and maybe came up on a ho tonight.

I walked up beside Tiffany, who was in deep thought about something, and said, "Hey, gorgeous. What chu thinking about, baby?"

"Our business." She smiled when she turned to see me. Naturally, seeing her smile made me smile. She had one of the most beautiful smiles I'd ever seen on a woman. She stood up from the stool and then we hugged.

"That dress and heels look amazing on you, and you smell wonderful, baby."

I knew that perfume. It was none other than OBESSION by Rihanna. Pinky had bought it for herself last week.

"Thanks, Damion." She addressed me by my first name. She always amazed me with her different styles of dress that fit her perfectly. She had on a red, tight-fitted, short dress that brought out every curve. Tiffany used to be a fat girl, weighing 296 pounds, a few years ago before I met her. Now her body was tight, right, and perfectly portioned, at 141 pounds. She stood at 5'8, thick and fine as an Amazon. She had long, straight, shiny Brazilian hair sewn in, that hung down over her shoulders. Red, short nails matched her dress, toenails, and the black red-bottom six-inch high heels. "Look at you, looking handsome as ever, and you smell wonderful as well."

"Thanks."

"You're welcome. I'm surprised to see you showed up on time, you usually be late."

"Yeah, I know. I wasn't doin' anything when I called you. Plus, I was looking forward to seeing you as soon as I could."

A pretty white brunette bartender walked up on us on the other side of the bar, smiling at us, and asked, "Excuse me, may I get you two anything?"

"Sure, give me a daquiri, light on ice, please," Tiffany told her.

"Okay, and you, sir?"

I didn't drink, so I ordered a glass of lemonade. When she returned with our drinks, she said, "Here you guys go. Enjoy. And by the way, that dress looks stunning on you. Where did you buy it from?"

"Thanks. I designed it myself. It's from Tiffany's Design and Collections. It's my—" Tiffany paused, looked at me, and said, "It's our clothing line."

Before she could go into her purse to get her business card, I beat her to the punch, got mine out my shirt pocket, and handed it to the bartender.

She stared at the card for a few seconds and then said, "I'll definitely give you a call. By the way, I'm Julie. And you?"

I wanted to show Tiffany some respect by not being on my phone and not trying to knock for a ho in her presence, but this bitch was asking for my pimpin'. A couple of minutes ago while she was pouring our drinks, I caught her sneaky ass eyeballing me when Tiffany wasn't looking. It was either my Ralph Lauren casual outfit, or maybe the Abercrombie & Fitch cologne, and the $80,000 worth of jewelry I had on. And according to how her mind operated, it could be my strong and smooth demeanor. Because even without all these accessories and clothes I wore, she'd still be feeling me. Either way, she was liking my campaign.

"I'm Monopoly. Good to meet you," I said while giving her a firm handshake. "And this is my son's mother and business partna, Tiffany. She's the brain, heart, and soul of our business."

They both shook each other's hand. "Nice to meet you, Tiffany. I'm new to Arlington. I'm from Tulsa, Oklahoma."

"Welcome to Texas. You're gonna love it here," Tiffany said.

"I have a feeling I am. Are you two celebrities or something?"

Tiffany laughed, because we'd been asked that same question before. I'd learned a valuable lesson from her a couple years ago. She taught me that when somebody asked you what you do for a living or thinks that you are someone famous because of how you dress or how you carry yourself, it means you are doing something right. And if someone asks that question and you're not what you want to be yet, don't deny it, because one day you will be, if you strive for it. It's not lying to yourself or anyone else. It's speaking it into existence and saying what you think you are. Tiffany and I were both salespersons, and we looked the part. We looked and acted like we were famous. A lot of people reacted to that.

"Yes, we are. We own one of the hottest fashion online companies and we're growing fast. And also, he's an R&B singer and songwriter."

"Are you really, Monopoly?"

"I am," I said, smiling.

"Where can I find your music at?"

"Just type Monopoly in on SoundCloud and YouTube. You'll hear my music and see my videos."

"That's so cool. Can I have your autograph, please?" She slid my card back to me with an ink pen. I signed the back of it. "Thanks so much. Are you two regulars here?"

"No. We come here every once and a while to shoot pool and talk business," Tiffany mentioned.

"Oh, okay." She looked down at the bar to see an impatient customer waiting that the other two bartenders hadn't got to yet. "Well, I have to get back to work. You two enjoy yourselves. I hope to see you again."

"You will, if you call," I told her.

"Sorry y'all, I have to go. I'll call you soon," she said as she rushed off.

Whenever she did call, I would be doing some obtaining and campaigning to knock her. She had a look like she could be a cheerleader for an NBA team. A cheerleader uniform was just what I would dress her up in to draw in tricks after I knocked her. She would fit perfectly in one. She had the gorgeous face, pretty, even teeth, white smile, and a tight body that would make a trick go broke to fuck with her. Her frame reminded me of the singer Carrie Underwood, but Julie was a little thicker. She had some tight daisy dukes on that hugged her little ass cheeks. Her skinny legs were flawlessly beautiful. Yeah, I'ma make that bitch my number one draft pick to get her to ho in this National Pimpin' Association.

Tiffany snapped me out my thoughts, saying, "Tunke, you ain't no good. And that bitch think she slick. I saw the way that bitch was looking at you." She shook her head.

I didn't entertain that comment. Instead, I changed the subject. She already knew what it was with me. It wasn't like I was still her man.

Pool was one of her favorite hobbies, so I knew that would get her feelings off of wanting to argue. I told her, "Let's get on this pool table. You beat me too many times the last time we played. I'm 'bout to get in that ass tonight."

"Oh, let's get it then," she said while getting down from the stool. "We can up the bet to $20 a game if you want to."

"That's a bet."

While we were playing the first game, she asked me what I wanted to talk to her about. She hit the yellow ball in the corner pocket then looked up at me. I told her about the concert that was in two weeks and how I wanted to pay to get my hoes' outfits made by our company. "Yea, I'll do it for you, but why you didn't ask me to go with you?"

"I didn't ask them to go. They wanted to go themselves, so I bought them tickets."

"It's okay. Umm, we gonna have to do it tomorrow because I'ma be out of town next week. I'ma be busy, so I need to get to work on their outfits as soon as possible."

"We can do it tomorrow," I said after I missed hitting the blue ball in the middle pocket by putting too much pressure on it. "What you got to present to me?"

"The other day I was thinking about how to advertise our business better, and it came to me. A fashion show," she said, excited. "What do you think about us doing one?"

"I think it's a great idea. When you talking about doing it?"

"ASAP. But I need your help on this, Damion. I need some of your connects."

"Okay, I got you. Let's schedule a date before you leave or after you get back to get together. We can put an outline together on everything we need for the fashion show. Like goin' over all expenses, models, artists, other designers, a good location. Shit like that. But we can definitely do it. And also, I'ma talk to some of my Mason brothers so we can get our business sponsored by someone and on the radio. I probably can even get you an interview on a morning show. I'll let you know."

"Really, Tunke? That'd be wonderful. Our shit will boom to the sky if we do that."

"Yea, I know. I'ma see what they say. If they don't, which I doubt it, I'll pay for it all out my own pocket."

"Ohh, thank you soo much, Damion!" she said while hugging me.

After seven games, with her winning four, and five daiquiris swimming through her stomach, Tiffany wanted to go home. I had a feeling she was going to ask me to come home tonight. So when she did, I didn't decline. I wanted to anyway. For one, I wanted some pussy. And two, I hadn't been spending much time at the house or with her and my son. Almost every conversation Tiffany, our four-year-old son, and I had in the past month was on Facetime. They really deserved better. Tiffany was a great woman. She did everything that I'd asked of her to do. She wanted the best for me and me for her. But I knew that as long as I was pimpin', they wouldn't get the time they deserved from me. I was dedicated to this game, and I didn't see myself giving up the game any time soon, especially not for any woman.

*** 

As soon as Tiffany closed our garage door and locked it, I pressed her up against the door with her back facing me. She couldn't go anywhere. "Tunke, what are you doing?"

I raised her dress up to her waist. A red thong exposed nothing but a bare, smooth, brown, phat ass. "All this muthafuckin' ass you got here." I spanked her hard on the right cheek, making her say 'ouch.'

"Uh, uhh, Damion, wait. Let's go upstairs."

"Shut up! I'm running this show right now."

She tried to get loose, but I overpowered her. I unbuckled my belt and stepped out of my shorts. I started kissing and sucking on her neck. "No, Damion, don't go in me raw. Please don't," she said while moaning.

I half-ass cared what she was talking about. I didn't think I had anything. All my hoes and I had gotten AIDS tests two weeks ago. Normally, I took one every six months, but since I had two new hoes, I went to get us all a checkup. Shae was the only woman I had sex with bareback within that time. Everybody's tests had come back negative, so we didn't have AIDS.

I took my dick out my Louis Vuitton boxers. I pulled her thong to the side then guided my eight-inch dick inside her wet, tight pussy. It felt like home sweet home. After a short while of pumping in and out of her, she started throwing her phat ass back at me while I sucked hard on her neck. Then I walked her to the washing machine that was six feet away from the door, while still inside her. I bent her over then put my right arm under her flat stomach and my left arm on the top of her upper phat ass cheeks. I started giving that ass a good thrashing, making her jiggly ass shake and bounce uncontrollably back and forth at me.

After fucking her from the back for a while, I reached over her to turn on the washer machine. I put it on the highest washing process. As the water started filling the machine, I long stroked her four times, pulled out of her, turned her around, then picked her up and laid her on her back on top of the washing machine. I slid her towards me until her lower back was on the edge of the washer. "Hold them sexy ass legs up in the air, baby." She obeyed my command. I put my arms up under her thick thighs. I lapped my tongue up and down repeatedly between her hanging cheeks.

After a couple of minutes had passed by, the washing process took its course, helping me please Tiffany better. It went around rapidly. I put my head at her love box, sucking and playing with her pearl tongue while the machine moved her. That treatment made her go crazy. She caressed her breasts and nipples with both hands. Then she touched and scratched at my shoulders. After that, she rubbed my neck and then my waved-up, bald fade haircut.

After she came, I scooted a stepping stool in front of me. With my left foot, I stepped on top of it then put my dick back inside her warm, welcoming pussy. The washer made her feel better, the way it rotated her. Her pussy walls grabbed at my dick every time I went in her, making me want to nut.

When she felt me pumping hard, trying to bust, she put her right hand on my six pack and said, "Tunke, baby, don't nut in me. I got too much going on. I don't want to deal with another baby right now. Let's wait, baby. Nut in my mouth, baby."

I respected her wishes and pulled out before I nutted. To tell you the truth, I felt the same way she did. I didn't want any more babies either. But I was just about to nut in her. The only reason why I couldn't stop was that her pussy was too good to pull out on my own. I was glad she stopped me.

I stepped down off the stool while jacking my dick. She jumped down from off the washer and pushed me to the wall. She dropped down to her knees and started jacking me off, then went to work with my dick in her mouth. She slid her tongue around my dick head, then sucked my head while jacking me off. After she swallowed every drop, she said, "Come on, baby, let's go to our bedroom."

We made love until the late night and fell asleep.

## Chapter 4

The sounds of pots hitting up against the wall of the sink woke me from a good sleep. I reached for Tiffany without opening my eyes yet. She must have been in the kitchen, because she wasn't in bed. The alarm clock on the night stand read 8:13 A.M. Even though I felt I just went to sleep a couple hours ago, I still got up and out of bed.

I put my Louis Vuitton boxers on, brushed my teeth, went to get both of my phones off the chargers, and then walked to the kitchen. Tiffany stood, chopping beef sausages. I walked up behind her, putting my hands around her small waist, and said, "Top of the morning, gorgeous."

"Good morning, love." Then she gave me a kiss on the cheek. "Are you hungry, baby?"

"Hell yeah, what you cookin'?" I asked as I walked out the kitchen to take a seat at our bar. Then, I turned my phones on.

"Breakfast burritos."

Seconds later, missed calls and text messages came to my throw-away touch-screen phone. It ended up being 54 missed calls and 28 texts from Selena, Pinky, and CeCe. I wondered why I didn't see anything from Shae. I started reading my texts to see what was going on.

Pinky ll:37 P.M.
Shae about to go to jail. I was in the car waiting on her. The police just questioned me. They let me go. Give me a call back.

Pinky 11:39 P.M.
Daddy, call me.

Pinky 12:00 A.M.
I been tryna call you but you not answering. I'm 'bout to go to my mom house.

Selena 11:43 P.M.

Daddy, R U OK? Do U still want us to work?
Selena 12:05 A.M.
Daddy, Pinky went to Fort Worth in the car. What U want us to do?

Selena 12:07 A.M.
Daddy, please answer the phone.

CeCe 12:00 A.M.
Daddy, Pinky hasn't come back in the car yet. Call us.

I stopped reading them after that one. "Ol' dumb ass bitch," I said out loud.

"What's wrong, baby?" Tiffany asked.

"This faggot ho of mine." Shaking my head. "Never mind her tho'. Shae got locked up for prostitution last night."

"Damn, that's fucked up."

"I'm about to call Selena and see if Shae called her. She knows not to call me from no jail cell."

I didn't want to talk on my main line about anything illegal, and I wasn't about to talk on this throw-away phone any more after I made a few calls. I would be erasing everything out this phone dealing with prostitution, break it, and then trash it. I didn't trust the laws at all. I knew they went through Shae's phone to see if she had a pimp. Checking her text messages, call log, contacts, to see who was posting her ads. My hoes had multiple phones. Every phone that Shae called would be trashed and replaced with new ones. See, the laws didn't want the hoes, they wanted the pimp. They thought he was somewhere close by when it came to a ho prostituting, and they pulled all types of tactics trying to catch him. You could see that in the way they had the laws set up for pimps and prostitutes. For example, look at the way they had all pimp charges set up. Pimping, attempted pimping, pandering, promotion of prostitution, compelling prostitution, and trafficking of a persons. They were all felonies. Now look at the way the hoes charges were set up, theirs were misdemeanors. The laws make real pimps look like we're making women prostitute and we're not. Real prostitutes who are with real pimps, prostitute and give the money they make to us willingly. They want to be pimped on. The laws put real pimps in the same category as sex traffickers, human traffickers, and gorilla pimps. Real pimps are not in that category. The system is fucked up.

I went to my Range Rover to get one of my throw-away flip phones to call Selena. As soon as she answered, her fast talking Mexican ass started going off at the mouth. "Daddy, we called you like crazy. We thought something happened to you. I called you like 15 times. You ok?" she asked on speaker phone.

"Yeah, I'm good. The two phones I carry on me went dead last night. Where did Shae get locked up at?"

"Arlington."

"What happened?"

"Pinky said her and Shae went on a out call together. When they left, Shae got another out call. That one was a undercover. Me and CeCe did a couple of in calls, but we stopped because we didn't hear from you. And Pinky still hasn't came back with the car yet."

"She what! When the last time you talked to her?"

"Last night at 12 something."

"Did she say when she was coming back?"

"No ."

"Don't worry about that ho. Pack up all her shit now. Everything. And sit it by the door."

"Okay."

"I'll deal with her later. Don't call or answer her phone calls. You or CeCe. I mean that. Don't let me find out y'all talked to her either, or y'all will be leaving with her."

"Okay, Daddy, I won't."

"Everything good over there, tho'?"

"Yeah, it's good."

"Cool. Don't do no calls from those phones. If they regulars, do them, but no new tricks. If you want to just chill, y'all can until I get there. I'm about to bond Shae out. I know she been waiting on me. We'll be there in a little bit."

I called Tight Game's bail bondsman company and had them bond Shae out.

"You about to leave or what?" Tiffany asked when I got off the phone.

"Nah, baby. I'ma stay for a little bit. I'm probably leaving after I eat tho'. It's gonna take about an hour for them to release her. What time do you want us to come over today?" I asked while deleting my hoes' ads off the internet.

"Come at 3-ish. I'll be ready by then."

"What you gonna be doing till then?"

"Pretty much just shipping boxes off to my customers. One of my workers from Atlanta should be here soon to help me."

"How's business been lately?"

"Wonderful, Tunke. I'm at an all-time high right now. You haven't been looking at your bank receipts?"

"I haven't lately. I look at it once every week. I barely spend money from that account." I had two accounts at two different banks. Our business account was at Bank of America. My warehouse job and the sales from all my music went to Chase. I bought things with cash more than I did with my credit if it didn't involve signing a contract to purchase what I wanted. Since I said I didn't look at my bank statements but once a week, from now on I would, just in case someone did some funny business. I wouldn't allow myself to get played if I could help it. But I trusted Tiffany in that area.

"Well, if you haven't noticed, business is great and getting better. I'm about to launch my first women's boutique in Atlanta in a couple months," she said, excited, while wrapping a burrito.

"I'm proud of you, baby. I remember when you just had the idea of wanting to design clothes and you had sketches on drawing paper. You came a long way from three years ago. I believe you can climb to higher heights on your path with your gift than what you have goin' on now. I'm glad I invested in you. I see what you've created has made you a happier woman. Look what you have accomplished with just a little help from me. An online clothing store. You're about to open up your own boutique. You're about to do your own fashion show. This is a million-dollar home we live in. You doin' it, baby."

"You a part of why I did it. I'm doin' it for us," she said while putting our plates of food that looked and smelled delicious on the counter where I sat. Then she filled up two clear glasses of freshly made orange juice and placed them on the side of our plates.

She came around the bar to sit next to me. "I thought by me building all this for our family that it would change you. And make you want to go legal and pursue your dreams wholeheartedly." She looked at me and placed her left hand on my thigh. "Baby, I'm doing my best to have patience with you. We really do need you."

She ran me hot a little bit with what she just said. I had to get on her ass talking about having patience with me. "I want you to listen to me and listen good. You can't change no motherfuckin' man. So, get that shit out your head right now. If a man changes for you, that means he loves you more than he loves himself. That's a weak nigga. A nigga like me can never do such a thing. I broke it off with you for a reason. Because I wasn't ready to lay this game down. No doubt, I love you and I appreciate how you treat me and everything that you've done for me. I really do hope you will wait, but if you feel that you no longer can wait, do what you gotta do for you. Life goes on. I'll understand. If what I'm doin' is hurting you, you can't continue to accept this from me. Live your life, Tif." I really wanted her around and her to accept my lifestyle and still be my woman. But I knew by her staying with me, she would continue to be a fool. Something she had been for too long now. She was better than that. She deserved better.

Her dreamy hazel eyes started to water. She put her left hand into my right hand and held it tight. "I don't want to leave you, Tunke. Your son and I need you in our lives. You're the reason for my happiness. None of what I have now would exist if it was not for you. I wouldn't have thought of some of the ideas, if wasn't for you. Yea, I know, eventually my business would have gotten started, but not like this. I've reached heights that I didn't know existed because of your motivation behind me. I don't want to lose you."

"You're not going to lose me. I just can't be your man, at least not right now. You'll be ok. I'll still be in y'all life." I knew it was time to leave this square shit here at this house and run to the game that I loved so much. Every time I came around her, she was with this bullshit that I didn't want to talk about. That was the after effect every time I fucked her.

Our relationship was better when I first met Tiffany. There was no complaining or problems about me pimping. That's what made me like her even more, because she accepted a nigga pimpin'. I had got on some square shit while still pimpin' and went on a bunch of dates with her. I wouldn't lie, I enjoyed every moment with Tiffany. Even though she had an outgoing personality, she didn't open her legs because I had money. That had me intrigued with her, along with her good company. I started to fall for her after a while, in the midst of getting to know her. It turned into love and we got into a relationship, then she had gotten pregnant with our son. I broke it off with her eleven months ago because she started complaining about me pimping. It was the same complaining a woman did when she wanted her man to get out the drug game. I wasn't about to put up with that.

A woman had two choices when fucking with a nigga like me, she could either accept my lifestyle without complaining or leave me the fuck alone, as simple as that. Even though she was jealous of me being around my hoes, it was more of the fact she didn't want me to get locked up again, which I could understand. I came to learn that it was hard to balance a committed relationship with a woman while pimpin'. A lot of square women couldn't deal with a nigga that was a real pimp. It wasn't like having a wife while you're in the dope game. It was different in a lot of ways. There's always going to be jealousy and envy. The same vice versa when it came to hoes.

The hoes would think you're not pimpin' and get on some bullshit once they find out that her pimp had a square bitch at home, especially if she wasn't contributing to the cause like they were. It didn't mix. It was better to just pimp. A ho was a pimp's woman just as a pimp was a ho's man. With some pimp niggas, you'd never know what one did behind closed doors. A bunch of them fronted like they were deep in game and it was straight pimpin' with them, but they'd never tell you what was really going on with them. Some of them would be married and some more shit. A real pimp is going to pimp, that's the only thing he's going to be committed to. That's why I left that square shit alone. I was disrespecting the game by doing that shit.

After I ate the delicious food, I took a quick shower and jumped fly in a new Versace casual outfit with a pair of white Versace loafers.

Before leaving the house, just to be on the safe side, I took 14 debit cards my hoes used for posting prostitution ads out my Range Rover and kept two that I hadn't used yet that still had over $200 on them. I cut the 14 cards in fours with scissors. I still had money on some of the cards I'd used, but fuck that money. I wasn't about to chance getting caught with them. I also took seven throw-away phones out my truck that had been used for only prostitution, took the SIM cards out them and then broke them. I placed it all in a black garbage bag. Upon leaving the house, I bust the bag and dumped everything into our neighborhood dumpster.

I drove from North Richland Hills to Arlington City Jail. Even though I trusted Shae, I was a little leery of being in front of the police station. Shae knew a lot about me. I been knowing her since middle school. I was the one who put her in the game seven years ago. The results of her telling on me could destroy almost everything that I'd worked hard to build. Truth be told, the proof was in the pudding. She'd passed a lot of my tests that I'd put in front of her to prove her loyalty. She didn't call me when she had gotten arrested. Instead, she called my hoes and had them tell me. Shae did what she was instructed to do if I had multiple hoes in my stable and she got locked up. She was my bottom bitch in every sense of the two words. However, I was still going to check her about not screening tricks good enough. She shouldn't have gotten locked up. It'd been a couple of months since I last checked her about something. I wasn't mad at Shae, but I believed she still needed to be checked. I couldn't let her get away without her being handled.

Shae walked out of a set of see-through glass double doors in front of the police station 37 minutes after I arrived. After she got inside, I took a look at my surroundings. I didn't notice anyone looking at my Range Rover. They couldn't see inside because of my 5% tinted windows. I sensed I was a little paranoid, so I calmed myself and attended to Shae.

I put my right hand under her chin while looking at her facial expression and into her eyes, searching for any signs of dishonor, disloyalty, frustration, or anger. But the only thing I saw was a little fear. "You okay, baby?"

"Yeah, I'm good. Glad to be out of there. I didn't have any money on me when I got arrested. Pinky should have gave you $500 to $600, if not more."

"We'll talk about Pinky and the money in a minute. What I want to know is did they question you?"

"Yeah."

"How many times?"

Two."

"What did they say?" I asked.

"The usual, wanting to know if I was working for a pimp. They went through my phone too, but I don't think they knew what name to go under since I had you under Danielle. Basically, that's what they wanted to know."

I grabbed her by her sew-in black hair, wrapped it around my right hand, then pulled her towards me. She started pleading with me. "Daddy, what I do?"

"Bitch, shut the fuck up, ho. You bet not be lying to me, ho. Now what I want to understand is you are a seasoned ho. How the fuck you let yourself get busted? You couldn't have screened him the proper way."

"I apologize, Daddy. He was a Mexican cowboy. I thought he was legit. It was a little slow last night. I was so caught up in trying to make some money that I just forgot. Sorry, Daddy," she said, trying to reason with me.

"I really do want to understand why this happened. I might be wrong, but I am about to find out if I'm listening good enough. Your actions are signs of being burnt out. You are the ho I would never think of letting herself get caught up in a sting operation. You stand firm as my bottom, but it seems like we are not on the same page right now. You stepped out of my program, ho. Because if you were on my program, you would have screened that Mexican cowboy, no matter what the fuck he looked like or what it seemed like. Are you burnt out, bitch?"

"No, Daddy, I'm not."

"I have an overseas account with $100,000 in it, ready for you to get at any time. You will be straight. If you feel like you want to quit hoing, you can leave. Let me know right now if you're sure about your decision," I said, testing her to see what she would say and meaning it at the same time.

"Yes, Daddy, I'm sure. You know I'm here for you for however long you want me to be here. I've proven myself to you so many times, and I still will. I will fuck all day and all night for you if you wanted. I'm here for you. I believe in you, Daddy. I enjoyed myself with you and I'm proud to be your bottom bitch. If I wasn't, I would have been left you. I fucked up, and I promise it won't ever happen again."

I let go of her hair. "Don't let it happen again."

"I won't, Daddy."

I believed most of what she told me. Only a thoroughbred would stay down with a pimp who got sentenced to federal prison. When every ho of mine including my ex-bottom bitch, Fancy, burnt off of me, Shae was the only ho that stayed down with me the whole time while still smashing for that ration. I trusted her. I even loved her. She was there when I needed her the most, at my lowest and darkest times. It would be inhuman if I didn't love her for that. But all that didn't mean she wasn't burnt out. I felt she was. Next time, depending on what she did wrong, I probably would let her go. I wouldn't want to, but it would be best for her. Like a pimp once said, "The game will wear down the toughest hoes." I'd just have to watch her more now to see if she was really burnt out. In due time, her actions would tell me.

At the red light, I dialed Selena's number on a throw-away flip phone. There was no answer. I redialed the number, same results. "Shae, call Selena on your phone. She didn't answer for me," I told Shae when I got on the 360 freeway.

A couple of minutes had passed by. "Daddy, she not answering for me neither."

"I wonder why the fuck she not answering the phone. I just talked to her two hours ago. Call CeCe's phone."

CeCe answered. My ears were open. I didn't want to panic, but this could mean a bunch of things. For example, it could mean that they chose up with another pimp or they became renegade hoes, or I could be trippin'. The reason I thought that was because I didn't answer the phone for them last night. As stupid as it sounds, a ho might leave because of that. You never knew with a ho. "Hell yeah, I'm out, bitch. Daddy ain't gonna let a bitch stay in that motherfucker. Anyway, Daddy was calling Selena. She didn't answer, so he had me call you. Hold on." She handed me her phone. "It's CeCe, Daddy."

"Wuz goin' on over there?"

"Selena had a regular come thru. He been here like 20 minutes already. He only wanted 30 minutes."

"What chu doin'?"

"I was using the restroom. I'm 'bout to take a shower now."

"Pinky there yet?" I asked.

"Nope. She called but you told us not to answer for her. She text me asking was you here and said she was on her way."

"When was this?"

"About a hour ago," CeCe said.

"Okay. Go ahead and get in the shower." After hanging up the phone, I told Shae, "You know Pinky didn't go back to that room last night?"

"No shit, Daddy. What she say when you talked to her?"

"I haven't talked to her," I said, not telling her why I didn't talk to her last night. I didn't have to explain myself to her. "She claim she went to her momma house. I know that's bullshit."

"And you know it," she said while shaking her head. "Daddy, I

68

hope she didn't fuck my car up. What you gonna do to her?"

I put on a devilish grin. "I'm still working on putting it all together in my head. But I am taking proposals. Since it is your car, you have any suggestions?"

"Pinky's my girl. I like her, but…" She looked down as if to think of something. "She do need to be taught a lesson. Because if you don't discipline her, she gonna do some mo' faggot shit again. And I know it's gonna be worse next time. I don't want to do it to her, but she fucked up. Trunk her. That should do it."

"If everything goes to plan, I'ma do it after we come back from Tiffany's house."

Two minutes later, upon our arrival to the hotel, we saw the white trick leaving the room going to a Ford 2011 Mustang GT. When he drove off, we went inside. There were a few snacks and a couple of soda bottles here and there in the room, but overall, it was clean. Far from what I expected it to look like. CeCe was still in the shower with the door closed. She had music by Kevin Gates on in the bathroom.

About four minutes later, while I'm counting my money that Selena and CeCe had made from the night before, I heard light knocks coming from the door. I looked at Selena. "Y'all expecting somebody?"

"Naw, not me. It's probably for CeCe. Or it could be Pinky," Selena told me, looking at her phone. "It can't be that trick that just left either."

"Probably." But I still took my pistol out from my waistband. I hoped this wasn't the police. But I thought again. The knocks were too light to be the laws. I looked out the peep hole. It was Pinky.

I opened the door to let her in. I closed the door behind her. "Your things are packed up already for you so you can go."

"What you talking about, Daddy?" she said with a confused look on her face.

"It's clear you don't want to be here, doin' that faggot shit you did. So, don't play dumb like you don't know what the fuck I'm talking about."

"I called you four times, Daddy, you didn't answer. And I text you saying where I was going. I really did need to go to my mom's."

I grabbed her by the hair from the back and pulled her hair until her chin was pointing up in the air, where she could see behind her. "Bitch, I don't give a fuck where you went. You should have brought yo' bitch ass back to this room where you belong, ho," I said, and then shoved her to the floor by the foot of the bed.

"I'm sorry, Daddy! I'm sorry!"

"I don't wanna hear that. You fucked up, now you about to pay, simple as that. Selena, you just had a date, right?"

"Yes, Daddy."

"Get naked. Lay on the bed close to the edge and open yo' legs. You about to get some of this amazing head she got to give." She obeyed my command.

"Daddy, come on, don't do me like that, please. I'm sorry," Pinky begged.

"I'm not doin' you like anything. You brought this upon yo' muthafuckin' self. Now, you either eat her pussy or I can call you a cab to take you to yo' mom's. Your bags are already packed. It's your decision. You better hurry up before I choose for you." Even though Selena didn't have sex with a bunch of tricks, I still thought it'd be humiliating Pinky by having her eat Selena after she had sex with a john, all in front of two of her sisters.

Pinky turned towards Selena. They looked at each other for a couple of seconds, as to say let's fake this shit and get this shit done. At least, that's what I got out of them looking at each other.

When Pinky went down on her, I picked up her white Michael Kors purse off the floor. "And, bitch, my trap better be right, too, or you really gon' get the fuck out my life."

I pulled out a roll of money that came out to be $515, which wasn't bad. She probably did go to her momma's house, but that didn't mean she didn't go to the drug dealer's trap to buy some heroin to snort either.

Selena had been moaning since Pinky laid tongue on her. Both of them had their eyes closed, but for two different reasons. I got up close to Pinky's ear and said calmly as possible, "Open yo' senses, bitch. I want you to see, smell, taste, feel, and hear everything. I told you we're a motherfuckin' business, ho. We don't got time for motherfuckin' playing. You see why when I gave you the rules of this game, I told you, ho, we're about business not pleasure, bitch. And you made last night all about pleasure. For that, you about to please my ho. You about to make her cum twice. She already came once. You got one mo' to go, ho. Clean that trick up off that pussy."

I stood up. "How it feel, Selena? Do it feel good or what?"

She nodded her head. "Your audience might not understand that language. We want to hear you say it. Do it feel good?"

"Yes, Daddy, yes!" she said as she moaned.

CeCe had come out the bathroom with a white towel wrapped around her body and one around her head. "What's going on?"

"She hooking Selena up with some of that good head."

"I hope she know she ain't take no shower yet after fucking with that trick," she said, making the situation harder on Pinky.

"Oh, we all know. This is one of her punishments."

After a couple minutes had passed, Selena moaned louder, lifting her back off the bed. "Oh, shit. I'm cumming. I'm cumming, Pinky! Fuck!" Selena grabbed Pinky's head and attempted to put her fingers in her hair, but she threw Selena's hands away from her and got up.

Pinky walked away in shame with her head down towards the bathroom. "CeCe, don't follow behind her. Don't help her do shit. Let the faggot bitch cry by her motherfucking self. And Pinky, don't take too long, because you 'bout to work and Selena need to shower. So do whatever you gotta do quick so we can go."

"I'm 'bout to go to the other room to take a bath. You want me for anything before I go, Daddy?" Shae asked.

"Yea, I wanted to tell you something, but I'll go head and announce it to everybody. You all are not gonna work today until I find out what's goin' on with these stings, who's operating them, when, and where. I should have gotten notified beforehand. Anyway, you three are free to have a little fun. What I mean by that is shopping and something that can occupy you queens' minds until I say times up. That don't mean go be a faggot and do what y'all want to do. Y'all are still under a pimp's law. I want you all back here at this room by two. Don't be late. Because if you late, that's gonna fuck up y'all's chances of getting y'all's clothes for the concert. We got to be on schedule. And delete all that shit out those phones so I can trash them later."

I gave Shae $5000 for their pleasures. While Pinky washed her face and brushed her teeth, I posted her on an escort site I knew the undercovers couldn't do any stings on.

While riding down Collins, Pinky had gotten a call, so I lowered the volume to "Space Age Pimpin'" by 8 Ball and MJG, because I didn't want to fuck up her opportunity of making my money. Seconds later, I recognized that she wasn't talking to a trick. "That don't sound like you getting at no paper, ho. Who you talking to?"

"My mom."

"You should have told her everything you needed to last night. Get off the phone."

"But it's my mom, Daddy."

"I don't care who it is. It can be the president for all I care. If you want mom to take care of you, I'll be glad to take you to her right now. But if you my ho, you better get off that phone. You on my time right now. Tell Momma you love her and you'll talk to her later when you can."

"I'll talk to you later, Momma." She turned my way after hanging up the phone. "Daddy, can I ask you something please?"

"What is it?"

"I've made you thousands of dollars over the last three weeks. I made you the most out of all my sisters since I been with you, and this is how you gon' treat me?"

As soon as I got in a parking space at CVS Pharmacy store, I turned towards her and said, "I been pimpin' for several years now and I came to learn to not let the big money a ho makes cloud my vision of a ho being a faggot bitch. To me, the most important thing is can a bitch follow my instructions, everything else will fall into place. That means I don't give a fuck about the money you bring me if your actions don't match up with your word. I'm not gonna let no woman play with my pimpin'. Now, I'm not no insecure ass nigga in no sense of the word. You been with me long enough to know I give you your freedom to do what you want to do in respect to me as your man. You should know how to please the nigga you with. I been drilling it in your head since the first day. I want you to answer this, though. I've been honest with you since day one and will remain doin' so until the second you depart from my pimpin'. Now, I want you to be honest with me. I believe you did visit yo' mom. But, I also know you went to the dope man trap too. Am I correct?"

"Daddy, I ain't gon' lie, I did. I'm sorry."

"I thought so. That's why I do what I do, ho." The way I see it, if you let a ho play with you and get away with it, then she's not going to respect you. I want respect. I admit, I tripped out by being at Tiffany's house. I should have been at the room with my hoes or answered the phone when they called. Maybe none of this would have happened if I was there pimpin'. But, that is beside the point. Pinky knew better, she should have went to the room. Because she didn't do it, there's consequences for what she did.

I went inside the store to buy her what I call a ho pack. It consists of a pack of condoms, a big box of body wipes, and a pack of Doublemint gum. She already had heroin to kill her pain, so I was about to max her ass out until it was time to go to Tiffany's house.

I took Pinky to a Hampton Hotel on the service road off of Interstate 20. While Pinky was inside paying for her room, I saw a pretty, short white woman walking back to an old grey Honda Accord in the parking lot. I instantly got out the car and made my way to her. Up close, she was more attractive than she was far away. First thing I noticed was her hair. Long dark hair hung down from all the sides of her head, except for the left side that was cut with a one guard on clippers. Her cloudless-sunny-day blue eyes looked me dead in the eyes as I got closer up on her. She stood about 5'7, slim built with perky tits poking out a white tank top with no bra. Blue skinny jeans hugged her slim legs and a pair of clean K-Swiss were on her small feet. Her frame reminded me of Taylor Swift, but she was shorter and a little thicker.

"Ugh, don't tell me you a pimp. You the second pimp that came up to me today. I'm getting tired of y'all. No, I don't want to fuck with you." She opened the back driver's side door and shoved a black trash bag inside.

Most times, when a woman had rejected a man's approach to talk to her, It was because she didn't give him any cues to come talk to her in the first place. Me, I didn't give a fuck either way, because I knew ways around the rejection. If she rejected my approach, I knew either my style of dress or the attitude of me being a boss and me acting like it's her loss might make her change her mind. If that didn't work, then so be it. Like I said before, it's her loss.

This wasn't the place nor the right time to check a disrespectful ass ho the way I wanted to. There were people coming and going out the hotel. I didn't want to overstep my boundaries in public, so I replied back in a positive, smooth, nonactive, and unaffected way that would be effective because she was probably testing me, trying to target any insecurity I might have and to see how I would react. "I haven't said anything to you for you to be so defensive. I know you didn't pick up a bad vibe from my appearance. So, don't be afraid of what I do without knowing who I am. I don't know what you've heard or have experienced with a pimp, but I'm not a vulture of the game."

I could tell from her tone of voice, facial expression, and body language that she was frustrated about something other than me. To be an outstanding pimp, you had to know how to read certain women you came across so you would know how to come at them. I knew if what I just said didn't get the bitch to break down at least one barrier, then adding what I'm about to say to what I just said would. "I don't think it's me being a pimp that's bothering you. Whatever you're going through, it will get better. I once heard a wise man say count your blessings. That means think about all the other times you weren't going to make it and you still made it. You'll make it this time as well. I don't know why you're so frustrated, but I do want to know one thing. I want to know why a woman as beautiful as you is not smiling? What got you so upset?" I asked as we stared in each other's eyes.

"I'm just having a bad day," she said, opening up to me.

"And why is that?" I asked like I really cared and wanted to listen to her problems.

She shook her head then looked away, probably trying to fight not talking to me or didn't want to talk about her troubles with me. Seconds later, she looked back at me and said, "I'm sorry, I normally don't act like this. It's a bad day. My damn car wouldn't start this morning. So, I was stuck at the club for three hours. I'm late picking up my son from the babysitter."

"I accept your apology. I understand how it can be sometimes. What's wrong with the car?"

"I really don't know. The bouncer at the club said it was something wrong with the transmission, but I don't think he knows what the hell he was talking about since it's running now after pouring some kind of liquid in it."

"Well, look, my papa's a mechanic. I can have him look at it for you for free if you want. And if he does fix it, it's already paid for." I had given my papa $2000 two weeks ago because he claimed he needed it for something important. When I gave it to him, we agreed on if I ever needed one of my cars fixed, I was bringing the car to him.

"Really?" she asked. "Don't be lying to me. Are you serious?"

"Everything I say is realism. It wouldn't be nothing to get it fixed. What will be better is getting with the team so you can put yourself in a brand-new Benz or Lexus or Jaguar by the end of next month."

"I don't know about all that. But I would like my car worked on, if you're really gonna do it for me." I had played on her weakness, hoping she would test what I said about getting her a new car, but she didn't bite. Once I got her car fixed, I'd apply more pressure on her.

"I got you. Give me your phone. I'ma give you his number and mine."

She handled me her iPhone. I saved both numbers in her phone. Then she told me to call myself from her phone so I could have her number. "My name's Rose. What's yours?"

"Monopoly."

"Nice to meet you, Monopoly. Sorry we met on a bad note," she said with a smile for the first time.

"Now there goes that beautiful smile I been waiting to see." She blushed a little, turning a bit red. "It's okay, tho'. I'm not trying to hold you up. I know you got things to do. We'll talk some other time. I'm throwing a Sunday Funday party at Joe Pool Lake tomorrow for the kids and adults. Food, entertainment, liquor, all free. You should come through, it's gonna be lots of fun. It'll be a good release from your troubles."

She took a deep breath and then said, "Yeah, you right about that. I might gather up my home girls and our kids and see what you got going."

Even though this was a ho, it was always good to meet a woman in public the first time you both went out. Whatever you're trying to get out of her, whether it was money, a ho, or sex, she'd be more receptive to game. Normally, upon meeting a square woman, to break down any barriers she might have up, I'd offer to take her out somewhere at that very moment of meeting her on my expense, if she was free to go. It was best to pick the place to show her your flavor and your style, or anywhere she wanted to go. By doing that, it initiated the first date. She'd feel more comfortable in public, telling me whatever I wanted to know once I asked. In the process of getting to know her, I'd be selling myself to her. Some might call it tricking, but it didn't matter to me because I never did it for sex, only to knock a square bitch into the game. Almost every time I'd used that game, it worked out in my favor.

"Do that. Well, I'ma let you get on your way and pick up your son. Just call me whenever you feel like it."

"Okay, I will. You do the same."

"I got you. Have a good day. Don't let your temporary problems affect your day when you know you gonna make a way to make it better."

She smiled. "Thanks for the encouragement. I gotta go, Monopoly. I'll catch up with you soon."

It seemed like this white girl had a good head on her shoulders as far as being smart and ambitious. I didn't like assuming things about a woman. I knew I had to mack then react. I planned to do just that as soon as I got a chance. One thing I knew about renegade hoes and strippers was that a bunch of them didn't have their own car and own crib. I didn't quite understand why that was. I knew that if they didn't have a pimp and still didn't have a car, house, or apartment, they were irresponsible and playing with themselves. A ho should have something when she's in control of all of her money. Most hoes without pimps spent their money on drugs and uncontrollable shopping. Their mindset was they'd make the money right back. I'd give props to the ones that were paying for school, the ones that were making a quick buck to take care of their kids, or hoing to do something important and an independent ho that was making big moves.

But the ones that were on drugs and didn't know how to budget their money were out of line for not hoing for a pimp. Most of them were not elevating at all and were in the same predicament they were in last year, and the year before that, or a worse situation. It just didn't make any sense to me. Even though these renegade hoes claimed they were independent and didn't want a pimp deep down inside they do', the way I saw it, all the good feelings an independent ho felt were really an illusion. A lot of them were faking it until they made it. I believed if they came across the right real pimp they were compatible to and liked, they'd choose up if they didn't have too much outside pressure on their decision. Only pimps could be compatible to a ho. They needed a man to talk to who wasn't a trick, because a square couldn't fully understand them and they couldn't accept them messing around with other men but them. A ho could be herself around her pimp. With all that's been said, I knew I had a good chance of Rose choosing me after I ran my tape to her. It was just a matter of time.

Pinky was leaning up against my Range Rover looking at me coming towards her. "She cute as fuck. What did she say?" she asked while we opened the doors to get her belongings out.

"She said she don't know about fucking with a pimp, but we still exchanged numbers, tho'."

"She probably just trying to see what you about first. Once she see, she'll choose."

"I represent Big game, Pinky. If that bitch don't see success in the game I present to her, that ho must be blind than a muthafucka. The bitch ain't got no choice but to get drunk off this pimp juice," I said, bragging to my queen, making her laugh.

"You bisexual or something?" I asked Pinky on the way to the elevator.

"Yes, I love females. I used to be in a relationship with a girl for two years. Shit didn't work out between us."

I thought back to the private party and the times I caught her staring at Shae. I could see now that she was bisexual. It didn't surprise me though. Most prostitutes went both ways. I did have to be careful with Pinky being around my other hoes. I didn't want to lose them over some lesbian shit. I just had to use it to my advantage to knock another ho. "I thought I saw tendencies but I didn't pay it no mind. What about CeCe, she fuck around?"

"Naw. She likes men only. The only time we did something together is when we did that two-girl show the other day. That's probably all I'll get out of her. I've tried to get her down so many times, but she loves dick. That's my bitch, tho'."

"How long have you two been friends?"

"Three years now. She went to school with my stepbrother."

"How long have y'all been hoing together?"

"A little over a year now."

Once we walked into the hotel room, I did something that I didn't like doing and fed her heroin. Under a high condition was the only way she would perform like I wanted her to. I made a promise to go ahead with my plan to put her in drug treatment next week sometime to get her off that shit.

When I came back into the hotel living room from pissing, Pinky was dozing off on the couch. It was sad to watch her. What made this beautiful girl want to even use drugs? I made it my duty to find out why after I trunked her today. She said she's been using for six months now. Her appearance looked like she didn't do any drugs, but her actions spoke it loud and clear. Even when people's physical appearance and health were in jeopardy from using drugs, they still didn't give a fuck. It was a shame. She was only 24 with so much potential. That made me think about myself as a pimp. A person would ask me the same question I asked about Pinky. Why did I pimp, take penitentiary chances, and put everything I had at risk when I was a millionaire and had so much potential to be so much more? The answer was, I loved this game with every breath I took. Even though I'd gotten the bad side of the game a couple of times, the game was still rewarding to me. And I pimped as a guard from not being pimped on. I wasn't tired of this lifestyle just yet, but when I did give it up, I was dedicating myself fully to my dreams and something legal.

After Pinky made four dates with some big-money tricks, it was time to pick my hoes up from the room.

Pinky got out and let Shae in the front seat. "Daddy, we bought you five silk Gucci boxers and a Gucci belt," Shae told me.

After I thanked them, we talked about what they bought from the mall until we arrived at Tiffany's house at 2:58 P.M. I felt I had to give my hoes a warning before we went inside. "You all behave while we in here. She about to take y'all measurements for some clothes to wear to the concerts. If y'all not getting along, come to me so I can handle it. Because if you take it among yourselves to handle it and it gets out of hand, there's gonna be some consequences. Am I understood?"

They all agreed, saying, "Yes."

Tiffany greeted us at the garage door. "Hey, Monopoly. Hello you all. Come on in. How you all doing?" she said as she stepped to the side, letting us in. They all spoke without much conversation. "How you been, Shae?"

"The same ol', same ol', but it's getting a lot better. What you been up to?" Tiffany and Shae knew one another through me. Shae used to do Tiffany's hair two years ago.

"Like you say, things are getting a lot better."

"I see. I like the new house and the living room set. It looks really good, girl." It was a beautiful house, inside and out. We had a 1.5 million-dollar, two-story house on lease in a gated community in North Richland Hills. It had five bedrooms with a study, game, and media room, covered patio and balcony, and three-and-a-half bathrooms. Our master bedroom had two large walk-in closets and a huge bathroom. The kitchen opened to a breakfast area and a family room with a fireplace, plus a three-car garage.

I recognized one of Tiffany's gay male workers coming out the kitchen. "This is Tim, you all. You already know Monopoly. This is Shae." She pointed at my queens one by one for them to introduce themselves. Shae knew she could talk and look at him, but CeCe, Pinky, and Selena looked at me for permission. I let them know they were good to talk to him.

"Nice to meet all you. Call me Tim. We're going to make sure you all look good in our outfits.

"Let's go upstairs to my work room so we can get started," Tiffany directed.

After two hours of looking through two binders of sketches and pictures of blouses, skirts, and dresses plus the closet full of new, unworn clothes that Tiffany had handmade herself, we picked out all four of my hoes' outfits.

We decided to all wear white to the concert. CeCe wanted my help on picking hers out. We decided on a pretty plunging neckline and a deep-cut, knee-length white skirt. Selena chose an off-shoulder, ribbed white dress. Pinky picked a tight white bodysuit that showed off every curve. Last but not least, Shae chose a shoulderless, tight-fitted white dress that came to her thighs, showing off her curves and a bunch of cleavage. A week from now, we were going shopping again for my outfit, our jewelry, their accessories, and heels. My hoes were going to be some of the baddest, sexiest, and the best dressed women in the Verizon Center that night. I knew I was gonna spend close to three to five stacks on just my outfit alone, and that wasn't including the jewelry. Shit, we might make a grand appearance and pull up in a stretch white Hummer like we were the stars. I was gonna make sure we all were dressed to impress and looking like we were living a luxury lifestyle. The way a real pimp did it.

I left my queens upstairs, letting them engage in girl talk and get their minds off hoing for a while. I went to the kitchen to get a glass of lemonade and two packs of nutty bars.

# Money Game

I took a seat on the love seat in the living room. It really did feel good to be at home. I missed being here. The house was usually filled with noise because of the kids, but they were at Tiffany's mother's house for the weekend. I looked up at the family portrait of Tiffany, our three kids, and me. I missed them. Even though her 11-year-old son and 13-year-old daughter weren't my biological kids, I still took care of and loved them like they were mine. They called me their daddy. According to Tiffany, their biological father wasn't anywhere to be found. She told me she made some poor choices with the dude who wasn't good for her. So, when she felt comfortable with me, letting me interact with her kids, they took a liking to me and I to them. We got pretty close within that first month. I even brought my daughter around them. I must admit that it hurt and I hated to break it off with Tiffany. Hurting her kids wasn't cool at all. I felt bad about that. Tiffany was a good woman to me, but like I said before, I didn't want a committed relationship. I knew better when that all started, but I still wanted her in my life some way, somehow. That was my reason for getting her pregnant and going into business with her. I knew I couldn't put her in the game, so I did that. No one woman could have all of me, only a piece of me. The game had me wholeheartedly.

My tattoo man finally got back with me after I texted him a week ago, asking him when he would be free to tat CeCe and Pinky. That same day, he text back telling me he was busy and he'd try to put me in his schedule at the end of the week. I knew he just wanted some pussy from one of my queens in exchange for tattoos. I texted him telling him to meet me at Shae's house at 7 P.M. this evening.

Speaking of Shae, that reminded me to call my Mason brother, Mark, who worked in the FBI's Human Trafficking Division. Tight Game introduced us to each other five years ago when I became a Mason. We all went to the same Masonic lodge. Whenever I called to ask him was a sting taking place in a certain city I was in, he let me know. Most of the time, he called me if they did any stings in the DFW area because that's where I was eight times out of ten. Knowing him had come in handy. The information that was given to me was passed on to some good pimps I knew.

When I called him, he told me he'd been busy with a sex slave case dealing with a child. He apologized for not letting me know beforehand, and told me he had gotten a call today about two compelling prostitution and trafficking of a person charges he should look into that got caught up last night. He sounded a little heated about it. Mark didn't care about a nigga pimpin' on adult women, because he understood that part of the game, as long as a nigga wasn't exploiting minors and forcing women to prostitute. He made it his business to find every little piece of evidence he could find to send them to prison for however long he could get them time. He promised to inform me if they did any more stings in Arlington and mentioned to be careful. Even though we were Mason brothers, I still had to be careful with him. I knew what he was capable of. He knew almost everything I was doing, so that meant he could easily set me up. Then again, he was a good friend with Tight game, and Mark knew a lot about him. No matter what, he wouldn't snitch on Tight Game. Because we were all Masons, he wasn't supposed to say anything about my actions, even if it was in his job description.

After the phone call, I got on Facebook on my phone because I had posted the party on there for three weeks now. I checked to see how many would be attending it tomorrow. So far, I had 346 people and whoever they brought with them. I was sure a bunch of people would show up since everything would be free to all whom attended. I posted it again like I had every day.

When we left Tiffany's, we went back to the hotel to Shae's car. Then we headed to her crib. I told everyone except for Pinky to go in. After they had gotten most of their bags out the trunk, I took out five shopping bags and sat them down on the ground. "Get that last bag for me, Pinky."

As soon as she reached and went inside, I grabbed her tightly by her neck and scooped her legs from up under her with my arms, then threw her into the trunk. "Get yo' faggot ass in the trunk, bitch."

I hurried to shut it behind her. She started yelling, beating, and kicking the trunk. I knew no one could hear her outside this two-car garage. She'd get tired of moving soon. I'd let her out whenever Tattoo Mike made it here.

# Smoove Dolla

## Chapter 5

About twenty minutes into being at Shae's house, I received a text from a chick named Claire while I sat on the couch surfing the web.

Claire

6:09 P.M. Saturday

Monopoly, I need a ride to get my check from my aunt's house in Dallas. I'll give u $20 if u can take me 2 pick it up. Let me know if u can.

Monopoly

6:11 P.M. Saturday

Give me $40 n I'll take you anywhere u wanna go. Send me ur address if u gon' do it.

She texted back seconds later, accepting my offer and sending me a Grand Prairie address. I added an extra $20 because she owed me and I knew she needed a ride. I could tell how eager she was in the text. I was going to campaign like a motherfucker when I picked her up.

Her asking for help brought me back to the first time I met her at a Valero gas station four months ago on a warm, sunny afternoon in Grand Prairie. I had one of my queens, named Diamond, pump the gas while I checked to see if my tire was flat or if it had a leakage somewhere. Come to find out, I did have a slow leak.

"Hey sir," I heard a woman's soft voice say behind me, right after I stood up. I stood up and turned around to see a hazel-eyed, caramel skin-colored, pretty, slim woman. "I really need a favor. Me and my little sister just had to push the car up the street into the gas station with my son in it. I ran out of gas. I really do need to get somewhere," she said, with one of the most desperate looks on her face.

I believed the only reason why she came up to me was because of how I was dressed and what I was riding in. I didn't have much jewelry on, but I did have on a Tom Ford three-piece blue suit with custom-made blue alligator Tom Ford dress shoes that cost $1500.

I felt she was sincere, so I made up my mind to help her out. But, I wanted to fuck with her to see where her head was at before

I did. Plus, I knew my queen was ear hustling to see what I was going to do. I really didn't know if she was a ho or not. My first impression of her was that she was a square, and I found out later that she was indeed one.

"How long has it been since you ran out of gas?"

"About 40 minutes."

I smiled at her. "You mean to tell me, as pretty as you are, you been out here 40 minutes and you haven't gotten any money yet with all these suckers around here?" I started pointing the suckers out. "There go a duck. There's another duck right there. Why come ask me?" I knew the answer to my own question as well as she did. It was being well groomed, looking stable, and like I had security that attracted her to me. I thought saying what I said to her, maybe it would sit thick on their mind. I wanted her to know that she had worth in my eyes, and that these tricks and lames walking around here can get played on. I also wanted her to know that I wouldn't be giving my money up so easily. I didn't care about that sad story shit.

"I've already asked three men already. They gave me nothing but damn change that added up to $2.19. I came to ask you because you look like you have money. Are you gonna help me or not?"

"You would have gotten what you wanted if you had asked in the proper fashion." I wasn't about to hand her no cash, so I took out my wallet to get my Bank of America credit card and my business card out. "Here's my business card. Call me if you want an opportunity to better your situation. Where's your car at?"

She pointed to a beat-up 1987 Cutlass, that I later found out was her mother's. She really did need an opportunity, I thought at that time. I ended up putting $15 in the tank with my credit card.

She ended up calling me the next day. We talked for a good thirty minutes. What I did for a living came up in the conversation. I told her I was a singer, pimp, and owner of a clothing business. I could tell she started feeling resentment towards me because she didn't want to go further into that conversation. Instead, she told me that she wasn't that type of woman, we can continue talking, but please don't come at her like she's a ho. She called me five different times in three days as well as texted after that, but I never answered any of it because I got the vibe she wasn't going to turn out. I didn't have the patience to run my game to her for weeks, maybe months, and wait on her to want to fuck around with me in the game.

I responded to her text because I had a trap for her ass. After texting her telling her I was on my way, I set up my trap I had for her. The trap was an attorney letter talking about an insurance claim. Tight Game had given me a copy of Christie's attorney letter without words but just with her law firm logo stamped on it. I put it in the scanner then saved it, and typed my own words over it. I printed one on my computer with last week's date on it. It read that I would be getting $106,327 by the end of next month for a company truck hitting my 2010 Rolls Royce Ghost. It was all a lie. I knew by her seeing those kind of figures she would open up to me, and maybe choose up with my pimpin'. I could have easily shown her the numbers on my bank stubs that had 11 times what I put in the letter, but I didn't trust her to look at that type of information. I sat the envelope flat on the console in my Range Rover. So when I left her in the SUV, I expected her to be nosy and read it.

It took me about 18 minutes to get to the address she had given me. She did most of the talking while I drove on Interstate 30 heading to Oak Cliff. I wasn't good at small talk. I was a straight to the point type of dude. I just listened as she went on talking about her unemployment and her seven-year-old son, who was in the backseat. I would use all that she had told me to knock her. It was only a matter of time before she was my ho.

When we got to her aunt's apartment in South Oak Cliff, her aunt Kim was sitting in a lawn chair along with a group of adults and children hanging around outside. Aunt Kim brought her niece's check to my SUV. Claire introduced me to her and her to me. She spoke to Claire's son, then we left to go to a corner store down the street to cash her check.

Since I hadn't eaten lunch or dinner yet, and I didn't need the gas, we went out to eat at the Spaghetti Warehouse. After an hour of being at the restaurant, we then headed to my penthouse. Still, up to this point, she hadn't fell for my bait yet. Really, I hadn't left her in my SUV until now.

I went up to my penthouse alone, leaving them in the AC of the Range Rover. I waited five minutes before calling her, telling her to bring along the envelope on the console and the door will open for them. She sounded like she still hadn't read it yet. I knew there was a great possibility that she would read the letter if she saw the attorney's sticker with Christy's name and firm address on the envelope. She would be forced to read it on the way up while riding the elevator. She would be curious to know what I had going on dealing with the lawyer.

I heard the front door close from the bathroom while brushing my grill in the master bedroom. "Monopoly," she yelled out. When she didn't hear a response, she yelled out again, "Monopoly, I'm here."

"I'm in the room. I'll be out in a minute. Make yourself at home," I said after rinsing my mouth out with water.

"Okay," she said.

To see if she had read the letter and gotten loose, I asked out loud, "You don't have anything else planned, do you?"

"No, I don't."

"So, you don't mind staying here for a couple of hours if you have to?"

"I don't mind. I can stay as long as you want me to. Do you live here alone?"

I had a feeling she read the letter because her tone had changed. It was softer, relaxed, and pleased, like she was willing to do whatever I told her to do. Or, it could be her being attracted to the penthouse that got her that way. Claire had seen me twice dressed up sharp in high-dollar outfits, she knew what kind of whips I was riding in, knew I was a singer and I owned a business. Now she saw how and where I lived. I knew whatever had gotten her comfortable had her thinking about being my woman. If I ran my game right, she would be my ho tonight. The effect of every move I made at this point was for her to wear that title.

When I walked into the living room she was looking at the night skyline of downtown Dallas. "Yep, just me, myself, and I. This is one of my spots I come to when I want to get away from everything and everybody. You like the view?" I said, catching her by surprise.

She turned around to see me coming towards her and her son. "Yes, it's beautiful. I've never seen it from the sky before. Lil' Dre, get your ass off that glass. You smudging the damn glass, boy," she said, pulling him away from the window. "Sorry, Monopoly, you got something I can clean it with?"

I had a spray bottle of Windex in my cabinet in the living room because somebody always seemed to smudge the huge window while here. "Yeah, it's a towel and Windex right there." While she handed me the envelope, I asked her, "Is it okay if I gave him some milk and cookies."

"Uh, uh, he already running wild like he ain't got no sense. He don't need none," Claire said, shaking her head.

Lil' Dre started begging Claire. "Please, Mama, can I get some cookies?"

I didn't like him begging, even if it was his mama. "I got him. Come on, Lil' Dre." I grabbed him by the hand and took him to the table where he sat in a chair. I poured him a plastic cup of white milk and gave him a plastic plate of about 10 chocolate cookies. "You want some Claire?"

"No, I'm good. I'm still full from the restaurant."

I left him at the table and walked over to the red sofa I had. She turned her head away from me then looked down while tapping her short yellow and white manicure press-on nails. "I have thought about dancing. I don't know if I'm sure that's what I want to do, but I am good at it tho'."

"I don't want you to feel that I'm pressing you nor forcing you to do anything. How about I set you up in the club tonight. If you like it, you continue doing it. If you don't, we'll find you something else to do. I know you can do that, can't you?"

"Yeah, okay, I'll try it out just tonight and see where it goes."

"Do you have anybody to watch your son?"

"My mama might. Let me call her and see."

Their conversation took about three minutes. "She said she'll watch him for a carton of Virginia Slims and $30." She saw my eyebrows raise then said, "Yeah, my mom is like that. She charges me for everything. That's why I'm in the situation I'm in now because of her."

"Don't blame that all on her. It's not all her fault. She's only a part of your current situation. That's another reason you should have chose me the first time. You wouldn't be dealing with that now. After tonight, you won't have any excuses for your finances. You're making the first step towards a new and better way of life. I will present you with the proper ways of dealing with life's difficulties, and all you have to do is believe in my word that everything I say is the truth and everything will be lovely."

Now that I talked her into dancing, I had to find a club she could work at where she could make the most money in an environment that would best suit her looks and character. I didn't want her at any black clubs because of how black tricks act and how they pay. In the middle of the living room facing the huge window, I called Claire over to take a seat in my lap.

"Why you looking at me like that?" I asked her.

"Looking at you like what?" she asked with a grin on her pretty face.

"Like you wanna eat a pimp up or something," I said, smiling back at her.

"I do," she said, then made a bold move and kissed me. We tongue kissed for about six seconds, and then I retreated, breaking the kiss.

"It's too early for us to engage in anything sexual. Plus, your son is here. I don't want to give him the wrong idea." I had her undivided attention, so I applied a bit of pressure on her, seeing if she would accept my game. "What we really need to be doing is engaging in conversation about improving our condition. I wanna go to the top and stay. I want the finer things in life. And so should you. You should be working to get money for Lil' Dre's college tuition and a better life for you and Lil' Dre, because you ain't going to get it with that check you get every two weeks. I have the opportunity to make those things and more possible, only if you want them."

"I'm not gonna be a ho, Monopoly, if that's what you talking about," she said while glancing back at her son at the table for a moment.

"In the game I'm in, it's not all about selling pussy, Claire. I have plenty of plots to make us a knot."

"Like what, Monopoly?"

"Boosting, dancing, modeling, escorting, which is just spending time with high-dollar tricks. Running checks and credit cards. And a bunch of other things. Do you see yourself doing one of those hustles?"

Claire was caramel and pretty, with long, black, natural hair and a slim, fine body, and she still had her California accent. She could pass for Latin American. I knew that would appeal more to Mexican men and some white men. I didn't want to call the girl I met today, but I wanted to know what club she worked at. I called Rose on speaker phone. "Hey, Rose, you busy?"

"Naw, what's going on?" she asked curiously.

"I called to ask what club you dance at?"

"Best Cabaret in Euless. Why, what's up? You coming to see me tonight?"

"Yes, I am. I'm coming to see you in the manner of pimpin', not ever tricking," I said, letting her know what it was with me. "I wanted to know what club you working at because I'm tryna put one of my queens in a club tonight."

"How she look? Is she pretty and fine? Black, white, or Mexican?" she asked, probably wanting to know what race of hoes I had in my stable.

"Of course, she's pretty. All my queens are in high demand. She's black, though she can pass for Latino. She's slim fine," I said as I looked at Claire from toe to head, stopping at her eyes. She had a shocked expression on her pretty face, indicating that she was surprised about what I had just told Rose.

"I'll take your word. But still, send me a picture of her. I want to see how she looks."

I went through Claire's phone, searching for a good body pic and selfie of her. Then I used her phone to send them to Rose. She got them in seconds.

"Oh, okay. She is pretty. Bring her through. The manager will let her work. I'll put in a good word for her."

"Thanks. Is the money good there?" I asked as Lil' Dre came over to sit on the side of us.

"Yea, on most nights. If she knows what she's doing she'll make some money."

I've never been there, nor had one of my girls danced in Best Cabaret. I'd only heard about it through other pimps and strippers, that it's a money spot with a lot of white girls. But I'd never taken the time to check out the topless strip joint for myself until now.

I took them both shopping at The Parks Mall in Arlington. I bought Lil' Dre three Louis Vuitton outfits, two Gucci outfits, and three expensive, popular name-brand shoes. I bought Claire a Burberry outfit to wear going inside the club along with a small Burberry purse, a bottle of Burberry perfume, two pair of three-inch high heels, a yellow G-string, a blue lingerie set, and some jewelry. I bought two Gucci outfits and a pair of Gucci loafers for myself. I picked all their outfits and I let her pick one of mine. She had good taste. I wanted her to see me in something she liked to see me wear. And the same vice versa. I came to learn most hoes loved for their pimp to pick what they wore on their body and head. They wanted validation, acceptance, and approval from their pimps. If a ho truly believed in her pimp's view, judgement, and liked his taste, she would want him to choose her clothes.

I got a little carried away at the mall buying shit. I spent over $6,000, and that was with the $510 from her check. Hopefully, Claire made between $800 to $1,500 tonight. It would take about two weeks to see a profit off her, making almost double what I spent on us at the mall. It was all cool, though. It didn't do anything but add points to my name. For doing that, it showed her that she would be well taken care of in my stable, and my queens had the best. The same way Claire saw it was the way I wanted Rose and other strippers in the club to see it. I was in little doubt about her letting me down when we got to this club. It's because she hadn't shown me anything yet. I didn't know if she could really dance. I was going to let Shae check her out and show her some things about dancing in the strip club when we made it to the house. That's why it's best to get paid first before you went all out for a new ho. But since I turned her out to the game, I guess it was cool to buy her and her son those things.

After stopping at CVS to buy Claire's mother a carton of Virginia Slims and Claire a box of body wipes, I dropped her son off at her mother's house along with the payment.

On the way to Shae's crib, I laid my rules and regulations down. Then I explained to her in depth on the proper way to talk to certain tricks, on how certain tricks wanted to be treated, what they wanted, how to handle them in different situations, what to think while she danced, how to clean herself quickly with wipes after finishing a dance on stage and after dancing on a couple tricks, and on what strippers and customers could and couldn't do at this type of strip joint.

I introduced Claire and my other queens to each other when we made it inside the house. Tattoo Mike had been here close to 30 minutes now, tatting CeCe up. The tattoo was the Monopoly man in a brim hat with a big diamond on top of a pimp stick in one hand and a leash in his right hand, holding three hoes down on all fours with a dog collar around their necks. MONOPOLY was tattooed at the top in bold letters. Pinky was next in line to get it on her front right thigh. Shae and Selena already had it on theirs. Claire wasn't going to get branded yet. She had some proving to do for me. She had to earn the right to represent me in that fashion.

I grabbed a cold bottle of water out the refrigerator then made my way to the garage. I picked up her small white Michael Kors purse off the ground and then went to sit in the backseat of Shae's Impala with the air conditioner on high, putting together some new laws for Pinky to follow.

I hoped she hadn't suffocated and died for being in there for a little over two hours. I would have been sad about that accident because I cared about her, and fucked up at myself that I would have to find a way to cover it up and not get caught up.

I pulled back the latch on the backseat from inside the car. I used Pinky's phone for a flashlight. Even though I didn't show it, I was relieved to see her alive and conscious. She was lying down with her head on a JC Penney plastic brown bag. She lifted her head up, turned to see me looking at her, then she turned back around and laid her head back down sideways on the bag.

"Get yo' ass up out that trunk."

She obeyed my command. She had to sit in my lap so I could put the seat back in place, but I kept her in my lap facing me. The only thing I could see in her eyes and facial expression was dehydration. I gave her a bottle of water to drink. She slowly opened it and then started gulping it down to one-fourth of the water left in the bottle.

I sat there quietly for about 45 seconds before saying anything to her. "The fact that you're sitting in my lap, tells me you still want to be down for my crown. I know while you were laying in the dark in that trunk you questioned yourself, whether you should leave me or not. You have the right to leave me, if that's what you desire. I don't force hoes to stay with me. Do you want to go?"

"No."

I slapped her hard across her right cheek. A look of surprise crossed her face. "Do you still want to be with me?"

"Why did you do that for?" she said, holding the right side of her face.

"Because I wanted to, bitch. Quit questioning a pimp, ho. I'm asking the questions. Do you want to be with me or not?" I only did that to see if she would get out of pocket with me by talking shit or throwing the water bottle at me, or wanting to fight me in this car for all that I did to her, but she didn't.

"Yes," she said, sure of herself.

"I wanna let you know that everything I did to you today is because of what you did last night. If you would have waited until you had spoken with me first, I would have let you do you. Now I'ma be very strict on you. Hopefully, it'll teach you some discipline. I've created more laws for you to follow. Now if you are still my woman, I want you to recite this to me with saying the numbers before the rule." I gave her the phone with a list saved in her memo and screen saver.

She quietly read what I put in her phone. Her eyebrows raised for a few seconds before she started reciting it. "Number 1, Lexi will think about you before I do anything and everything. Number 2, I will stay off and away from heroin. Number 3, I will respect my daddy and my sisters. Number 4, I will honor and be loyal to only you." She looked up at me.

"Those principles are not just for you to master but to recite to me three times a day on schedule so it can become your life. If I don't answer, I want you to text it or voice it to me. I want you to know that I care about your well-being, your mind, and your life. To allow you to destroy yourself with drugs is a sin on my part as being your pimp. I want you hooked on nothing but me. I want you healthy, and to look as beautiful as you are right now when it's your time to leave my pimpin' to fulfill your life's purpose. My hoes will never be drawn out like one of them drugged-up hoes on Lancaster you see every day, selling pussy in their thirties and forties. My hoes will succeed in their dreams with the game I bless them with. I want you to be that strong, smart young woman I know you are and shake that monkey off your back. I know it's a struggle, but we gonna make it through this. You gon' have to, if you still want to be a part of this family. So after you run out of the heroin you bought, that's it. I'm not supporting your habit, and I don't pimp hoes that use heroin, meth, bars, crack, nor cocaine. Tomorrow, I'll let you know what we gonna do about that situation. What I want to know is, what made you get on heroin in the first place?" She looked down in shame. "You don't have to be ashamed, Pinky. I want to know your pains and hurts so I can understand the woman in front of me. I stand as your man as well as your pimp. It's my duty to know these things about you so I can help you with them. Now tell me, why did you start using heroin?"

"When I was eight, I got molested by my mother's brother. And I got physically abused by my mom's present boyfriend growing up.

# Smoove Dolla

My ex-girlfriend turned me on to it. I got..." She stopped talking, shook her head, and then put her head down, but I could still see her eyes, which were starting to get watery. "Daddy, can we please not talk about this right now? I don't want to talk about it." She went for her purse and tried to open it, but I stopped her. I knew she was going for the heroin. I saw tears coming down her face, falling to my hand.

Her reason for using drugs was like a couple of hoes I'd pimped in the past. It was crazy how some males would sexually touch and abuse a child. And some mothers let it go down because of some bullshit love they had for their so-called man. There's a bunch of things I questioned about God. I didn't understand why God would create men that raped and molested kids. That was very weird to me, but that wasn't for me to understand, only God.

I looked into her eyes. "I really do hate that you went through that. I apologize for their faults and what they put you through. I promise as long as you are in my life and under my law, that will never happen again. That's my word. Now you have a real man who will love you, care, and appreciate your mind, your body, and heart, and soul. I want you to believe in yourself and believe in me as your man and pimp to make things better for you."

Some pimps would probably disagree with me apologizing to her, but it was all on the behalf of the man that caused her pain. I wanted her to know I stood as a real man. Majority of the women that had gotten molested, sexually assaulted, or raped had lost respect for all men, didn't trust men, hated men, and didn't give a fuck about men. Some of those same women even hated their own selves and had low self-worth. I knew deep down inside those types of women wanted to forgive men and still needed men in some form or fashion. A lot of those same females were the ones that over-indulged in sex, were addicted to drugs, partying, sex, and alcohol. A lot of them were bisexual, some were playing roles of men in their relationships. Those females were all unbalanced and were living in unhealthy conditions. My plan was to give Pinky the knowledge, wisdom, and understanding on how to forgive all males so she could free herself from the hurt she had experienced. It's my job to rebuild

96

love and respect for herself, and in me as her man, and to make her believe that my game would make her successful in life. It's a cardinal sin on my part to feed her drugs or even allow her to use drugs. I wasn't about to let her up, not down and destroy her. Either she let me help her get off heroin or left my pimpin' alone. I wasn't accepting that shit, and I meant that.

"Everything's gonna be fine, baby. If you ever want to talk about anything, let me know. I'm here for you. Anyway, you gotta new sister named Claire. She won't be hoing. Instead, she will be dancing in the clubs. Make her feel comfortable, okay?"

"Okay."

"You, Shae, and Claire will be going to Best Cabaret tonight with me, so after you get tatted, go take a shower and dress for the occasion."

"Can I work at the club as a waitress ?"

"Only if you can do something for me."

"What is it?" she asked eagerly.

"You remember the white bitch I met today at the hotel?"

"Yea, I remember."

"I want you to do whatever it takes to get the ho to choose up with me. Get in that ho's ear for Daddy, okay." I could have done it myself, but the chances were greater of her choosing me if I got Pinky to do it.

"Ok. That won't be a problem. I can do that."

"Alright, we gon' see. Come on, let's go inside."

After CeCe finished getting tatted, I sent her and Selena in Shae's car to their hotel rooms to work. I let Tattoo Mike get a quickie with Pinky and gave him $250 for tattooing my queens.

While Shae made Claire's real hair look good and Pinky was getting dressed, Shae laced them up on things they both needed to know.

I walked out the room once Shae started showing Claire different dance moves, and dressed into something that would get her attention in the club. I put on a Hermes Jagger fit with Chanel sneakers. I barely wore the sneakers I had in my closet, but when I did I dressed to kill like I always did. Most of the time I wore some kind of dress shirt and slacks or a suit with dress shoes. Since I had hoes in their late teens and early twenties, it was good to dress like my age of 24 and switch it up every now and then. I also wore my platinum 50-pointer chain, diamond-cut pinky ring, diamond-cut Rolex, and bracelet, that was all worth $80,000. A bitch had no choice but to choose with my pimpin' tonight.

    \* \* \*

When we walked into Best Cabaret, my queens had smiles on their faces, and they were dressed to attract patrons. I sent Claire and Pinky to fill out an application. Since Rose had put in a good word for Claire and the manager loved how good Pinky looked, he hired them on the spot. He wanted to see how they would perform for the night. If they did good, they could continue to work there.

I got us a spot in VIP. From our view, the whole club was eyesight, looking from one end to the other where the bar was stationed.

The club was nice and roomy with two main stages and a bunch of small stages here and there around the club. For about 15 minutes, nothing but pop music blasted out the speakers since I walked in the door. This club didn't have all the fine, big booty dancers that Memphis, Tennessee strip club, The Queen of Hearts, or Dallas, Texas, Onyx, nor Houston, Texas, V-Live, all had, but it was definitely a good money spot for white, Mexican, and mixed women. It was 80% snow bunnies, 15% Latin girls, and 5% mixed girls working around this joint. There were a variety of races of men, but mostly truck driving looking white men. I couldn't tell if there weren't any pimps in the building. I really didn't care if there was or not. I wasn't here to make a pimp buddy. I was here to add hoes to my stable and, of course, to make money.

After Claire left to put on her yellow top and G-string, she came into the VIP and sat on my lap. She really did look good. Her light makeup was perfect. Her thick black hair was in an afro style but all in curls with three curly bangs hanging in front. Her stomach was flat to where you couldn't tell she had any kids. She had a pair of amazing runway model legs. "You look amazing, Claire."

"Thanks."

# Money Game

"You look nervous as well."

"I am," she said, slowly nodding her head.

"Go take about two or three shots of something to the head so it can get you loose. No more after that. Don't over-drink yourself. Just take a couple of deep breaths. You should be less tense after that. Keep in mind, these guys are tricks. Look around, they're here to give their money away. Just do what you're good at and what you were taught to do, and they'll give their money to you. Go do your thang, baby," I said, giving her a little motivation. I also gave her a kiss on the cheek then sent her on her way.

After she went to the bar and did as I told her to do, she started walking around the club. The first three white men she went to turned her down. It wasn't because she didn't look good. It was because most of the guys came here to see mainly white girls or they were one of the stripper's loyal customers.

The next man she walked up on, she danced for him. If you saw her dancing in front of this heavy-set white man, you would say she was a stripper before. But as we know, if you're gifted in rhythm then you can damn near dance to anything. That's Claire. She was dancing with grace to a hot 2012 pop song.

Pinky was looking amazing in an white one-piece lingerie as she blessed the club with her lovely presence, serving drinks and food to the patrons. From what I could see, everywhere she went inside the club, a man was trying to get her attention by grabbing her arm, or walking up on her, ordering drinks just to have a conversation with her. She handled them in a proper fashion and kept a big, beautiful, white smile on her pretty face.

She made me smile just by looking at her enjoying herself. She had been making me a lot of money since I copped her and had brought a bunch of value to my stable. I wondered how long that was going to last. I believed she wanted to quit snorting, but she wasn't strong enough to shake that monkey off her back by herself. Monday, I was going to take her to set up an appointment with Fancy at the rehabilitation center she worked at. That should do the job. I hoped...

Pinky and Rose had been interacting with each other throughout the night, every time Pinky came across her in the club. She was doing a good job at getting Rose loose. One of those times, they put on a little kissing show for a white patron, which he loved and tipped her big.

The first time Rose and I got to talk to each other was at 11:45 P.M. She came over and sat next to me. "What's up, Monopoly, you having a good time?"

"Time is money. My queens are making money. So, to answer your question, yes, I'm good. I like the scenery. How are you?" I said and then smiled.

"I'm good too. Just tryna break these tricks. Oh yeah, I see you snuck your girl Pinky on me. Nice game."

"That's what she told you?" I said, laughing.

"Naw. Game recognize game. I like her, though. You mind if I spend the night at her room tonight? She told me to ask you." I liked this ho already. I could tell she wasn't a lame and she was a thinker.

"Yeah, if you don't mind paying a pimp. You can work alongside her all you want. You gotta pay to play like everyone else."

She laughed. "Uh, uh, I don't know about all that just yet. We'll see. I just want to have a little fun with Pinky, if you don't mind."

"I was half-ass playing with you. You good. Do what y'all do." I wasn't worried about Rose knocking me for Pinky. It would go in my favor either way it went. This would prove how much she loved females versus how much she wanted and liked me as her pimp. This would prove she really wanted to change her drug habit and wanted a better life for herself that only I had for her. If she did run off with Rose, I think she would come back to me eventually on down the line. Majority of the time gay and lesbian relationship never work out long. She would really have to work extra hard for me when she do come back. Hopefully, Rose chose up before the morning came and we wouldn't have to go through all that. "What time you leaving the club?"

"Probably around 2. Why?"

"Because you going to breakfast with us, on us. Just meet us at the door at 2:05."

"Okay, I'll be there."

"I ain't tryna stop you from making money. Go make your money. I'll get at you later."

A little later, after Rose walked off, I saw a cute, baby face, blonde-headed white girl tagging alongside of Shae, coming from the ladies room. "Daddy, I met her in the restroom. I overheard her talking to another girl about how she was tired of her pimp and she's thinking about leaving him. I approached her, telling her how good it is with you, and she should choose up. She wanted to meet you first," she said, as they stood in front of me.

"My name's Monopoly. What's yours?" I asked her, flashing my fifty-thousand-dollar, princess-cut, platinum, 16-piece grill at her, eight at the top and the same at the bottom.

"Stacey," she said, as Shae walked off, leaving us alone to talk.

I didn't want her to sit in my lap because she hadn't taken a shower. Ain't no telling what she'd done in this club tonight. So, I positioned a chair directly in front of me.

"Sit down so we can correspond and create a bond."

I followed her eyes as she sat down. They pointed to a black dude in all blue looking at us. "That blueberry over there with that mug on his face must be your pimp?"

"He was. I can't do it with him anymore." Her eyes started to water. She looked away from me, and then put her face in both of her hands.

"'Do you want a therapist, ho, or a real pimp?"

She looked up in surprise with a tear rolling down her face. After five seconds of her not answering the question, I asked, "Which one is it, Stacey? I ain't got all night."

"A pimp," she replied.

"Keep yo' head up if you want to be my queen. I don't want no weak ho." I could see pain in her eyes, so I told her, "My queens are a reflection of me. My queens are strong, smart, and successful. I see that you are strong for breaking the chains that gorilla forced on you. I also see that you are smart for wanting to choose with a real personified player of the game, because I'm all you need to be successful in this here game. How long have you been here tonight?"

"About four hours now."

"How many days you been working at this club?"

"For two days."

"What's his name?" I asked, moving my head towards her ex-pimp.

"JP." He was a nigga I never heard of before.

"You know where he from?"

"In Dallas somewhere. I don't know exactly."

"How many more hoes do he have?" I asked, just in case I wanted to knock the rest of his hoes.

"Just one. That's his bottom bitch dancing on that white guy over there," she said as she pointed to an attractive, tall, skinny, white brunette five tables away. She looked like she used drugs. She was supposed to have a little more weight on her but still looked good.

Immediately, I asked her, "Do you do any drugs?"

"I smoke kush," she said flatly. If she was lying, it would come out sooner or later.

"How much money have you made tonight already?"

"Probably, a little over 300."

I took a dollar bill out her small polyester bag. "Look, this is what I want you to do. Go make what you can make until I say it's time to leave. Don't worry about him, I got him."

When she walked away, I walked out of the VIP area and made my way over to JP's booth. He still had that gorilla mean mug on his face. I already knew where this was headed. He wasn't the type of pimp that lived by the principle, cop and blow. He was the type to want to kill the pimp for knocking him and abuse the ho for choosing another pimp.

"Wuz up, P, I'm here to inform you, your ex-bitch just chose me."

"Man, get the fuck away from my table," he said, in a slur. He sounded like he had been drinking. You know what happens when people drink and can't handle their liquor and their problems mentally. They resort to the physical plane and get violent.

I laughed at this clown. I dropped the dollar on the table. "That's a dollar on the bitch towards a new outfit. You might catch a bitch and keep the one you do have." I knew that probably triggered a button to bring trouble to me, but there wasn't too much we could do before the big white bouncers stopped the confrontation between us.

He stood up. He was a short, built nigga. I could tell he had a short-man complex, but his traps, biceps, and chest muscles were poking out his 50 Cent blue tank top. His muscles gave him his confidence. "Nigga, I said get the fuck away from this table, nigga, before you get it in this muthafucker. I don't wanna hear that shit. Fuck you and that ho."

"Aight, aight," I said smiling, with my hands up in the air while backing away from him. After four steps, I put my hands down. "You got it. I don't want no trouble. We pimps, remember, JP." I turned around and walked back to our table in the VIP section.

If he left out the front door before me, I'd have to leave right behind him, just in case he started some shit on the way out. If I didn't have my pistol in the car, I would've called my homies from the hood here to make sure I made it out untouched and to do my dirty work. I wasn't about violence unless I was pushed into that corner. Hopefully, he didn't try shit on the way out.

Thirty minutes before 2 A.M., I talked to the club's manager, Derek. He really didn't like the fact that I was a pimp because of what illegal trouble prostitution brought to strip clubs. He said some of the girls might have pimps, but none of them had ever come to talk to him. In fact, I was the first pimp to ever come talk about having a ho work in this club within the three years he'd been manager. The reason I talked to him was to let him get familiar with seeing my face and know who I am. One day in the future, I might knock a female with no ID that I wanted to work the first day and didn't want to wait on the identification card to come in the mail. I could use him if I knocked for a woman who had a prostitution charge on her record that wanted to dance in the club. So it was good to get in good with him.

To my surprise, JP didn't try anything on the way out. However, he did glance at me with that same mug glued to his face, when he walked to his blue '97 Cadillac. That was too much blue. This nigga had to be a crip.

When we left, Pinky, Claire, and Shae rode with Rose. Stacey rode with me. On the ride from the club in Euless, I told Stacey some of my rules until we arrived at the IHOP's parking lot in Arlington, down the street from Selena and CeCe's hotel room.

About twenty-three minutes into being there, I got a call from CeCe. "Daddy, where you at? This punk ass Mexican trying to take his money back. He pissy drunk." Then I heard Selena struggling in the background, saying, "You not getting the money back!"

"Excuse me, y'all, I'll be right back." I stood up from the bench and rushed away from the table, out the restaurant towards my Range Rover.

"I'm up the street, I'm on my way. Tell him the police is on the way so he better leave."

"Okay. Stay on the phone, Daddy."

I put the phone on speaker while I drove. I made it to the Extended Stay in four minutes. I got out the car and ran into the hotel building, heading to room 127. I slid my key card into the lock with my gun in my other hand, then went inside the room quietly.

When CeCe saw me, she attempted to run towards me, until I stopped her by holding my hand up. I snuck up behind the john while he was over Selena, wrestling and trying to get the money back. She was putting up a good fight with the john. I hit him with a powerful right hook to the left rib, making him hunch over. He fell over, landing on his right side, holding his ribs. I kicked him dead in the face like a punter did in football. "You bitch ass john! Didn't she say she not giving it back!" He started pleading with his right hand blocking his face for me not to hit him again or shoot him. Blood leaked badly from his mouth. "Y'all hurry up and get y'all shit packed up."

"Everything?"

"Yea, everything. Y'all leaving and not coming back." CeCe was going too slow for me, so I told her, "CeCe, speed yo' muthafucking ass up so we can get the fuck up out of here. I wanna get on yo' ass anyway for not helping your sister! Bitch, we a family, ho! All that scary shit gotta go. Family sticks together, ho. One fight, all fight, no matter who it is," I said as I looked at her while she packed.

"Sorry, Daddy."

"Bitch, I don't want to hear that bullshit. Sorry not gonna do a muthafuckin' thang. Do better next time, ho. Now, hurry ya ass up and get that shit packed up."

I took the john's wallet out the back of his tight Wrangler blue jeans and looked at his ID, then threw it on top of him with his money still inside. I wasn't about to jack him and risk catching a robbery charge if he decided to call the laws. He might want to cover the fact he paid for some pussy and not tell his wife the real story of why he got beat up. "I want you to leave in five minutes after we leave out that door. I know your address, so don't come back to this room and don't tell the police what happened. If you do, you will die, that's a promise."

After they gathered everything, leaving the room messy, I helped carry the few bags they had to Shae's Chevy Impala. My girls weren't going to be doing any dates for the rest of the night or tomorrow unless it was a regular that had big money. I was going to get Stacey a room by herself here to work to get the rest of my choosing fee, and have Selena and CeCe watch her room door to see if she was going to let JP in the room. But I canceled that plan because of this incident with this Mexican john.

Selena drove the Impala and followed behind me to IHOP. Everyone was still there talking or on their phones. As soon as Shae saw me, she asked, " Is everything okay, Daddy?"

She had called me three times and texted me while I was gone, so I said, "Yeah, they had a little trouble with a john. Everything's okay now." I didn't want to say too much in front of everybody, because it wasn't everybody's business.

I ordered CeCe's and Selena's food. They ate and then we all left. Pinky and Rose went back to Pinky's room at the Hampton Hotel. CeCe, Selena, Shae, Claire, Stacey, and I went to Shae's crib, took a shower, and then we all watched the movie *Temptation* on her 80-inch flat screen in the living room until we all fell asleep.

## Chapter 6

The following morning, I woke up at 8:38 A.M., got up, did my hygiene, put some clothes on, and hopped in the Caprice. Then I went to Wal-Mart to get more eggs, corn tortillas, sliced jalapenos, cheddar cheese, bananas, and a gallon of milk. Even though we just ate about six hours ago, I was going to make them breakfast this morning.

Since the Hampton was down the street from Wal-Mart, I went to pick up Pinky. The room was up at 11 A.M. anyway. I wasn't going to be around or free at that time to come back and get her. I picked the covers off Rose and Pinky's naked bodies. They were so tired that they didn't wake up, they just shifted in bed. I could see they had some fun because of the dildo and vibrator in the bed with them. I slapped Pinky on her soft ass. "Pinky, get ya ass up."

She screwed her face into a pout then laid her head back down. A few seconds later, she got up and then woke Rose.

I was used to seeing my queens running around the room naked, but my dick got hard this time from seeing their sexy bodies in bed together. They looked like they would perform great in a threesome. I prided myself in having discipline. I knew Rose would have been game to fuck me, but I would have been disrespecting the game by putting my dick in her. To tell you the truth, I wanted to see how Pinky's pussy felt and fuck the shit out of her, but I prolonged my desire. I knew I could control her better by not fucking her. I knew that if I had already, things with her would be worse. I needed to fuck her mentally as much as possible. And I wasn't about to fuck Rose because for one, she hadn't paid my fee to become my ho yet nor given me any money.

Rose told me she didn't have to pick up her son until noon today. So, she followed behind me to Shae's house. I started breakfast as soon as we got there.

I began with frying bacon. I cut the corn tortillas into small chips. I took the turkey bacon out, then fried the chips in the bacon grease, mixed it with eggs, sliced jalapenos, chopped onions, cilantro, and cheddar cheese. All that together created what was called Migas. And I also made banana milk. I made enough food for eight people to eat a small portion, since we were going to eat at the party.

I woke everyone up in the house as well as Rose and Pinky, who went back to sleep, and then we prayed and ate.

"Damn, Daddy, where did you learn how to cook like this?" CeCe said, while steadily eating what was left on her plate.

"My grandma Medea. Yea, I learned a lot from her when it comes to this cookin'."

"Monopoly, you did great. It's delicious, I love it," Rose told me.

They all thanked me.

"Y'all welcome. This is just a little appreciation for what you all do for me."

After I finished eating, I called my dopefiend detail man, Fred, over. I fed him a plate of Migas then he helped me wash and detail all our cars around the corner at the car wash. That took about an hour and a half. I then took my queens shopping to get them and their kids swimwear. We picked up Claire's and Rose's sons and Selena's two kids. Stacey had two daughters but didn't want to take them because of problems she was having with her kids' father. Something in me told me she was holding something back from me. Tomorrow, before she started hoing for me, I would make it my duty to find out everything about her.

I took Stacey, CeCe, and Pinky along with me to help me set up at Joe Pool Lake and left the others at Shae's house since they had kids with them. Fred used his truck to carry the tables and equipment in.

I rented five ski boats and fifteen jet skis from a commercial business that had a lot on the lake's property. I put out tables with chairs, blew up a bounce house for the kids, and set up the cotton candy machine all in the area we were going to be in. I was glad that Tight Game volunteered to buy all the liquor and beer and barbecued all the food that he bought. I called him.

"What's going on, big bro?"

"Getting ready. I just finished barbecuing. Did you take care of your end at the lake?"

"Yeah, everything is taken care of. I'm waiting on you and Cedric now." Cedric was setting up the music equipment and the DJ.

"Okay, I'm about to take care of a couple things. I'll be there within an hour or so."

\* \* \*

Mack Trill and Serious Jones played dominoes against Bel-Air Fish and Mr. Selfish. Tight Game and I sat in chairs close by, waiting for the next game. My pimp partnas, C Pro, Luxury P, P Money Know Love, and Versace Boss, along with other men and women, played on tables nearby.

Five minutes later, when Tight Game and I sat down to play Serious Jones and Mack Trill, Tight Game declared, "This week I made a decision...I'm retiring from the game you all." There was a brief silence around the table.

"You serious, TG?" Mack Trill asked, surprised.

"Yea, it's over for me, Trill. I've earned my name in this pimp game. I'm a veteran in the game. It's time I sit back in a rockin' chair, give y'all the game, and watch you all do your thang. It's been a long, lovely journey on this Pimp Highway. I've seen a bunch of shit in this game. In the 80s, 90s, and 2000s, I won Pimp of the Year seven times, two of them were in a row from '90 and '91. I been pimpin' over twenty-six-plus years now. I've pimped in damn near all 50 states, over 100 cities, and pimped on hoes from about 13 foreign countries. Yea, it's my time to get out the low level of the game completely. I've mastered it. I'm reaping my rewards."

We all learned something from each other's game, mistakes, troubles, and success, but most of the pimps here looked up to Tight game. He was an OG compared to most of us young pimps that were here today. We all called upon Tight Game when we or our hoes were in trouble, because of his bottom bitch Christie's law firm. Tight Game's name rang as the biggest pimp in Texas. His girls didn't do what our girls did. Their tricks were millionaires and businessmen. Tight Game was considered a high-class pimp.

He went on, "I've made it without ever getting caught up. The only way I made it without falling in the trap of the law is by dealing with the game in its proper perspective, Christie, the information I possess, and the gift of gab. My conversation put pussy in my possession. The game I was taught and learned thru experience is my backbone. Something that sold and brought big money to me. I remember when my younger siblings and I were starving, Momma only had money for the bills and Daddy was nowhere to be found. Game got the money to feed us. When I didn't have a place to stay, game got me shelter. When I needed clothes to dress good, game got me clothes and kept me fly. I can go on and on with this here, y'all get the picture. Pimpin' is the best game to be in, if you live it to the fullest.

"Prostitution has a thousand faces. Matter of fact, the next time you watch television, just look at all the commercials. Most of them, no matter what kind of commercial it is, it can be the television, newspaper, local news, radio, and billboards advertisement. Majority of the time, everything's advertised with a woman. It's the way to market, to bait in customers. If a woman uses her voice, her body, or anything of a woman to advertise something to make money, it's still prostitution, no matter how you put it. The government is a pimp. They just been doing it smarter and on a bigger and better level than we do it. They've been pimpin' the masses for centuries. They do it in taxes, slavery, religion, and in some education. They do it in all laws that govern our society. They are the best that ever did it. Those are the things we must know and understand so we can get our share. It takes a true pimp to wake up and realize how to truly get the money you really want out this legal system.

"I advise y'all to invest in a higher level of the pimp game. Something like a spa, a porn company, an escort business, a car shop, something legal. I know you all probably just love pimpin' this way. If that's you, then do it, continue to break a bitch. I'm here to tell you, I'ma vet in this game, and if you have any brains, the skills, and gift to control a muthafucker, you can pimp up in the corporate world as well. You'll still stand as a pimp, which is a Boss. You'll still have hoes, which will be your employees. You have to elevate from the low level of the game to the top. Hustling to ball or just to survive to make it to the next day, week, or month is a fucked-up state of mind. That's what's wrong with our people today. You got these fake ass, weak, wanna-be ass pimps with these part-time ass hoes in the way fucking up the game for the real ones.

"You gotta go all out in this game and pimp to the end of you. It will pay off. A lot of niggas in the dope game and pimp game just want to be seen as being niggas that's on without a real plan. I can't lie though, you know having big money and having hoes break themselves feed a nigga's ego and makes a man arrogant in a way. It's not wise to hustle in that state of mind. Don't let the money pimp you. You stand as the pimp and you have to have control over yourself in order to pimp properly. Don't get the same results that a lot of these niggas get, prison or death.

"These laws ain't no joke. And a bunch of you are breaded up off ho money and from doing whatever else you're doing. Use that money to get you a business going. I know you love it when it comes to pimpin' in the streets, because I love it. I love it when you can cop a bitch, work a bitch, and then break the bitch or just meet a ho and have her break herself. I love it when a muthafucka know what I stand for. I'm a muthafuckin' pimp. People know it when they meet and see me, I'm pimpin'. They know a hoe out there sucking, fucking, seducing, twerkin', poppin' that ass, doing whatever for me to make that cash and bringing it back to a pimp. But if you love and respect this game at all, pimp on something legal.

"There's more to it than the low level of the game. You can get yourself a legal business and still get your money out these tricks and suckers. You can't really call yourself a pimp if you can't advance to that level. You have to elevate."

Since Tight Game had started talking, two dominoes games had come to a pause. There were a few pimps standing around our table listening to what he had to say. I took in everything he had said. It was true, Proper Game. I took heed of everything he had said, and he had me thinking hard. I knew I had to do something with myself.

I knew this wasn't forever. Eventually, I would have to change to live a better life and enjoy my rewards with my family. I didn't want to end up back in prison, like many who had played the game, or worse, dead.

My nine-year-old daughter, Nayla, came over and pulled me away from the domino game. She wanted me to drive her around on the jet ski, so I excused myself and played with her. We rode around for about 45 minutes, enjoying ourselves together.

After my daughter had gotten off, I saw Rose sitting with one of her friends on her phone, so I pulled her away and took her for a ride. We rode for about 20 minutes. Then we started talking while she sat in front of me on the jet ski.

"So, this is how you do it, huh?" she asked me.

"Yea, I funded most of this. Some of my brothers and I take turns every month or we all pitch in and do something for the kids, the fam, and whomever else wants to participate in the fun we provide. We gotta give back to the people."

"I like that. I can't lie. I've liked everything you've done so far. I didn't know pimps were like that. Two of my homegirls over there, had pimps before. We all do our own thing now without a pimp. But they say they went through hell with their pimp."

"My kind is rare. I'm like this because I'm a Mason and I love and respect this game to the fullest. I'm true to this game, Rose. I do my best to pimp in its proper manner and find out the game things I do not know so I can master this game all around the Monopoly board. I'm not one to cheat or extract from others. My motives are set higher than that. My game will get a queen whatever she's striving for," I said passionately.

We were being watched by Tiffany and Rose's renegade crew. Both of my baby mommas attended the event. I knew Tiffany hated the sight of me being close up on another girl, especially a white one. My daughter's mother didn't care because she had a dude here she was dating. And Rose's homegirls were either feeling me too or despised a pimp. They were to faraway to tell. From what she told me, they probably were talking bad about us. I used that to try to knock her.

"You know, you're being looked at like you're doin' something wrong right now. But if it didn't feel right to you, we both know you wouldn't be sitting with me right now. You'll be like them, drinking up all the liquor you can consume and taking advantage of everything free here. You should know you have your own happiness to fulfill, your own life to live. I know they're your girls, but don't worry about them. Don't let them get in your head. Think about your own wants and needs. Deep down inside, you know you can't be independent in every aspect of your life. You cannot deny that somewhere inside of you wants a man. And I'm that stomp-down man that's gonna attend to your needs.

"I'm here for you. I'm here to help, not hurt you. You don't have to choose up with me today. Just think it over for some time to see if it will be the best move for you. When you do choose, bring me $2000."

As we talked a bit more, I found out that she was the leader of the renegade crew. I knew if she chose, Rose would tell them how it was with me, then the other three white girls would be right behind her sooner or later, like ants following behind one another. They were all seasoned hoes, so they knew the ins and outs to hoing. From the looks of their cars and possessions, it seemed like they were doing okay with the money they were making. Three of them had cars, that's including Rose. They weren't expensive cars, but they still had their own rides. All I would do was present them with an opportunity to make more money for doing less work, but my instructions and guidance had a big price tag on them.

I took her iPhone out her hand and then turned it on by a push of a button. "Put your password in for me."

She put the four-digit number in and then asked, "What you going to do with my phone?"

I didn't answer her, I just went to her gallery then tapped on the camera. I put the phone in front of us and then started snapping away. I took eight pictures of us, one of them included me kissing her on the side of her left cheek, and another one was of us hugged up. I started going through them, showing her how we looked together. "We look good than a muthafucker together, huh?"

"Yeah, we do."

I went to SnapChat in her phone and put hearts and sunrays in one of the photos we were hugged up together in. I showed her. "You like that?"

She nodded her head while smiling. Since she liked it, I replaced the red roses she had as a screen saver with the last photo I just showed her. That picture would have me on her mind every time she went through her phone. "Uh, uhh, you doing the most, Monopoly," she said playfully.

"I know. You don't mind, do you?" I asked and smiled.

"You done already done it. I don't mind, tho', it's cool." I knew she wanted a man in her life. It was all in between her words and body language. The tone of her voice, her blushing, her leaning into my chest, her caressing my arm, and licking her lips towards me all indicated she liked me. I accomplished a lot in the short time with her. It was like we were on a date by ourselves and I gave her my undivided attention while I was in her presence. I knew the senses with her I had touched was enough to make her choose. She had already seen that I was different from what she had heard about pimps, and on top of that, she saw how I treated my hoes. All I had to do was wait now. Sooner or later, she'd be my next queen.

Tiffany looked at me crazy. It wasn't anything new. I got that every time we threw a party and my hoes attended it together or other females that came trying to holler at me at a party.

Majority of the time, I would talk to her about it. She would always say in the middle and end of our conversation that I should give this lifestyle up. I didn't want to hear that shit today, so I paid her no mind. I was pimpin' and would never change that for no woman.

There were close to 400 people that showed up. I was glad no one got into it with anybody this time like sometimes happens when certain people get too much liquor in their system. We had all kinds of entertainment, ski boats, jet skis, and plenty of games for everyone. My homie, Cedric, DJ'd and we had live music from him, my brother Tony Staxx aka Juice Leroy, and an artist that I'd written a couple songs for and recorded a duet with. I even performed two of my songs, which everyone enjoyed.

The rest of the day went wonderful. Most of us ended up staying at the lake until I shut it down at 9 P.M. Tight Game, his two queens, my five queens, their kids, and I all went to Shae's house. They talked about their girly things at the long glass dinner table while the kids ran around playing. Tight Game, Lil' Dre, and I sat on the sofa while talking and watching old boxing matches of Muhammed Ali on the 80-inch flat screen.

I went to the bathroom to piss. As soon as I opened the door, I saw Stacey sitting on the toilet without using it, on the phone saying, "Just wait."

This ho looked like she was on some sneaky shit. If this bitch was talking to that nigga JP, I was firing the ho for disrespecting my pimpin' and being sneaky. He could have the bitch. "Who the fuck you on the phone with, ho?"

She hurried and said, "A trick, Daddy." Then she got back on the phone. "I won't be working tonight, baby. I'll call you when I am," she said seductively and then disconnected the call.

"Bitch, give me that motherfuckin' phone, ho! You up to no good!" Before she extended her arm, I snatched the phone out her hand.

"He's just a trick, Daddy. He's obsessed with me."

I looked through her Android phone. A name Tricks appeared over ten times on the call log within an hour. "Damn, ho, he want you that bad?"

"I'm good at what I do."

"Is he paying big money?"

"Of course. He spends a few hundred every time, sometimes just to talk."

"Okay, here." I gave the phone back to her. "If he calls or texts again, tell him you're available."

While I peed, I made a mental note to see what was up with that bitch Stacey later on tonight. I couldn't put my finger on it, but something wasn't right with her. I'ma make it my duty to find out what it was.

Tight was ready to go two hours later. "Yeah, Monopoly, it's about time we get out of here. I enjoyed myself today. It turned out great."

"Yeah, it really did," I said, agreeing with him.

"We'll have to plan ahead of time on something else for next month. We'll do something bigger and better next time around, young blood."

"Yes indeed, big bro. Just let me know something."

As the four of us headed to the front door, I saw Stacey on her phone again, texting this time, sitting at the table. "You on that phone again, huh? He called again?"

"Yeah, he won't stop."

"Tell him you're available." I was about to go ahead and get this money out this ho after I talked to her after Tight game left.

"Get that money, pimp," Tight game said while smiling.

When I opened the front door, I saw three gunmen wearing all black. "Get back in there, bitch ass nigga," a mask man said, pointing an AK47 at my face.

"What the fuck?" I asked out loud, still standing in the doorway in shock.

"Get yo' bitch ass back in there before I pull this muthafuckin' trigga, nigga," he demanded again.

We went backwards into the living room with our hands in the air. I heard Tight Game mumble something but couldn't make out what he had said. Before I even saw Stacey walk past them out the door, I knew what had transpired. This bitch had set us up. The power in the three gunmen's hands stopped me from going over there and snapping that bitch's neck. I couldn't believe I allowed myself to get played on like that.

"You two niggas get on y'all knees. The rest of y'all, lay on the floor and shut the fuck up," the same gunman said, which was the shortest one out the three men. He had to be JP.

Claire and Selena screamed at their kids to come here, and once they had them, they then shielded them with their bodies. At that moment, I felt like shit, like nothing. I was supposed to be their protector. There wasn't any way to protect them but to give the gunmen what they wanted so they could leave everyone alone, unharmed.

JP frisked us while the tall, slim one pointed another AK at us. My Glock was in the car and the other one was in my room. I sure wasn't about to try to take theirs with three guns pointed at us.

He took $1200 in hundreds out my wallet, tossing it before retrieving the five thousand cash from my pocket. He got a wad of money from Tight Game also. Then he took our Rolexes, our diamond, gold pinky rings, and snatched the fifty pointer chain off my neck.

While that went on, the third one with the pistol went to the back of the house.

"JP, is that you?" I asked the shortest one.

"Shut the fuck up, nigga!"

"You got what you wanted. I just ask that you don't hurt us. You—" He butted me on the side of my head with the stock on the AK, making me fall to the floor.

"Nigga, I said shut yo' bitch as up. Nigga, I ain't playin' with you. Next time, it's gon' be a bullet. Speak when I ask you something."

I felt my head leaking blood heavy, and I got a little light headed from the blow. If I had gotten hit any harder, I would have gotten knocked out. I said a short, silent prayer, asking God to protect the girls and kids in this house. I hoped they took whatever possessions they wanted and left us alive.

The one with the pistol came back in the living room. "Let's get the fuck up out of here."

"Was there a safe or money back there?" JP asked.

"Hell nah, but I got a lot of jewels, tho'," he said, holding up a long pillowcase full of stuff.

"That ain't enough. I want the money," JP stated. He ran over to the dinner table where my hoes and their kids were, and then picked Claire's son up. "Let him go, bitch, before I pull this muthafuckin' trigga."

It took her four seconds and a cold stare from JP for her to let go. She started crying harder. He dragged Lil' Dre over in front of me. "Where the rest of the money at? I know y'all got some more somewhere in this muthafucker. Break it off, if not, I'm killing him," JP said, with the AK still in his hand, pointing it at Lil' Dre's chest.

My mind was racing, thinking of something I could do. That's all the cash I had here. The rest was in the bank, in my safe at my penthouse, and buried in the backyard of my momma's house.

The only thing I kept at Shae's crib was 30% of my clothes and some of my jewelry. It was no money here but what they had taken from out my pocket.

Tight Game spoke up, "Young gangsters, I'm not about to stand here and play with you all. I know y'all mean business. If you want big money, I got you, just leave the babies and the women alone, please. I don't have any money on me but the little lousy few thousand y'all got off me. Just give me a chance. I'll put you in there with thirty Gs, each. That's enough for all three of you," he said on his knees with his hands up in the air.

I didn't know if he was telling the truth or not, but it sounded like the truth. From Tight Game's reputation and knowing him personally for almost eight years, I knew it would be consequences behind that. He had a lot of pull and plugs in high positions, so I knew they wouldn't get away freely.

"Awight, take us to it." He pushed Lil' Dre down to the floor, making the seven-year-old boy cry harder. Claire rushed to her son's aid. "If you lying, I'm killin' you!"

The one that had the pillowcase in his hand said, "Fuck that, bro. We can't trust that shit. We good, bro. Let's get the fuck up out of here."

"Nall, bro, I need that money. I believe him," JP said.

The gunman with the pillowcase raised his pistol up at Tight game and then pulled the trigger four times. "Nigga, I said let's go! Now come on!"

"Noooo!!!" I yelled as I made my way towards Tight Game. Within four feet away from him, three shots stopped me in my tracks. I fell to the floor face down next to Tight Game. I managed to turn my head, looking him straight in his eyes as he quickly lost consciousness. I anxiously wanted to scoot over and close the two-inch space that was between us, but I was afraid of getting more bullets put into me and that possibly leading to my death. I heard JP say, "Why you do that, bro? I needed that money, Rida, damn bro."

He pushed JP hard with the hand he had the gun in, making him stumble back a couple feet.

"Nigga, you fucking tripping right now! Chill out! Fuck them, I couldn't trust that shit. Let's go."

They left out the front door, leaving behind screaming and crying women and children. I felt three pairs of feminine hands on my body and heard nothing but mumbling coming from them until my eyes closed and I lost consciousness.

Maybe one day I'll settle down
But for now
I'll just play around
And I'll make them feel good
That's how I get 'em
Making all feel special
Then I'll forget 'em
So I won't hurt
I keep a lot of them
'Cause they think I love 'em
But I love 'em all, love 'em all ye-yeah
need another one to get over the other one
Another one, ye-yeah
'Cause they think I love 'em
But I love 'em all, love 'em all ye-yeah
need another one to get over the other one
Another one, ye-yeah
—K Michelle "Love 'em All"

# Smoove Dolla

## Chapter 7

The first thing I felt when I woke up in a hospital was both of my hands being tightly held. To my right, my momma's head rested on a fluffy white pillow on the side of the bed. To my left, Shae was doing the same. In a chair by the window, Tiffany had her head down on the table, sleep.

My momma raised up because she felt me move. "Hey, Tunke. How you feeling?"

My name woke Shae and Tiffany. Shae stood up, looking at me like she was worried about me, while Tiffany rushed over alongside of Shae.

"Yes ma'am, I'm good," I said without knowing what she was really talking about. At first, I had asked myself how the fuck I end up in the hospital, but the event that caused me to be here slowly popped up in my mind. I thought about Tight Game getting shot. "What happened with Tight game?"

No one answered me. "Don't tell me he dead," I said while shaking my head. "Is he ok? What happened to him?"

My momma spoke up. "He in a coma, Tunke."

My heart dropped. That answer hit me hard. I fucked up. I started to feel anxiety coming inside me, fear of losing Tight Game, and regret for not screening that bitch like I should have. I needed to see him and try to talk to him. I started snatching the patches off my chest, then took the IV out my arm. When I reached the halfway point of getting out the bed, I felt so much pain in my chest and stomach. All I could do was lay back down and close my eyes.

Since Tiffany had been a nurse in the past, I told her to put the needle back in my arm. After she did that, she squeezed the morphine bag. It felt so good, but not good enough to kill all the physical and emotional pain I felt right now.

"I hope this wakes you up and makes you realize you only playing with yourself," Tiffany said.

"What?" I asked, surprised. "Shut the hell up. You must have forgot that it was pimpin' that got you where you are today. You knew what you were dealing with at the beginning. So don't ever come at me like that again!"

"That's enough, Tunke. Quit talking to her like that. Y'all don't argue in here."

"Oh, it's alright, Ms. Ebony. I've had enough of him. I was a damn fool to wanna be with you. I'm done. I'm out of here," Tiffany said, throwing her hands up in the air, then started heading towards the door.

"Tiffany, hold up, let me talk to you about those clothes before you go." Tiffany and my momma walked out the door together, leaving me and Shae alone.

"Hey, Daddy. I'm glad you made it and you're okay," Shae said once the door closed, then we gave each other a long kiss.

"I'm glad to see you too, baby. How long have I been here?"

"Two days. You been through a surgery too. Oh yea, a detective came by here wanting to talk about what happened that night. I told them I couldn't tell who it was. The night you got shot, before the ambulance got there, I made everyone leave except for Tight game's girls. They didn't want to leave him. I told them to say they didn't see who it was. That white bitch, Stacey, left with them niggas too. We tried looking for her in Arlington and Euless, but we couldn't find her. Oh yea, Claire and Selena left you. They say they couldn't deal with everything that was going on and you put their kids in danger. But Rose chose up with you yesterday." She dug inside her big Michael Kane purse. "Rose's choosing fee is in it, too, along with what we made since you been in the hospital. It's $6300. Here's your phones."

"Thank you, baby."

"You're welcome. Daddy, I got to tell you something. I don't want you to get mad at me tho', Daddy." I knew it had to be something she had no business doing since she said it like that. As far as me tripping on what she did, it depended on what took place. "I was only trying to make back everything they took. They took all our jewelry, Daddy."

"Tell me what happened, Shae, and quit beating around the bush." I was trying not to get on her ass, but I was about to because she was making excuses for whatever she had done. I couldn't lie,

I was a little heated about our jewelry getting taken, but that really didn't matter. What they took was material shit. All that could be replaced. Some of it was insured anyway.

"I got locked up again."

"You got locked up again?" I asked, not believing what I just heard her say.

"Daddy, I'm sorry. I was just—" Since my right arm was wounded and had an IV in it. I threw the huge stack of ironed money as hard and best I could with my left hand, hitting her dead in the face. She stumbled back. "Shut yo' bitch ass up, burnt out ho."

She looked at me, stunned. "Damn, Tunke, after all I've done for you, that's how you gon' do me? Nigga, you burned out. Fuck you, Tunke," she said, then stormed out the door.

She must have really been fucked up about what I just did. She'd never talked to me that way or even came close to before. She'd always shown me respect. Yeah, her hoing career was over. I was glad she left without picking up the money she had given me, because there was no way I could stop her from getting it in my condition.

My momma came back into the room a minute later, taking me away from the thoughts of revenge on the niggas that caused me to be in the hospital. "Damion, what you do to Shae? I just seen her getting on the elevator crying."

"Forget her."

"Damion, you wrong for what you doing to them girls. They ain't did nothing but be good to yo' no-good ass. You ain't gonna realize until you lose Tiffany because of some nasty ass hoes. I had a dream you were gonna get robbed, and look what happen to you. You better wake yo' ass up, Damion. You got so much potential to be somebody great, but you want to be a pimp out of all things. You got your head screwed on wrong. Won't you work on your music and leave that bullshit alone? You know I'm not gon' live forever. I'm 48, Damion. I want to see my only son accomplish a lot more in life."

"I am, Momma."

"I really do hope so. Why you got all this money on the floor?"

"Pick it up for me, please." After she picked it up and placed all the bills in neat stacks, she asked, "Damion, you need this money? If not, let me have $2000 please."

Just to mess with her, I said, "It's prostitution money, you still want it?"

"Boy, you better quit playing with me. Can I have it or what?"

"Go ahead and get it," I said then yawned.

She got twenty hundreds out the stack of different bills and handed me the rest of the money. I put it behind me and laid on it. "You gonna be okay by yourself?"

"Yeah, I'll be good. Who all been up here?"

"Just me, Tiffany, and Shae. Some girl named Pinky and a white girl was up here yesterday for a little bit. I'm about to go, Damion. I'ma try to come back up here later to see how you doing. If not, I'll be up here in the morning." She gave me a kiss on the cheek. "I love you, Damion."

"Love you too, Momma. Be safe."

All three women that I loved were gone, but their fragrance still lingered around the room. It made me miss them and wish they were still here with me. I inhaled deeply then slowly exhaled to calm myself so I could think better. I thought about what just happened a few minutes ago. I let my emotions get the best of me. I was really upset at myself for slipping. That shit was killing me inside right now. I had to get full control of myself before I emotionally and mentally self-destructed. I couldn't believe I let myself get caught up like that after I'd been a jacker myself, and I knew how niggas misused females to manipulate and deceive their targets. I should have peeped that whole play. Recognizing all the red flags when I saw the mug on his face, not accepting the knock for his ho. Another flag was when she didn't want to bring her kids along to the Sunday Funday Event. The last red flag I remembered was when I busted her on the phone talking to JP in the bathroom.

The game was fucked up. A bunch of so-called pimps and hoes weren't playing by the rules. They weren't playing the game a hundred percent. They were double breasting, doing other hustles making it hard for a real player in the game. A bunch of hoes now were renegade and getting away without suffering the consequences of being a renegade ho. Some of them were stealing and robbing tricks, making the game sour. Now I could see another reason why Tight game gave up the game. It wasn't the same as twenty years ago. Even though the low level of the game was fun and rewarding, it still wasn't worth playing because of the bullshit that went on nowadays. Maybe it was time for me to give it up. I would give that hard thought while lying in this hospital bed.

I admit it hurt me to see Shae not here by my side at my weakest times, when she had been there at all the other difficult times. But like true pimps say, Bottoms are to be respected. I disrespected her when I threw that money at her. I tripped out. I should have rewarded her for her efforts on hoing for me when she wasn't instructed to do so. Shae was my true queen indeed. I should have just taken her out the game without asking her when I sensed she was tired of hoing when she got arrested weeks ago. She would have happily accepted that without questioning me. Shae was taught by Fancy, who was the best at screening new johns. Shae would have never gotten caught up if she had been using the technique she was taught to do. Shae had been in a lot of states where detectives were hard on prostitutes and it was hard to screen johns because some cities allowed undercovers to lie, touch, as well as fuck the prostitutes without nutting before arresting them.

I believed the only reason why she stayed down with me so long was because she loved and cared for me. We'd been knowing each other since we were fourteen. She'd been hoing for me for seven years now. We met when she moved from West Dallas Fish Trap Projects into Turner Courts Projects in South Dallas. I was the first boy she had talked to in our seventh grade class at Pearl C. Middle School. From that day forward, we had become cool and later friends with each other in Lincoln High School until now. When I was blessed with the Proper Game from Tight game, I introduced her into it. She had no problem hoing for me and turning our friendship into a pimp-ho relationship.

She had already been a down for whatever rider since seventh grade. She had given me money when I didn't have any. She stole and burglarized alongside of me, letting me have most of the money we made, sometimes all of it. Shae had even helped me fight when I got jumped by two older South Dallas Dixon Circle crip niggas at their corner store after getting out of school when we were fourteen years old. We both got bruised up and my new red, white, and black Jordans still got taken then burned right in front of us. I stole off on the one who poured gasoline on my kicks and then lit the flame. I still ended up getting beat up worse the second time we fought. I had two black eyes and a busted lip, and Shae came out with a swollen jaw, all over gangbanging. We both were bloods back then. But when pimpin' and hoing came into our lives, repping a set came to an end. It was all about the game and the Money. I'd really gotten so comfortable with Shae being around that it actually hurt losing her.

Shae had always been good to me and there for me. She'd been the best ho I'd ever had in my career. We were very compatible to each other in a lot of ways. I hated to lose her. But even if she wanted to come back, I wouldn't accept her back. She'd done enough, her time was up. It was her time to fulfill her life dreams. I was going to do everything in my power to make them tangible. Whenever I got out of here, I was going to find her a building to rent for her beauty salon and pay to decorate it. Then I'd use my sources to promote her business. She deserved that and a lot more.

I understood my actions after I flipped out on Tiffany and Shae. I took my frustration of being in the hospital out on them. I got defensive when Tiffany criticized and complained about my lifestyle. I should've let her talk to get her feelings out instead of responding defensively to her conflict, because I understood it was in a black woman's nature to want to argue. Even so, I still stood as a pimp. A pimp didn't allow any woman but an elderly woman, his mother, and grandmother to talk to him like that. A pimp was going to live life the way he wanted and the best way he saw fit, without caring what anybody thought or felt about it. It was what it was. A pimp was going to check what needed to be checked. Although, I could've responded in a calm and positive manner. The truth was, I felt powerless in this hospital bed, that's why I responded to them that way. I knew everything Tiffany needed, was concerned about, and how she was feeling. She needed me to be there for her and the kids. She felt I was being irresponsible about our business and my duty as a father. Tiffany was concerned about me living and dying. To tell the truth, it's all true as far as being an irresponsible father, not being a good friend to her, and the lack of communication between us. She was fed up with me. The man in me couldn't blame her. I would've said fuck me and left too if I was in her shoes going through the same shit with someone who didn't want to be with me. I'd call Tiffany or go see her sooner or later and make it up to her, but we were done with being in a relationship. I wasn't about to do that square shit anymore.

As far as Claire and Selena went, I didn't much care about them leaving. I understood their departure, though. I was supposed to be their protector. That night, no one was protected in that house. Claire was dead with me though. I didn't gain anything with fucking with her. Selena never had given me any problems for the four months she had been with me. She was a good ho. I would help her if she wanted my help with whatever, and I would accept her if she wanted to come back.

A dark, pretty, older nurse in her late forties came into the room. "Good Morning, Mr. Johnson. How are you feeling?" When the hanging wires from the machine caught her eyes, she asked, "What happened here, Mr. Johnson?"

"I snatched everything off trying to go see a brother of mine, but realized I was hurt too bad to move like I wanted to."

"You know, you're blessed to be alive. You almost died the other night, Mr. Johnson. You lost a lot of blood. One of the bullets was an inch away from the heart. I hoped you thanked God for letting you live. What's your brother's name?"

"Hobert Washington. I heard he's in a coma."

"Oh yea, I remember him. He's on the third floor," she said with sympathy all in her eyes and face. It told me she loved her job and was a caring person.

"I need to see him. You mind getting me a wheelchair and taking me to see him?

"I'm doing my rounds and about to eat lunch. If no one has come to see you by then and taken you by the time I'm done, I'll take you to see him," she said with a sincere smile while she hooked new patches to my chest.

"Okay, thanks."

After she left, I got on my phone. I had a lot of messages in my DM on Facebook, Instagram, Twitter, and text message notifications that blew up on my personal phone. I had a lot of missed calls as well. I didn't want to be bothered with anybody asking me what happened that night if they couldn't help me find who shot me. So, I didn't bother to return anyone's texts or calls at the moment. But I did call some of my homeboys to come to the hospital today when they got time.

I started feeling hungry. I didn't feel that way when my momma was here, but I was hungry as fuck. I wasn't about to eat this hospital food. I called Rose to see what they were doing. I wanted something to eat. "Hey Monopoly," she said when she answered.

"What's up, Rose? Where y'all at?"

"Me and Pinky at the dentist office getting the little man's teeth cleaned. It's good to hear your voice again. How are you holding up?"

"I'm good. Just hungry as a muthafucka. How long y'all been there?"

"Since 8:15. It's 8:38 now. They should be calling him soon."

"Okay. When you all done, bring me 50 garlic hot wings with fries from Wing Stop. And bring me a lemonade drink."

"I got you as soon as we take Chris to school, then we'll get your food and make our way to you. Is that okay with you?"

"Yeah, that's fine. As long as you don't take all day."

"I won't. I wanna see you anyway."

"I wanna see you too since you done paid your way. I don't hear Pinky, where she at?"

"She went to the car about five minutes before you called. We were just talking about you. She's gonna be glad to talk to you."

"Don't tell her you talked to me then. Just come up here after you get the food."

# Money Game

"Alright, Daddy."

\*\*\*

A little over an hour later, Rose and Pinky walked inside the room. They spoke and greeted me with hugs and kisses, seeming excited to see me awake. Rose handed me a Wing Stop bag along with a large cup of lemonade.

"Where Shae? I thought she was up here," Rose asked.

"She was. She left not too long ago." I didn't bother telling her what happened with Shae and I yet. I didn't want them calling her right now asking questions. If I had told them, they probably would think she left for the same reasons as Selena and Claire did. I knew Shae's separation from me would leave a huge question mark in their minds, knowing how down and loyal Shae was to me. Shae was probably the reason why Pinky and CeCe were still my hoes, and Rose chose. So I kept them in the dark for now until things calmed down with Shae. I'd call her later to let her know all the information to get her money from the overseas accounts, since she was no longer my ho anymore.

"Did she give you your choosing fee and the money I made last night? It's $3100."

"Yeah, I got it." Since we were talking about money, I started telling them how I wanted them to make money. "I don't want you all hoing unless it's with a regular. All I want y'all to do is work the clubs for now until I tell you otherwise. This is for y'all safety. I don't want nothing happening to y'all while I'm in here. Pinky, you still can be a waitress if you want. Don't do no extra shit, we good on cash. All I want you to do, Rose, is dance and date regulars. Am I understood."

"Yes, Daddy," they both answered back.

"Rose, I want you to see if CeCe's dancing is qualified for the strip club. If so, I want you to teach CeCe everything there is to know about working the club. Take her to Men's Paradise and have her fill out an application. Can you handle all that?"

"Yeah, I can handle that," she said, nodding her head.

"Monopoly, I called your grandpa earlier. He wants me to take the car to him at 12 to see what's wrong with it."

I looked at the time on my Android phone, it was 10:42 A.M. "You still got a little time to kill. It takes about 25 minutes to get to South Dallas. You got some money on you?"

"No. Shae left me with $50. I only got $13 left."

I gave her $500. "Give him $100 and use the other $400 for whatever y'all need along the way. If everything goes right and as planned when I discharge, we gonna get us two new cars."

"For real, Monopoly?"

"Everything I say is realism, Rose. My word is bond. I got chu, Rose."

She thanked me and gave me a tight hug. I knew she'd love getting out that old car into a new one. I wanted her to look forward to something she really wanted. Also, I knew she would show off her new car to her renegade homegirls, raising the curiosity within them to come fuck with me. Pinky didn't care about getting a car. The things she wanted the most were a father figure and heroin. Although, I knew she'd be fucked up at me for giving the bottom bitch title to Rose and not to her. It was a great possibility that Rose was going to be my bottom now, because she had the experience in leading hoes. I was going to teach her my game then let her be an example of my game. Pinky wasn't bottom bitch quality. She was only good for catching other hoes to knock, making my stable look good, and making big money. She didn't have that leadership I needed to be a good example to my other queens. If she wasn't on drugs, she probably could be a good bottom. But then again, when I thought about it, if she was hoing and sober, she probably wouldn't be a good bread winner.

Like most hoes, they needed the dope to cope and go along with everything in their lives. Shit, I knew a bunch of pimps who did heroin, wet, powder, crystal meth, drank syrup or liquor to cope with the shit that went on in the game to not drive themselves crazy. But a pimp wasn't supposed to be no addict, at all. A man that was a real pimp had discipline over himself and his weaknesses. Sometimes I wanted to smoke kush to cope, but I immediately would kill that desire. I still admit it was hard sometimes to deal with the shit that went on, but I still got through it without driving myself crazy. I was a strong motherfucker, I didn't need any drugs. Plus, I loved the game, so I had to accept whatever came with it.

Rose, picked up her Gucci purse off the bed then said, "Come on, Pinky, let's go."

Pinky looked at me and said, "Daddy, can I stay with you please?"

"Damn, bitch, you don't want to ride with me? You gon' have me go by myself? That's fucked up, Pinky," Rose said.

"I wanna stay with Monopoly. I need to talk to him about something, it's important."

I really wanted Pinky to stay. I wanted the company. "Where's CeCe at?" I asked the both of them.

"She at the room. And she probably still sleep. We probably won't make it in time if I go get her," Rose replied, disappointed.

"Just call and see. If she's sleep, just tell her to get up and go with you. She ain't gotta be dressed up to go. Anyway, it's a straight shot on 30 from the hotel. Y'all will make in time."

"Alright, then. I'll be back later."

"Alright. Call me if you need me and when y'all make it there."

When Rose walked out the door, I asked Pinky, "What you gotta talk to me about?"

"I just wanted to have some alone time with you."

"Is that right?" I asked her.

"Yep. I'm glad you're alive," she said as she started rubbing my arm.

"Shit, me too. I just hope my bro wake up soon."

"Daddy, that shit was crazy. That shit scared the fuck out of me."

"Yeah, I know. I want to apologize to you for everything that happened that night. It should've never happened."

"It's okay. You're alive, that's all that matters."

"I see that you called and texted like you were supposed to yesterday and this morning. And I also see that you're high right now, too, but I'm not going to trip on you. I understand. Whenever

I get out of here, I'ma schedule you an appointment with a friend of mine at a rehabilitation center. I still do want you to recite those laws to me. I believe it'll help you in the process of getting off."

There were two things I could do with her, keep her or let her go. In actuality, I didn't want to lose her. Other than the fact she was on dope and she did that faggot shit the other week ago, she had been good to a pimp. I'd come to really like Pinky and even grew to love her. Now, let's not get that confused with me being in love with her, because I could easily get over Pinky if she left me right now and wouldn't be fucked up about it. I didn't need her at all. I wanted her in my life, so I accepted her drug habit for the time being, until I had time to put her in rehab. Now, if she got out and went back to drugs, I was done with her, because not only did she waste my time, but I stood on not fucking with bitches that did hard drugs. "You got anything you want to say or ask me?"

"No. I'm just glad to see you." Her eyes and face expressed happiness.

I smiled. "I'm glad to see you too, baby." Pinky was looking good as hell in a tight, sky blue Dolce & Gabanna dress. It amplified her beauty. Her entire look and scent made me horny as a motherfucker.

I did something I'd never done with any of my hoes except for Shae. I tongued Pinky down. A short time after kissing, she reached under the white sheet and under my gown, then grabbed my dick with her soft hands. She started jacking me off until it was brought to life. I'd been prolonging fucking Pinky for controlling reasons. But right now, I couldn't care less about that. I wanted to feel her pussy. She'd earned the dick anyway. Plus, I didn't get a chance to build Pinky up after I trunked her. I was glad she stayed down after the tragedy that caused me to be in this hospital. Now it would be a good time to give her what she wanted.

She unlocked our kiss then went into her Dolce & Gabanna purse and pulled out a watermelon Fruit Roll-Up. "What chu gonna do with that?" I asked.

"You 'bout to see," she said, and then started smiling while opening the wrapper. She took the candy out, tossed the wrapper in the small trash next to her on the floor, and then wrapped it around my dick like the food, pig in the blanket. She went down and started sucking my uncovered dick head. She did that for about 35 seconds then went down until every inch of me was in her mouth and touching her throat. She gagged and hummed on my dick while her right hand massaged both balls.

Several minutes later, Pinky placed her mouth on the side of the bottom of my dick and started going up and down like she was sucking the side of a popsicle about eight times. Then she went up to my head and did the other side until the fruit roll up dissolved. She went down to my balls and put them into her mouth, circling her tongue slowly around them while jacking me off.

Personally, it wasn't nothing like a pretty bitch knowing what she was doing when it came to giving head. It looked really good. I wanted to feel how good her sex game was. "Climb yo' fine ass up on this bed," I said as I lowered the bed so she could get on the bed easier.

After she took off her pups and climbed up, she stood right in front of me, raising her dress up to her waist. Her pussy print flaunted in a blue thong. Beyond her love box were two phat butt cheeks perfectly hanging from her rear, eating up her thong. It was a sight to see. I grabbed my phone and started snapping away like I was a photographer. I took about ten photos of her smiling, playing in her hair, some with her 34-C breasts and pussy exposed along with other playful photos. I could use those pictures to post or sell them as jack shots.

I put my phone down then ran my right hand over her pretty yellow feet up to her calf muscle, up between her thick and soft inner thighs, then stopping at her love box. I started massaging her pearl tongue with my thumb. She moaned as soon as I touched it.

I dragged her juices from her wet pussy to her asshole. I rubbed my middle finger around her rim a few times and then went back to her pearl tongue with my thumb. "Ease down and ride this big motherfucka."

As she squatted down, she held on to the rail with her right hand. She started bouncing on the head. I couldn't take the tease, so

I grabbed her ass cheek with my good hand and eased her down on me. The tightness of her made me think about making her get on the bottom while I got on top and beat her flesh in, but I couldn't because of my lack of strength.

I started forcing her up and down on top repeatedly with my right hand. "Oh, shit! I'm 'bout to nut Monopolyyy!" she yelled aloud.

It got to the point where I let go of her because she learned how I liked it. To keep her balance and to be safe from falling, she held on to both sides of the plastic rail while she rolled me. We both moaned out loud in pleasure, getting lost in the moment.

Minutes later, it got so good to me where I couldn't hold in my nut anymore. The beautiful sight of her riding me and the unbearable feeling of her love compelled me to explode inside her just like a volcano erupting. She continued the ride, until a couple minutes later she came again, then she collapsed on top of me.

We ended up fucking again until we both fell asleep.

\*\*\*

The sound of something hard getting hit against plastic woke Pinky and me. We looked up to see my homie 8ball hitting his pistol on the rail of the bed. "Get yo' ass up, nigga."

"Wuz up, bro?"

"You told me to come up here. I'm tryna find out them niggas that shot y'all? You good?"

"Hold up y'all." I tapped Pinky on the side of her ass cheek. "Go sit in one of those chairs over there and face the wall. Get on ya phone or something."

My cousin Bobby and two of my homeboys were in here too. My hoes and my homies weren't allowed to talk to each other unless I allowed them to. Right now, there was no need for them to talk to each other.

Pinky put her dress down over her ass, grabbed her phone and purse, and then got off the bed. Before she walked off from the bed, I got four Tic Tacs out her purse and popped them in my mouth,

134

because I smelled my own breath kicking. All my homies and my cousin watched Pinky's ass wiggle as she did as I told her to do. To get their attention off her and on to the reason why they were here in the first place, I spoke up. "Yeah, I'm good, bro, just in a bunch of pain, but I'm making it tho'." I started giving them our hood handshake.

"You can't be in too much pain you in this bitch getting pussy."

"Shit, this morphine killing most of the pain. Them muthafuckin' bullets ain't no joke. They hurt. You been shot before, you know how it feels."

"Yeah, you right. They do hurt." 8 Ball had gotten hit five times by some Park Row niggas. My hood niggas had beef with them for about nine months until they called a truce due to both hoods losing niggas. 8 Ball had too many bodies on his rap sheet and beef with niggas. For that reason, he didn't leave home without a gun. Sad to say, but I believed he would have taken it to church.

It would have been waiting on him in his car off safety. He didn't slip. We called him 8 Ball because he favored the rapper 8 Ball that rapped with MJG from Memphis, Tennessee.

"What up, big bro? I thought I'd never see you like this in the line of work you in," my little homie, Kendrick, said, who stood next to 8 Ball. Lil' Ken was barely 18 years old. He is a straight-up killer. He had five bodies that I knew about by the age of 16. He made a name for himself early. I hated that he dropped out of school just to be a gangsta. The little homie could really hoop his ass off. I believed he would have been a major figure in college and probably would have made it to the NBA later on in life. He was that good.

"This shit comes with any game you in. I'm just lucky to be alive, bro."

"I'm glad you made it, Monopoly," my 20-year-old homie, Poppa, said. He was a well-respected youngin' who had earned his name at 17 years old from murkin' niggas. Poppa really meant Pop Ya. That's exactly what he would do if you crossed him the wrong way. He was a quiet and serious dude who sold powder in one of the big homies from the hood trap houses. After I started working eight months ago, I used to have him as my enforcer when I wasn't around. Poppa was my nigga. They were all bloods. Even though I laid down my flag and picked up this pimpin', they still had love and respect for me, and the same vice versa.

"You know who shot y'all?" Poppa asked.

"I do, but I don't know where to find them. All I know is the one that set me up is a fake ass pimp nigga named JP. The nigga that shot us was a nigga named Rida. I don't know who the third nigga is. I think JP was a crip. He gotta be from what he wore and said to me that night at the club."

"What club y'all was at?" 8Ball asked.

"Best Cabaret up in Euless."

"I don't know shit about that club, but it shouldn't take me long to find out who JP and Rida are." 8Ball got around. He knew a lot of niggas in Dallas. He was 34 years old, a head bouncer, and promoter for Dallas Live, the biggest and livest club in Dallas-Fort Worth. He was well respected in a bunch of hoods in the DFW. So, there was a great chance he could gather some information about them niggas.

"What happened? How you get set up?" Bobby asked. My first cousin knew a lot of niggas also. He had two wet and coke houses in the Greedy Grove, Oak Cliff, and South Dallas. He came up from jacking a big-time Mexican in East Dallas for 30 pounds of coke and 42 bands when he was 19. He never looked back since. He was now 23 years old in the big league with all the big ballers. Bobby owned a smoke shop, two soul food restaurants, as well as sold drugs.

Halfway in telling them what happened, the door opened, in came the same nurse from earlier. She looked at Pinky first then at the five of us. When she noticed the gun still in 8Ball's hand, immediately, her good mood turned into a surprised and scared look. She started walking backwards towards the door, leaving the wheelchair where it was.

"Put that gun away, bro," I said while tapping him on his arm. While he tucked it in his waistband in his pants, I told the nurse, "Sorry about that, Ms. Perkins. They're family. Ain't nothing going on. They don't mean no harm."

8Ball sensed it was a good time for them to leave, so he told me, "Hey, Tunke, we finna get outta here. I'm 'bout to see what I can find out. I'll holler at you when I know something." We said our see you laters and gave each other dap.

"I don't know what to say about you youngsters. Y'all better be careful. I could have been the wrong person coming through that door. Mr. Johnson, are you ready to go see your brother?"

"Yes, I'm more than ready," I said and looked at my people. "Y'all going to see Tight game?"

"Nah, man. I don't know about them, but I can't see him like that. That shit gon' really have a nigga mad, ready to go get at them niggas who did it. Nah, I'm good on that." Bobby, Poppa, and Lil' Ken all agreed with 8Ball. Before they walked out the door, 8Ball told the nurse, "My bad for scaring you. You have a good one."

I felt them on not wanting to go see Tight Game. Since I was the reason he was in the hospital, I felt obligated to see him, even though he was in a coma.

The nurse put the morphine bag on a tall, metal, portable stick on wheels. They both helped me into the wheelchair and then Pinky pushed me onto the elevator up to the third floor.

When Pinky rolled me into Tight Game's room, I got shot ugly looks from Christie and one of the Asian hoes that were there at Shae's when we got shot. I could tell the hateful looks were blame. They were blaming me for what had happened. I knew they were going to, especially when they assumed everything about what took place. It was okay though. I didn't have to answer to them. It was possible Christie would go to our Mason brothers and make a big deal about Tight game getting shot. They probably would come talk to me or want me to meet up with them at our lodge or barber shop to hear my side of the story. Hopefully, they believed and understood me. But I wasn't worried about it if they didn't. I knew the truth, it wasn't on purpose.

"Excuse me. I want to be with him alone for a minute, please." They remained sitting in their chairs on their phones without saying a word. I waited five seconds for them to move before I said something. "I apologize for what happened. I'm fucked up at myself right now. However, this shit goes along with the game we're all in, so don't act like you don't know it's a possibility a nigga might get robbed and shot. I'm getting tired of explaining my muthafucking self. I want some respect in this muthafucker and some alone time with him. Now get the fuck up and get out this room!"

Two seconds later, Christie got up while telling the Asian chick, "Come on, Mimi, let's step out."

After Pinky rolled me over to his bed, I had her step out as well. This was my first time ever being in the presence of anyone in a coma. He looked as if he was asleep. I could see that his dark-brown skin on his face still looked smooth. His long permed hair that was usually hanging down his back was now in two thick braids.

I started talking to him. "If you hear me, I just want to let you know, I apologize for what happened. I should have known better. I hope you find you it in your heart to forgive me. I will appreciate it and take advantage of the game you've given me. I love you, big bro."

I couldn't stand looking at him any longer. I got madder and more emotional by the second, looking at him in this condition. The niggas that did us like this were about to suffer the consequences when I found them.

Pound for pound, car for car, jewelry for jewelry, woman for woman, I'm undefeated cross-country.
- Young Lace


If you let the little shit go, after a while, it mounts up to disrespect. The smallest problem is actually the biggest problem, because if it was really small, she would have known not to do it. Some things hoes do purposely to get your attention, just like any other broad. The difference with a ho is, you have to check her ass, or you're getting knocked off. A real ho will not pay a chump.
— *RoseBudd BitterDose*
*American Pimp*

# Smoove Dolla

## Chapter 8

I had to stay in the hospital for an additional two weeks due to internal bleeding. I was so ready to get out of here, that it didn't make any sense. It felt a bit like being in jail. But in this case, I could leave if I wanted to. If I did, I would die sooner or later from not having the proper care my body needed to survive. The day had finally come to discharge me. Now I waited in the room for Shae to pick me up.

During the course of the two weeks, Shae and I got back cool with each other, and had been talking on a daily basis. She wasn't hoing anymore, but was on to a new chapter in life to fulfill her life's dreams.

A lot of people had the game misconstrued when it came to building their hoes up, and helping them pursue their gifts and talents. A real pimp took care of his hoes, especially upper-class pimps. This went for good-graded hoes, because you would come across hoes who weren't striving towards any good goals, some that had no idea of what their purpose in life was, and there were some who didn't want anything worth having in life. The only thing a pimp could do with those type was cop and blow. I loved what Tight Game had done with Christie. That was big pimping. Before I went to prison, I came across a ho that wanted to be a porn star, but I didn't capitalize on that opportunity to build my ho up in that field. Let that happen now. I would make it my duty to have that ho's name bigger than Cherokee and Roxy Reynolds. If a pimp's hoes were being true to the game and stayed down, he had to be true to the game, making sure at the end of her hoing career she would be straight, and on the road to fulfill her life's purpose. If they had any children, I would even start putting money into their college tuition. Especially a queen that was his bottom. A down queen like Shae deserved it all for what she had done. I would love to see how beautiful it was to be her man and husband. She was really an incredible, lovely, respectful, and smart woman.

But my love was deeper for this game than the love I had for her. Maybe when it's time to get on the square shit and she was still available, I'd marry her.

Since it was Mother's Day last weekend, I gave two tickets for the Tank concert to my mother and sister along with $5000 apiece. I gave Rose, Pinky, and CeCe the other three tickets, along with $20,000 for shopping money and to do whatever they wanted to do for Mother's Day weekend.

After the concert, my hoes flew to Hawaii for three days. My homie, 8Ball, ended up finding out who Rida was. Our homeboy, Cory, was friends with him on Facebook, who's a rapper as well as Rida. Rida promoted his song and the show he had coming up at an after-hours club in Fort Worth this weekend. Cory recognized Rida's name and let 8Ball know.

We found out that he was from Highland Hills in Oak Cliff. Even with the information we had, we still couldn't locate JP. 8Ball had asked two crackheads he ran into when he went to the Pink's apartments in Highland Hills, to holler at a chick he knew. He offered them $40 to go to the White's and Brown's apartments to see if they could find any information on JP and Rida, but they said they be all over Highland Hills, and they'd never heard of them. Maybe they lied to him, I didn't know. It didn't matter, because I was discharging from the hospital today, where I could make his show Saturday night. He would be taken care of then. Hopefully, JP would be there or Rida could lead us to him.

\*\*\*

As soon as we made it on the southside of Arlington, I laid out a blue, Tom Ford, tailored two-piece suit, a white dress shirt, a white-and-black-colored tie with blue Tom Ford dress for my business purposes today. I knew it would feel great to get out the hospital gown, take a shower, and into some real clothes. I checked myself out in the long body mirror after getting dressed. The only thing I disliked about myself was that my nose was too pointy. Back in the day, when I was in elementary school, I used to get jokes cracked on me about my nose. When I first started hustling, I just bought and wore designer glasses and dressed nice to cover it up.

But no matter what I thought about my nose, since I was a baby boy until now, I'd been told thousands of times how handsome I was by numerous women. I had no doubt about that. I popped my collar. I looked damn good in my new suit. Even though I lost 17 pounds since I had been in the hospital, I still had my sex appeal with a cut, slim, and hard body. Protein drinks, good eating, and light workouts four times a week would shake me back to my normal weight of 180. To top my business look off, all I needed now was a haircut, a Rolex, and a pinky ring.

Since we were in Arlington already, I drove to a barber shop on Cooper St. and Park Row, close to UT of Arlington. My number one barber shop I went to was in Big T Bazaar in Oak Cliff, but I still had to take care of some things in Arlington before I headed to Dallas, so we stayed out this way.

Even though I still had a two-inch wound in my head, I could still get my usual cut, which was a bald fade. While getting my hair cut, I had Shae look up a good building for her hair salon.

On my way to The Parks Mall, we talked about the office spaces she had chosen and whether or not it was a good location. She found a space in the Greedy Grove on John West and Buckner. The second one was in Oak Cliff off Lancaster and Fordham. The third one was on the eastside of Arlington on Arkansas and Collins. Since Arlington had been a growing city and the closest to her house, we decided to go check it out first. She called the white guy that owned it and he told her he could meet up with her there in two hours. We fucked off at the mall shopping for jewelry and a few outfits until 10:30 A.M.

As we sat in my Range Rover waiting on the owner, Shae looked at me and asked, "I know you not leaving the game alone, but when are you planning on it?"

"To be honest with you, Shae, I don't know. I gave it some thought when I was in the hospital, but my addiction to this game is strong to the point I don't want to give it up. Pimpin' is in my mind, body, and soul. And it goes deep, Shae. I know one day I will grow tired of this lifestyle. It ain't no telling when that will be, tho'. I remember when I first turned out. I can't lie, shit was hard on a young pimp. I was 17. Even though I could take care of responsibilities when it came to our necessities, I didn't have a clue or any understanding about life. I didn't even have any understanding about pimpin'. I was just going through the motions, things I saw, and the little game I was taught. It took me paying my dues, going to prison to fully understand how shit really is and works. I think different compared to seven years ago. I have more now compared to what I possessed back then. I know why you asked me that question. I know what you want."

"What I want, Tunke?"

"You want me. And you know what, Shae?"

"What?"

"I want you too, Shae. I wanna be your man and have a real family with you one day."

Shae had two strong desires that I'd always fulfilled. One of them was to have a family that she'd never had. The only real family she did have was her grandmother, who passed away five years ago. She had no siblings, that's why I had my hoes calling each other sisters instead of wife-in-laws. She never knew nor ever seen her dad. Her mother was a whore and heroin addict in West Dallas before she died of an overdose ten years ago. Her grandmother got custody of Shae when she was 14, when she moved to Bunton projects in South Dallas. Her second desire was fear of losing me.

That's because I took her virginity. I was her first and only father figure, best friend, and big brother. I damn near taught her everything. We were never a couple because at the time Shae and I first met, I was with my daughter's mother. We became close friends until I got introduced to the game, then I turned her out. I've learned it's always best to find a person's weaknesses and their greatest desires if you want to control them and keep them around.

"Really, Tunke?"

"I'm serious."

"What about Tiffany?"

"She's a great woman and I do love her, but she's not enough for me. Love is not enough for me. Loyalty means more to me than love. I know if I go to prison right now, she'll leave me and find herself someone else. Even though I believe she might do little shit for me here and there, that's not what I want. You've given me everything I've ever wanted and more. You're perfect for me, Shae." Then I put my right hand into her left hand and said, "I know if it's been this great on this side of the game, it has to be even better on the square side. What you think about that?"

"I know it will. You're the only man that I've ever loved in my whole life, and the only man that I ever wanted to love. I don't't know who my biological father is. But it doesn't matter because you've been more than a father to me. You've been my everything since we were teenagers. I know it's gonna work with us. I really do love you, Tunke, with everything in me."

"I love you too, Shae." When she was talking, I saw a tall, heavy-set white man get out of a grey 2500 Ford truck and then walk in his office space he had for rent. He had been inside for over five minutes now, so I told Shae, "Call that dude and see if he's ready for us to some in. He just walked in a while ago."

It took 27 minutes to look around and convince her to want to rent the building. After I paid him $1000, he gave her a receipt, two contracts to sign, and then two sets of keys. He wished her luck, said he'd see her next month, and then left.

She started to pace the big floor in an energetic way and said excitedly, "I'm finally about to do it, Tunke." Then she started giving me a description about where she wanted her station booth to be, where she wanted the beautician, the barber booths, the colors of her chairs, what pictures and images she wanted on the wall.

It made me happy to see my queen happy. I was really proud of myself for keeping her around seven years, accomplishing the things I had with her, and now helping her accomplish her dreams. In my mind, I gave myself a pimp's pat on the back. "We'll have to get together in the morning or sometime Monday so I can show you how to order everything you need off your business account. This is it, baby. You about to make it happen."

We wrapped our arms around each other. "Thank you so much, Tunke. Thank you, thank you, thank you."

"You're welcome, baby. Thank yourself as well. I want you to accomplish everything you want to do in life, Shae. I want that vision in your mind to come true. You have to work hard, stay dedicated, and continue to move in the direction of your goals with perseverance. You have that in you. You can do it. Four years ago, you were afraid to get your own shop. You had your business, little money doing hair here and there. That was your first step. Now, this is your second step towards success. You made this possible. I'm behind you all the way, no doubt. You can do it. Let me hear you say, I'm doing it!"

I felt tears on my neck. "I'm doing it, Daddy."

I had her say it two more times. I wanted her to have confidence not only in me and my abilities as the man in her life but in herself, her own decisions, and the gifts she possessed. I understood that it took two to accomplish things in life, so it was my job as her best friend and teacher to remind her of her inner strength, the commitment to her dreams, and to be self-reliant.

I gave her a kiss and said, "Don't ever stop. Come on, let's lock up. I gotta go to CVS to get my prescription then go to my job."

We made it to my job at 12:37 P.M. I parked right on the side of partna, Jay. I saw him in his white 2010 Camaro SS, asleep.

Everyone was on break at this time. I got out and tapped on the passenger window three quick times, waking him up. He unlocked the door for me to get in once he saw it was me.

"What's up, my boy? I heard you got shot. You aight?" he asked after I had gotten in. We gave each other dap.

"Yeah I did, a pimp good, tho'. What's up with chu?"

"I been aight. I'm tired as fuck. I was up all night fucking with this little bitch in Irving. I should've took my ass home last night. I ended up staying and fucking on her all last night. Mane, I got two hours of sleep," he said, then put a Doublemint Fresh chewing gum into his mouth.

My partna, Jay, was a high-yellow pretty boy that be fucking with them hoes. I used to pay him a finder's fee to direct the biddies my way so I could turn them out to the game. Most of the referrals he'd sent me had hoed for me. He sent Selena my way five months ago. "What you doin' up here?"

"I'm 'bout to holler at Scott, let him know I'm quitting."

"What? For real, bro? Why you quitting?"

"I got too much going on to be working a regular job. I did it for a couple reasons. It's in the way now." The main reason I had a job in the first place was because I wanted the laws to believe I was a working man who loved working, if anything jumped off.

I wanted to keep them off my ass. Plus, I had people that I knew and worked with that would vouch for my character. And the other reason was to put together those little private parties I threw for tricks.

"Damn, it's gon' be boring than a bitch around here, pimp," he said, shaking his head. "I'ma miss running game with you and talking about these hoes."

"Yeah, I'ma miss you too, bro. I'ma still fuck with you, tho', outside of work. We still gonna go out and fuck with some hoes."

"And you know it. Did you ever hit that bitch, Jasmine, up?" he asked me.

"Hell nah, I keep forgetting. You said the bitch already hoing, right?

"Yeah, but she let me fuck for free. All I did was smoke a sack of kush with her."

"Oh, she one of them bitches, huh? This might be easier than I thought. I'm 'bout to see what's up with her right now."

I got on my Galaxy phone and pulled up my Facebook app. Jasmine was my Facebook friend under Jazzy Hustle. I went to her DM and text, "Hey, Hustle, U look like the only thing you missing is a BO$$ & betta direction in ur life. Grab you a piece of this game and hop on this MONOPOLY board to Elevation. I can take you places. Please let me know if you have room in yo' life 4 somebody that will show u a betta way 2 do what u doin'."

"She should hit me up after reading that," I told Jay.

"She ain't nothing but a little freak. She'll hit you up," he informed me.

I saw an unread message from two and a half weeks ago from a white girl named Bre'Anna. It read, "Wuz up, Monopoly? When we gon' chill together."

I didn't know anything about her except that she was from the Northside of Arlington and she was 23 years old. I couldn't recall how long we'd been friends on social media. All I knew was it had been for a few months. I scrolled through her timeline on her page and looked at a few of her photos in her gallery. I could tell she either liked black culture or she wanted to be black, because she wore nothing but Jordans tennis shoes on her feet in every photo. Normally, I didn't fuck with white girls that talked and acted like they were black. Most of them were ruined and for some white johns, it was a turn-off for them. I figured if I could accept a woman that's lesbian, I could accept a white girl that acted black. Both were confused, abnormal, and a degree of being fake.

I messaged her back. "Hey, Bre, I don't do the chilling thang, not for free anyway. I'm in the game like EA Sports. Come hop on the MONOPOLY board and live a luxury life. We getting money over here. Fuck wit' me and get some money, baby?"

Chilling was a new word for fucking and smoking. None of that was going on with me for free. Normally, I wouldn't come at a square like that, but I knew she liked a nigga's style. I knew she had gone through my photo gallery to see how I was livin' and everything I had posted on my timeline to hit me up in my DM like that. Even though I knew seeing beautiful women around a man created curiosity in most women, I didn't have any woman in my photos with me other than women of my family and my Eastern Star sisters. The feds weren't about to start investigating me by having my hoes in my pictures with me. Although, I did campaign hard by stunning in most of the 4000 and something photos I had on Facebook by the outfits I wore every day, the things I bought, places and events I'd been to, with every picture posted having over 3000 likes or better.

"What they been saying about that private party I threw?"

"That bitch must've been off the chain, 'cause that's all they be talking about. They want you to throw another one. I hate I missed it, bro."

"Yeah, it was live. My hoes put on for a pimp. You should have came. I would've let you in for free. I'ma throw another one soon."

The bell rang to let everyone know that break was over. We got out his car and then talked to each other until he made it into his work area. I spoke to some of my co-workers along the way to our manager's office.

I knocked on his opened, hollow wooden door. He looked up at me from his computer, smiled at me, and waved me in.

"Hey, Monopoly. How are you?" he asked, calling me by my pimp name. He stood to shake my hand. We were cool with each other like that. Scott wasn't the average white man. He still acted white, but he was in love with black people. His ex-wife was black and he had mixed children. Whenever Scott wanted to date one of my black hoes, I let him for free. He had helped me by letting me come back to work for him after I'd quit the first time, and he had let me call in a lot. He knew I was a singer, pimp, and owned a successful business. He didn't trip on me because I had good work ethics. I did my job when I was here.

"I'm good. How 'bout you, Scott?" I asked as I felt my phone vibrate on my hip,

"I'm great. It's good to see you. I heard about what happened to you. I wanted to come see you in the hospital, but I've been pretty busy. What brings you here so soon after being out the hospital?"

"I came to let you know I'm quitting."

"Are you serious? Why are you quitting, Monopoly? Is it because of your injury from getting shot?"

"No, it isn't that. It's just so much on my plate right now. And things are steady piling up."

"You're one of the best fork workers we have here. I hate to lose you. How about you take leave for a month since you were in an injury incident. I'll even raise your hourly pay up $2 when you come back. How about that?"

"Sounds good, Scott, and thank you, but I still want to quit. I have to take care of my business."

"I hear you," he said as he nodded his head. Then he stood up and extended his hand, which I shook. "Just think about that offer. It's still on the table. Give me a call if you accept it."

"I'll think about it and call you if I do. You take care, Scott. Call me if you need me." Before I got shot, it was a burden on my schedule working five days a week while pimpin' at the same time. So, not coming back here to work was a relief to me. Although, I would miss it because I liked working here.

After I left my old job, I dropped Shae off at the house and then left to go to my queens' room in Arlington to pack their things for another hotel in North Dallas. I put the address in Rose's GPS to the Sterling Hotel and sent them on their way while I went to my insurance company. They gave me a check for $173,494. Rida took damn near three hundred thousand dollars in jewelry from Shae and me. We lost a big amount of money, but it was okay since I got majority of the money we spent on jewelry back. I went to a credit union to open an account with them and deposit my check.

After I left the credit union, I went to the Sterling Hotel. I sat in my Range Rover in the A/C, checking my messages from Jasmine and Bre'Anna.

Jasmine wrote back saying, "Yea, I'll fuck with U but can we make a deal on 50/50?"

I hit her back immediately. "I'm NOT about to wheel a deal wit' YOU, baby. This isn't the show *Let's Make A Deal*. I'm MONOPOLY, baby. I'm representing REAL PIMPIN' over here. I want it all or nothing at all. And it's a G for my pimpin'. Holler at me when u get it."

I went to check Bre'Anna's message. "I'm down. What I gotta do. 817-451-1275 Call me."

I didn't call her right off the bat. I was going to take my time with her so she could have a clear understanding about what I did and her duty of being my queen. I had too much of my info on Facebook to allow this bitch to take me down.

Jasmine messaged me back within seconds. "I don't have any money to post. Can you post me and I'll let you know when I get the $1000."

"Send me ur #. U have a car, right?"

After I sent that message, I called Rose and told her to step outside. Locking my queen Rose to my game was more important right now than trying to knock for a new bitch. Rose possessed the qualities I wanted in a ho, and I needed her to be a part of my family.

"Hey, Monopoly," she said after she closed the car door.

"Hey, baby, what y'all doin' in there?"

"Me and Pinky just finished packing. CeCe still trying to figure out what she want to pack."

"CeCe is a lazy bitch. She always taking her fucking time doing shit," I said, shaking my head.

"You right about that, Daddy," Rose said, agreeing with me.

For the most part, CeCe was a good ho in her effort in making her quota despite the fact that she wasn't in high demand. I let her bring me no less than $700 a day. She accomplished that faithfully. But when it came down to something like cleaning the room, packing, , unpacking, and posting her ads, etc., she was slow to act on them and took her time doing it. She liked to lay up in bed and sleep a lot. I'd
never tripped because my trap was always right. I gave her a call.

"What you doin' CeCe?"

"I'm packing my stuff."

"You been packin' for three hours altogether today, ever since we were at the last hotel. What's so hard about packin' five outfits, lingerie, and heels?"

"I don't know what I wanna take, Daddy."

"You lazy bitch, if you don't find something and walk out that door within the next five minutes of hanging this phone up, I'm leaving you here by yourself."

"Okay, Daddy. I'm finishing up right now."

"And everything better match, too. It's 3:27. If you not out here by 3:32, I'm leaving you. You wasting my time, I got shit to do," I said and then hung up the phone. I turned towards Rose. "I did some thinking when I was in the hospital. I like your leadership and your performance since you been mine. I have faith in you to help me lead this family where I want us to go. For those reasons, I want to give you the title of being my bottom. I know you can handle that, right?"

"Yeah, I can handle it, Daddy," she answered as she stared me in the eyes. I put my right hand on the top of her left hand and started rubbing it.

"Upon you becoming my bottom will require a lot of explaining for the next couple weeks, because it's important for you to know and understand everything it takes for us all to stay successful in this here game. Anyway, we'll talk more about that later after we get you a new car."

"You foreal, Monopoly? We about to go get me a car right now as we speak?

"My word is my bond, Rose. You doin' your part, I have to do mine. It's law."

She thanked and hugged me as Pinky and CeCe walked out the room to the car.

The four of us made conversation about Rose being my bottom now and what we wanted to do tomorrow as a family the whole way to Big Star car dealership in Lewisville.

Big Star has Bentleys, Rolls Royces, Lamborghinis, Bugattis, and Maseratis.

I searched the internet last night for a car, so I already knew what I wanted. I fell in love with the 2007 Rolls Royce Phantom sedan. Once I sat my pimpin' ass into the white leather seats and test drove the arctic white over cornsilk-colored car, the love grew deeper. I knew I wanted it. Rose test drove a 2008 Rolls Royce drophead convertible. Then she saw a 2012 Bentley Mulsanne and ended up getting it. I dropped $7000 to lease the cars in our names.

I had CeCe follow behind me in my Range Rover. In the hotel's parking lot, I took a picture of me standing on the side of the car with the driver's door wide open. I posted the picture on Facebook and the gram and said, "PicturePerfectBack@ItLikeINeverLeft...MONOPOLYTHEBO$$."

Rose had done the same thing with her car and tagged me in. Even though we were leasing those cars, I wanted it to seem like we had bought them and that I shook back fast. It was my first post since I got shot. I came to understand shit could be fake, but if a person could make the illusion look realistic, people would believe that it was true and real. It's just like the magician who was skilled in performing tricks, the crooked pastor who preached about the word for self-gain, the president who promotes change and to make things great again. Like the beautiful woman who talked faultless and posted flawless photos of herself on Instagram. The masses didn't like to be fooled, but they would take face value about things without doing good research. The way I saw it, people liked to fill in the blanks with their own imagination and fantasies. That's why imagination was often more exciting than reality.

I packed all their bags they had left at the hotel into the trunk of my Roll Royce, and then Rose followed behind me in her Bentley to my penthouse downtown. The whole way there, I explained to her on our Bluetooth everything she needed to know early on about how to live and stand on my Word. Also on how to communicate my vision, enforce it, and motivate my other hoes to really want to win.

After putting my queens' bags up into the hall closet, I sat on the sofa to look at the likes and comments I received on social media. Next, I went to my messages. Jasmine messaged me back twice, the last one was her number. I called her up. "Hello," she said once she answered.

"What's up, Jazz?"

"Who dis?"

"This Monopoly," I told her.

"Oh, hey. Are you still gonna post me?"

"No. I have a better idea. I'ma have you working with someone until you get my fee right. Send me your address. I'll be on my way when I get it."

"Alright, I'm about to do it now." Then we hung up.

After getting some good mouth service from Rose, I talked to the white girl, Bre'Anna, on the Bluetooth while driving to pick up my homie, Poppa, in 4Deuce in South Dallas. I needed him to be around for what I had planned for tomorrow and to be my enforcer for my hoes.

Bre'Anna claimed she was ready for the game. I made it as clear as I could in her duties of being my ho. She had no problem with that. I would be picking her up as well.

Since a pimp was really seeing some money and making big moves, bitches were falling in my lap. Early in my career, bitches didn't come this easy. With some hoes I'd pimped on in the past, I had really put in some work to knock them. I'd been blessed by the Pimp God, Jared, because I'd never experienced the game hoeless. I'd been blessed to have two good bottom bitches in my career.

It was very rare to find these types of hoes to fit your pimpin' like Fancy and Shae had fit mine, unless you knocked them young and fresh at 18 years old, and mold them into what you want them to be. Even though Rose would be a good bottom, she couldn't compare to what Shae had been to me, no matter what I did for Rose to make her go harder for me. She didn't have the history Shae and I had built before we got into the game. There was a good chance that another pimp could come along and knock me for all my hoes by knocking Rose from me. If Shae had ever chose with another pimp, she would have come back to me sooner or later. Just what I predicted would happen about Shae leaving the game happened. Tiredness of the game brought her to the exit door.

Jasmine lived in her own apartment on Collins and Brown on the Northside of Arlington. She was 22 years old with an 18-month-old daughter who was staying with Jasmine's Mexican mother in West Texas for the last two months now while she'd been hoing. She'd been trying to stack some money but hadn't been able to hustle up the type of money she thought she'd get. When I investigated why she was making short change with her good looks, it came out to be that she wasn't posting properly, unconsciously. She told me she was about to give up the ho game because it wasn't working out for her. I guaranteed her that my game would provide the right tricks and make her successful. She took me up on the offer.

Jasmine rolled a luggage behind her while she walked towards the car. I got out the car to help her put the luggage in my trunk. She was looking good as hell. She was yellow bone with a round face. Her petite body fit perfectly in a Dolce & Gabbana dress that had floral patterns all over it, with some pointy-toe booties on her feet that looked like they were Calvin Klein. She had a few tattoos on her body. The only visual one I could see in the low light area we were in was of a baby's face that might have been her daughter on her left arm. She had small breasts and not much ass, but she looked really good and was good to go. The only thing that I saw that needed improvement was the color of her hair. Adding awkward blue to most of her black hair would increase her sex appeal.

I walked up to her and grabbed both of her hands with mine. "You lookin' good than a muthafucker tonight. Who the hell you trying to impress, me or the tricks that's waiting on your fine ass?"

"All y'all," she said shyly and then smiled.

I smiled at her. "The best way to impress me is to bring in the most cash you can make and follow my instruction. That's gonna get me every time. You made a wise choice choosing up with a certified pimp today. You on your way to greatness, baby. Go get in the car." I put the luggage in the trunk, closed it, and then got in the car.

I made it to Bre'Anna's grandparents' house on the southside of Arlington in 13 minutes. She was seated on the wooden steps leading to the porch. She stood up once she saw me pull up.

I laughed at her appearance inside without showing it on the outside. It was terrible. She had on a white tank top and dark-blue jean shorts with a pair of white, black, and blue new Jordans. She was a cute blonde girl with freckles all over her body. After a pimp's makeover, she'd be ready to be sent on her hoing way.

She had two boxes of Air Jordans shoes in two Wal-Mart plastic bags and a green suitcase that sat on the porch.

"What's in the suitcase?" I asked curiously.

"My clothes and stuff."

"You got that big ol' suitcase and that was the best thing you could find to put on?" She nodded her head. "That's not good enough for the tricks I want you to attract. Come on, I'm about to take you shopping at The Parks Mall."

I spent fifteen thousand dollars between Bre'Anna, Jasmine, Rose, Poppa, and myself at the mall. I bought Bre'Anna a whole new wardrobe. I bought my new queens a bunch of cosmetics as well.

After leaving the mall, we went to Shea's house so she could dye Jasmine's hair aqua blue. Bre'Anna took a shower and changed into one of her new outfits I bought her. After Shae helped them with their makeup and hair, we left for North Dallas to get a room off of I-75 and Northwest Hwy. I didn't want them to be at the same hotel ass Pinky and CeCe because they didn't properly pay me my choosing fee yet.

Before going to the hotel, I stopped at Jack N The Box so Poppa could get him something to eat. While waiting in the line in the drive-thru, I checked a text message that Claire sent me.

Claire:

Hey, Monopoly. I'm glad to hear that U R alive. I'm sorry 4 wat happened. I wanted it 2 work out between us. I couldn't take my son being in danger. I hope U can understand why I left. I text 2 ask 4 a favor until I get my check next week. Can U loan me $50 please Monopoly?

6:49 P.M. Friday

Me:

This isn't Quicken Loans, Claire. I can't solve that problem 4 U. Sorry.

7:21 P.M. Friday

By the time I drove up to the order menu. I received another message from her.

Claire:

Please Monopoly. We really need it.

7:22 P.M. Friday

Me:

NO! I STAND FIRM ON THAT. GET OFF MY LINE IF YOU NOT TRYING TO PAY ME 4 US 2 LIVE GOOD.

7:23 P.M. Friday

I heard Jasmine ordering food after my homie, Poppa, did. She was going against my rules that I just broke down to her. I wasn't tripping on her eating. More than likely, I would have let her eat something light and cheap if she had asked me first. On the other hand, I was kind of glad she got out of pocket so I could check her ass. It was a good time to stomp down on this ho so she could know

I didn't take no shit from no ho and my pimpin' real. I turned around in my seat to look at her. "Who told you, you can order something?"

"Nobody."

"You must have some money on you or something."

"I don't have no money, Monopoly. I haven't eaten since 12. I'm hungry, Monopoly."

"I understand that, but you owe me, Jazz. I bought you everything you need to make money. Tricks can't see what's inside yo' stomach. You ain't even shown a nigga you worthy of a pimp's game, any-motherfucking-way. Show me how bad you wanna be with a pimp by paying me properly first, then you can eat."

When I pulled up to the first window, the mid-30-looking-year-old Mexican woman said, "That will be $13.48, sir."

"Excuse me. I want to erase that #5 with Sprite and slice of cheesecake. Add a cup of company water, please." Then I gave her a $10 bill for Poppa's order.

After getting my change, I drove to the next window. I gave Poppa his food and drink then sat the water in the cup holder on the side of the door next to Jasmine. "There you go. That should hold you till later. And it bet not get wasted in my car, either."

Poppa bust out laughing. "Monopoly, you a fool, bro."

"Poppa, bro, you can't let no ho think she getting her way without paying properly. I don't know what she think this is. Bitch ain't paid me a penny yet. I put her in some of the best designer shit and she want me to feed her too. No! No! No! I ain't no trick, I'ma motherfuckin' pimp. Bitch, make my mothafuckin' money." You can't let a person think they getting over on you unless you playing them and setting them up for failure. A nigga had to check their ass. If not, they were going to do it again and label you as a sucker. And that I was not.

I ended up taking her out to eat at IHOP later on that night at 12:30, just her and me. It was a must I checked her ass earlier. I didn't want something that small to mount up to something disrespectful. I had already went too far out for the ho when I took her shopping, spending thousands of dollars on her. Buying this ho food too was going over the limit. A real ho ain't paying a chump.

157

Smoove Dolla

A bunch of no-good hoes would have tried to get over on me without paying me if I hadn't got on her ass. That's why a ho should come with a choosing fee, breaking herself before she enters a pimp's door.

Game comes in all flavors. If you don't have some kind of game that works in your favor, you will fall in a trick and sucker category when dealing with women. Game is just having the upper hand in every situation you encounter.
— Smoove Dolla

## Chapter 9

All six of my hoes, Poppa, and I went to Austin the next morning. We went out shopping, bowling, to four different bars on 6th Street, and a restaurant named Mr. Jims. I posted all that on Facebook with only Poppa in my pictures to show that I was out of town. I also checked in a local lodge in Austin to make it official.

Now, Poppa and I rode in my Range Rover with Rose and Pinky in her Honda heading to Fort Worth. I left my personal phone and our new cars in Austin because I knew they had trackers on them.

Before I left 6th Street where my other hoes were, I posted my location again and then put my phone in my Rolls Royce. In two hours from now, I would have Bre post again for me in a different location while I was out here in the DFW. I wanted to be all the way on point just in case I got questioned by the laws of my whereabouts tonight when I took care of Rida and hopefully JP too.

Since we were five minutes away, I Facetimed my hoes about what was going on tonight while Poppa drove. Pinky held the phone to the right side of her so I could see them both. "Hey, Queens. You both look amazing tonight. Y'all might be a little out of place at this after hour. I hate that we're not going to a photoshoot for a magazine or an upscale establishment amongst stars so we could show off our success. Those days were coming soon, tho'. Tonight, at this club, I don't want you in none of these niggas' faces. We're not here to make money. I don't care how much they're offering. Do I make myself clear?"

"Yes, Daddy," they both said in unison.

The reason why I didn't allow my hoes to deal with young black men was because of the problems that came along with most of them. Truth be told, other races played dirty games also. The only thing a ho had to watch out for with a white trick was the crazy ones, and there's not that many of them. The same with the Mexicans. Overall, they were good business. Majority of the time, the problems were with young black tricks. So, to save me the trouble of rescuing my hoes from being robbed, raped, and tricked, I didn't let them date black men unless they were verified by me or through someone I knew that could vouch for them of being good business. Anyway, today was all about us having fun until now. A pimp was about to get into some gangsta shit. I wanted my two queens to help my homegirls as a decoy, if needed, so that's why they tagged along with me.

It was a one-way in leading to The Warehouse. The parking lot and the side of the street had a lot of parked trucks, SUVs, and cars, but we still managed to get a parking spot and then we walked to where my homeboys and homegirls from the Bonton Projects cars were.

The outside of the club scene was live. It looked like a mini Kappa Beach weekend or East Atlanta Day. I really did want to take some pictures with my hood niggas and my hoes, but I was supposed to be in Austin right now like I had posted I was.

We ended up going inside at 12:17 A.M. after an hour of talking and fucking around in the parking lot. I was glad the club still operated on a low level. They had bouncers instead of real police officers. My plan would have never worked if the policemen were security. Four of us gave our guns to the females to get in with because they weren't getting searched. I paid the door woman $140 for seven of us to get in. I let the other eight people with us pay their own way inside.

As soon as we walked out the entrance hallway, passing up the restroom, the smell of weed invaded my nostrils. Smoke floated in the air like heavy clouds in the sky.

After passing the bar, the club was damn near sardine packed, shoulder to shoulder. I did a perimeter check, starting from the right to left, looking for a place we all could post up at. The stage was on the right of us along with these small stages that were connected to it with strip poles on each of them.

Deeper into the club in the far right corner, there was room enough for about 40 people to fit in along with three big pool tables that were occupied by a big dice game and two pool games. Outside of the room to the far left was a long area full of chairs, tables, and a long black sofa. Beside all that was a huge patio with a bunch of chairs, plastic tables, and crowd of people standing around. We posted up in a spot between the patio and the bar, having a full view of the dance floor and stages.

Some of my homegirls and both of my hoes went to get them a drink, and couple of my homies went to join the dice game while I stood there looking for Rida. I didn't see him anywhere. I was so anxious to the point where I was about to send Rose to ask the DJ was Rida still going to perform, but I decided not to. I checked his Facebook again for the eighth time today to see the flyer he'd been reposting all day. I knew he would be here shortly, so I just stood there ready and waited impatiently on him.

As I observed the crowd a little more, I noticed a few groups of niggas by the color or images on their clothes, and by them throwing up their sets and hoods. I recognized hoods from Hoover Land, Agg Land, East Wood, Wood Haven, and Stop 6, as well as cliques from Arlington and Dallas.

I recognized a girl I knew from the 3rd Gate in Stop 6 named Erika. She was dancing to a hot lil' song by Kendrick Lamar by herself, about fourteen yards away from me.

The music brought back the memory to when I first met Erika ten months ago. That day, she stood at a bus stop on Rosedale and Miller on the Eastside of Fort Worth as I came from a homeboy's crib in Polly, who was a big dope boy in Funky Town. I almost drove my candy red box Chevy Caprice into a 2009 Audi in front of me by staring too long at her. I would have been fucked up about that. That would have fucked up my candy paint, 30-inch Forgiato rims, and the body of my Caprice. Even though I had the latest Range Rover and Benz at that time, the Caprice was my baby. That was the same car Tight Game had given me back in 2005, I just put over 10 stacks into the car to make it pimped out.

She didn't see me pull up in the huge parking lot because she was too busy in her phone. I parked right behind the big bus stop and then turned on "Beauty" by Dru Hill on my Pioneer stereo system, turning the volume up. I couldn't have it turned up too high because I had four 12s in the trunk, and that song had a bunch of bass in it already. The beat stole her attention away from her phone.

I saw her head do a little bob, and her body attempted to move before she caught herself then looked back at me walking towards her, smiling with my door opened and music still playing.

"I hear you. You jamming, ain't chu?" she said, looking me right in the eyes, then looked away seconds later.

"Yeah, because of you. When I saw you, this song popped up in my head." It was a little corny, but it made her smile.

"I'm impressed. I normally get approached by dudes still in their cars. They never get out of their cars."

I believed that a bunch of niggas weren't blessed to drive in an expensive car or slab and hop out dressed in designer. I approached her in a Louis Vuitton outfit that cost nearly $3500, and had over $40,000 worth of jewelry on me, all worth more than the slabs itself I was riding in. Some niggas spent all their money on their slabs and tennis shoes. Then they tried to use that to cover up their wardrobe. Hoodrats and ghetto bitches fell for that game and didn't care as long as they were seen riding in the car. Some of the men just didn't have conversation, courage, and confidence to really walk up to a woman. To play the game properly, you had to be well rounded. That's what it takes to leave a deep stain on a woman's mind to have her really interested to get to know you.

"I guess they don't know how to be a real gentleman. I'm Monopoly, nice to meet you," I said then smiled, extending my right hand at her for a handshake.

She smiled and then shook my hand. "Nice to meet you too. I'm Erika."

"Where you headed?" I asked.

"Home. I'm waiting on my sister. She should've been here by now. She left me at the library while she went to pick up my niece from the babysitter. Speaking of her, here she is pulling up now."

A 2010 grey Ford Taurus sped inside the shopping center's parking lot bumping a song by Rich Homie Quan. "Give me yo' number before I go," she mentioned to me.

After we exchanged numbers, her pretty, caramel complexioned sister asked, "You got some kush?"

"Nah, baby. I don't smoke or sell drugs. I can direct you into the direction of who has some, tho', if you want."

The expression on her sister's face turned into a "yea right, nigga, you sell something, nigga" look. A bunch of people who didn't know me mistook me for a drug dealer because of what cars I drove and how I dressed. Erika and her sister didn't find out I pimped until she called me that same night. Her older sister didn't want her to talk to me, but Erika said that she was feeling our conversation and wanted to know more about me. I found out she just got out of prison from doing a three-year bid for a dope charge. She was riding with a homie from her hood and they got stopped for a traffic stop by the law in a drug-infested neighborhood. She stuffed a half oz of heroin inside her panties, thinking they were good until a cop called in a dog to sniff around. She didn't snitch on anybody or take probation. She signed and served the whole three years in state prison like a G. I knew it was all true, because I did a little research on her. I respected her for not snitching.

The reason why we quit talking to each other was because I felt she wasn't trying to help herself. Since she didn't want to ho for me, I tried to get her a job at a beauty supply store in Meadow Brook after she lost her job at a call center. As stupid as it sounded, she didn't believe that black females didn't work at that store because a Chinese couple owned it. I was fucking on the girl that worked there, who told me that they needed another girl to hire. I used to get hookups on free hair from her for my queens. I cut Erika off after that by not calling her and answering her calls, until she stop calling altogether.

I walked over to where she danced while taking my hoodie off my head, and grabbed a hand full of her soft, left phat ass cheek. She grabbed my arm and roughly threw my hand away from her. "Nigga, get yo' muthafuckin' hands off me," she said while turning around to see me. "Monopolyyyy. Boy, I thought you were one of these other niggas. What's up? How you been?"

We hugged each other. "I been good, baby. Elevating in life, that's about it. How 'bout you?"

"It's been going alright."

Erika had the skin tone of a brown Hershey Kiss. Long weaved braids came down to the small of her back. She had a pretty face with thick, full lips. She had small breasts but had a huge, wide ass, standing at 5'6 in a black dress that was netted on the side. "I see you still looking beautiful, better than when I saw you the first time. That's what's up," I complimented.

"Thanks, Monopoly," she said, smiling. "You still pimpin' or what?" I think she asked me that because I wasn't dressed to impress like I normally did every day. I had on all black from my head to my Adidas for this occasion.

"I'ma pimp to the death of me, baby. Why, what's up, you want an application?" I asked, looking into her eyes.

"Boy, you crazy. Who you come up here with?" she screamed over the loud music.

"My people and two of my queens," I said, pointing to where they stood at. I did a double take at the sight of a nigga and Pinky talking and flirting with each other. The nigga was caressing her body and whispering in her ear. She was smiling until she saw me, then she pulled away from him.

Erika grabbed my attention away from Pinky and back to her by asking, "What are you doing after y'all leave here?"

"Heading to Dallas. Why, wuz up?"

"Can I come with y'all?"

"It's alright with me. I just don't know when I'll be back out this way, so it's on you if you coming with me. But I don't mind," I advised. "You got a car now?"

"Nah, not yet."

"Who you came here with?" I asked, wanting to know.

"My sister and some people from Stop 6. I been with they ass all day. I'm tired of them. Do you know what time y'all leaving?"

"Nah, not really, but I'll let you know when we do."

"Ok. Please do, Monopoly, because I'm tryna get away."

"I told you, I'ma let you know. I got you," I assured her.

She must wanted to fuck. My mind wasn't on sex right now. Revenge was on my mind.

When I looked back where my people were, the nigga Pinky was talking to was no longer in sight. Rose was heading towards me.

"Daddy, I know you seen what happened. The dude approached her and started feeling on her. She let him, it was like she didn't care. I told her to quit talking to him, but she didn't stop until you saw her. She says the dude sold her heroin."

The only thing I didn't like about Rose was she wasn't aggressive enough. My ex-bottom hoe, Shae, would have checked that hoe verbally for disrespecting my pimpin'. I was surprised any of my homies didn't say anything to the nigga, but then again, they didn't know I warned my hoes before we came to the club. Only Poppa knew, but he was somewhere else in the club, probably shooting dice.

"I'm not worried about Pinky. I'ma take care of her after we leave. You good?"

"Yeah, I'm good. Just looking at those tricks raining money on these trash ass bitches. You mind if I get up there and get you some money, Daddy?"

"Go ahead, I don't mind." I needed to get back some money that I spent today.

The two females that were dancing on the stages had to be hoes. Rose wasn't lying, they were trash looking. Both of them were a little chubby. The blackest one was ugly ass fuck but somewhat fine. The other was okay but had a bunch of baby fat. These hoes looked like they were the $40 special hoes that fucked around this part of town from Interstate 20 to Riverside on Interstate 35. Even though they couldn't dance exactly like a stripper, they probably could follow instructions. Plus, it looked like they were about their paper, no matter how they looked physically, and they weren't bad dressers either. Any other time, I would have tried to knock them 'cause they had potential to be something better with the right pimp, but I wasn't looking for a ho at the moment. I was looking for revenge. My mind was set on Rida and JP.

Rose did her thang on the third pole, making niggas shower money on her and making the other two dancers look ridiculous, making them stop dancing after a while.

I walked over to where my hood niggas stood. Pinky tried to talk to me, but I cut her off with the quickness. "Bitch, don't say shit to me, ho. Keep whatever you gotta say to yo' muthafuckin' self."

"But, Daddy, that was—"

"Bitch, what the fuck I just say, ho. You know what, I'ma deal with you later. Get the fuck outta my face."

I turned to talk to my homegirls from my hood. "Y'all, keep an eye on my ho up there for me." I had to make sure my white ho was protected.

I knew some of these bitches was hating because she was white, looking and doing a whole lot better than them, making these niggas drop out that cash and creating a desire in the black man to fuck a white girl.

Two rap songs later, the DJ announced that Rida would be performing in five minutes.

My homie, Ken, tapped me on the shoulder. "There that nigga go right there."

I looked his way. This nigga had the nerve to wear one of my chains to this muthafucker. It was my platinum 50 pointer chain with a five-inch stack of money as the medallion. He had four other niggas standing around him. One of them was built like the third gunman that was with Rida and JP. Blood started to boil inside my veins. I was so anxious on murking these niggas, my hand tightened around the handle of my Glock inside my hoodie pocket.

I put the hoody back over my head then told my homegirls to go get my hoes, and head to the cars. Our move on Rida had to be while he was performing, or either right after he finished. I couldn't see it going down when they left the club. They probably would be on alert. And, I really didn't want to follow behind them anywhere. Getting at them while on stage was the best plan I kept coming up with.

Rida and his people were crips, 247 crips. Four of them had on a bunch of blue, except for one who had on all black. The one in all black was a tall and heavy-set nigga that had the face of a killer. He looked like he was ready for something to pop off and might have a gun on him. I whispered in Poppa's ear, telling him to pop him first before I moved in on Rida, because he was the armed one.

When he started performing, I looked around to see if Rida had other people on the dance floor. There were a couple of dudes and females shouting Rida's name out close to the main stage to the left of me. I told four of my youngings to get behind them and as soon as they heard gunfire, to pop their ass before they made a move. It seemed insane and bold the way we were going to kill them, but they had to get it. I didn't want to wait any longer. Now was the time. I had to give him props on his music, though. He had a lot of people rocking in here. It was a hot club song. His rapping skills were good enough that I would do a song with him. It was fucked up he was about to die and not get far with his talent. He would have blown up in due time. That's the way it goes when a nigga is in the streets doing dirt, and a street nigga found out who robbed and shot him.

Poppa and I went through the crowd to the front of the stage. My right hand had been on my Glock for about five minutes, ever since I saw Rida. Finally, I was about to use it. I eased it out my hoody pocket then slowly aimed it up at Rida with my wrist on top of the Glock so it would be out of eyesight from everyone. As soon as Rida came close enough to the edge, Poppa fired shots into the big armed man, and then I shot Rida three times. After nine shots, all four of them were laid out on stage. A few seconds later, I heard more gunfire.

While people screamed, ducked, and ran, trying to get to safety, I grabbed Rida and pulled him off the stage to the floor. He looked right into my eyes with shock on his face. "You fucked with the wrong nigga this time," I said, then put a bullet in his head.

Someone ran into me. I pushed them to the floor then pointed my gun at them. Out of all people in here, it had to be Erika.

"Monopoly," she said with surprise.

I pulled her up by her hand to her feet. "Be quiet. Put this in your purse." I handed her my Glock and she did as she was told. I had her do that because she had seen me pointing it at the dead man on the ground, and so she wouldn't tell anyone anything about what just took place. Later on, I was going to make her feel that she was an accessory to this murder, but in reality, if I did get caught up, she wouldn't be in jail for my actions. I wouldn't let her suffer for something I did.

I quickly went through all his pockets, gathering his wallet, a small knot of cash, a cell phone, took my chain off from his neck, and then put everything in my hoody pocket. Before I grabbed Erika's hand and joined the running crowd, I took off my pair of black gloves.

We had to pass my homies' cars to get to mine. Poppa handed me a GAP shopping bag with five guns inside. I told them to head to Dallas and that I'd catch up with them once I take care of my ho.

As we walked off, I gave her the keys and the bag I was given. "You driving. I'll be there in a minute."

I turned towards Rose's Honda to the passenger's door where Pinky was. I could tell the door was locked, so I started hitting the window with the side of my fist, trying to put fear in this ho. Their eyes were like a deer in front of headlights of an oncoming car. "Rose, open this do', now. Open this muthafuckin' do'."

I opened the door after she unlocked it. "Daddy, what's going on?" Pinky asked, leaning backwards all up on Rose in the driver's seat.

"Bitch, you know what's goin' on. I warned you, and you still did what I told you not to do, faggot ho."

"I'm sorry, Daddy. That was my brother's homeboy. He came on to me."

"Bitch, I don't give a fuck who that was. You faggot ass ho. I'm done with you, ho. Go ahead and beat yo' feet like the Flintstones, because I don't want you no more." I grabbed her arm and yanked her out the car. I picked up her Gucci purse off the floor and chunked it at her, which she caught. "I'll have Rose bring your belongings to your mom's house later."

"So you just gonna put me out and leave me out here without a ride and no money? How am I supposed to get to my momma's house?"

I thought about giving this ho some money for a cab, but the thought of her buying some heroin with it had me thinking. The police in the near distance had me think about her making a mad move to the cops, telling them that I assaulted her or something crazy, so I gave her $100 from Rida's stack. "Call a cab."

Then I turned towards the car and said, "Follow behind me, Rose."

I ran to the passenger side of my Range Rover. As soon as Erika got into the short line of traffic heading out the one-way street, I told her, "Get on 35 then get on 20 and head to Dallas."

"Why you do that girl like that?"

"Because she didn't know how to follow simple instructions. She hard headed than a muthafucker." I took the blame for what she did. Because if I didn't bring her along, left her in Austin where she was free to do what she wanted in respect to me as her man, what she did wouldn't ever have happened. I knew there was a chance she might know somebody here at the club since she was from Fort Worth.

What got me heated was when she went against Rose's word and mine. And the bitch was smiling when that nigga was feeling on her. She was letting a nigga touch on her who wasn't going to spend bread. I knew if he was really her dealer, the only thing he was giving her was a bag of heroin in exchange for sex. I'd give her a break away from my pimpin'. I'd let her come back if she wanted to for a small fee. I just did that to her to show her I wasn't playing with her and that I didn't need her. I wanted Rose and Erika to see it too. Just because a ho looked good didn't mean that I needed her to make money for me. If a ho wasn't following my instructions, I was dismissing the ho, faster than the ho came into my life.

I pulled out Rida's phone and made an attempt to go through it, but it was locked. "Fuck!" I said out loud.

"What's wrong?" Erika asked.

"This damn phone locked," I said as I shook my head.

"All you have to do is Google how to unlock it. That's a Android, ain't it?"

"Yeah," I said in doubt, half-ass believing her because I'd never heard of it before.

"Just Google it. It's on there."

I Googled it. And what do you know, it came up with 58 results.

# Smoove Dolla

As soon as I tapped on one of them, Erika said, "The laws turned on their lights. They're behind us, Monopoly.'

"Fuck. Aight, just hurry up and pull over."

I called Rose and told her that I had gotten pulled over, to get off at the next exit, and wait on me. I didn't know what this was for. If it was for a traffic stop, I was good. But if Pinky had told the laws on me about anything, I probably would be going to jail.

I hate I didn't remember that on most nights there were a bunch of patrol cars on Interstate 20, especially on the weekends and with the mass shooting that just took place at the club. Knowing the police were going to be on high alert, I could've gone another way to Da Trip to avoid this situation.

"My license is expired, Monopoly, and we got all these guns in here. I'm not tryna go to jail," she said in a panic.

"I was just going 66, six over the damn limit. Muthafucka ain't have to pull me over."

"Bitch, just chill. Be calm. I got us. Follow my lead. If he ask where we're coming from, tell him we just came from our friend's house on the southwest side," I said while handing her my insurance and registration with my Masonic traveling card on top. I wanted it to be the first thing he saw, to make him cancel his plans on writing her a ticket and/or searching my SUV. "After you let the window down to him, then ask him is there something wrong. Okay?"

"Okay. I got it, Monopoly." When he stopped at the driver's door, she did as I said do to the white Fort Worth cop. "Hello, Officer, is something wrong?" she said and then smiled.

"Yes. You were speeding, going 66 in a 60 miles per hour speed limit."

"Really, I didn't notice that I was speeding, Officer Cox."

"May I have your insurance, registration, and driving license, ma'am?"

She handed him all that I handed her. He examined my travel card for about six seconds, and then looked at my other information for two seconds. He looked at me and then asked, "Are you Damion Tunke Johnson?"

"Yes, I am."

"Can you step out the vehicle?" he asked me.

I thought something was wrong for a second, but then I thought about it, and he probably wanted to separate me from Erica so he and I could talk in private. "No problem, Officer Cox."

I got out slowly and met him at the back of my Range Rover. "So, brother, with which lodge are you affiliated?"

"Frederick Lodge No. 111 on Malcolm X in Dallas." I peeped out he checked out how I stood in front of him and the way I had my hands.

After talking with him for about ten minutes, I found out he was 42 years old, a third-degree Mason, what Lodge he attended in Downtown Fort Worth. I told him I'd been a Mason for almost five years now, and that I was a third-degree Mason as well.

He asked me what did for a living, which I told him that I was a professional singer, songwriter, and owned a successful clothing line.

"Well, Mr. Johnson, I'm going to let you get on your way," he said while extending his arm towards me for a handshake.

While my right hand was in his hand and my left hand on top of his right hand, I said, "Getting pulled over reminded me that I didn't put my Square and Compass emblem sticker back on my bumper after I got my Range Rover painted four months ago. I can put it on there tomorrow for sure."

"Yes, do that. It would have saved me the time of pulling you over, but it was a pleasure to meet you. But due to a lot going on tonight and her speeding, I have to follow procedure."

"It's okay, you gotta do your job. And it's nice to meet you too. You have a great night, travel Light Square," I said, hitting him with some Masonic slang.

He smiled then said, "You do the same too, Square."

I walked to the passenger front door to get in, and he headed to my driver's door. "Hey, young lady, drive safely and at the speed limit." He tapped lightly on top of the SUV's roof three times and said, "Y'all have a safe trip."

"Thanks, Officer Cox," Erika told him.

"You're welcome."

When Erika got back on the highway, she asked, "What was that about? That was weird. I never seen no shit like that before. What all do you do?" she asked, knowing something was going on.

I remained silent. I had to be secretive about that type of information. I didn't answer her. Instead, I called Rose and told her to go wherever she wanted to go until I called her. I didn't need her around me while I finished my business with JP.

"Why did you kill that dude at the club?" Erika asked.

I looked at her, suspicious, but then thought to myself that she didn't mean any harm by the question. Plus, she probably wanted to know why I got out of character, because I wasn't the violent type. "I'm not the one to resort to violence unless I have to. Them niggas violated. They robbed and shot me and my bro. They had to get dealt with. Simple as that.

"Damn, Monopoly, you got shot?" she said with sympathy in her voice. "When did this happen?"

"Almost three weeks ago. To remind you of what just took place at the club, you touched that Glock too. You are an accessory to what happened at the club. You touched the gun, you saw what I did without reporting it to that cop. He saw you driving, so that makes you the getaway driver. I hate to drag you into this, but you know what I did. I'm not saying I'll let you go down with me if anything does happen, because I won't, as long as you don't tell nobody what went down tonight. And I mean nobody. If anything does happen, I got money and connections I can use for us both. You just witnessed that with the cop back there. I want and need for you to keep this between you and me. Can you do that?"

"Yeah, I can do that. You don't have to worry about me saying something. I'm a G bitch," she said with meaning.

"I like that. If you that queen I been searching for, we gonna go a long way and accomplish a lot together. But we'll see how down you are when it's time."

When we made it to Arlington city limits, about 13 minutes out from the club, I saw a patrol car parked on the service road. About every 60 to 80 yards there was an Arlington patrol car. I saw two other cars, but none of them were my homies that were pulled over by the police. It was better if I quit talking to Erika and let her concentrate on driving since Arlington police were known for pulling people over. "Let me look through this phone so I can throw it away. We got all night to talk. Concentrate on driving, baby, so we don't get pulled over again."

When I unlocked the phone, I went straight to the contacts. I put JP in the search bar. No results came up. Then I typed in Bro. It came up, but it had Tricks behind it. Stacey had him under that name in her phone too. So, this was what people close to him call him. That's why no one knows him by JP, except a dope boy from Dallas that Tricks robbed for some dope and money. I got that information from 8Ball.

After I put Tricks' number in Erika's phone, I noticed a familiar female face I had seen before on the small contact picture on the side of her number. The contact was right above Bro Tricks. I tapped on it to blow it up bigger. It was a pretty selfie shot of Stacey, whose real name was Brittany. I went through his gallery in his phone. He had numerous photos of her. I came to find out that Rida was Brittany's baby daddy, with two beautiful mixed young kids, a boy and girl. So, that's why she didn't want to bring her kids along to the Funday Sunday Event.

Now pieces were starting to fit to the puzzle. I saved Brittany's new cell number inside Erika's phone along with Rida's mom's number, just in case she had to get kidnapped to get to Tricks.

I was debating whether or not I needed to trash Rida's phone right now. I wanted to find Brittany and Tricks within the next hour. If I didn't, then I was going to find them later. Within the next hour, it was a possibility that Tricks would find out that Rida had gotten killed. He would be on alert and in hiding after that. I needed another way to get at Brittany without calling her and her knowing it was me. She might be posted on an escort site. If so, I could get at her that way. I googled her number and the results showed that she was posted on two escort sites as Sugar.

I called her on a throw-away phone. "Hello," she answered sleepily.

"Are you available, Sugar?" I asked in a low, sexy tone.

"Yes. How much time would you like to spend with me?" It sounded like she had raised up from lying down.

"An hour."

"That will be 300 roses, baby."

"That's okay with me. Your pictures are lovely. I gotta see how sweet you are. Where are you located?" I used a line I heard a trick say to one of my hoes on speaker phone.

"In Red Bird. On Camp Wisdom. At The American Inn. You know where that's at?"

"Yeah, I know exactly where you at," I told her.

"Okay. How long will it take for you to get here?"

"I'm in Mesquite. It won't take that long, about 30 minutes tops."

"Ok. I'll be hot and ready for you. Call me when you make it to the hotel."

I called Poppa. He was asleep in the back seat of Lil' Ken's car until I called and told Lil' Ken I'd give him $500 if he would let Poppa drove his car to Red Bird so he could do something important for me. He accepted the offer and said they were within five minutes of 8Ball's crib in 4Deuce in South Dallas, then Poppa would be on his way. I gave Poppa the location and told him to call me when he was headed this way, so I could run down the plan to him.

Poppa and I met up at the Exxon gas station on the corner of Camp Wisdom, and I gave him his gun and the $300 for Sugar. After she text me back with her room number, we headed to the hotel.

I pulled up on the other side of the hotel two minutes after Poppa did. I had my eyes open for any movement in and outside of the rooms and cars in the parking lot. Tricks could have been in another room around here peeping out the window, or close by watching her door. Poppa had me on the line on his phone in his pocket. I listened as he got out the car, walked up to the door, and knocked.

The door opened. "Hey, you," I heard Sugar say.

"Hey."

"Come on in, handsome. How has your night been?" The door

closed.

"Good. And yours?" Poppa said in a low tone.

"Good as well. If you don't mind me asking, what do you do for a living?

*Duuh*

It sounded like she had gotten pushed to the floor and hit the wall. I knew he wasn't going to waste any time talking to her. Poppa wasn't a procrastinator.

"Please don't hurt me. I'll do what you want, just don't hurt me," she told Poppa.

Poppa got on the phone. "I got her, Monopoly. You good, you can come in now."

"Alright, I'm on my way."

As I walked towards the door, I scanned everything in my surroundings. I was glad this hotel didn't have any cameras outside. I didn't want to be seen by anyone. I might have to kill her after I received the information I needed from her.

Once I closed the door behind me, I took my hoody off my head and got my Glock out. I smiled at her while walking towards her, looking her dead in the eyes. "Get that surprised look off your face. You had seen enough to know you were fucking with a major nigga. What, you thought I wasn't gonna find you, ho?"

She scooted back to a wall behind her as I came closer to her. "Monopoly, please hear me out. I'm so sorry. They made me do it, Monopoly." She started crying, making an ugly face. "They made me. I had no choice."

I knew better than to believe that shit. A bitch that associated with niggas like Rida and Tricks was just like them, and might have been worse than them. A lot of bitches and hoes could be and liked to be conniving, sneaky, sly, and play games if an opportunity presented itself to do so, especially if that person on the other side was lame, or they did it because they had some kind of hate in their heart about something that happened in their past with a man and woman. That's why a lot of hoes and bitches couldn't be trusted. When you take a look at why they were like they were, majority of the time it comes back to something that happened in their past.

Even when you get a bitch like that and you are a real nigga who does what you say you will do, it's hard to change that programmed mindset they're in. That's why it's good to let people evolve on their own instead of forcing it.

I'd learned that with Pinky. I knew a woman was a reflection of her man and would follow behind her man in good and bad. If she didn't, they wouldn't be together too long, unless she saw him as less than a man and she wore the pants in their relationship. I said all that to say this, Brittany was probably just following behind her man, Rida. No matter what, she was on their side and was a part of the plan to rob me. No matter what, they used her to get her to Hollywood act like she was really my ho. That shit got me hot, but I couldn't get mad at nobody but myself.

"Bitch, save that bullshit." I grabbed her blonde hair and pulled her up. "Get yo' bitch ass up, ho." I pulled Rida's phone out my pocket. "I already took care of your kids' father. Bitch nigga is dead. Now, if you don't want to join him, I suggest you tell me how to find Tricks."

"I don't know where he is."

The barrel of my Glock made contact with her forehead. "Bitch, you think I'm playing with you? Where he at? You better tell me something, ho, before I pull this muthafuckin' trigger," I threatened.

"I told you, I don't know where he is. I heard he has a warrant out for his arrest. I heard he's on the run. I don't know where he's at. Please, don't kill me, Monopoly. I'm sorry. I'm sorry, Monopoly," she said and then started crying hard.

Even though I was getting tired of looking at this bitch, I had second thoughts about killing her by my trigger finger. Killing this ho wouldn't do anything for me. Rida was my first body ever. And to be honest, killing the man that shot and robbed me didn't satisfy me none. I thought killing them myself would do justice inside me, but it didn't. I wasn't a killer, and I didn't have any desire to kill again. That's why I had Poppa here with me. She still had her attractiveness and good looks, but I could tell she was using some kind of drugs. She looked like she had dropped 10 to 15 pounds since the last time I saw her. It was a dark spot barely noticeable, hidden behind makeup, like she had been punched. There had to be drugs in this room somewhere. "Poppa, watch this bitch for me while I look around."

Poppa pointed the pistol at her while I searched the room. I went through the nightstand, but there was nothing inside but a blue Bible. I looked around the room to her big, pink no-name-brand purse hanging from the straps on the restroom doorknob. I went through it. There were eight condoms, a package of Kleenex, a pair of sunglasses, a few cosmetic items, and a big brown cigarette pouch, amongst other bullshit I looked over. I opened the pouch. There were three hypodermic syringes, a little over $20 worth of meth in a twenty sack, two blue lighters, a silver spoon, eight cigarettes in a soft pack of Newport's, and seven Xanax pills inside of a dime bag.

I placed the hard black substance on the spoon then applied heat from the lighter at the bottom of the spoon. After a while, the substance turned into a liquid, then I filled the syringe with the liquid.

"Poppa, I'll break you off if you can knock that ho out and shoot her up until she overdoses. Place her sitting up on the floor at the end of the bed."

"I got chu." Then he swung a quick hard right hook to her chin, catching her by surprise, knocking her out cold.

I put the syringe on the bed while saying, "I'll be waiting on you outside."

I knew I didn't have to tell him to make sure she died. He'd put a bullet in her head if he didn't think she had died from the drugs, just to get the job done.

After giving Poppa $5000 for himself and the $500 for Lil' Ken, I drove to the Trinity River to throw all our guns and phones into the river, then we headed to my penthouse.

As soon as we made it, Erika started on breakfast for the both of us, cooking blueberry pancakes, scrambled eggs, beef sausages, and turkey bacon with orange juice.

After eating a good meal, we took a long shower together. I did something I normally didn't do, I went into her raw, a woman I barely knew and who hadn't paid me yet. I fell for her banging body and the heat of the moment. I quickly erased the thought of her having any disease. That would've spoiled the fun out of the sex, and I wanted to enjoy every moment of it. We fucked from the shower to the living room, to the kitchen, and ended up in the bedroom. We laid in bed, exhausted from being out all day and all night and from fucking three hours with pausing in between my ejaculations.

I must tell you about the vibes I got from the knowledge of Erika's character and connecting with her sexually. Erika was a good and loyal woman. She was the type of woman to make a man happy and proud. I knew she was the woman I desired to be by my side in this game I lived and breathed.

I made an attempt to make her mine. "You got a million-dollar sex game, so I don't know why you playing with yo'self."

"I'm not playing. Why you say that?" she asked.

I started rubbing her bare pussy. "You got some good pussy. And you put it down on a pimp. You got men out there that'll pay big money for some of this loving you got."

She didn't say anything, not a reaction I expected. I stopped rubbing her love box because our conversation was about to get off the subject of sex and on another approach. I had the light dimmed inside the room just enough where we could see each other. I looked into her eyes while we laid in bed facing each other.

"I want you to know the reason I stopped calling you and answering your calls is because I cut you off. I felt that you were on some bullshit. I respected you enough not to come at you like a ho and offered you a 9-to-5 job, working with my homegirl at a beauty supply store. I hate you passed that opportunity up, that would have been a good look for you. The funny part is, you didn't believe me. I told you when we first started getting to know each other that I'll never lie to you. I stand as a real man. I ain't gotta lie because it is what it is. You either like what I say and do or you don't. I'ma be me. And I want RESPECT above everything else. But I guess I haven't shown and proved enough to you yet. Why didn't you believe me?"

# Money Game

"My past, Monopoly. I got trust issues. Niggas I've fucked with said they'll do this and that but never follow through. That's why I didn't believe you, Monopoly. Niggas play too many games for me. I need a real nigga on my side. I'm a down bitch and all I've had was some no-good ass niggas talking good. I don' know why niggas can't keep it real," she said in disgust.

I believed what she said, but there was something that she was afraid of or either uncomfortable to admit to me. I might be wrong, but I felt she was afraid to take that opportunity, either because of some inside fear or the questionable unknown feeling working around that environment with Asians. My job at this moment was to give her validation in my abilities, to reassure her in herself as a woman, to conquer her fears, to persuade her that with the game I supply and demand, she would have no choice but to succeed in life, and give her knowledge on how some of these niggas' thinking process was.

"I totally understand you, Erika. Only if you knew how fucked up these niggas think and how emotionally disturbed they are, you'll understand why they're the way they are. It's so hard to get niggas out that fucked up mindset they're in. You can only encourage a man so long with what you know how to do. Right in front of you is a stomp-down man, a true pimp in heart, who will live out everything he says he will do. Here and now, you have a choice to choose a better life for yourself, for me to be your man, your lover, your pimp, your supporter, your protector, your provider, and everything you need to succeed in life, or you can go back to that life you are comfortable with living, where you really not doing nothing with yourself. See, with me, you're living the luxury life you never had and setting up for everything you want to be in life. Erika, do you know the difference between a ho and a bitch?" I asked, changing the gears in our conversation. I knew it was a good time to give her more things to consider about hoing.

"Nah, what's the difference?"

"I really want you to understand that a bitch fucks without getting paid. A bitch fucks a nigga because she's drunk, high, or because she's attracted to a man in some form or fashion. Some bitches fuck for the thrill of sex and doing something spontaneous. I look down on a female who gives away her pussy for free A real ho is highly respected and is a queen in my book. A ho is the only woman I want and love to be around, because we have something in common. We understand the way the world works, we know our places. See, a real ho will never open her legs for a man if he didn't pay her first. A queen will never go through what a bitch goes through when dealing with a man. Only a bitch will get nothing but a sore throat and cum running down her ass. A queen knows that her conversation, time, looks, and service cost money, and if a man wants any of those things from her, he has to pay to play.

"As simple as that, Erika. I'm not trying to force you into this lifestyle, because that's not what I do. Understand, Erika, I'm just trying to get you to understand that a lot of men out there in the world will pay for what you've just given me, and this game is a chance to better your life not worsen it. Now if you're interested in what I'm saying and want to see me prove what I say, I want you to say, 'I choose you, Monopoly.' If not and you want to keep things as they are as friends, that's fine with me too. I will accept either one. What's your choice?"

I hoped she didn't say no. It seemed like she was in a pleasant mood because she was smiling. She had to be after getting fucked down good, busting five orgasms, all in between these red silk sheets. Now I was smoothly feeding her this good game face to face, so she had no choice but to choose up with my pimpin'. It was written all over her face that she was into me. I knew I had her under my spell.

"I choose you, Monopoly."

"Are you sure you want to fuck with me in this game, baby?"

"Yea, I'm sure. I wanna fuck with you," she said then put her arm around my waist.

I smiled along with her and then kissed her full lips. "You made a wise choice. Don't worry, baby, everything's gonna be just fine." I talked to her about how good the Life was in the game and about most of my and some of my hoes accomplishments. She fell asleep on me a few times, but I woke her up every time. I wanted to keep her mind set on me and hopefully, once I let her go to sleep, she would have good dreams about me. Since I had been up all day, I started yawning and dozing off myself after talking to her for three hours. I kissed her and we both went to sleep at 9:17 A.M.


You had to use reverse psychology in the game. She was an amazingly attractive, beautiful creature. All eyes were on her. But she was feeling herself, so she acted conceited and pretended to be ignoring you. You should mirror her actions. You seem annoyed when she speaks to you. This will get her attention because in her mind, you're not responding to her sorcery she's conducting. She will go out her way trying to win your attentions. This is when the old saying comes in.


"Talk to everyone in the room besides the one you really want. And she will fall into your lap."
— MUNDO MONEY

# Smoove Dolla

Money Game

## Chapter 10

We woke at 12:45 P.M. After we took another shower, she put back on her clothes that she had on yesterday. I put on a new Givenchy outfit with an iced-out platinum Rolex, a platinum, diamond-cut bracelet, two platinum diamond earrings, and a long, platinum, custom-link chain made out of small, thick Monopoly men connected all the way around, all worth 120 bands.

The whole time I was getting dressed and on the way to Shae's crib, I gave Erika my law that she had to follow if she wanted to be with me, and I mentioned to her what I wanted her to do while I handled my business. I gave Erika three racks to buy her some outfits, shoes, heels, good hygiene products, and whatever else she needed to look her best for me and the tricks she would be satisfying. I had her drop me off while she went to the stores I told her to shop at.

While Shae made me a cup of hot green tea, I found the painting service on the internet that my Mason brother owned. I had her call and give them the details on what she wanted on the walls on the inside of the beauty shop. They said they would start on the job Tuesday. Next, I logged on to a couple websites where she could order the booth chairs, hair dryers, sinks, big mirrors, hair equipment, and products with her overseas bank account. Also, I told her about what alarm system was best to use and how to apply for it.

While I was breaking down how to get insurance on everything, I heard a door close in the back of the house. The first thing that popped up in my head was a nigga being here. My body tensed up, but I kept it player. It wasn't like she was my woman or my ho, so I couldn't say anything about her doing her, but I felt some type of way. "Why you didn't tell me you had company? We could have went out somewhere and did all this."

She looked at me crazy. "Really, Tunke? You really think I'll disrespect you like that by having another nigga here while you here? If a nigga was here, he would have been gone early this morning before you even got here. But I don't need another when I

183

got you. I still got you, right?"

"Yeah, you still got me, as long as you want me to be yours. If it ain't no nigga here, then who is it?"

"That's Pinky, Tunke," she said, rolling her eyes, and then softly pushed me. "You know a bitch love you."

"I know. I love you too." I gave her a kiss on her full lips. The reason why I thought a nigga was here was because you never know with a woman. I wasn't a fool. A square nigga could have been her motivation to get out the game. I knew she loved me a lot, but you just never know at times when it comes to women. "Let me guess, she called you last night to come pick her up?"

"Yes, and I was gonna tell you."

"I ain't trippin', do you." I sensed she was lonely and wanted company when she told me she wanted to go out last night but never did, and since we had got back cool, she'd been calling me a lot to talk.

"Last night we had a long talk. She told me she wanted me to help her get off drugs."

"And you believe that game?" I asked, surprised. She knew not to fall for shit like that.

"She didn't have to bring that up last night. We were talking 'bout some mo' shit. She brought it up out the blue. Even though I'm not in your stable no mo', I'm still Pinky's sister. If she needs my help, I'm here for her." Here was Shae with wanting the family she never had again. But it was all good, though. Helping Pinky was cool with me, I just hoped it did some justice, because I did want Pinky off heroin.

Before I could respond to what Shae had said, Pinky walked out the hallway into the living room. She probably had heard us talking, because it was so quiet that I heard the toilet flush and then running water inside the bathroom with her having the door closed. I wanted her to know that I didn't believe her. Maybe it would push her to prove herself to me. "Hey, Daddy," Pinky said.

"When you see people talking, excuse yourself," I told her, letting her know to show us some respect.

"Excuse me. Hey, Daddy," she said in a different tone of voice this time.

"Wuz up, you aight?"

"Yes. Are you?" Her tone of voice had changed for the third time now. I could tell I made her feel better by speaking to her.

"Yeah, I'm good. I'm blessed. I woke up this morning with more zeros added to my bank account and a fresh turnout. I can't complain at all, baby."

"I'm sorry for what I did last night. You still mad at me?" I laughed inside my head at her question. She thought I was mad, but I only did what I did to stomp down on her. I knew that would bring the effect I wanted, more respect for me.

"I was never mad at you, Pinky. I was disappointed in you because you disrespected me. That's why I did what I did. What are you gonna do, leave with me when I go or stay here with Shae and let her help you?" I asked, testing her to see what she would say.

She looked at Shae and then at me. "I'm staying here with Shae."

I nodded my head. "That's wuz up. Anyway, we were in the middle of something important before you walked up. Whenever we finish, I'll talk to you then."

"Can I sit in here with y'all?" Pinky asked.

"As long as you don't interrupt us, I don't mind." I scooted over towards Shae to give Pinky some room. She sat in between the end of the sofa and me.

Writing all the information on paper and breaking down everything took close to six hours in all that I'd been here. I called Erika and then Rose, telling them to come to Shae's crib.

Rose told me that two of her homegirls she ran with wanted to choose up with me. For them to choose, she had to be telling them everything that I did for her and how I ran my operations. "You must've been bragging about Daddy over there."

"Yes, I have, Daddy." I could tell she was smiling and that her homegirls were around from the way she was talking. It sounded like she had me on speaker phone. Since they were listening, I bragged a little bit to them through Rose. "That shit I did for you already ain't nothing compared to what I got planned for us. You fucking with a Giant Pimp now, baby, with nothing but Big game. That means I got a million and one money schemes so me and my queens can live a luxury life. Fucking with me, you got no choice but to succeed in this life. Tell your homegirls my choosing fee is two grand. Give them my number. Tell them to give me a call when they get it and then we'll go from there, alright, baby."

"Alright, Daddy, I will. I'll be there within 15 minutes."

Giving Rose a little freedom paid off. I wasn't expecting her to go around her homegirls last night. I thought she would go spend time with her son. Just what I said would happen with Rose and her crew, happened. It didn't go exactly as planned, but she influenced two of her homegirls to choose. The one who didn't choose was either not there with them or she would probably wait for what the other two would say about me, and if she liked what she heard, she might give my pimpin' a chance. I didn't know her, so I didn't know any possible ways to knock her by myself, only through her homegirls, which was better if you ask me.

When they finally made it, I put Erika's bags inside Rose's Honda, leaving the Range Rover at Shae's crib, because we didn't need all our cars out of town. We headed towards South Dallas to pick up Poppa. I definitely needed an enforcer while I was going cross county, city to city, and probably from state to state after I left the Mason function in Houston I said I would attend.

As Rose drove down I-20, I turned around in the passenger's seat and looked through the things Erika had bought from Saks, Fifth Avenue and the Chanel store. She had taste. She picked out some nice and sexy clothes that I knew she'd really look beautiful in. They weren't too hoish, but they would do for now until I went shopping with her.

She caught on to me very quick. After going through three bags checking tags, she said, "Oh, here go your change." She went into her new red Chanel purse that cost about $600 to $900, and then handed me a few bills and coins. "It's like six hundred and something dollars. I didn't get everything I wanted. I really wanted to stop by Bloomingdale's. You think when we get a chance we can stop by there?"

186

"We'll see. I'ma see how good your productivity is first before I spend any more money on you. What you have now is enough to last you a few days."

After picking up Poppa, we made our way to Austin. Bre texted me on the way there, telling me she and Jasmine had an out call for an hour. I texted her back okay, leaving out the part that I was almost there. I wanted to surprise them and see what they were doing. They could've been doing some out of pocket shit while I wasn't around. We made it to the hotel at 8:31 P.M.

CeCe and Claire were in bed asleep. Both of them should had been up at 7 P.M. I didn't trip, because I had them working the escort websites late night, as well as had them up the whole day yesterday shopping and having fun. Since the room was a little messy, I woke them up and had them clean up both rooms. Bre and Jasmine made it to the room 26 minutes later, after I arrived. I sat on the couch, and Erika sat in a wooden chair by the small kitchen. I could tell she was absorbing her surroundings, curious, like a square or fresh turnout ho would be around an unfamiliar territory, females she didn't know, and a lifestyle she had no knowledge of. Every ho except for Rose eyed Erika and she eyed them, probably thinking about whether or not they were going to like each other and sizing each other up. Bre, being the friendly person she was, was the first one to speak to Erika. I was glad that happened before I asked them to. With them doing it on their own, it would make Erika feel more comfortable and accepted.

I sat all six of my queens down, let them all introduce themselves one by one to Erika and then her to them. Next, I started telling them what I expected out of them tonight, what hotels they would be working out of and with whom. I had Bre work with Jasmine, CeCe, and Erika until I left the strip club, then I would take her to Extended Stay Hotel on Burnet Rd. and Highway 183 where Rose will stay when they get off from the club. At the moment, we were at the Extended Stay on Capital of Texas Highway.

After dropping Rose and Bre's luggage off at their hotel in our new cars, we rode to a North Austin strip club named XTC.

I told Rose where to fill out an application at while Poppa and

I walked ahead of them towards the back, where I usually sat in the very back, and met up with Serious Jones.

Serious Jones had been in Austin a week now. He had three of his white hoes dancing here also. He was a good pimp at 31 years old, who was from Wood Town in Oak Cliff, Dallas, Texas. Although he was very serious when it came to pimpin', he often cracked jokes and made fun of a lot of things. He was a good entertainer to the people that were around him. He had some money-getting hoes in his stable as well, each of them ten toes down for him, who kept him with the jewels and tools he wanted and needed to succeed in this game. A pimp we both knew by the name of Trill Black had put Serious Jones on game over a decade ago, so he had more experience in the game than me.

Although I was only 24 with seven years under my belt, I had surpassed him as far as owning a successful business, zeros in my bank account, and money I had stashed. There was a lot more I still had to learn about this game and women. I'm a player personified who wanted to know the game inside and out and around the whole board. Along the way of knowing Serious Jones, I'd learned and picked up some things from him by watching him in action. He was one of the few pimps I had mad respect for. He and Tight Game were the only pimps that held me down in the feds with books, magazines, money, a couple of visits, and thousands of photos to show niggas how big Dallas pimps did it. And I could easily name over fifty pimps that I knew and had met before I went to prison. That should tell you something about those two.

Even though today was Sunday, there were a lot of dancers and a bunch of patrons in the club. I really liked being around this type of environment amongst white, Mexican, and mixed dancers, and the patrons alike. At cabarets like these, the customers didn't come with much drama, and the dancers didn't have to work extra hard for a small amount of money like they did with black men. I still liked the environment of a black strip club because there's nothing like the sight of a fine, pretty black woman. But since there was big money being made here, I was where I needed to be.

There weren't many girls that came to our table. Pimpin' and

Serious Jones were the reasons. Even though he was from Dallas, he was a regular here at XTC. He visited Austin often because of the money being that good here. There were big events year round in Austin, so people from all over the world came to attend them.

Some of the girls here already had pimps, most of them were renegade, and they knew what it was with him. A couple of girls I'd seen here knew I was pimpin' because either I told them so, my ex-hoes had told them, or my association with Serious Jones. Plus, I carried myself like a pimp. One thing for sure, we weren't throwing or giving no money to none of the dancers for anything. That was the main reason why they stayed away from us.

There was this one cute white girl I saw after she finished dancing on a trick. Two minutes before, I was in conversation with Serious Jones about what went down with Pinky, not paying this dancer no attention until I checked my surroundings. I saw her staring at me while she was whispering in the trick's ear.

Once I locked eyes with hers, I didn't look away. The look I gave her along with a smile made her look down, unlocking her eyes away from mine.

Seconds later, the white trick gave her a 50-dollar bill, then she got up, said a few words to him, and then started walking towards my path. I stood up, blocking her path before she could pass me, makin' her stop a foot in front of me. "If you not trying to spend no money, you wasting my time," she mentioned immediately and seriously.

"Fucking with me is never a waste of time. I'ma mogul in this game, everything I touch go platinum, baby. I'm Monopoly the Pimp," I said with a smile without extending my arm for a handshake. She still had that look on her face, that she didn't want to be fucked with. I pulled out my wallet clamp that had two of my credit cards, five Vanilla One cards, and a few of my business cards in it. I took out a business card, bent it long ways up the middle, then placed it in her G-string in between the bent part. "You should go out on a date with me so we can enjoy ourselves and get to know one another. It'll all be on me."

She snatched the card out her G-string, looked at it for four

Smoove Dolla

seconds, then crumpled my card in her fist. "I might. I'll think about it," she said and then walked around me.

I liked to show my business cards to females that played hard to get, the ones who didn't want to talk to me, to show them that I'd been successful in my pimpin', and to prove to them that I was investing in business with the money I was getting from a ho. Most women would look into it just to see if it was legit, and maybe surf through the website to see if what you were selling was likable. Majority of the time, the woman would gravitate to a nigga after that. She probably would give me a call since she didn't drop it on the floor or try to give it back.

Afterwards, Serious Jones and I chopped it up about the game. Then the three of us joked around for about 25 minutes, until I received a call from CeCe telling me that Jasmine and Erika were fighting.

"What they fighting for?" I asked.

"Jasmine say she caught her stealing," CeCe told me.

"Put me on speaker, CeCe," I said as I got up and headed to the men's restroom, because I could barely hear.

On the way, I could hear her telling Erika to stop, Erika was cursing Jasmine, it was a bunch of commotion on the other side of the phone.

"Daddy, you on speaker now," CeCe finally told me.

Once I walked inside the restroom, I told them, "If you hoes don't quit fighting, I promise you, I'm sending you bitches back on the next Greyhound bus back to Fort Worth, and y'all can kiss my pimpin' ass goodbye forever. And if you think I'm playing, I can show you better than I can tell you." A young Mexican woman patron stepped around me, laughing as I stopped in the middle of the restroom.

I heard Bre and CeCe breaking it up. Erika said, "Aight, aight, I'm backing up off the bitch." Bre was telling Jasmine to stop walking up on Erika. "Monopoly, this bitch keep walking up on me. She keep on, I'ma give the ho what she want," Erika said.

"Erika, just walk out the room, go somewhere until I get there. I'm on my way now. Bre and CeCe, hold Jasmine back until she calms down. Y'all hear me?"

The both of them responded back with okay. "Jasmine, if you want a rematch, I'll let y'all get it again. I just gotta be there to referee, 'cause I ain't letting you two hurt each other. I'm on my way."

If it ain't one thing it's another. Shit like this happened when a pimp had multiple hoes in one hotel room. Fighting wasn't a big deal, because hoes got into it with each other, no matter how much you demanded them not to and to get along. It happened because of many reasons, but mainly jealousy. Erika stealing something didn't sound true to me, though. It didn't even sound like something she would do, when all she had to do was call me and ask could she go buy it, but I'd find out when I talked to them one by one.

I told Serious Jones what happened. "Two of my hoes were at the room fighting. I'm 'bout to go straighten this shit out. I'll holla at you later, Jones."

"Aight, P, handle yo' business, pimp. I'll holla at you," Serious Jones said as he downed a glass of the most expensive champagne here and then poured himself another glass out the bottle.

"Poppa, you staying here or you leaving with me?"

"I'ma stay. I'm tryna get off some of this work," he said, referring to the powder, meth, and ecstasy pills he had for sale. Even though I'd never sold drugs, I knew that strip clubs were one of the best spots to sell upper and downer drugs.

If the drug dealer knew some of the dancers and waiters at the club, it would be best to have them help him get off supply to other strippers and tricks that used it. Rose was helping Poppa get off his drugs.

My hoes were in the bathroom when I quietly walked into the hotel room. They didn't hear me come inside the room or close the door behind me. I stood to the left outside the bathroom door, listening to their discussion. "Wasn't stealing, just looking at some of your clothes," I heard Bre say, catching her at the end of her sentence.

Then Jasmine said, "She lying like a bitch. She wasn't looking at my clothes. That bitch had the tampon box in her lap while still going through other shit when I walked in the room. Fuck that bitch. I'm 'bout to beat this bitch up when Monopoly come."

Something in her voice was suspicious. She was giving the idea of Erika stealing from her too much strength, like she was trying to cover up something. I was going to find out what it was.

There was nothing said after that. My guess was they knew she was the one getting beat up and was going to lose the next fight as well. At least that's what I got from the commotion I heard on the phone and now the silence.

"Bitch, be still, I'm tryna make it stop bleeding," CeCe told Jasmine.

I walked into the bathroom, making my presence known. After they told me I scared the shit out of them, Jasmine started telling me what happened, which sounded like a bunch of bullshit. I wanted to hear Erika's side of the story before I made judgement on what I would do. Although, I still wanted to give Jasmine a fair shot at a rematch. "Do you still wanna fight again?"

"Yeah," she said with doubt.

"Are you sure?" I asked, making sure.

She said "yeah" again, nodding her head.

"CeCe, get me a clean, dry washcloth. Do one of you have Vaseline around here?"

"Yeah, I got some in my bag. I'll go get it," Bre said as she got up to get it.

Her wound wasn't deep enough for stitches. I applied pressure to her one-inch cut above her left eyebrow with a white washcloth for a minute, then I put Petroleum Jelly inside her wound and all over her face. "I really don't want ya fighting, but if you really want a rematch, you can. I put the Petroleum Jelly on your face so if you get hit in the face, it'll protect you a little bit. Her fist will slide off, depending on what angle she punches you in. I want you to swing back and block her punches. Do what you gotta do, stand up for yours. I'm 'bout to go get her."

After collecting the money they had made while I was at the club, I left the room. Erika was in the other room, seven doors down. When I walked in, she was sitting on the couch messing around on her phone. "Put your phone down. Why was you in her bag after you got the tampons?"

"Monopoly, I wasn't stealing shit. Why the fuck—"

I cut her off. "Bitch, excuse you. You in a pimp's presence, ho. I want some muthafuckin' respect, ho. You ain't gotta do all that muthafuckin' cussing to tell me what happened. Tell me like you got some sense," I said, reminding her that she was a pimp's ho and not in the ghetto anymore.

She sighed and then said, "I'm sorry, Daddy. Okay, I found out I started my period when I got back to the room from a date. I called and asked Jasmine did she have any tampons I can use until I go to the store. She was in this room at that time. She told me she'll come over to the room to get it for me, but I couldn't wait. The blood was coming down heavy. She walked in the room while I was looking through her bag at her clothes I liked. I wasn't stealing at all. I was about to give her a compliment until she started popping off at the mouth and calling me bitches, so I ran up on her and beat her up."

"I believe you, but don't do none of that shit no mo' if you not cool with one of my hoes yet. Next time you need anything, just go buy it so it won't be no shit. Always have your own shit so you won't have to ask them for anything. She said she was coming to get it for you, you should have waited. And don't put yo' hands on no ho of mine without my consent unless she hit you first or run up on you. Do you understand me?"

"Yes."

"Yes what, Erika?"

"Yes, Daddy. But it's whatever. I won the first time and I'ma win the second time too. I didn't wanna fight her in the first place. I was just liking her style. She ain't got nothing for me," she said with confidence.

Back in the other room now, Bre and CeCe watched in between the two beds while Jasmine and Erika posted up ready to fight each other in the open space in the room. "When I say fight, y'all do what y'all do." I stepped back eight feet and then gave them the word.

Erika posted up like a nigga that could fight. She moved her arms, ready to block every punch that her opponent threw at her.

Jasmine threw a wild right hook that Erika swiftly weaved, then Erika connected a left hook, followed by a right body shot to the rib, making Jasmine fold up, and then she slowly went down to her knee.

"Don't hit her no mo', Erika. You alright, Jazz? You still wanna fight?" I said while stepping in between them.

She nodded her head. I stepped back out the way, giving them some room.

Eight seconds later, after she stood up straight, she ran up on Erika throwing wild windmill punches. She hit Erika a couple times in the head, but it didn't faze her not a little bit. Erika side stepped to the right and hit her dead in the jaw with a mean left, then pushed her hard onto the bed. She probably would have knocked her out if it wasn't for the Petroleum Jelly making her fist slide off Jasmine's face.

"That's enough, Erika, get up off my ho." I kind of felt sorry for the ho and regretted letting them fight. Even though Erika was about 30 pounds heavier than Jasmine, I thought Jasmine would get with her the second time around. I didn't think about the fact that she grew up in Stop 6 and had been to prison, until now. I knew she had to learn how to fight from those two experiences in life. Jasmine was just a pretty bitch who couldn't fight.

I gave Erika the keys to my Rolls Royce and told her to head to the car after cleaning herself up in the other room. After she left, I told Jazz, "Don't feel bad, at least you tried, baby. Y'all follow her to the bathroom and help her get cleaned up for me."

Jasmine stopped in front of me. "Daddy, may I go back to Arlington for a week, please? I should be good enough to work after that."

I looked at her yellow-toned face. There were dark-red rings around her eyes and scratches on her neck and face. Her jaw was swollen as well as her bottom lip. Blood slowly leaked out of the cut above her eye through the Petroleum Jelly. She took a good beating. There was no way she could work looking like this. Her face would probably take about six to eight days to heal, at least to where she could apply makeup to the remaining bruises. "Yea, you

Money Game

can go home until I say you good to work. Y'all, go help her clean her face again."

When they went into the bathroom, I looked around the room at my hoes' bags. I noticed one that was out of place, that looked like someone stuffed everything back in it, and it belonged to Jasmine. There was nothing but clothes and a box of tampons inside, nothing out the ordinary. I started going through the bags and pockets of her clothes. In the third blue jeans I checked, there were five blue hundreds inside it. So the bitch was cuffing on me. I thanked the Pimp God Jarod for letting the episodes that took place reveal to me the truth about Jasmine.

I put the money back inside her pocket. This was a time in the game where I felt I shouldn't physically abuse this ho for trying to get over on me. Getting sent to prison and hearing stories about how other pimps had gotten caught up for pimpin' had me cautioned about how I pimped. I wasn't about to allow this situation to get me arrested for physically disciplining this ho. Plus, Erika had already beat her up, And that was enough. I didn't want to add insult to injury physically, but somehow, emotionally and mentally. If a bitch stole from me and she knew what kind of pimp I was, then I couldn't trust her, and she didn't deserve my pimpin'. She stole a one-way ticket out my life. It probably would be best to confront her when I dropped her off in the morning, or whenever she asked for some money, which I knew she was. And if I allowed her back in the future, she would definitely pay me extra. I was tripling my chosen fee to come back. She could get it since she was shown how to post ads properly.

I went outside and got into my car. Erika was sitting in the passenger seat listening to Future.

"You okay, baby?" I asked her.

"Yeah, I'm good. I ain't gonna lose no sleep over that. You know none of that didn't have to happen. It was all a misunderstanding."

"I'm glad you beat that bitch up. That ho had cuffed $500 of my money in her clothes. That's why she pulled that little stunt on you, trying cover up what she did."

"Ohhh, now it's making sense. I had a feeling something was wrong with that bitch from the way she was acting, I just didn't know what because I don't know her."

"Next time you have a feeling about one of my hoes, tell me about it, okay baby?"

"Okay, I will."

"You fight harder than a muthafucker. Where you learn how to fight like that?"

"The streets and the pen. I'ma hood bitch, Monopoly. I'm from Stop 6. You know how it goes down in Stop 6. I had a lot of fights in prison too. Bitches hated on me a lot because them male guards used to fuck with a bitch hard."

I could see that to be true. She was very gorgeous. She was also a little too aggressive as far as fighting went, unlike Rose, whose aggressiveness went into hustling. Erika fit perfectly in my stable, I just had to teach her how to transfer that aggressive fighter into being an aggressive hustler.

"So, how long do you be on your period?"

"Between five to eight days."

"I still want you to work tonight," I said, testing her to see her reaction and how down she was for me.

She gave me a confused look. "You want me to fuck while I'm on my period?" she asked, surprised.

"Yeah. As long as you ain't got arthritis, lockjaw, or gingivitis, you're good to go."

"How you gon' do that?"

"I know a way to cover that period up."

We went to CVS Pharmacy to buy a bag of makeup sponges, two bags of douches, and a box of tampons, and then headed to the hotel on Capital of Texas Highway.

After she finished cleaning herself up, I put five makeup sponges up inside of her pussy. Tricks didn't have any idea if she was on her period or not, and they couldn't feel nothing but the inside of her pussy. I used to do this with Shae when she was my only ho and was on her menstruation. A bunch of hoes and strippers did this as well when it was that time of the month and they needed to keep hustling. I did this to her because she beat my ho up where she couldn't work tonight, so she had to take her place. I broke that down to Erika so she could understand why she still had to work tonight. She didn't trip, which was good. It would only be for one night anyway. I had something planned for her and Rose tomorrow.

Jasmine got her own room to sleep in so Bre and CeCe could work out of the two rooms we already had at the other hotel. I worked Erika until 3 A.M., and CeCe and Bre until 5 A.M. Rose got off at 4 A.M.


"Baby girl, no one can play this game alone & win... You'll need a like-minded partner to succeed, just like with everything else you do in life. So, if you gone believe in something, why not believe in me?"

Excerpt from: Chosen
*True Pimpin'*

# Smoove Dolla

## Chapter 11

Rose woke me as soon as she got up at 9 A.M. I woke Erika up, who was asleep on the other bed. There were a bunch of missed calls and unanswered texts in my phone from last night and this morning. I only returned a couple of them, and that's including the three from Claire. She had texted me five times, damn near begging me to come back. She must be really doing bad. Claire and I talked for about fifteen minutes, making things clear on where we stood and how things would continue to go on between her and me.

Once I got off the phone, I told them, "I want y'all to put on something nice and presentable. Y'all gon' be cashing checks today. Erika, take them sponges out and douche real good afterwards."

After calling Jasmine to wake her up, Erika yelled out the shower, "Daddy, I need your help, there's one still in me. It's too deep, I can't get it out."

After getting off the phone, I went into the bathroom. I slid the curtains back then turned the shower knob off. Erika's curvy, naked body made me think about sex, but I quickly erased those sexual thoughts out my mind. I washed my hands then dried them with a clean, big white towel. I sat down on the toilet and told her, "Come closer to me and squat a little bit."

I put my index, middle, and thumb fingers inside her opening. As I went deep inside her, I felt around trying to see if I felt the sponge. After about ten seconds of feeling around, I started scratching at something soft. "You feel me scratching you?

"No, that must be it."

"Alright, put your leg up here," I said, patting the edge of the tub with my left hand. "Do your best to push it down while I claw it down." Seconds later, I had it where I could grab it with two fingers, pulling it out of her. The sponge only had blood on half of it. I tossed it in the commode and flushed it. "You sure that was the fifth one?"

"Yea, I'm sure. Thank you, Daddy."

"You're welcome," I said as I was washing my hands again.

When I picked up Jasmine, I warned her and Erika. "I don't want no fighting in my car, so I suggest you two do whatever y'all gotta do to squash whatever beef y'all still got against each other. Because if y'all argue or throw one punch in this muthafucker, I'm putting both you bitches out on the side of the freeway, and I'm changing my number." That was true and it wasn't. If anything did happen between them, I was blaming it all on Jasmine. That would give me another reason to do something to her ass. Erika was good with me.

Jasmine's apartment was the first stop when we arrived in Arlington. Jasmine looked at me crazy when I didn't get out to help her with her bags. After getting them out the trunk, she sat them on the sidewalk, and then walked to my car window. "Daddy, I need to send my momma some money for my daughter, and I need some spending money while I'm out here. Can I get $700, Daddy?" Most bitches ain't shit and would try to play your ass if you're not hip to their games.

"Fuck no, bitch! Use that $500 in your pants pocket you could have asked for and would have gotten but cuffed on me. You just stole a one-way ticket out my life, ho. Bitch, fuck you," I said then sped off on her standing there looking stupid.

This was a good time to warn my queens. "I advise you two to never try to get over on me because eventually, I'm gonna find out. I can see through bullshit. And when I do find out, you will be gone like that bitch. Always remember, I want you in my life, I don't need you," I said as I rode down Collins Street. I knew they knew about my slip up and how I got tricked by Brittany, but so be it. I didn't let that stop me from being the pimp that I was. We all knew niggas in some kind of game, whether it's the dope game, pimp game, even gamble house game, that had gotten robbed. Niggas slipped once in a while. Everything a nigga did was not going to be air tight. Somewhere, there would be a loose hole. I learned from my fuck ups. I had to continue on with my pimpin', allowing nothing to get in my way of my success in this game.

By the time we made it to IHOP in Lewisville for brunch, Jasmine had called Rose and me multiple times as well as sent us a bunch of texts that we never answered.

While eating, I received a text from an Austin number.

Unknown
WYD
12:42 P.M. Monday

Me
Who this?
12:43 P.M. Monday

Jennifer
This Jennifer from XTC. We met last night.
12:45 P.M. Monday

Me
Can you talk? If so, call me.
12:45 P.M. Monday

Two minutes later, she called. "What's going on?" I asked when I answered.

"I'm bored. I was just calling to see what you were doing. Since you said you'd take me out, I wanted to know if you want to do something today."

"Mmm, I'm in Dallas right now handling some business, but I'll be back in Austin by 7:30. Will that be okay with you?"

"Yea, sure, it's cool," she said, sounding a little disappointed.

"You sound disappointed. Don't worry, it's gonna be worth the wait. I'll give you a call around 7, okay?"

"K. I'll be waiting. Talk to you then," she told me then hung up.

Afterwards, we went to my white homeboy's house down the street. Nate made fake identification cards and fake employment checks that looked like the real deal. I bought Erika, Rose, and Claire fake ID cards and six $1150 Waste Management employment checks apiece, along with the work gear and clothes for $6200. They dressed out in the work clothes at Nate's house. On the way to a corner store in North Dallas, I laced them up on what to do, how to act, and what to say to them and to each other while they waited for their money since it was Monday.

I took them to two stores each in North Dallas, Greedy Grove, and Oak Cliff to cash checks. Afterwards, we went to my penthouse in Downtown so they could change back into their regular clothes.

Before we headed to Austin, I took Claire grocery shopping for her mother's house.

Then we dropped her son off and the $150 worth of groceries as well as $400 to her mom.

We made it to Austin at 7:18 P.M. I picked Jennifer up at a La Quinta hotel off Highway 183 and Interstate 35. When she got into my Rolls Royce, I said, "I hope you don't mind three of my girls tagging along with us. We been running around all day handling business. They can use some fun right now also."

"No, I don't mind. I'm okay with it." I was glad she was cool about coming along with me and my hoes. Some females were skeptical about that while most females would feel safer with other women around. Some of us knew and had heard stories of gorilla pimps who had pimpnapped a ho. Most gorilla pimps would beat a female up or let his hoes jump her and force her to prostitute for him. Some pimps used drugs to get girls and control them. I wasn't a gorilla. I was a pimp with class. I didn't like for my hoes to use drugs at all. Although, because a pimp did come across a lot of hoes that did drugs, I did accept hoes that used, only if I felt I could pimp them without any major problems. I just didn't put women on drugs that weren't on them from the jump.

Whoever said that it's better and easier to pimp on a druggy ho was a lie, and he couldn't have too much good game. The reason why I thought Jennifer called me and asked me out was because I learned that Rose had a short conversation with her about me being her pimp and how I operated. She told Rose she would think about it and get back with her. Since she told Rose that, I would use Rose to knock her if I didn't get her to choose tonight. It wouldn't be long before she was in my stable, as long as she continued to talk to either one of us.

I took them to a Speed Zone where I knew all of us would enjoy ourselves. After riding go-karts on different race tracks for about two hours, Jennifer sat on my thigh as I sat on a wooden bench, while Rose, Claire, and Erika continued to ride go-karts. I read sadness in her pretty blue eyes. "You okay?"

"Yeah. Why you ask that?"

"Seems like something's troubling you."

"Nah, I'm good." Her tone told me different.

"No, you not. You can talk to me about anything. Tell me what's wrong."

"I don't want to bother you with my problems. I'd rather not talk about it," she said as she looked away.

"If something's troubling you, talk about it. I'm all ears. How you feeling right now?" I said, not taking no for an answer, really wanting to hear what had her in her feelings.

She inhaled and exhaled deeply then continued. "I just broke up with my ex-boyfriend of three years. Really, he broke it off with me. He put me out of his apartment. It hurts living without him. I'm so used to him being around."

When she finished, I said, "That explains that look in those pretty eyes of yours. So, you been at the La Quinta since he put you out?"

"Yeah."

"Why he broke up with you?"

"He got back with his baby momma. That bitch was over there when I went to get my stuff. They threw all my stuff outside the front door," she said with tears in her eyes.

As we talked, I felt I had to give her some time to heal from her breakup. When a woman was going through something, if she didn't ask for any help, all she needed was an ear. I sat there listening and holding her for about an hour. Since she was the one who called me to go out, I told her, "Come on, let's ride some more go-karts."

"Good idea, I'm not trying to think about my problems anyway," she said as she stood up after me, and then we headed for a short line for the two-seater go-karts.

We left for Mr. Jim's restaurant to eat after being at Speed Zone for four hours. The conversation of her choosing up didn't come back up again that night. And I didn't want to bring it up anyway. I knew just like she had called me to go out, she'd call me when she was ready to choose. It was better that way, I thought, knowing if she did that meant she had a strong attitude toward my pimpin', wanting to make me a substitute for her ex.

*** 

The next time I heard from Jennifer was the very next morning at 7:21 A.M. from Austin's Travis County Jail on a collect call. I accepted it.

"Hey, sorry to be calling you like this. Last night, I—" Before she started telling me what happened, I cut her off. I didn't want her to say anything she did or that might incriminate her, making her sound guilty of any crime, over this phone.

I asked her, "You need me to do anything for you?"

"Can you bond me out, please? I'll do anything. I promise I'll pay you back," she begged.

"I got you. What's your name?"

"Jennifer Green."

"Okay, I'll hop right on it. You'll be out within three hours."

"Thank you so much, Monopoly," she mentioned happily.

When I hung up, I called Christie, hoping she was available at the moment and not mad at me for what happened with Tight game.

"Good morning, Christie," I said when she answered.

"Good morning, Damion," she spoke back, calling me by my real name.

"You busy?"

"No, I'm having coffee at Starbucks before going to the court building."

"How you been holding up?" I asked her.

"Not so good. I've been a little depressed, but I'm making it. What's going on with you? Is everything okay?"

"Yea, with me it is. I called because I need you to bond someone out for me."

"Okay. What's their name and what county did they get arrested in?"

"Jennifer Green. She got locked up in Austin, Travis County," I told her.

"I don't usually take cases out the city unless it's worth it or Tight game wants me to. But since it's you, I'll do it. I know an attorney out that way that owes me a couple favors. I'll give him a call and he'll bond her out through his firm," Christie said.

"I appreciate that."

"You're welcome. Since I'm doing this for you, I want something done for me as well."

"What is it?" I asked curiously.

"Well, you know I've been taking care of a lot since Tight game's been in the hospital. It's been frustrating and exhausting me. We both know there's a possibility that he might not make it or recover from the coma. I'm just going through a lot and I'm lonely," she mentioned, still beating around the bush, not saying what she wanted from me.

"So what exactly are you askin' from me, Christie?" I asked, confused.

"I want you to spend the night with me."

"Okay, and do what? I know you ain't talking about fucking."

"I am. I need you tonight," she said in a low tone of voice.

"You done lost your fuckin' mind or something? I'm not doing Tight game like that. If you lookin' for a male escort, you know where to find one. You not finna get it out of me."

"Please. Just one night. I'll pay you $5000 and Jennifer's case will get dismissed," she begged and bargained.

Even though this was a win-win situation for me, I didn't know about taking that offer. It sounded like a sweet deal, but at the same time, it felt like I was betraying Tight Game in a sense. He was my big brother, a friend, and father figure. I had no doubt that he wouldn't be mad at me for doing something like that. He was too much of a big player to sweat me fucking Christie. It's not like he said he was going to marry her, but that didn't have to be said to see that. Plus, she'd fucked plenty of men for him and herself to advance them both and to add on to what they both had. So, was I wrong for getting money? I believed not. I knew I was a true player who loved the game deeply. So, I asked myself another question. Would I be mad if I my woman fucked and paid one of my pimp friends? Honestly, I couldn't get mad about it if I was in a coma. A real player didn't get mad about shit like that even if he's awake.

They get over it and play on. A part of me felt that it was right to do what I was taught in this game. And that was cash first before a bitch's ass. Plus, I was about to add Jennifer to my stable, so it would be a bonus by getting her charges dropped. But deep down inside, I felt a little bad, because Tight Game was more than a mentor to me. He became like a father figure to me. I had mad love for him. He was the reason I was alive, pimpin', and rich today. Plus, I'd made an oath to the Masons that I stood firm on. Even with all that justifying, it still didn't stop me from wanting to take Christie's offer. Even though we were Mason brothers, at the end of the day, we were still pimps.

For me to accept her offer, she would have to pay me more than five racks, for one, because it wasn't enough and two, for her disloyalty. "Make it $10,000 along with the case dismissal and we got a deal, or nothing at all.'

"Hell no, Damion, that's too much. I'll give you $6000 and the case dismissal. I'm not giving you any more."

Since she said that, I'ma see about that. "Time is money, Christie, you know that. I'll be wasting my time driving all the way back to Dallas for $6000. I guess you don't wanna be pleased tonight. I'll take care of the case myself, thanks tho'. You have a good day, I gotta go," I said and then hung up.

She called me right back. "What's up?" I said when I answered.

"Okay, Damion. I'll pay you $10,000 and case dismissal."

"Alright, I'm in Austin right now. Where we meeting up at and what time?" I asked.

"Uhhh, will it be convenient if you can meet me at The W downtown in Dallas at 9 tonight?"

"Yeah, I'll be there."

"Damion, please don't tell anyone about this, please."

"Believe me, I won't," I said, feeling a little guilty inside.

At 10:04 A.M., I received a call from an 817 number I didn't recognize nor have saved in my phone. I answered anyway out of curiosity. "Hello."

"Hey, am I speaking with Damion Johnson?" a white man asked.

"Who wants to know?" I asked politely and curiously.

"I'm Detective Pollok with the Arlington Police Department. I want to ask you a couple questions about the night of May 4th, the night you and Hobert Washington got shot."

I didn't want to lie to him telling him I wasn't Damion. That would be a dead giveaway if I lied and he knew this was me speaking. Evidently, he knew this was my phone number since he asked for me. I didn't think he was calling to investigate or interrogate me for a crime, so I acted friendly and said, "Yes, I'm Damion Johnson. How may I help you, Detective?"

"Is there any way you can come into my office today to talk, Mr. Johnson?"

"Not at this moment. I'm out of town."

"Well, I'd like to ask you some questions concerning the suspects that shot you both that night."

"Yes, go ahead."

"Do you know a guy by the name of James Ford aka Tricks or JP or KB?" he asked, saying names I'd never heard before.

"I would have to say, no, I don't, Detective. It don't ring a bell."

"Well, he's been attacking, robbing, and killing his victims in the Dallas-Fort Worth area. He's been wanted for a couple of months now. We finally caught up with him at a hospital the other morning. He has a brother that goes by the name Rida, who recently got murdered. It was probably behind the robberies they did. You might have been one of their victims. I'm just trying to connect the dots here, Mr. Johnson. He's a known notorious pimp in Dallas. And I see that you have a prior federal human trafficking charge. He might have been an enemy to you, Mr. Johnson."

"Yes, I was convicted of that. Although, I was wrongly accused. I didn't do anything wrong, Detective. Anyway, what does that have to do with anything, Mr. Pollock?" I said defensively, before he started to think that I was still pimping.

"No, no, Mr. Johnson, I'm not accusing you of anything. You're the victim in this investigation. I just want to find out who shot you and Mr. Washington. Do you think maybe one day this week you can come in to take a look at a few photos and identify the shooters?"

"Yes, it's possible, but I don't know when that will be. Like I said before, I'm out of town at the moment. I have been since I been out the hospital."

"This is my office number. I'm Detective Pollok, please give me a call if you remember anything that happened on May 4th so you can find some justice out of the tragedy."

"Okay, I surely will, Detective Pollok. Thank you very much, Detective," I lied. "I want to see whoever is responsible for robbing and shooting us get prosecuted."

As soon as we hung up with each other, I called Christie. "You busy, Christie?"

"Kind of, but what's up?"

"A detective just called me. Do you know a Detective Pollok from Arlington?"

"Yes, I do. What did he say?"

"He called asking a bunch of questions. Look, I don't want to talk about it over the phone. I'll just talk to you tonight when I come over."

"Alright. Have a good day."

"You too," I told her, then I disconnected the call.

I wonder how this detective got my fucking number, my personal number at that. Even though he didn't sound like he was trying to arrest me, I still couldn't trust him. Detectives played trickery games. I didn't know if I should get a new phone number or keep this one. I didn't do anything on this phone that could get me arrested. For that reason, I knew one thing, I didn't need to do any pimpin' in Dallas-Fort Worth.

A couple hours later, I picked Jennifer up at the firm that bailed her out, across the street from one of Travis County jails.

As soon as she got in the car, she said, "Thanks so much,

Money Game

Monopoly. I called my brother and mom, they say they were busy. And my damn mom complained about me getting locked up again, saying she really didn't want to help me this time."

"I told you I got you. You don't have to worry about the bond or your case. There's a lawyer that's handling everything." Then I got straight to the point. "So, what did you mean by you'll do anything to pay me back," I said while staring her in the eyes.

"I meant I'll do anything to pay you back. I don't know about choosing up with you, Monopoly. I've heard the stories from the girls at the club. I don't want to go through that." Her eyes and the movement of her fingers indicated she was feeling dreadful.

"Look, Jennifer, you don't have to be afraid of anything. Their stories might be true, but I know you didn't hear any of that from my queens. I operate a whole different way. You had to be curious about a pimp in some kind of way, because you called me. And I don't know anything about your family, but I was there for you today when you needed my help. I got you right out, using one of my connects. And that will happen every time if you were mine." I changed the subject, letting what I said sink in, and asked, "What did you get locked up for?"

"DWI. It's a felony now."

"Did they tell you what impound yo' car went to?"

"Yep, where it always goes. It's on the north side. I'll show you where it's at," she told me.

Before we made it to the impound, Jennifer said, "You know what, Monopoly, I'm choose up with you."

"Are you sure about that?"

"Yes, I'm sure. I like you."

"What made you choose?" I was curious on why, so I could keep it up and appeal to her liking when I was with her.

"I like your style. And you're handsome. You're good company too." I could tell her ex was black also. I could tell from the way she looked at me. If I was her first, she would have said so. It was like any man and woman who were messing around with someone outside their race for the first time. Majority of the time, they would have made it known.

# Smoove Dolla

I nodded my head. "Best choice. You got taste. Since you with me now, there's some things that will have to change so you don't end up back in this situation. I don't want you driving while you been drinking. I don't want you catching any more cases like that. One of my other hoes will drive you if you want to drink, okay."

I laced her up with my rules on the way to impound and then on the way to her hotel room on our phones.

For the rest of Monday, I was with my hoes while they were making calls, until it was my time to head towards Dallas. I let Poppa stay at the room with my hoes to protect them if they needed it while I was away.

I chopped up game with Erika the whole way to The W Hotel in Downtown Dallas. I took her along with me because I didn't want her at the room with my other hoes. She was on her period, and didn't make any sense for her to be around if she wasn't working. We got a room on the same floor Christie was on. After I showered, did my hygiene, and dressed up in a casual Polo fit, I went to Christie's room.

When Christie opened the door, I was in awe of what I saw. I couldn't stop my eyes from roaming up and down her amazing body. She greeted me with a lovely white smile. Her straight, long blonde hair was hanging down her back, a few inches from her plump ass. Her eyebrows were arched and thin lined, and she wore red lipstick with gold, triangle-shaped earrings to match. Her face was made up lovely with a little bit of makeup, and her big juicy breasts were poking out of her red lace bra. Her waist line was small and her stomach flat. Her camel toe hung down in red lace panties between her toned legs that were in red stockings that came up to her mid-thighs. She also had on a pair of red, six-inch heels. At age 46, she could put a lot of younger women to shame. I never imagined that I would have this opportunity to fuck Christie. Shit, it wasn't like I had been wanting to or was planning on it. It surprised me that she wanted me to.

"You look amazing, Christie," I told her.

"Really, you like?" she asked while waving her hands down her body.

"No, I love it," I told her.

She smiled and then said, "You look good yourself, Tunke."

"Thanks."

She grabbed my hand and said, "Follow me."

A part of me wanted to pull back because of Tight Game, but a big part of me wanted that money, and I was curious about the experience of having her sexually.

As I walked through the hotel living room, I masked my face and put on an act. After sitting down on the couch, she handed me a thick white envelope. "Here's your $10,000."

I ran my thumb through the new blue one-hundred-dollar bills. It looked like it was all there to me. Without folding it, I put it in my front pocket.

She opened a black leather briefcase. It contained a thick three-foot long, red-painted wooden paddle, a red vibrator, a big black whip, a black belt, red plastic nipple clamps, lubrication, and five different sizes of red pussy and anal balls connected together. "As you can see, I like pain. I know you can handle that, right?"

"Of course, I can," I said as I thought differently. I wasn't into this pain shit, but I was sure I could handle it.

"How big are you?"

"Nine inches."

"Pull it out for me, let me see it," she demanded and anxiously helped unbuckle my belt and unzip my zipper on my shorts and pulled my meat out. "Oh yeah, it's perfect," she said, excited, and then she ran her small hand up and down my semi-hard shaft.

"Before we go to the back room, I want to suck your dick." As soon as she pulled my shorts and Gucci boxers down a little more, she dropped to her knees and her mouth went over my dick, and she added both balls inside her mouth with the help of her hand.

After a short while of sucking, my dick swelled inside her mouth. When I grew too big to fit in her mouth, she began to gag, and a few seconds later, she released me and then went up to my dick head while staring me in the eyes. She licked her tongue around it about eight times, and then started sucking on both balls while jacking me off. She hummed on my balls while I fondled both of

Smoove Dolla

her nipples. After a few minutes of sucking my dick, she went up to the head while I ejaculated. She swallowed every drop of nut that came out of me while jacking me off. I could tell she was an old ho. She knew exactly what she was doing, especially making a nigga's toes curl with that good ass head. She got up from the floor and wiped her mouth with a dry face towel and asked, "Did you like that?"

"Yeah, you got some fire ass head. I didn't know you were doing it like that."

She smiled and said, "Oh, you ain't seen nothing yet. Come on, let's go to the back and get to it." While closing the briefcase, her Note 5 got my attention when it started ringing. The name and a photo of Detective Pollok popped up on the screen. I looked at Christie, who had a suspicious look on her face that she tried to cover up. That look told me something funny was going on. And I was gonna find out what it was.

"Answer that motherfucker." I wanted to hear how and what they were talking about.

"I'll talk to him later. I don't want to spoil the moment," she said, while grabbing at my semi-hard dick.

I pushed her hand away from me roughly. "Bitch, I ain't no motherfuckin' sucker, ho! Don't try to play me. Bitch, you either gonna answer this phone or I will. Either way, bitch, I'ma find out why you looking so motherfuckin' crazy. You know what, bitch, I'ma do it for you, fuck you," I said as I touched "Talk," faking like I was going to slide it to the right to answer her phone.

"Okay, okay, Damion, I'll tell you everything," she said as she tried to stop me from answering the phone.

"Well, bitch, get to talking. Why the fuck this fucking detective calling my personal phone?"

"Don't get upset."

"Bitch, you better open your motherfuckin' mouth and tell me what's going on."

"I gave it to him, only to find—"

I cut her off by saying, "Bitch, you what? What you mean you gave it to him?"

212

"To find out who shot Hobert—" I got madder. Before she could finish her sentence, I pushed her over the arm of the couch. I hurried over to her, as she was in a sitting position against the wall. I put my left hand out and started squeezing her face with the palm of my hand and fingers.

"Bitch, keep yo' fucking mouth closed, bitch! That shit has already been handled, stupid bitch!"

I released my hand and slapped her hard with my right hand. When she flicked her head back towards me, making her hair come off her reddened face, an evil grin appeared on her face. "You crazy, pain freak ass bitch."

"Let me get the fuck out this room," I said to myself while I pulled my shorts up, zipped up, and buckled my belt.

I started walking towards the door. "Where do you think you're going? Come back here or give me my damn money back." I continued to walk without saying anything, then she said, "You know, I can call the police and tell them what you just did to me. Tell them how you just robbed and attempted to rape me."

I looked back at her, giving that bitch a look like I'll kill you if you did. She still had that same smile on her face. I changed my mind from going over there and smashing on her. That's what she wanted me to do, she loved pain. I wasn't going to give her the satisfaction she wanted. I knew she couldn't and wouldn't call the police, but I still took two pictures of all the sex toys inside the briefcase and her in lingerie as quick as I could, just in case she did do what she spoke of doing. Anyway, we were both dealing with the Masons and we both had power, so we couldn't just do each other that way. She was just running her mouth, wanting me to react.

I went and sat in my Rolls Royce for a while, trying to calm my mind. Instead of going back to the room where Erika was, I went to go see my daughter Nyla since I was in Dallas. The sight of her and love from her could always humble me and put a smile on my face.

I went to Nayla's mother's house and spent the night with my daughter. My daughter's mother, Cassie, was cool with that. She was my best friend. I didn't have any drama from Cassie. I wanted it to stay that way between us. Communication and not having sex with her was the reason. We got along better and easier without sex for seven and half years. Having sex with any and everybody you meet or friends you have in your life wasn't cool and no good to me. Some people don't know how to deal with and control the anxiety that came with sex. Basically, sex cut short some friendships that would otherwise deepen and last longer. It lessened the drama for me. I gave Cassie seven grand for the both of them and gave Nayla $1000 to put in her closet if she ever needed it for something.

It was 9:55 P.M. Since Nayla was happy to see me and a night owl like her daddy, I let her stay up until midnight. We talked and played until midnight arrived, and then I made her go to sleep for school tomorrow. Cassie and I talked for hours until we fell asleep.


And believe if a hoe jump outta pocket in my stable, she gone get gone like a rocket. I refuse to beat a hoe physically, I'll settle to whoop that bitch brain and leave a stain of my game.
— Professor


Real game is not transparent. The key is to train yourself to read game. Once you peep it, you will enter into all situations with boldness and confidence.
— Pimpin' Ken
The Art of Human Chess
A Study Guide of Winning

## Chapter 12

Early the next morning, I woke Nayla up for school. Before I took her to school, we had breakfast at IHOP for forty minutes. Afterwards, I picked Erika up from The W Hotel then chilled at 8Ball's crib in South Dallas for hours, and then headed back to Austin.

The next day around noon, I got a call from Rose's homegirls, Sarah and Heather, and I talked to them both for 17 minutes before I told Rose to go pick them up in her new 2012 Bentley Mulsanne. I made up an excuse that we already had too many cars out here and we didn't need any more, so Sarah didn't have to drive to Austin in her car. I only did that so I could listen to their whole conversation on the ride to Austin.

While Rose made the two-and-a-half-hour drive to Arlington, I laced her up on what to do and she laced me up on her friends' likes, dislikes, what motivated them, where they were from, and how long she had known them.

She left me on the phone when they got into the car. "Heeeeey, bitch!" one of them said excitedly, happy to see Rose.

After the three expressed their greetings and exchanged compliments towards each other, one of their friends turned the radio up loud and said, "This ride is sick, Rose."

"Damn, Heather. Turn that shit down. Anyway, this is the perfect time to ask me whatever you want to know, because things are going to be different now," Rose mentioned.

"How different, Rose?" Heather asked curiously after the music was turned down

"Just a little different, not in a bad way. We down with pimpin' now. We gotta follow a program that I know will be good for us all. The old way of doing things is over. Plus, we will be making triple the money for doing less work. Monopoly is everything we ever wanted in a man. Everything we ever wanted to accomplish, we can with Monopoly as our pimp. Look at me, I'm riding in this year's Bentley. And it only took three weeks of hustling to get. It would've taken me months to get on my own." Rose was running her tape. Hearing her made me proud of her and my decision on making her my bottom. I copped a winner for sure.

"Is the car in your name or his?" Heather asked.

"Of course, it's in my name. He's not like that. Plus, I worked for it. And yes, if I was to leave him right now, I can take my car with me. But I won't be leaving him. I'm so far gone into him that I feel I love him."

"Damn, bitch, you love him now?"

"Yeah, I got love for him. I'm not complaining about nothing he does. I love how he pimps, and who he is. He's a good man and he's a man of his word. He hasn't even demanded the pussy yet like some of these fake pimps do, so I can't do nothing but respect and love all that," Rose said defensively.

"Destiny said he brainwashed you, but I see why you're so into him," Sarah mentioned. "I knew there was something special about him when we went to that party he threw."

"He is special. He really is a good pimp. I'm for him all the way, and I need y'all to do the same. Y'all my girls, y'all both know I got y'all back and I wouldn't put y'all in a situation to get hurt and fucked over. Thanks for choosing Monopoly. I needed y'all here with me. I just hate Des didn't choose, but I do understand what she went through with that pimp."

"Yeah, I went through the same abusive shit with that piece of shit pimp I was with. I feel her pain. I hope Monopoly isn't on no gorilla shit," Heather said in annoyance, really wanting some more reassurance about me from Rose.

"Trust me, bitch, he isn't. He will check an out of pocket ho quick, but he's cool, you'll see," Rose confirmed.

"How many girls does he have in all?" Heather asked.

"I don't know, I think he has a few more out of town. All I know is the five hoes at the room with us."

"Are they bread winners or are they busted up?" Sarah asked.

"They look good. They're good at what they do, but they gone have to step their game up fucking with us, tho'. You know how we do it when we get together."

"Hell yeah, you already know how we do it. We get money, we

get money," Sarah yelled out.

"Y'all bitches are crazy," Rose said while laughing. To me, it sounded like Sarah was dancing and Heather was showering money on her. "Y'all bitches chill before we get pulled over."

"If we do, I'ma just shake my ass for him so he can let us go," Sarah told Rose. I could tell they liked to have fun, so maybe I could manipulate them with that tactic, amongst others I would use individually on each of them.

"Damn, bitch, what got you so hyped up, you rolling?" Rose asked.

"I'm ready to meet Monopoly! I can't wait to see what he's all about!" Sarah said excitedly.

"You sure about to see. Pick that money up off the floor," Rose said then started giving them a run down on some of my rules.

I stayed on her line a little over an hour before hanging up on their way to Austin. I had faith in her that she would do her job properly without me listening.

When they finally arrived at Extended Stay, I had them come to one of the two rooms where I was waiting. I recognized Sarah and Heather from the Best Cabaret, the event I threw at the lake, and from the photos Rose showed me in her phone of them. Both were tall and very attractive white girls. Heather looked the best out of the two. She was a brunette who stood about 5'9, weighing about 130 pounds. She was very pretty with gorgeous skin that looked like the color of vanilla yogurt. Her hair was curly and came down to her shoulders. Her eyes told me she was curious, but her shoulders said she was feeling a little awkward. Sarah, on the other hand, walked in the door with her nose in the air. That indicated that she was a proud ho and happy to be meeting me. That was what I needed, a ho that was in love with the game. This blonde stood about 5'7, weighing around 115 to 125 pounds, with a nice little ass and a good set of paid breasts on her, resembling Savanna Chrisley in the smile, skin tone, and hair color. They were both ready hoes. I would make sure I sent them on their hoing way after I broke down my game to them.

I introduced myself to them after they came in and sat their bags down on the floor. Hey, I'm Monopoly," I said with a smile as I looked Heather in the eyes.

"Hi, I'm Heather."

"It's nice to meet you, Heather."

"Nice to meet you too."

I turned towards Sarah, who had a smile on her face the moment she walked inside the room, unlike Heather, who seemed a bit suppressed. After Sarah introduced herself, she broke herself with the $4,000 for the both of their choosing fee. I trusted Rose's judgement on her friend, but I wanted another perspective on Heather. I probably would sneak Jennifer on her since they would be dancing at the same clubs. I would use Jennifer to help break down Heather's barriers also. I didn't know if she had hidden objectives for revenge or not. You never know until you find out how the ho's mind ticks. You have some hoes that are like that, going around the city and state getting pimps locked up as well as ruining a pimp's stable. I had to keep eyes on her.

Sarah, on the other hand, I believe we would hit it off good just on the strength that she was into me from Rose drilling into her head about me.

After speaking to Rose and giving her a kiss on her cheek, I escorted them to the sofa to sit down, and Rose sat in the middle of them. I pulled up a chair backwards five feet away. Facing them, I began to lay the foundation down by letting the girls know my game from A to Z, and not Z to A, so we would all be on one accord. From the word go, I let them know that if they had any type of cash flow, then they needed to drop it like it's hot before it gets cold. In other words, a ho needs to break herself coming through my door as Sarah just did. From there, I let them know that I'm Monopoly and Monopoly their Daddy, and I prefer Daddy over everything. Therefore, they shouldn't see, hear, or adhere to none but me. On the other hand, whenever they're out and about, then they should always call, text, or let a family member know their whereabouts at all cost, for their safety. From there, I let them know the house rules and what I expected from each one of them. Next, I told them about getting knocked and if they chose with another pimp, have him call to serve me. Then, I let them know how they should carry and conduct themselves in my company and outside my company.

While I was saying all of this, I couldn't help but notice how Sarah was just staring at me, and how her eyes sparkled every time I said a word. Sarah was definitely into me and probably couldn't wait until she had an one-on-one conversation with me.

After giving them instructions on what I wanted them to do tonight, I went to the other Extended Stay where Bre and CeCe were staying. I didn't want all eight hoes around me or each other. Since CeCe and Bre didn't have kids and didn't have any ties to anything but family, I decided to send them out of town. I gave them a choice of cities they could go to, cities that I had already been numerous times and knew all about, like the hot spots in that particular city. They chose Miami, Florida over Seattle, Washington and Phoenix, Arizona. I bought them their plane tickets for the next day at 3 P.M. The next morning, I took them both shopping at the mall and a couple of other stores in Austin for new clothes, jewelry, and cosmetics for the perfect ho appearance. I also gave them money for a rental car, mace, stun guns their security, and for a lot of condoms. Before sending them to their destination, I gave them a bunch of motivation as well as game.

In the meanwhile, my other hoes danced at a couple clubs until the next morning came around, and then we headed to San Antonio. I got three rooms at the Hilton right by the Riverwalk so we could sight see at the tourist sights. We had made a few days of money out here.

That same day, I got a text from Shae.

Shae
Pinky pregnant
1:36 P.M. Thursday

I hurried up and stepped outside the hotel room in the hallway to call Shae. I didn't want my hoes to hear my conversation. "What you mean Pinky's pregnant, Shae?"

"That's what the text said. You got a baby on the way, Tunke," she sang playfully, then said seriously, "When she was going through withdrawals, she said she think she might be pregnant because she was throwing up too much, so I bought her a test and it came up pregnant."

"Put her on the phone."

Seconds later, Pinky said, "Hello."

"Who else you been fuckin' raw, Pinky?" I asked aggressively.

"Nobody but you, Daddy," she said hurtfully.

"Bitch, you bet not be lying to me. We gon' see when you have the baby. You gon' make me chop yo' ass up." I didn't know whether to believe her or not. She played too many games. I hoped the baby was mine. If it wasn't, I still would take care of the baby as long as she stayed down with me.

There were hoes that got pregnant by their tricks by having unprotected sex and being careless, which was a sin because safety was very important in my stable. If it wasn't mine, it was one of her tricks or her heroin dealer's. I was going to be in their life regardless of whose baby it was. As long as she wanted me to be a part of it, I was there. Although I disliked her drug habit, I still had love for her. "Put Shae back on the phone."

"Yeah," Shae said once she got back on the phone.

I didn't want to talk about Pinky anymore, so I asked her, "I'm glad you texted me. I had thought about your birthday coming up. What do you have planned for your B-Day?"

"It's on a Sunday. I'll be on a plane Saturday morning to Paris. I might be out there till Monday after next or that Tuesday. I'm surprised you remember my birthday."

"Come on, Shae, how can I forget? We been together since we were teenagers. I do something for you every year."

"Since I'm not your bottom anymore and you have a lot going on, you ain't been calling me, so I figured you forgot about me," she said, wanting me to reassure her on how I felt about her since I hadn't been showing her any attention nor had I been calling her.

"I could never forget about you, Shae, ever. You still mean a lot to me and always will. What you doin' that Friday?"

"I have nothing planned. Why, what's sup?"

"We spending Friday together then, okay," I told her.

"Ok. You know I'll love that."

After three days of making money, I took my hoes out on the town of San Antonio. The sun in mid-day was a hot, blazin' 95 degrees outside. Since they wanted to go swimming, I took them to Six Flags Wet N' Wild after we went shopping on the River Walk.

Later that evening, we went to a Mexican restaurant called El Rio Grande on the Riverfront. I was told by a couple of San Antonians that this restaurant was the best Mexican food restaurant in the city. Mexican food was my favorite food, so I couldn't wait to try their food out.

Seconds later, after the waiter left our big table from getting our orders, I noticed two Hispanic chicks eyeing me and giggling. One of them darted her eyes when I looked at her, while caressing her glass. I excused myself away from my queens then made my way over to their table.

"Hey, I'm Monopoly, how are you two ladies doing?" I asked with a smile.

"We're doing good, Monopoly. I'm Nicole," the chubby one said with a big smile on her face.

Then I looked at the pretty, petite one. "Hello. Anna," she said in a strong Mexican accent.

"I see you both haven't eaten yet, won't you two join us? I'll take care of the tab."

"Ok," Nicole said, and then told Anna something in Spanish. I guess she didn't speak English.

Anna nodded in agreement with no hesitation and with a grin on her face.

After talking with them for almost an hour, I found out they were cousins. Nicole was born and raised in San Antonio. Anna wan born and raised in Mexico and had been living here in San Antonio for almost seven months now with her mom. She and her mother were both immigrants from Mexico. Nicole was 21 and Anna was 19. I found all that out through Nicole. My guess was right, Anna only spoke Spanish. When I found out Anna was an immigrant, I changed my mind about letting her in my stable. I wasn't about to make the desperate move some young pimps as well as up and coming pimps made when they came across a young, ready teenager or immigrant woman. That shit would have a nigga facing federal charges. I didn't want that. Even though I did want to pimp them, my best move was to move around away from them. Although, I did get their numbers and would call them when I found out a way to have Anna around legally.

My hoes and I left the restaurant after being there two hours. When Friday came around, I met up with Shae at Cedric's house in Mesquite to take some photos together for her birthday. Since she liked boxing as much as me, we went to a Friday fight that was displayed in the Uptown District in Dallas in the daytime and outside. Next, I took her shopping at the North Park Mall and the Galleria, spending close to 25 grand. We went to Arlington to drop off our bags at her house along with her Chevy Impala. At 7 P.M., I took her to a comedy club in Arlington called Improv. We had fun and enjoyed ourselves together that whole day, like we always did when we went out, especially when fun was our objective.

While we were talking over "Emergency" by Tank in the parking lot at Randall Mill Park, I received a call from Pinky. This past Wednesday, I let her go to her mom's house. According to Shae, she was off drugs and didn't have any symptoms of having withdrawals. I let her go to test her to see if she would go get high. I hoped she was staying strong and not using. It would have really hurt to find out she was back using heroin again while my seed was inside her.

My phone was hooked up to my AUX cable in my Rolls Royce, so when I answered the call, the sounds of Pinky crying blurted out the speakers. "Please don't shoot me, please!"

"Bitch, shut the fuck up! You about to make me some re-up money!" a man with a deep, raspy voice said, sounding like he was high on something.

"Ok, ok, I'll do it. I'll do whatever want me to, just please don't hurt me, please. I know a trick in Arlington. He'll pay big. I'm supposed to be meeting up with him."

"Yeah, call him. Hurry up! Put him on speaker too, bitch!"

I put my phone on mute and then looked at Shae to see her looking at me with a confused look on her face. It probably was the same look I had on my face. "Do you believe this shit? This shit gotta be a set up. What you think?"

"I think it's real. Got to be real. She's a faggot bitch for sure, but she wouldn't set you up, baby. She loves you, she wouldn't do you like that. This is real, Tunke."

I couldn't hear the wind hitting up against the phone anymore, so she must have disconnected the phone call. A few seconds later, she called right back. "Hey, can we meet up right now?" There was no way she was off drugs. She couldn't be off in this type of situation. I shook my head at this shit. If this bitch wasn't pregnant, I probably would've hung up the phone and let her deal with this on her own, but she was, and I had love for Pinky.

"Yea," I said dryly.

"Ok. What would you like to do with me?" she asked in her sexy voice.

"I want 30 minutes, head and pussy."

"That'll be $450."

I'd been dealing with hoes for seven years now, so I knew the way tricks talked to them. I wanted to sound believable, so I bargained, "That's too much. I got $400 for you."

"That will do. Are you at home in Arlington?"

"You can't come to my house. My wife is home. I'm at Randall Mill Park off Fielder and Randall Mill. We'll have to do something in the car like last time."

She slightly moaned. "That's cool with me. I can't wait, I'll be there in ten minutes," she told me.

When we hung up, I quickly told Shae my plan. Shae got out the passenger door to get in the back seat and waited until they arrived.

As soon as I saw lights coming down the dark road nineteen minutes later, I picked up my pistol out my lap, hurried out the RR, and went to hide behind a huge tree in the near distance. Every street light out here was on and shining bright, but there still were a bunch of dark spots around the park, especially where we were. There were three cars in the waterpark and baseball field parking lot. There was one car in the pond's parking lot with us, but they weren't inside their car. The only thing I had to watch out for were the people who were out walking and running and coming back to their cars.

He parked two car spaces away from mine. From my view, Shae was just a dark figure in a car. I couldn't tell the gender of the figure. She was slumped down, posing as me.

Pinky got out the truck, then started walking towards the Rolls Royce and opened the back door. She paused for a few seconds and then returned to the old black pickup truck, to give the dude the $400 that Shae had given her. She headed back to my car and got in the backseat. Shae and Pinky both laid down where no one could see them anymore.

The dude in the black pickup truck looked at the Rolls Royce for five seconds and then started doing something on a phone, because I could see the reflection of the light from the phone on his dark face. I started creeping up to the truck from the side. I hoped he didn't look up and see me coming towards him, because I didn't want to kill him nor get shot myself, but I was sure the phone had his attention.

When I got to the truck, I opened the door while pointing my gun to his head as fast as I could.

"Don't try to reach for that gun of yours. I'ma kill you if you do. Now, put yo' hands behind yo' seat." The dark-skinned man was sweating hard like he was on an ex pill. He didn't move or say anything. I knew he was thinking about his next move, so I said, "Don't play with me, I will kill you."

While he was putting his hands behind the seat, he attempted to reach for his gun, but he was too slow. I was ready for him to make a move. I already had my gun sideways, so I hit him four times in the mouth with the butt of the gun, making him yell out in pain. Blood instantly gushed out from me splitting his shit wide open. He put his hands up over his face. "Bitch nigga, I told you don't move."

I put my gun in my waistband to grab Pinky's phone out his lap. Thank God he didn't read our text messages to one another, because he would have caught on to our play. This stupid motherfucker was

224

looking through her photo gallery.

I put Pinky's phone in my pocket while I pointed his pistol at him. I reached over him, took the keys out the ignition, and then threw them to the floor of the passenger's side.

I found an open area on his head that he didn't have protected with his hands and arms, and started pistol whipping him. "You bitch ass nigga. A real pimp is a gentleman. I hope you catch a bullet next time you pull this shit off," I said as I hit him for the 10th time.

While he yelled in pain, he laid his head on the steering wheel, holding his face in his hand after I stopped.

I could've went into his pocket to get his wallet if he had one, but I didn't want any blood on me. I shut his door, hurried around to the passenger door, opened it with my shirt, and then went into his glove compartment. I took a bunch of his documents and stuffed them into my pocket.

Even though I would always remember how he looked, I still wanted to know his name and address just in case he found out who did this to him. I wanted to be on my toes.

I took my shirt off, put my hands in my shirt, wiped the gun off, and then threw his pistol into the pond. I got in the backseat of my car. "Shae, get in the front seat and drive."

Trying to calm myself and not hurt Pinky was hard for me at the moment. The thought of her being back on drugs caused me to get madder. She didn't have to tell me she was using again or prostituting on the track again. I already knew, her actions told me. What just took place would have never occurred if she wasn't doing those things.

While Shae drove on the road through the park heading out, I rushed Pinky, choking the shit out of her, pressing the whole side of her face into the light tinted window. "What the fuck is wrong with you, bitch? Huh, bitch? You done lost yo' fuckin' mind or something, huh, bitch?"

"No, Daddy. I'm sorry. I'm sorry, Daddy," she said while crying heavily, holding my wrist.

I pushed her head into the glass, causing a loud thump noise from the impact. "Bitch, you ain't sorry, ho, funky ass bitch. Every time I turn around you doing some shit you ain't supposed to be doing, you faggot, hard-headed ass ho." I hit her head up against the window hard once again while still choking her.

I felt the car stop and then a hand touch me on my shoulder. "Please stop, Tunke, please. She pregnant with your baby. She can be helped. We can help her. Please stop it, this not you, Tunke," Shae told me.

I almost forgot Shae wasn't my bottom anymore. I was about to check her for getting in a pimp's business, but I changed my mind. Anyway, I couldn't get mad at her. She did the right thing telling me to stop. Niggas only hit and put their hands on females when they felt they didn't have control over the situation or the woman, or weren't able to handle her verbally, or the man was insecure and weak, lacking control of himself. The reason why I put my hands on Pinky was because I was so caught up in my feelings about Pinky that I lost control. Shae recognized that and brought me out that state of mind. A man had to learn self-discipline and come up with mental and verbal ways to deal with these kind of situations, if not, he would self-destruct. In situations like these, the war was not physical.

I released her from my tight grip and asked her, "What hotel you staying at?"

"I haven't been staying at no hotel," she said while crying.

"Where all your shit at?

"Everything's at my momma's house. That's where I been since I left Shae's house."

I was a little skeptical about taking her to her mother's. She might want to stay there. If she did that I would have to abandon her and our baby for some time. I want allow her to be my down fall so the best thing I could do is let her go and forget about her. A person could only help or be down with someone for so long without seeing progress in that person. If they can't help themselves you can't help them, you have to let them go. Just maybe one day, after my child was born, if she's not off drugs, I could take Pinky to court for custody of my baby.

"You getting off drugs while you pregnant with my baby,

Pinky. I'm putting you in rehab tomorrow. If you relapse when you get out, you lost me forever. Shae, you remember where her mom lives on the Southside?'

"Yeah, I remember."

"Head that way, that's where we going."

We made it to her mom's duplex in Fort Worth in seventeen minutes. I put on a white t-shirt I had in my truck before going inside with Pinky. I walked inside with her to make sure she comes out with me and to help her get her things.

Inside the house there wasn't much furniture but only a grey long couch, a love seat, and a glass table in the middle of the living room. There were two lamps standing up on two small tables. different color sheets instead of blinds were covering all the windows in the duplex. There were two old televisions, the oldest and biggest one was on the bottom of the other one. She introduced me as her man to her white mother and mixed younger sister who looked the age of 12 years old. Then I followed her to her room which didn't have nothing but a queen size mattress on the floor and a bunch of cloths in clear plastic bags around the room.

She handed me $650. "That's what I have left. I was gonna give my momma $200 when I got back. Can she have it please? She really needs it."

"Yea, I'll give it to her. Where the heroin at?"

She looked down in embarrassment. I lifted her chin back up with my finger. "This is the only way you can get off Lexi. Where is it?"

"I don't have no more. I snorted what I had." I gave her a look like I didn't believe her. "I'm serious. I don't have no more."

I didn't say anything else, I just picked up her big Gucci bag and then we walked into the living room. I put the bag down then pulled out the money she just gave me, peeled off three hundred-dollar bills and handed them to her mom, Sandra. The only reason why I gave her $300 was because it seemed like Sandra and her little sister, Kimberly, needed it from the way things looked in their home.

"I hope you not pimping my daughter out," her mom said to me.

She had to say something about Pinky's lifestyle. It was only right I added my two cents in about what Lexi was doing in the streets, so I told her in the most respectful way I could think of at the moment. "I hope you not blaming me for her prostituting and using drugs. If I had the choice of her life, she wouldn't be doing nothing of what she's doing. I picked her up like this when I met her months ago. I'm just tryna dust off these bad habits she picked up. You probably the reason why she doing it. Oh yea, she told me about how you put men before her. And how you allowed yo' boyfriend to abuse her and punch on her." I became mad at that thought. So many times I'd heard stories from some of my ex-hoes about getting raped, molested, and abused in some kind of way by men in their house growing up. Some males were fucked up and didn't deserve to live. "Well, let him do it again. I promise you, he'll be a dead man. Go to the car, Lexi."

"Lexi, don't leave this house with him. You can stay here. You don't need him. We can get through this together," Sandra said, pleading to Pinky.

"I have to, Momma. I do need him."

I opened the front door and said, serious, "Go get in the car, Lexi."

She walked out the door, looking sad with her head down. "And Ms. Sandra, you don't have to worry, she won't be prostituting or using drugs, if I got anything to do with it. She about to take care of herself and our child that's inside her. You got my word, I'll bring her back so you two can fix y'all relationship as mother and daughter. I won't keep her away from you. I want her happy and doing good in life too," I said, then followed Pinky out the door and closed it behind me.

On the ride to Shae's crib, I called CeCe and Bre to check up on them. They should be good because they worked in a ho house in Miami. Most ho houses provided protection and certain needs for hoes. That made it where I could pimp from afar for a couple weeks until I visited them or made them come back to where I was.

After I finished the phone call with them, I called my bottom bitch, Rose, to check on them.

"Hey, Daddy," she said as soon as she answered.

"Hey, baby, what's goin' on?"

"The usual. Getting at this money out here."

"That's wuz up. Them hoes been in pocket over there?"

"Yes, Daddy, they are. Everything's going good so far."

"I didn't want anything, just calling to check on y'all. I don't know if I'ma be out there tomorrow. I'll let you know in the morning. Wire that money to me in the morning, okay."

"Okay, I will. Is there anything else you want me to do?" Rose asked.

"Naw, that's it for now. I'll call you tomorrow and you can call me whenever."

Thirteen minutes later, we walked into Shae's house. Pinky followed me to my room. I sat her bag down on the floor at the foot of the bed.

While I was taking her phone and purse away from her, I said, "Go get in the tub. I'll be back in here to talk to you, to let you know what the plan is."

"Okay," she said while picking up her Gucci bag, and then sat it on the bed.

I went into Shae's room, put Pinky's phone in her purse, and sat it on the dresser.

"So, what do you have planned for Pinky?" she asked while putting up some of the things we bought today.

"I'm taking her to a rehab center in Irving where Fancy works at."

"Damn, she do work at a rehab. I forgot about that."

"I just hope it works this time. If it don't, I'ma have to cut all ties with her completely. I'm not 'bout to waste any more of my time fucking with her."

"I hope it works too. I like Pinky. I believe it'll work, but we shall see."

"Yeah, we shall see."

Shae handed me a big, long, black gift jewelry box. "I know it's early, but I won't be here Sunday. Happy Father's Day, Tunke. Thanks for being a father figure in my life."

Damn, I totally forgot about Father's Day being a day away, let alone this month. I'd been doing so much since I been out the hospital that I paid no attention to the holidays.

I opened the box, and there was a thick yellow-gold chain that was about 25 to 30 inches long.

Van Cleef diamonds and princess-cut white sapphires were on top of the chain and gold medallion. The initials AOH, which meant ALL OFF a HO, was a custom-made bit medallion. "Thanks, baby, I love this." I kissed and then hugged her. I looked back at her and said, "I'm curious, how much did this cost?"

She smiled. She already knew where I was going with my question. "It cost 95 hundred. I know I spent too much, but I couldn't resist buying you something big for Father's Day to show my appreciation for everything you've done for me."

I wanted to say something about her budgeting her money, but it wasn't an appropriate time to do so. The thing I could do was get lost in the moment with her and not mention how careless she was with the money I put up for her business.

After talking with Shae for about half an hour, I went back into my room. Pinky was rubbing raspberry lotion on her pretty, short legs. "You alright, baby?"

"Yeah," she said as she started rubbing it on her cute feet.

I sat on the bed, took her well-pedicured feet, and lifted her leg on top of my thigh, then squeezed lotion in my hand and started rubbing it into her skin while massaging it at the same time with both hands. I did that for a while then got up behind her and started rubbing on her neck and back.

"You know I care about you and I love you, right?" I asked her.

She waited five seconds before she mumbled, "Yea."

I turned her back around so she could face me as I stood. "You don't sound too sure about that, Lexi. I understand why you feel that way, tho'. I'm hard on you because you need it, and I want the best for you. It hurts to see you using drugs. Sometimes I be wanting to give up on you. But since you're pregnant, I'm gonna do my best to help you get off that shit. I want to see you doing good in life. You're gonna have to learn how to fight and have control over what you're going through in order to quit using. I know you can do it. I believe in you. If I didn't think you could, you wouldn't be here right now, believe that. Anyway, we'll talk in the morning. Get some rest. I'm taking you to a rehab in the morning. A friend of mine will be helping you."

"Thanks, Daddy," she said with a baby face look.

"You welcome. You know I got chu. Good night, baby. I love you."

"Good night, Daddy. I love you too."

Majority of the girls in the low level of prostitution were on drugs. I'd seen some of the most beautiful, gifted, and talented women using drugs. Either they were shooting it, snorting, and/or smoking through pipe or lace, sometimes even going so far as to putting drugs in their anus to get higher. As I took a look back at my childhood in my projects in the ghetto streets of sunny South Dallas, I'd seen a lot of people hooked on all types of drugs, turning beautiful young girls and women into ugly females. The same with the males. I'd witnessed people at the young age of 11 using drugs. It wasn't that I looked down on drug users, it was the fact I didn't like them because of what they did to people. They destroyed.

So, I made a vow to myself when I was 16 to not fall victim to drugs. I was a pimp. How would it look to my hoes if I was high all the time...? Stupid! My hoes would follow my lead. How could I control, supply, and protect my hoes if I was high and drunk? At the beginning of my pimp career, I listened to my hoes' life stories and problems, and I came to realize that we all had problems of some sort that needed to be solved. Most people used drugs to hide from reality, to escape pain, amongst other reasons. So, I understood Pinky's background and problems she was dealing with. Plus, she was a product of her environment. All that was a big part of why I kept giving her chances. When I told her I loved her, I meant that. I wasn't in love with her at all, but I did have love for her. How could I not? Pinky had made me happy in many ways by putting money in my pocket, being my companion, giving me love, and sex. So it was only right I did something for her in return by getting her off drugs and taking care of her. I owed the best to me and mine.

I gave Pinky a long kiss and then returned back to Shae's room. I took my grill out and brushed my teeth. Afterwards, I got in the tub with Shae.

About forty minutes later, as we let the water out the tub, Shae said, "I love you, Tunke."

I turned her head towards mine and lowered my head. "I love you too, Shae," I mentioned before I started tongue kissing her passionately. About five minutes later, I began to rub her big breasts and then fondled with both nipples.

A while later, I reached my right hand down to play with her pearl tongue. She moaned while we kissed and grinded her hips against my fingers.

"Stand up and face me." When she did that, her body stood up like a beautiful, curvy, brown female statue. Her body glistened with water. Her fat, wet pussy was directly in my face. I started sucking on her pearl tongue. I licked up, down, and around her pearl. I couldn't get in between her legs like I wanted to, so I had her put one foot on top of the side of the tub. I got on my knees in the tub. I feasted on her pussy like it was the Muslim Eid and Thanksgiving. Her leg started to buckle and shake while she held on tightly to the shower rod and wall.

Minutes later, I lifted her up and eased her down on top of me with her legs over my shoulders. As I went inside her, I felt her walls moving, welcoming me with the best greeting ever. I fucked her slow, lifting her up and down on my dick, then I started fucking her fast. I knew she wanted to have an orgasm, so I fucked her like she wanted me to, fast and hard. As I fucked her, she yelled out my name, told me she loved me, how much she missed me, and to keep fucking her, all in that order.

Minutes later, she yelled, "It's coming, Tunke baby, it's coming, baby! Oh my god!" Then she got down off me and started rubbing her pearl tongue roughly.

Seconds later, cum began to squirt out as if she was urinating. Afterwards, we went to her king-sized bed. As I hit her from the back, I smacked her fat, jiggling ass while pulling her sew-in weave with my other hand. About 50 strokes later, I switched positions. I

# Money Game

had her lie on her side with her legs bent, knees on down, hanging off the bed.

She started rocking back at me and we locked eyes for about a minute, and then she looked away, losing herself in the moment of me going in and out of her. About 40 rough strokes later, I ejaculated inside her. My body jerked as I still pumped a few times in her before I collapsed on the side of her. As we laid facing each other, Shae said, "I want some more, baby."

"You know how to get this muthafucka hard again."

After about 40 seconds of her sucking me up, the door opened. It was Pinky in her birthday suit.

"What you want, Lexi?"

"Can I join y'all?" she asked.

"You gon' have to ask Shae. This her time," I told her.

"Shae, can I join in?"

Shae came up from giving me head and then said, "Yeah, come help me keep this dick hard."

As Pinky walked towards the bed, Shae put Marsha Ambrosius' Pandora radio station on her surround sound connected to her phone. Marsha Ambrosius' "Late Nights Early Mornings" was the first song to blast out the speakers. I wanted to talk some shit while I fucked both of them, but the music was loud. Although it was loud, it really did make the mood just right. I would just have to let my body talk tonight since she set the mood she wanted.

The both of them sucked my dick at the same time. Shae had the head of it in her mouth, and Pinky had the side of it in hers. Next, Shae started going up and down while Pinky sucked my balls. The next song to come on was "Freakin' Me" by Jamie Foxx featuring Marsha Ambrosius.

Shae got on top of me in a cowgirl position. Shae eased down on my dick, and then started bouncing her fat, jiggly ass. Pinky watched my facial expressions as Shae put it down on me. Pinky then grabbed two handfuls of Shae's meaty ass cheeks, picking her ass up and slamming it down on me. It felt so good being inside Shae.

Two minutes later, Pinky got on top of me and started riding my face. I had my arms up under her legs, hugging her thick thighs as she held on to the brown wooden backboard.

About two R&B songs later, Pinky lay on her back with her legs behind her head while I pounded her pussy, standing up on the floor. Shae was on all fours on top of her, with her ass tooted up in the air. While I gave Pinky backshots, I had my face in between Shae's ass cheeks. Shae's cheeks bounced and jiggled all over my tongue, ears, and the side of my face. As Shae grinded on my face, my tongue danced back and forth from her asshole to her clitoris multiple times.

After a while, I had both of them bent over on their knees side by side in front of me while I stood up off the bed. As I fucked Shae from the back, I fingered Pinky's asshole with my middle finger and then after a while, with two fingers. They tongue kissed. I spanked Shae hard twice on both cheeks and then I did the same to Pinky, who was fondling her nipple.

Once Shae got her nut, I went into Pinky from the back.

After I made Pinky cum, we all got into the shower together because we were all sweaty. I swear these two girls were some freaks. We ended up freaking in the bathroom. Pinky stayed in the tub playing with her pearl tongue, sitting down in the tub with the water from the shower head spurting directly to her pearl tongue. Pinky watched me as I had Shae in her favorite position, holding on to the sink bent over, pounding her from the back while we looked into each other's eyes through the mirror.

We went on a fucking marathon until about four something in the morning.

Money Game

## Chapter 13

The next morning, I woke up early feeling exhausted from the night before, but I still got out the bed. Tomorrow was Shae's birthday, the same day as Father's Day. I wanted her to stay asleep and wake up to see her gift beside her while Pinky and I were gone. I took a quick shower in my bathroom, then put on a new Versace fit that looked really good on me. Next, I woke Pinky up quietly, holding my pointing finger up to my lips, making her get out the bed as lightly as she could.

While she was in the shower, I went to my Rolls Royce to get Shae's present. It was in a small, pink bathroom trashcan that had small hearts decorated all over the outside. Inside the trashcan was some red, thin decoration paper neatly placed along with a 24-karat gold woman's wrist watch in a black jewelry box that cost me $1,850 from Kay Jewelers. There was a message in my gift to her. The trashcan symbolized waste. The watch represented time. I also wrote a poem expressing my feelings for her on a pink-colored paper. It read:

You mean more to me than a bitch that's my bottom
You're my ride or die through any situation or problem
In this game, we've seen times of joy and times of misery
In this life, you and I can continue on making history
Whatever you need, it ain't nothing for me to provide
Especially, since you've always been by my side
Most women ain't built for this let alone designed
But you came in it ready to get money and grind
I would tell you all of my goals and plans
That's why you deserve this watch in a trashcan
You never ran when it turned into a struggle
You stood by me and we continued to hustle
Out of all the girls you're the only one that I want to keep for a lifetime
This watch in this trash means life without you is a waste of time.

Even though the gift was concerning her life as my bottom bitch, it was the thought that counted when bringing her a gift, the sweet words, and remembering her birthday that mattered the most. I knew it was the small things that mattered when it came to a female, so I knew she would love my gift. Plus, she loved jewelry.

Before I left, I put the trashcan in front of her phone on her nightstand. Her flight didn't leave until 3 P.M., so I could leave her asleep. I knew she would be reaching for her phone to call me, asking why I didn't wake her up before now.

Ten minutes out from our arrival to the rehabilitation center, Shae called thanking me for her gift and that she loved it. We talked until we reached our destination. I wished her fun on her trip, and then we hung up.

Fancy was on her computer typing when we walked up to her office door. I cleared my throat to get her attention. She looked up and greeted us with a white, gorgeous smile. "Hey you, come on in. It's a surprise to see you. What brings you here today?"

"You know what they say, you can't forget about your first." Fancy was my first real ho in the game back then. The ho that Tight Game jugged me with when I was seventeen years old. She was one of my top money makers back then before I went to prison for pimpin'. When I went to prison, she decided to get out the game, do something legal with her life, and became a counselor. She kept it real and stayed in touch with me in federal prison and after I was released. Most times, you don't get that loyalty out of hoes. That was very rare for a ho to do.

"Yeah, yeah, whatever," she said.

"I know I didn't call you ahead of time to schedule an appointment, but it's really an emergency. She's pregnant and hooked on heroin. I know you're good at what you do and you can help her.

"Of course, I can help," she said seriously with sympathy. "That is if she wants the help."

After I introduced them, I left the office, letting them talk alone for about twenty minutes. After they finished talking, Pinky and I talked in the waiting room area. "You ready for this change, Lexi?"

"Yes, I'm ready," she said with confidence. "Thank you so much, Tunke, for getting me help. I 'preciate it."

"I told you I got chu. You in the best of hands. You just gotta do your part. Do what you gotta do for yourself, for us, and ours. It's gonna be hard, you know that, but all you gotta do is fight and believe in yoself. You got this, Lexi, you can overcome this shit."

"I am. Thanks, Daddy," she said while giving me a tight hug.

"You're welcome."

"I love you, Daddy."

"I love you too. I'm about to go. Stay strong and stay firm."

She cried and squeezed my arm tighter and said, "I don't want you to leave, Tunke. Can you stay for a little bit longer, please, Daddy?"

"I can't stay. I gotta get back to business, baby, but I promise you when you get released from here, we gon' spend the whole day together. If you want to talk to me, just let Fancy know, and she'll call me for you."

After I left from talking with Pinky, I went to Fancy's office. The door was cracked an inch. I tapped on it until it opened wider, where I could see with both of my eyes. She was standing behind her desk on the office phone. As I walked into her colorful modern office, she put up a finger and mouthed, 'hold on a minute.'

I sat in her chair for about ten seconds before her looks started to get the best of me. She stood tall, wearing a blue, tight-fitted designer dress. I got up and closed and locked the door. I was about to fuck with her, to see if I still had my way with her sexually. The last time I fucked her was a year ago when she was engaged. She was married now.

She looked at me when I got up behind her, but I didn't pay her no mind. I raised her dress up over her bare ass, exposing a blue thong. I rubbed my hand up between her thighs then up her ass cheeks. She instantly moved my hand out the way and pulled her dress back down while still on the phone. I stood up from the chair and pulled my dick out. I raised her dress up again, moved her blue thong out the way, and then stuck my raw dick inside her pussy. I put my hand on her back and then lowered her back to where she was bent over, making her drop the phone. She slightly moaned while I pumped in and out of her. She picked the phone back up and said, "Baby, I have to go to a group meeting. I'll have to call you back when it's over, honey." Ten strokes later, she said, "Yes. Uh, uhh." It was a long pause, then she said, "Okay, love you too, honey."

When she hung up the phone, she looked back at me with a beautiful fuck face, like she was loving every thrust inside her. "Ohhh shit, Tunke," she yelled while her whole body shook.

Three minutes later, I felt myself about to nut, so I pumped harder. "Don't fucking nut in me, Tunke."

A few seconds later, I pulled out while ejaculating. I started stroking myself, nutting on her phat ass cheeks. "Damn, that pussy still good and wet like I like it," I said, breathing hard.

She turned around quick and pushed me hard back into the wall. "Why did you fucking do that? I was on the phone with my fucking husband, Tunke," she said, angry.

"You better quit tripping up in this muthafucker, I know that much. It ain't like I forced you to do it. While you were throwing that ass back on me, you should've been pushing me off you then. Don't act like you didn't like it, like you didn't cum."

"You know I liked it. But I can't keep doing this with you. I'm married now, Tunke. We have to move on from the way we used to live. You got me lying to my husband. Can you please quit doing this to me? Respect my marriage," she said while wiping my nut off her ass with a couple of Kleenex. "Is it all off?"

"Yeah, you got it all."

"Is there nut on my dress?" she asked as she pulled her dress down over her ass.

"Naw."

Fancy always liked to fuck me when she was my bottom bitch. Now, since I'd been out of prison and with her being married, it'd been hard for her to resist fucking me when I came around. I only fucked her five times since I'd been released. The only reason why I fucked this time was because I wanted to see if I still had some power over her, and that dress looked amazing on her. More than likely, I would grant her wish and not fuck her again. I did owe her that much for all she'd done for me.

"You know, you could have at least waited until I got off the phone. You didn't have to do that while I was on the phone with my husband, Tunke."

"I couldn't help it, look how sexy you are in that dress."

"Whatever, Tunke." She shook her head then changed the subject. "Anyway, Lexi's beautiful. Where did you find her?"

"In Fort Worth walking the blade."

"Has she been on heroin since you've known her?"

"Yep. You know I normally don't fuck with hoes on heavy drugs, but I gave the bitch a chance because I liked her looks and I knew she'd make a pimp a lot of money. It's been hell dealing with her too. The only reason why I gave her a chance after chance is because she's pregnant. Or else, I would have been left her alone."

"I will do my best, but you know it's all up to her. She's gotta be willing to change," Fancy stated as she took a seat in her recliner chair. I walked around her desk to sit down in the chair in front of it.

"Yeah, I hope she is."

"I heard what happened to you and Hobert. Are you ready for a change after experiencing getting shot and robbed?" she asked. I knew that question was coming up sooner or later.

"Nall, I'm not ready to stop pimpin'."

"You should think about changing your life before you get yourself killed or go back to prison. You know if you go back to prison for pimping, it will be a big setback for you. After all, you have worked hard for what you do have right now. Just think about that, Tunke, okay?"

Fancy sounded just like my mother, Shae, and Tiffany. She was right, but I wasn't ready to change my criminal lifestyle yet. I believed a man only changed when he was tired of living the way he was living, or when he was tired of getting the same results or something else took its place. I wasn't bored with my lifestyle as a pimp. Sometimes, I did think about my exit out the game as well as the consequences of my criminal lifestyle, and how it could cause me to lose a lot. I knew I would have to make a transformation for the greater good of my life as well as make the relationships with my family and friends better sooner or later, because I didn't want to lose anybody close to me over my choices in life. "Ok, I will," I said as I nodded my head, wanting to leave already.

"Do you think Hobert's gonna make it out the coma?" Fancy asked.

"He has the best doctors, which are brothers, monitoring him, so I really hope so. I do believe so. I miss him like a muthafucka."

"I know you do. You two are like father and son. He's a strong man, he'll pull through," she said confidently.

We talked for about 25 minutes, and then I left.

For Father's Day, my daughter gave me the biggest bottle of the latest Polo cologne and the latest Jordans. My four-year-old son didn't give me anything but his presence, which was the perfect gift. My hoes gave me a custom, Tacori Royal, diamond-cut pinky ring and Rolex watch that had to both cost at least $12,000. My traps had been a little over their quota, which meant they had been grinding hard and working together to produce their set quota and buy me that jewelry.

I wanted to do something big for Father's Day, but I hadn't planned for it. I regretted forgetting, because I would've thrown a Father's Day event. Tiffany didn't allow me to take all her kids out to Six Flags Hurricane Harbor, only my son. More than likely, if I had thrown an event, she would have come along with all her children. I really wanted to spend the day with them all, but I understood why she didn't allow them all to come. We hadn't said a word to one another through any source of communication since the day she walked out on me at the hospital until today. I knew her and how her mind worked. She was thinking, since we weren't together, there's no reason for me to take her kids out. Especially when I hadn't been consistent in showing her and my kids no attention that I wanted to be in their lives.

She was right. I'd been selfish, always wanting things to go my way, but it didn't work that way every time. It was a two-way street in any relationship. I could tell she was upset when I went to pick up my son from our house. She barely said fifteen words to me. She made up an excuse so she wouldn't have to be in my presence, talking about she had to be somewhere in thirty minutes. It sounded like some bullshit to me. For her to deny me to spend Father's Day with her children, who saw me as their father, she had to be dating another man. I'd bet money that she was, but I could totally understand why. I hadn't been there. I was always running the streets. She deserved to be happy with a good man that was going to be there for her emotionally, mentally, physically, as well as sexually. As long as she was happy, I wasn't trippin' on her being with someone else. I was cool with that. To apologize for my wrongdoings as her son's father and business partner and get some understanding on things, I would have to plan a date where Tiffany and I went out to eat so we could talk about everything that was going on with us, so we could make things better between us. That would probably be after I got back to the metro plex from being in Houston, Texas.

My Father's Day was perfect. Five of my hoes, three of their young kids, my daughter, and my son all spent six hours at Six Flags Hurricane Harbor. We all enjoyed ourselves. The fun that occurred today had me thinking deeply. It was a beautiful thing seeing my kids happy and enjoying themselves. They were so happy to be in my presence, that it made me feel bad for neglecting them. I made a vow to myself, no matter what, even if I had to sacrifice my time, losing money, or my hoes, I would do whatever I had to do to be in my kids' lives.

Today also had me thinking about my past with my father, on how growing up without him affected my life as a boy. Even though I could call him whenever or just pop up at his house these days, most of my siblings and I weren't close to him like we should be. The only bad thing I could say about my dad was he really wasn't a good father to some of his children, and that had rubbed off on me. I wasn't going to put it all on him, because some of it was my fault also. I could say this about him, he was a good man who was living his purpose in life, which was coaching sports and teaching. Thanks to Tight Game, I had a stand-up man to look up to and be a father figure in my life. I was very grateful to have met and be brothers with Tight game. I'd learned a lot from him. He was a true leader indeed.

The next day, my hoes and I went to Houston, Texas. I got three rooms at the Plainfield Motel off Bissonnet and Highway 59 on the Southwest side. Bissonnet was a popular blade, one of the best tracks in Texas. It was in my top five in the United States. I hadn't fucked with the track out here in about two years. It felt good to be back in the city limits of Houston, Texas after so long. Since we were at the Plainfield Motel, known as the Playin' Field where a lot of pimps and hoes were staying, I made sure I was on my game because I wanted to knock a few hoes out here, and I didn't want to lose none of my hoes. If I did lose mine, so be it. Hoes come and hoes go. The game goes on. All I knew was I was going to pimp hard, at my best, and send my hoes to go make my money.

The money CeCe and Bre were making in Florida, I had them send it to my younger sister in Dallas to hold majority of it for me. The money my hoes made in San Antonio, I had put up in my safe at my penthouse yesterday. I only had $1000 in my pocket now. I didn't need much money on me because I wasn't planning on buying anything that cost a bunch of money or taking my hoes shopping at the Galleria until this coming weekend. Plus, I had about $1700 combined on four debit cards for my hoes, and 2.6 million dollars in my bank accounts from my clothing business, my last job, the small recording deal I signed almost four years ago, songs I'd sold, and songs I got royalty checks for. There wasn't a need to have a lot of cash money on me at one time, especially when my hoes would be going to work tonight to make more money.

A little after we arrived in Houston, I met up with my pimp partna, Pimpin' ANT, on the third tier of the motel, looking out on the balcony at the busy street on Bissonnet.

"That wanna-be cop be threatening hoes, tryna get free pussy from the hoes. Some of these renegade hoes be running to the nigga when Ps be sweating them. This nigga works Thursday thru Monday." As ANT laced me up about what's been going on at Plain Field and the black security guard that worked there, a white, slim,

# Money Game

pretty brunette in a white halter top and blue-jean booty shorts with red house shoes on walked our way, recklessly eyeballing us.

ANT started checking the ho. "Damn, ho, you looking at us like we a movie or something, ho. You know it's pimping going on around here. What, you like this Oscar-winning picture, uhh, ho?" he said as he put his hands on his waist, posing for the ho. "Yeah, put yo' choosing shoes on and nominate this pimpin', ho."

She didn't reply back. All she did was put her head down towards the pink plastic mesh laundry basket full of clothes she was toting, and walked past us. "Yeah, you better keep yo' eyes where they belong before you be my next ho. I'm pimpin' ANT, bitch."

"Who ho is that?" I asked, wanting to know whose loose ho that was.

"My ho if that bitch come back through here," ANT said, and then we both bust out laughing.

"She lucky she wasn't on the track. I would've broke on the bitch for everything. And another ho added to my team." ANT was a dog when it came to pimpin'. He was from Dead End, a hood that was on the southeast side of Houston. He was one of the few good pimps I associated myself with out here in Houston.

The next time I saw the ho ANT checked was at the RaceTrac gas station on Bissonnet, down the street from the motel, later on that evening. I saw her when she walked inside the store before I poured myself a 24-oz cup of tea.

"Hey, handsome, can I talk to you?" I heard from behind me.

I turned towards her, making eye contact with her. "Yeah, wuz up?"

"I wanna choose up with you."

"It cost two Gs to fuck with my pimpin'," I told the ho and then held out my hand, palm up.

"I don't have any money, I just got put out the car with nothing. He kept my phone too."

"Why the fuck you bring yo' pretty ass in this store if you don't have no money?" I said, remembering how ANT got down on the ho the wrong way. She wanted a nigga to soft mack her.

"I saw your car parked outside that I seen you driving earlier, so I came in to choose. I can make that two racks tonight. Just let me post and walk the track at the same time, I'll get it," she said in a New York accent.

"Alright, we'll see, don't come up short. Wuz yo' name?"

"Syn. You gonna call Finesse to serve him?" I knew this Finesse nigga was doing some pimpin' when she brought up serving him, or she just mentioned that so I could call him to make him feel some type of way because she chose up with another pimp. I really didn't want to accept this ho and call this pimp without her properly paying me. But she didn't have her phone nor any clothes, except the ones on her back, so I was going to accept the ho and see what she made tonight. If she didn't make $1000 and up on my choosing fee, I was going to do something to make her leave me on her own. I wasn't tolerating no ho playing with my pimpin'. I thought the ho was making a mad move anyway.

When I called the New York number that she gave me, it took Finesse five rings to answer. "Yo, who this?" he asked.

"This Monopoly. I got some news for you, pimp. Yo' ex-ho, Syn, just chose up, Jack. But I need to know this ho's profile before I accept her in my stable of hoes." I stepped up to the counter to buy two big boxes of Trojan condoms for Syn along with the iced tea for myself. "You got time to chop it up about the ho?"

He must have heard the cashier telling me the cost of what I just bought, because he asked, "Yo, P, you at RaceTrac?"

"Yeah, why, wuz up?"

"I'm about to pull up. I'm two lights away. I'll just come up there to talk to you, kid. I'm in a money-green, 2012 Aston Martin Rapide. It's the only money-green one in the world, so you got no choice but to see a pimp."

I chuckled and then said, "Alright, I'm walking out now. I'll be waiting on you."

We posted up on the side of the ice bag deep freezer, right in front of my Rolls Royce. As I looked out for his Aston Martin, I saw nothing but a bunch of clean and candy-coated slabs, foreign whips, SUVs, and trucks sitting on big rims, and swangas at the gas pumps and parking spots. I couldn't forget about the loud bang in a couple of their trunks that shook the concrete. It was a Monday night, and it was looking like a car show out here. This was an everyday thing for Houston.

If there were cities being nominated for best pimped out rides or best slabs for the Hood Awards, they would have to add Houston in that category. Houston had my vote. H-Town was the home of the swangas, candy paint, pop trunk, screwed and chopped music.

A minute or so later, Finesse pulled up in the Aston Martin at gas pump fourteen with two white girls in the car with him. Now I could see why he had bragged about his car like that, other than the fact he was letting me know he was really getting at some money. He was on stage, and his hoes were his audience. One of the arts to keeping a ho was to brag about your pimping to a ho. When he got out the car, I observed the pimp I had talked to on the phone a few minutes ago. He had a fly and flamboyant style, a style I actually liked. I could tell he was on his shit and really pimping because of what he had. Syn mentioned serving him, and his hoes weren't looking at me at all. Not even while I was walking up to his car.

As we talked at the gas pump, I gathered information about Syn. He let me know she wasn't a Suzy Choosy ho, and that he was her first pimp of almost two years. She smoked kush and didn't use any other drugs. She was a very jealous ho, especially when she didn't get her way.

Before we parted, he gave me her Android phone and purse that he just took away from her before he put her out his car, and we exchanged phone numbers. One day, I might take that trip to New York, and I would need to know the pimp spots and ho strolls to go to. New York was a city I'd never been to before but always wanted to visit during the summer. "Hit me up, kid, when you ready to get her shit from the room."

When I got inside my whip, I started screening Syn. "Before I drive off with you, let me know if you making a mad move. I don't have time to waste with a mad bitch. I'm in this game to win." If she said that she did or hesitated about the question, or if it sounded like some bullshit lie, I was going to smash the gas on this ho's ass tonight until the ho decided to leave me.

"I'm not making a mad move. I like you. Ever since I seen you at the room today, I wanted to know you. Actually, I saw you two times today. The first time you were with that pimp, and the other time you were with all your hoes. I really like what I saw. I been wanting something new for a little minute now, I just haven't ran into the right pimp yet," she said in a New York accent.

It sounded like she was telling the truth to me, so I moved on to my next question. "Finesse told me you were jealous. Why was that?"

"I don't know. I just feel like I wasn't getting the attention I needed and used to get since he got those two new bitches." From Finesse telling me that she was jealous meant that he'd fucked her and/or Finesse was fucking up showing another ho more attention than he did her. I'd made that big mistake in my career by fucking a couple of my ex-hoes in the past before going to prison. It cost me losing some of my hoes in my stable because of the hoes running them off. I'd learned a big lesson, it wasn't good to mix business with pleasure unless you knew how to capitalize off it and still stay on top of your game.

"So, that's what you want?" I asked.

"I mean, for the most part, yeah. I make money, I have no problem supporting my pimp. I just want to be loved and feel taken care of by my Daddy."

"I can give you that and more. That's not a problem for a pimp like me. With my pimpin', there are things you're gonna have to learn. In my stable, there's no need to be jealous. You're a ho just like the next ho. What makes y'all different is how good you are with following a pimp's instructions. And that will determine how special it will be when we're alone together. Listen." Then I started breaking down some of my rules and regulations to her.

It was 9:16 P.M. After I finished serving Syn my rules, I decided to work her on the blade.

None of my hoes had worked the track yet. I didn't think I would be putting them down on the blade, except for Syn. The track prices were too low for my hoes. The escort sites and strip club was where they needed to be to make my money. Earlier, I decided to let Jennifer, Rose, Sarah, and Heather dance at a majority white club named Girl's Collection. I had Erika and Claire dance at V-Live.

I got Syn's things from Finesse, and then had her put on something very hoish, a tight pink dress that fit like a small shirt, showing off her little ass cheeks and pussy print with pink, three-inch high heels. I showed her how to post two ads of her on two big-money clients' escort sites, and I gave her money to get her own room to work out of.

Before I put Syn on the blade, I told her all the prices to charge on the blade and internet. They were going to be different prices. I knew the prices on the track but added $20. Then I told her, "Get the trick to touch you on yo' titties or pussy or fondle his dick to determine if he's a law. If you go to the room with a trick, text me so I can keep an eye on you, if I'm around. Don't get into a car with more than one trick," I said, and then sent her on her hoing way.

Not even five minutes had passed by when she got her first bite. A white truck slowed down trying to get her attention. He stopped and pulled up to the curb. Her big breasts were bouncing as she walked like a model on the runway towards the truck. She bent down and put her left arm on the lowered window of the car door with her right hand on her waist, clutching her handbag purse. They engaged in a brief conversation through a passenger window before she looked around at her surroundings and then got into the truck. The trick drove around the corner in the back of the Sears shopping mall. They returned in seven minutes. I watched and waited while sitting on the hood of my car from the corner of the motel's parking lot.

Within minutes, an old-model, blue Suburban stopped on the side of her after she flagged him down. She repeated the same thing she did with the last john. They were finished in nine minutes. As she neared my car, she reached into her bra and dropped a small stack of folded bills into the passenger side window that was down. I didn't want the laws to see a ho give me any money if they were watching. Before she walked off, I told her that I was about to go down the street for a couple of hours, and to call me if she wanted me for anything as well as text me when she had a date.

# Smoove Dolla

In Houston, Texas, there was a spot that a lot of pimps, players, macks, and women of the night hung out at every night. It was a pool spot right off Bissonnet named Moe's Pool Hall that I came to almost every single night I stayed in Houston. Moe was an honorable ex-pimp at 65 from Fifth Ward in Houston, Texas who still had love and respect for the pimp game. He had owned this spot for over two decades now.

At 10:30 P.M, Moe's Pool Hall was the place to be whether you were inside of it or outside. The inside was where the highsiders, drinkers, and the gamblers were at. On the outside was where you wanted to be at socializing with other pimps. Personally, I was always posted up outside, because I liked watching the outside scenery where the track was in full effect. Almost every other four to six minutes, you see a hoe or hoes coming in and out paying their folks, and then going back out on the blade getting more ho dough. This was where the real action took place for me.

You saw all types of whips you could possibly think of from pimps that were all over the USA. It really felt good being in the midst of pimp game.

Serious Jones, Versace Boss, Sir Success, Pimpin' ANT, and I kicked game as we stood around our cars. Inwardly, I admired the pop trunk ANT had in his candy blue, 1983 Cadillac that read CHOOSE PIMPIN' ANT in blue neon lights. Every time his trunk opened up, you'd see that, which was a set trend in Houston if you could afford it. It was a style we didn't have in Dallas hoods.

This nigga ANT was known for popping trunk on every track in Texas while driving up and down the blade spitting pimping out the window. He'd knocked a few hoes campaigning that way. My pimp partna, Sir Success, got my attention off of ANT's 'lac when I heard him campaigning and politicking. "Say...Hoe! Yeah you— this pimpin' ass Success internationally known and not a local joker! I'm known cross-country for breaking bitches adding to my riches. They call me Mr. Don't Stop, because I always have a hoes' cock for sell. So, dig these blues, while I tie your tennis shoes." Right then and there... all that fine black ho did was place her head down to the ground, and beat her feet to the concrete.

248

That's when we all said, "That ho is under some real live ass instruction." Come to find out, the ho stepped to a pimp across the parking lot and broke herself by putting money in his pocket. The nigga was flyer than a motherfucker. He was dressed to impress with a red three-piece suit on with some red gators by Stacey Adams, and diamonds in his mouth, watch, and ring. I chucked up the pinky for pimpin' and a nod of approval.

The whole three hours I was outside of Moe's Pool Hall, I didn't see Finesse nor his Aston Martin. I was going to buy him a drink, all off my new ho, if I had seen him. I guess I'd catch up with him some other time. The clock on my Rolex read 1:27 A.M. After bullshitting with some of my pimp partnas for thirty more minutes, I shook the spot, and went back to the motel.

Syn did exactly as I told her to do. She texted me before and after every date. She made $860 from the time I put her down on the blade and the time I drove back into the motel's parking lot. That was all from working the track dates and in calls.

By 4 A.M., Syn had finally made a total of $2480 doing in and out calls. She didn't catch an attitude nor complain about working the long hours. It wasn't like I would've cared if she did. Either she was going to leave me or keep breaking herself. I was serious about getting my choosing fee. I wanted her take my pimpin' serious as well. I felt by taking no shorts on my choosing fee, she would see me as the real player I was. I really liked her work ethic. I knew she was going to be one of my top money makers in my stable, that's if she kept it up.

Saturday morning, Rose, Erika, and I went to buy us a couple of outfits at the Galleria Mall. We all picked out something casual since we were going to be outside today in 89-degree weather. I made sure I put on my 24k gold Rolex and two-toned ring that both had the Masonic square and compass embedded in the center facing outward.

There were hundreds of people here at Memorial Park who attended this function us Masons did for charity for the community. There was something going on at this park every day of the week. I guessed because it was beautiful as well as one of the biggest parks in Houston, and located near Downtown, south of Houston. People of all races, but mostly black, were talking and laughing amongst each other in different groups around the park, some adults and kids enjoying the free entertainment and eating the endless amounts of delicious foods.

Events like these were going on around the world twice a year, sometimes more, depending on what city you were in, for the community to come and enjoy themselves with the entertainment we provided. Normally, when I attended a function I had to perform songs I'd written for entertainment because I was a recording artist, but singers had already been chosen for this event. I'd sung for a bunch of my Masonic brothers and Eastern Star sisters' weddings, charity causes, nonprofit awarenesses, and some of their organizations. Singing was my main craft, and if any one of them needed my services, I had to provide it. I still got paid for my services, but it was my duty of being an active Mason. There were lawyers, doctors, police officers, judges, entrepreneurs, entertainers, athletes, and chefs as well as other professional career holders here, who would do the same for me if I wanted it, and even for free if I needed their services.

To tell the truth, the only reason why I came was because I got invited. High-degree Masons from my lodge would be here as well as some from other lodges around Dallas and Houston, all that Tight game knew. When I was in the hospital, two of my Mason brothers that I was close to from my lodge had called me, asking did I need their assistance in seeking revenge. I told them no, thank you, and I didn't mention anything else about what happened. One of the two was here today. This would be my first time speaking to them on what really happened the night we got shot and robbed. I wanted to clean up all false rumors, if there were any on my name.

I spoke and introduced my queens that were on the side of me to about twenty-five of my brothers and sisters that we came across in different groups walking around the park that I knew and hadn't seen in several months. When I introduced Rose, I said, "Joshua, I'd like you to meet my friend, Rosemary. Rosemary is a model and dancer. She's in the process of working on opening her own pole dancing class. Rosemary, this is my friend, Joshua Carter. He plays professional football for the Houston Texans."

When I introduced Erika to my Eastern Star sister, I said, "Erika, I want you to meet my friend, Ashley Taylor. She's a doctor at Methodist Hospital here in Houston. Ashley, this is my friend, Erika. She's a model and dancer as well as an up and coming actress." Both of my queens looked at me, surprised, like they couldn't believe I had said that about them the first time I introduced them, until they went along with it the second time. I'd been observing them since they'd been with me. I knew their skills if they were unconscious of it themselves, so I could see them doing what I introduced them as. If they wanted to pursue it, I'd help and do my best to make it happen successfully. After we left, I'd bring it back up. How I introduced them was the art of introducing someone. At a social event, it was a conversation igniter and a way to network.

Before I excused myself away from my two hoes, I told them, "I'm about to talk to a few people. Y'all go mingle. If people ask y'all about modeling, dancing, and being an actress, go along with it. But the key is to get them to talk about themselves so you won't reveal much about yourself. Let me get over here. I'ma talk to y'all both on why I introduced you two that way." Then I made my way to a circle of six, where four of my brothers from the lodge I attended were talking to two other brothers from Houston.

Minutes later, after my brothers finished talking about upcoming events, one of the brothers from Houston brought up me and Tight Game getting shot. I ended up telling them what happened from the time we all stepped into Shae's house to the point when we got robbed and shot. The thing I was ashamed of in my life was not being a good enough father to my children, not being a pimp. A lot of people looked down on and wanted nothing to do with a pimp. That's because of all the shit gorilla pimps and sex traffickers made us look like. Even though I knew all that, I still told them how I got deceived by a girl that set me up. Five of them knew that I pimped as well as what Tight game used to do before he gave it all up. It ain't no secret.

One of my high-degree brothers that was very close to Tight

game got angry and said, "IfHobert doesn't make it, that's your ass, Damion. You'll be seeing me personally. That's a promise." He touched my chest with his index finger with every word he said, and then pushed me hard. He was bigger than me by 90 pounds, weighing around 260, standing at 6'3, so I went back four steps.

When I tried to run up on him, my close brother, Timothy, grabbed me. "Please don't fight out here."

"Fuck you, Jerry. That shit wasn't my fault." See, I had a lot of respect for Jerry, almost on the level I had for Tight game, but he had gone a little too far with disrespecting me. He was serious about what he promised me. He could easily get at me and get me killed. He had a lot more power than I did, but I wasn't scared of him at all. I wasn't no punk on no degree. I stood up for me and mine.

"Come walk with me, Damion. Let him calm down, man. He's just upset right now," Timothy said while holding my arm. Jerry was heading the opposite direction with two of our brothers. Some people were looking our way, noticing the conflict, so I started walking off with Timothy.

"He down bad for that shit, bro," I mentioned.

"I know. He's just hurt. He's afraid he might lose his best friend."

"I am too. You think I'm not?"

"I know you are. We all are," Timothy said.

We sat at a bench right in front of the pond where a bunch of kids were playing. Timothy was really a good dude, always striving to be better as a person. He was a good role model as well. He always kept a positive attitude. I'd never seen him mad before, and I'd been around him a lot. He was 28 years old, happily married with a beautiful wife and with kids, very family oriented. He worked for his father, who was also a high-degree Mason at our lodge, who owned one of the biggest construction businesses in Dallas. The reason why we were so close was because of his love for music. He was a fan of my music and because of that, he helped me get the recording deal I had four years back. I couldn't say anything bad about him.

Timothy talked to me for about 41 minutes about my life and

where I was headed if I continued this lifestyle. He broke it down to me in Masonic terms to where I could fully understand. It really had me thinking deeply about where I was headed in life.

He really fucked me up when he said, "A bunch of brothers wanted to get at you because you put Hobert in harm's way with your poor choices. It was my father and I who broke it down to them that Hobert brought you into that lifestyle you're in. And you love him as if he is your own father, so they can't get mad at you, suspend you, or kill you for what took place. I told them to go after whoever shot you two, but you said you didn't want any help, so they left it alone for now."

"Thanks for everything, Timothy. I really do owe you, man. You've been helping me out since I've known you."

"It's nothing. That's what us brothers do, we help each other, no matter what, even if we don't deserve it."

"Thanks. I want you to tell the brothers I took care of who shot us except for one of them. He's locked up at Lew Stewart. His name is James Ford. He got locked up on May 5th. If they want to help, tell them to take care of him. He's the one that set it all up," I had told Timothy.

"Yeah, I'll check into it. Looks like Jerry left. I wanted y'all to talk this out before you two left the park because it's all a whole misunderstanding. You need to come to the lodge on the next two Thursdays so you two can talk about what's going on."

"Alright, I'll make time for it, no problem."

"You be careful in those streets, Damion. Remember, it's not what you do, it's how you do it.

Being around this environment and listening to Timothy talk had me really thinking about pursuing other things in life. The crazy part about that was I didn't want this feeling of changing to go out the window. You know the feeling when the preacher at church preaches or the Iman at the masjid gives a good sermon. For some people, it really had you feeling some type of way until you stepped foot out the building and went on with the rest of your day. Just as I was the best pimp I could be, I had to do the same with being a Mason. As a Master Mason, I should strive to live an upright life and not waste a moment of my precious time I had left here on earth. That time for change had come too soon. What I needed to figure out now was what I was going to do with every ho in my stable, because all of them weren't ready for a change.

Once we got into my Rolls Royce, after they expressed how much they liked the function and the people they met, I told them, "The reason why I said that earlier is because I'm changing my game soon. I want you to pursue something legal other than prostitution. You two have potential to be so much more. Rose, did Shae ever tell you what I did for her after she left my pimping and got out the game?"

"No, she didn't tell me anything. What did you do for her?"

"For almost six years, I was putting money in a overseas account for her to pursue her dreams and some to fuck off for her pleasure. I recently just got her space for her hair salon. I plan on doing the same for y'all. Really, for all my down hoes." I pointed towards the park. "Y'all witnessed who I know, I got a lot of connections. Whatever you want to do, it can be done. We can start building whenever you two want to. We can start today, tomorrow. We can start next month, next year. Whenever you feel you are ready. The right time is now, tho'. As your pimp, I have to switch my game up so we can sustain as a family and be more successful in life. As y'all pimp, I'm here for you in every aspect in life. You two are my most trusted queens. I need you two to motivate my other queens in doing the same as I'm doing with you at this moment." I talked to them the whole drive to the motel, giving them motivation and inspiration on pursuing something legal in life.

Rose and Erika knew a bunch about me. I wasn't scared of them snitching on me, 'cause they really couldn't prove anything anyway. It was my word over theirs. Still, though, it was my job to make sure they were good, to make sure they knew they were cared for, that I was there for them, and trusted them so I could be trusted more. That way, I could lock them into my game, block other pimps' game, and whoever was trying to destroy everything that I had going on.

# Money Game

The only way to a man's heart as my mama says is his stomach. Well, I agree to disagree, because the only way to my heart is through my pocket full of profit copies as a form of an able ho being under these proper instructions.

— Professor

# Smoove Dolla

## Chapter 14

Since I promised my daughter, Nayla, that I would take her shopping on Monday, late Sunday night, Jennifer and Syn followed behind me in her car to Arlington. I left my other hoes in Houston to dance and ho until I made it back that way. We had been in Houston a week now, and we'd probably be out there for another two to three months since we were making a lot of money.

Early the next morning, I had Jennifer post them an ad to do a few calls to make back what we spent on two rooms and on the trip to and from Arlington. The date she was about to perform was her second call this morning. After their fifth date, I'ma let them chill and sleep till the night came around while I spent time with my daughter.

While she performed the date, I went down to the pool area where Syn was. I wanted to check on her to see what she was doing. When I entered the indoor pool area, Syn was sitting on the edge of the pool with her feet in the water. She couldn't see or hear me because she was facing the opposite direction from me with her Beats by Dre wireless headphones on, connected to her phone.

I didn't bother her yet, I just sat on a metal bench on the wall that was about seven yards behind her, checking my Instagram.

Out of nowhere, Syn started singing Adele's "Rolling in the Deep" song. She caught me by surprise, making me stop what I was doing to listen to her. She didn't quite reach Adele's range, but she had a wonderful, unique falsetto voice that could make it in the music industry. A couple of minutes later, she started singing "Realize" by Cobie Caillat. I was very attracted to her amazing voice. She could really sing.

Minutes later, she looked around to find me behind her. "Daddy, how long have you been in here?" she asked as she took the headphones off her head.

"For about eight, nine minutes. Come here."

She made her way towards me, and then sat in my lap. "Yes, Daddy."

"Sing Cobie Calliat again, baby," I demanded and then smiled.

"Really, Daddy?" she asked shyly.

"Yeah, really, sing to me. You said you want attention. You got my undivided attention right now," I said while putting my phone inside my 24k gold clip attached to my Versace shorts. "I want to hear you sing. You sound amazing. We the only two in here, go ahead and sing."

My compliment to her made her blush. "Thanks, Daddy. Okay, here it goes." She closed her eyes while exhaling, and then started singing with all her might. Singing was her gift in life. If she pursued it, she would make it, no doubt about it. It was crazy that I had caught a bitch that could sing. It must really be meant to be to change the game up. I didn't care what she said, she was pursing this singing shit.

I wanted her to know I was a singer as well. I knew the song by heart, so I sung along with her when she got to the last chorus of the song. "If you just realize what I just realized." She stopped singing when she heard me. "Keep singing," I told her before we started singing together again. "If you just realize what I just realized, we'll be perfect for each other and we'll never find another."

When we stopped, she said, "Daddy, I didn't know you can sing. You sound really good, Daddy."

"Thanks, I'm a recording artist with a record deal. I can get you in the studio, if you want in. Have you ever thought about it before?"

"Hell yeah, I have. You just don't know how bad I want to sing, Daddy," she said, excited.

"Then why haven't you been doin' anything with your voice?" I asked her.

"I've been wanting to, but I've been in this lifestyle. I've been with Finesse for two years now. I asked him twice can I record and go on *American Idol*. He said he'll see but didn't do nothing about it for almost seven months. I liked Finesse, so I stayed with him. I didn't find nobody I liked more than I liked Finesse until I saw you. If you can get me in the studio, Daddy, I'll do anything and everything for you. I just wanna sing."

Being a singer myself, I knew how bad she wanted to get her voice heard by the world. I felt similar to her before I gotten my deal. The good thing about it was she already had a strong desire to want to be a singer and had the confidence she needed to make it in the industry, so I didn't have to waste the time to talk her into wanting to sing. Everything she just told me was good to know. I was in a position to do something her last pimp didn't want to do, something that meant a lot to her and benefited us both. He definitely didn't know what he had. Syn was a gold mine. I was shaking my head.

"I'ma help you, fo' sho. I'ma make a call to schedule you some studio time. We will get together soon to write you a song or two so you can record it. I'ma let you know what's up later on after I get back, ok?"

"Okay. Thanks, Daddy," she said as she hugged me. "It's so fucking crazy yo, that I met you, and you are a singer. I knew it was something about you. Something pulled me right to you. It's a reason why we met."

I checked my text I got from Jennifer a minute ago.

Jennifer
Daddy, I made ur money.
10:55 A.M. Monday, July 1, 2012

Me
Good girl, I'll be up in a min.
10:57 A.M. Monday, July 1, 2012

Jennifer
k
10:58 A.M. Monday, July 1, 2012

Syn wrapped a towel over her small waist, and then we got on the elevator heading up to the fourth floor. When the elevators opened on our floor, something felt wrong. Out of being cautious, I made a quick look to the right to check my surroundings before I walked into the hallway. I saw two black men and a white guy looking at our hotel room door like something was happening. I was glad a white woman in her early thirties went into the elevator going down. I pulled Syn close to me in the elevator.

As soon as the doors closed, I asked the woman inside the elevator with us, "What happened up there?"

"I don't know. There were men going in and out the room like they were policemen. They didn't have on any police uniforms."

"Were they coming out room 236?"

"Yes, they were," she said as she nodded her head. "My room is 241."

After she said that, I pushed the second floor button and instantly gave Syn my phones, my wad of money, debit cards, and my pistol. The woman beside us took four steps back into the corner when she saw the gun. "There's nothing to be scared about. I'm not wanted for murder or anything, ma'am. I didn't hurt anybody, and I'm not gonna hurt you. What happened up there is about prostitution." I was careful not to tell her that I was a pimp, because some people hated and disliked pimps. She didn't say anything, she just stood up against the wall in silence.

I'd gotten caught up in a sting once before. I knew how detectives operated when it came to prostitution and pimpin'. I knew it was a sting. I didn't know who to trust right now. Jennifer had snitched on me. I couldn't say that Syn would do the same or not if she had gotten caught up, but I had to trust her at this moment. She was all I had in my presence. I needed her to get in contact with Rose. She knew everything she needed to do in this situation, but I wanted Shae to know as well, so I told her, "Remember this, call Rose and Shae. Their numbers are in that Android. Call them on yo' phone. Tell them what happened. Tell them that Jennifer ratted me out. They know what to do, baby. Don't mess over me, Syn. Messing over me will be messing over yourself. Remember what we talked about. I got us."

"I won't mess over you, Daddy. I promise, Daddy, I got you," she told me.

Ideas of getting out of this hotel without getting arrested were flashing in my mind. I thought about paying this white woman to drive me out of here, but I couldn't trust her. If we got pulled over on the way out the parking lot, she probably would lie, say I put a gun to her head and threatened her to help me escape. I just said a quick prayer to help me with this situation that confronted me, and took a chance on escaping alone. The white woman in the elevator with us didn't look like she needed any money from her decent style of dress, but everybody needed money, even if their appearance didn't seem like it, so I told her, "I'll give you $2000 if you can take my girlfriend down the street to another hotel for me please."

She thought about it for a few seconds, and then said, "I have an interview at 12:30, but I'll do it." The elevator doors slid open.

"Thanks so much. Syn, give this woman her money." Before anybody could board the elevator, I took off the big thin towel around her waist and then placed the towel flat on the floor. "Put the pistol and that phone in the middle of it."

After she did what I said, I neatly folded the towel five times. "Keep this under your arms until you get into the car. Let's hope I make it out safely, baby." I gave her a kiss on the lips and then hauled ass down the hallway to the stairway.

I jumped five steps at a time until I made it down to the bottom floor and out the door to the hallway on the first floor. I looked out the clear glass side door heading to the parking lot, and no one was in sight. *I might make it,* I thought. I stepped out the side door, heading to my car like everything was good and normal. As soon as I was within a few feet of my Rolls Royce, I heard a policeman yell, "Police, freeze, don't move!"

I stopped all movements. I didn't want to be another black man shot by the police or want to run and make it seem like I was guilty of any crime. "Now, put your hands up where I can see them and turn around, slowly!" the policeman demanded. I put my hands up and turned around and asked the detective, who had a gun pointed at me and who wasn't an uniform cop, "What's going on, Detective?"

"You're a suspect. I'm detaining you until I'm told otherwise. Do you have any weapons like guns, knives, or blades on you?" he asked, as I saw my hoe, Syn, and the woman driving out the parking lot in a green Ford Cherokee.

I looked smoothly at the detective because I didn't want him to notice my ho getting away, and said flatly, "No."

After the detective searched me, he asked me, "May these two cops search your vehicle, sir?"

"Yes." I could have said no, but they would have gotten a search warrant to search the car, after towing it to the police impound, and then tore and ripped my Rolls Royce up just to be on some hateful shit.

While he searched the car, I stood by an undercover car for about 30 minutes, when a detective by the last name of Patterson came up and told me he was taking me to Arlington Police Station.

Riding in a car handcuffed and being taken to jail was one of the worst feelings ever, even if you knew you were bonding out as soon as you got there. Especially when you were going down for a felony, and you didn't know what the outcome might be. In my situation, I was going to Tarrant County Jail after I was finished in Arlington City Jail, where it was damn near impossible to beat cases in their courts. Majority of its jailers had signed for time or gotten found guilty at trial. It was fucked up in there.

As soon as we got inside Arlington City Jail, I was taken to a small interrogation room by the detectives. I sat alone in that room for 27 minutes until two detectives came inside to interrogate me.

There was a dark, tall, heavy-set guy in his early forties. He had a low haircut, but it was bald in the front and the middle of his head. He had on a green, cotton, button-down shirt and khaki pants, wearing a pair of Adidas tennis shoes. The white detective was a tall man who looked to be in his late thirties. He had on blue jeans, a blue and white button-down shirt, and all-white New Balance on his feet with a TCU cap on his head.

The white detective sat down in a chair six feet away in front of me with a table in between us, and then said, "As you know, I'm Detective Patterson and this is my partner, Detective Allen."

He pointed at his partner, who stood by the closed door looking at me. "We're with the Human Trafficking Unit here in Arlington. I'd like to help you if you can help me. Tell us what's your relationship with Jennifer Green."

"I'm not talking without my lawyer present."

"So, you don't want to tell your part of the story?"

"No, I don't."

Detective Allen walked over and placed his palms on the table top while peering down on me. "Tell us, where did you get the money to buy all those diamond rings, watch, the grill, and the necklace you have on? Is that what you buy with the money you get from prostituting these women?"

I wanted to tell these motherfuckers I was a whole multi-millionaire, and had probably 20 times what they had combined together in their bank accounts in mine off legal moves, but I all I said to them was, "Man, take me to a cell. I'm not tryna talk to y'all."

"Okay, Johnson, you're facing a bunch of charges here," he warned, trying to make me fold. "You should have helped yourself." The two detectives walked out the door together without me.

Even though I was anxious to know what I was being charged with and what had been said that I did, I wasn't about to ask nor say anything else to them. It wouldn't have made a difference anyway. Talking would have made things worse. I knew one thing was, it was going to be hard for them to convict me on whatever charges they put on me. They had no solid proof.

I sat in that room for almost an hour before they returned, read me my Miranda Rights, and arrested me for compelling prostitution. I used the free phone as soon as I got into the holding cell waiting to get booked in. The first person I called was Shae.

"I've been waiting on you to call me. You alright?"

"Yeah, I'm good. You called Christie?" I asked her.

"I called her six times, left voice messages and texts. She's not answering or responding to any of them. That ain't like her, something's wrong."

"You don't have to call again. Thanks, tho'. I'll just bond myself out tomorrow. You just enjoy yourself on your vacation. I'll call you a little later. I love you, baby."

"Love you too. I'll be back in the states tomorrow night. Make sure you call back baby, foreal," she said, worried and seriously.

"You know I will. Aight, baby. Talk to you later."

Next, I called my mother. "Boy, what yo' ass doin' in jail, Tunke?" she asked as soon as she accepted the collect call, making me regret I even called her. But the reason why I did was because I didn't want her to be worried about me. I did talk to her every day, and plus, I need her to take Nayla shopping since I couldn't. Now that I had gotten myself locked up again, she show 'nough gonna worry.

"I don't know, Momma. They said something with some girl."

"How much is your bond?"

"I just got locked up a couple hours ago, so I'm not gonna have a bond till tomorrow. Are you doing anything today?"

"No, why?"

"I was supposed to be taking Nayla shopping. Can you take her shopping for me, please?"

"Yeah, I'll call her to see if she still wants to go shopping without you," my mother told me. Nayla probably would be sad that I was locked up again and wouldn't want to go anymore.

"Thanks, Momma. I'll give you a call back later. I'm 'bout to make some calls to check on a few things." I had to hang up with her because I didn't want her to say something that would make it seem like I was guilty of something. I couldn't talk on the phone with her knowing that the phone conversation was being recorded.

Later on that evening, I built up enough courage to call my daughter, Nayla, for missing our day together. I could hear the hurt and disappointment in her tone of voice like every time I was absent for something that was important to her. Even though she forgave me every time, I couldn't continue to let her down. From this moment forward, I was going to make the effort in changing. I was gonna take a big step away from my hoes prostituting. If I didn't know the tricks, my hoes wasn't fucking them, only escorting tricks to dinner and events. Also, they would be using the web cab sites, dancing in clubs, and performing at parties I threw for them. Nothing else until I said otherwise. Doing those things would minimize my chances of getting locked up again. I had too much riding on the line to fuck it off. Everything I'd worked hard for would be thrown out the window if I was convicted of another felony. Plus, I was really hurting my loved ones. Yeah, I had to do something better. Being locked up was being stagnated, it wasn't what's up.

The next morning, the judge set my bond at $300,000 for a compelling prostitution charge. That bond was too high for a second-degree felony. I wasn't bailing out on that bond amount. I'd just wait until I made it to Tarrant County and get my bond lowered then. I knew what they were doing. They were still investigating, trying to borrow time so they could find more charges to put on me. I wasn't dumb. I knew the State of Texas wouldn't find anything else on me. The only way they would was if Jennifer told the feds that I had hoes in Houston and Florida. I would make her look silly and seem like a liar on camera, because I knew they would be recording her testimony. I was ahead of them. Syn had called Rose and Shae to tell them what had happened. Rose had told all my hoes to shut everything down, delete all their posts, and don't answer their phones for anybody they didn't know.

Later the next day, the guards called me out for an attorney visit with Christie. As soon as I sat down in the booth, I asked her, "Why haven't you been answering yo' phone when Shae called you?"

"I've been busy with business and work. And I don't recall I was supposed to be taking orders from you, so get off my back. I made time for you, I'm here now."

"Bitch, don't get smart with me, ho. You need to stay in yo' muthafuckin' place. You here to be my muthafuckin' lawyer. Now, tell me what's goin' on. What's been said? What do they have on me?"

She looked down then back up with a disgusted look on her face and said, "I don't have anything yet, they're still investigating. They won't talk to me about anything, but they did give me your affidavit for the compelling prostitution charge."

"Let me see," I said anxiously.

She gave me two pieces of paper through the paper slot in our visitation booth. It read:

CASE NUMBER DIDO15398437
THE STATE OF TEXAS IN THE MAGISTRATE COURT
CITY OF ARLINGTON IN TARRANT COUNTY, TEXAS
AFFIDAVIT FOR WARRANT OF ARREST AND
DETENTION
The Undersigned Affiant, who after being duly sworn by me, on oath, makes the following statement: I have good reason to believe and do believe that:
Johnson, Damion Tunke, Black Male, 08/28/1988
On or about the 1st day of July, 2012, in the incorporated limit of the City County of Tarrant, Texas, did then and there commit the offense of:
Compelling Prostitution
2nd Degree Felony
On June 25, 2012 at approximately 8:55 A.M., the Arlington Police Department emergency 9-1-1 system received an anonymous tip from an unknown woman saying that a man named Damion Johnson was threatening and forcing a woman by the name of Jennifer Green to prostitute. She also gave both Green and Johnson's number. The anonymous tape recording was sent to my office on June 26, 2012. After I was given the tape, I immediately started my investigation.
On July 1, 2012, we tracked Jennifer Green's cell phone number on the internet. I found out that she had an advertisement posted to www.frontpage.net[frontpage], a website frequently used for prostitution service providers. The advertisement contained Green's photographs and phone number. I scheduled a full service (sexual intercourse) for $400 at 10:45 A.M. at an Extended Stay hotel located at 1492 Avenue J in Arlington, Texas. At 10:30 A.M., two police officers, my partner and I, arrived at Extended Stay in two unmarked vehicles. Detective Allen and the two officers monitored the parking lot looking out for our suspect, Damion Johnson, while I continued my investigation with Jennifer Green. While inside the hotel room, Jennifer received a telephone call and I overheard her telling a caller that for an hour of her time, it would cost him $3500.

266

I then put the marked $400 on the counter and after she finished her call, she took the money and disrobed quickly. I asked could I get a blow job. Jennifer replied, "Yeah. Take down your pants." That's when I arrested her for prostitution and then read her Miranda Rights.

Upon speaking with Green, I learned that on or about the June 9, 2012, she met Johnson at a gentlemen's club in Austin where she worked as a dancer. They went out on a date, and the next day she started working for Johnson. Green said that Johnson promised to provide her an apartment and a car if she would work for him as an escort. Johnson provided her a room at the Extended Stay in Austin. Johnson had her post three Frontpage advertisements. Each advertisement provided a different phone number in an effort to increase visibility on the website. Johnson also set rules for the victim to follow. The rules included not disrespecting him and to always notify him that she had a customer, and he slapped her with an open hand. Victim told Johnson that she wanted to go home after this incident. Johnson refused to let her leave. After this incident, Victim remained with Johnson out of fear.

On or about July 1, 2012, Johnson and Victim left Austin for San Antonio in a Rolls Royce. They stayed in the Hilton near the Riverwalk. Johnson had victim post advertisements on Frontpage. On that night, Victim made approximately $1600 on both incall and outcall appointments.

On or about June 16, 2012, Johnson and Victim left the Hilton to Houston where they stayed at Plainfield Motel on the Southwest side of Houston. Victim made approximately $13,000 on both incall and outcall appointments in the Houston area.

On or about July 1, 2012, Johnson and victim left the Plainfield Motel to Arlington Extended Stay located on Avenue J. Victim told Johnson multiple times that she wanted to go home to Austin. Victim asked for money back. After continuously asking permission to go back home, Johnson drove a red Rolls Royce into a car wash stall where he physically attacked the victim, slapping her approximately six times in the face. Johnson told Victim, "Bitch, you ain't never going home, I own you!"

Victim stated that she made approximately $36,000 having sex with men for money, and gave all the money to Johnson. Victim would see customers in her hotel room or would meet them at their location (incalls and outcall). Johnson set the rates that Victim was to charge. The rates for "full service" (sexual intercourse) were $150 for a half hour and $300 for an hour. Johnson also provided Victim with condoms.

I have probable cause to believe that Johnson did commit the offense of compelling prostitution. Johnson knowingly caused Victim by force and threat to commit prostitution. Victim initially worked for Johnson voluntarily, but he began using force against her the first time she broke one of his rules. He continued his violence once Victim voiced her desire to return back to Austin. Victim stated that Johnson has threatened to kill her if she were to leave him.

Subscribed and sworn to before me by said affiant on July 2, 2012, I hereby acknowledge that I have examined the foregoing affidavit and have determined that probable cause exists for the issuance of an arrest warrant for the individual accused therein.

Magistrate, Magistrate Court, Arlington, Tenant County, Texas $300,000 Bond

Arlington Police Incident #15—3462898 Detective F. Patterson.

After I finished reading the affidavit, I said, "This is a lot of bullshit, and you know it! I didn't force no bitch to prostitute! This punk ho lying! This case should be easy for you to beat."

"I don't know, Tunke, with your background and everything, you—"

I cut her off and said, "You don't know! Bitch, I know you better do something to get this case dropped with this weak ass evidence! You know I didn't do this shit. I done saw you beat a bunch of niggas' cases that were guilty and you talking 'bout you don't know! Don't fuckin' play with me, Christie. I want you to beat this fuckin' case!"

"I can try my best, Tunke."

"Bitch, don't try, do your best. And when can you bond me out of here?"

"Whenever you make it to Tarrant County. I'ma have to get your bond lowered first."

"Alright, Christie. Just do what you do as fast as possible." I was about to apologize for the way I had talked to her just a moment ago, but I remembered that she mentioned getting me locked up, and she gave that detective my number. Plus, I wasn't sorry about shit I did to her. I just got up without saying anything else.

This fucking affidavit had me hot. It seemed a bit funny. Really crazy. It didn't mention anything about my other hoes, which was a great thing. But I still felt like I had to hold my breath because they still could be trying to build another case. I couldn't believe Jennifer said I assaulted and forced her to prostitute. But then again, that's what some hoes did when detectives put pressure on their ass. When the detectives started talking about putting cases on them, years they would get if they didn't help them, detectives mentioning they could take their kids away, getting them deeper in their emotions so they could snitch and lie on the pimp so the case could stick. They went so far as giving hoes assistance from the state and government, giving them checks, food stamps, and housing as long as they came to court and snitched. That's why a pimp does what he do with most hoes to keep them in the blind, because you can't trust them fully.

My mind was going so all over the place that I forgot to tell her to find out who tipped the police off. I searched in my mind for every possible person I could think of that would do some bullshit like that. No one knew Jennifer's full name except for Christie and some of my hoes. None of them knew my name but Christie and Rose. Even though I knew hoes could be shiesty, untrustworthy, deceitful, and cunning, I didn't believe my hoes had anything to do with tipping the laws off. Christie was the only one left. I'd bet a $100,000 that she was behind that call. Thinking back on what happened at her hotel room on how she threatened to get me arrested and how she was ignoring my hoes' calls to her when I got locked up, yeah, it was her.

Even though she went to a different lodge than us, she was probably the one that was telling them to suspend me and going along with Jerry about suspending and killing me. I really had to figure out a way to beat this case without Christie as soon as possible. I didn't want the Masons to look bad, knowing this case could give our organization a bad name and backlash, saying we were sex traffickers, which was very far from the truth. To tell you the truth, I needed them for my business connections and my singing career to blossom in a major way. I also felt being a Mason could help me on becoming a better person. If only I kept my head on Masonry, that could happen.

Three days later, I got transferred to Tarrant County Jail. It was 7:13 A.M. Wednesday morning when I finally made it upstairs to the pod in the towers. There were two tiers in this 48-man tank with two-man cells. Only about ten cells had one-man cells. They gave me a cell by myself, which I was glad to get, because I didn't want a celly.

I sat my towel roll, bed roll, and indigent pack down on the bunk of the cell, pissed, washed, and then walked to a phone to call Rose collect. "Good morning, baby. You okay?" she asked sleepily.

"Yeah, I'm good. I made it to Tarrant County last night. I'm downtown. I want you to get up right now and come visit me. And put $500 on my books too before you come see me."

"Okay, I'm getting up right now."

After I got off the phone, I walked up to the desk where the pod officer's desk was at. The young, fine, pretty, dark-skin female officer was conversating with a tall, brown-skin older male officer who brought six of us to this pod.

As I stood alone behind the red-taped line that we couldn't cross that was eight feet away from the desk, I overheard their conversation. "Up in central today," catching the last words of a sentence from the male officer.

"Did your wife make you lunch or are you eating out today?"

"You know that heffa didn't make me nothing. I'm eating at that catfish cafe on the westside," he mentioned.

She was running game on this old nigga. All she did when she brought up his wife was remind him that his wife wasn't doing her part as his woman and made him think about what she would do if she was with him. She had it so down pat that she had to be running the same game to a couple more of her male co-workers. I bet they bought this fine woman all kind of shit. She looked like that type to me.

"Since you couldn't take me out for my birthday two weeks ago, the least you can do is buy me lunch again today. I'm really hungry. I didn't eat breakfast this morning," she said and switched her body weight to her other leg, making her hip poke out, and then tilted her head the same way.

He pulled out a small stack of twenties, fives, and a bunch of ones out of his left pocket trying to impress her. Most niggas that did that upon meeting women were tricks. It's just like one of the rules in the hood with pulling out a gun, 'never pull it out if you not gonna use it. When a man pulls out a stack of money to impress a woman, he gives out a signal that he will buy her things and take care of her financially, or pay for sex. So never pull out your money if you don't intend to trick off, unless you are trying to trick a woman. Some players do it to trick women into investing in him. If a woman knows you for having money or has seen you with money more than two or more times, more than likely, down the line she will invest in you and give you money. "You know I got you, baby. How much you want?"

"What time are you going on break?" she asked.

"Around 10:30, 11:30, why?"

"You going before me, just buy me four pieces of fillet fish, four hushpuppies, and fries. Get me a large Sprite too. Don't forget to get some ketchup."

"I got you, baby," he said, smiling a white smile at her. "Whenever I leave to get the food, I'll be right back so the food will be hot."

"Okay," she said while looking at me standing there with a soft smile on my face. I wanted her pretty, fine ass. She was dark skinned like rich chocolate. Short at about 5'4. Thick in all the right places. She had small breasts. Flat stomach. Small waist. Big hips. Phat ass. She had to have trouble putting them pants on this morning the way her dark-green uniform fit perfectly tight on her fine body.

Other than her body, her pretty face was her best asset. Round chin. Full, sexy lips. Pretty white teeth. Cute pug nose. Sexy, light-brown eyes. Eyebrows arched. Makeup done perfectly. She had about a week old brown sew-in hair that hung down to her upper back. The only thing that threw her face off, that I didn't like, was the hole in her nose from a nose ring that she couldn't wear to work. The nose ring meant she was insecure in some form or fashion.

One thing I knew about a lot of women from the south, you easily attract them with seeming like you're interesting. If you were an on nigga or made it appear like you're living the good life, you can grab their attention. With Cartier glasses on my face that's worth $2000 because of the diamonds in the 14-carat frames, 80 grand in my mouth, and standing with assurance told her I'm someone to know, I'm a known nigga, and that I made a great first impression;

"What you smiling at?" she asked curiously after the black officer walked out the pad.

"You got some game on you, I see. I like how you playing that sucker."

She grinned slickly and then said, "I gotta eat and pay my bills."

"That's wuz up. To give you a good tip on him, since you're young and he's old, pushing 50, act more innocent around him. Act like you have little experience about certain things, and ask him about them. Refer to him as Daddy. That's the only way you goin' keep on your pants and still get whatever YOU want from him, whenever you want. Do you understand everything I just told you?"

She smiled and then said, "Yeah, I get it. Thanks."

"Oh, you welcome. You can do that or we can just blackmail him since he's married," I said smiling, making myself seem exciting.

"I can't do nothing like that to him. He's a cool old man."

"You can, and you would if you had to. I'm just playing with you. Anyway, do you have any chemicals so I can clean the cell? I just moved to this pod."

"Yeah, I got bleach, water, and bibby. You want that?"

"Yeah, that'll do."

She bent down and then came up with a bottle and a small brown bag. My had rubbed against her fingertips when she handed the bottle to me. She didn't say anything. I must add, she had pretty, short, blue, square press-on nails on. "You need any rags?"

"Nall, I'm good, I grabbed an extra towel when I was in intake. Thanks, tho'. I want you to check something in the computer for me too." I knew I could have her, but it wasn't about sex nor nowhere near wanting a girlfriend with me. I wanted her to accept me as I was, a mother fuckin' pimp. If she didn't choose pimpin', we could only be cool with each other and maybe be friends.

"What's your name and Cid number?" I handed her my ID card.

"What you want to know?"

"I want to know how many charges I have and my bond amount."

After she typed my information in, a surprised look appeared on her face. She looked at me, looked me in my eyes for two seconds, and then back at the computer. "It says here, you have one charge of compelling prostitution with a $600,000 bond."

"Thanks. I'll bring the bottles back after I'm finished with them."

"Okay," she said, with a interested look in her eyes, probably wondering why I didn't continue to talk to her.

When I turned around, there were five black dudes looking at me from two near metal tables. I guessed they were peeping me talking to the bitch. I could tell from two of their facial expressions they didn't want a real player around so they could get with the officer themselves. Understand, a real player don't give a fuck who's around, he's gonna get at the woman. If she's already someone's woman in here, then I might let a nigga make it until she reckless eyeballed me. But to tell you the truth, as long as a woman worked in a place like this, a woman was fair game to all because she worked around hundreds of men. She would always like and be interested in other men that were incarcerated here, and probably act on the thought of fucking with someone else while she's already with someone. Only a certain type of woman can keep it 100 and be faithful to her man in the midst of plenty temptation. What most niggas didn't understand was the unity of a players circle we could form to have in this situation. If we worked together using our abilities, we could all come up or get what we wanted. There was always a nigga better and badder than you out there that we could learn from. And, of course, you feed the land where you stayed. That way, everyone ate and it lowered the jealousy, keeping the haters at bay. A bunch of niggas didn't want to do it because a nigga wanted to be The Man, which meant he'd never be in it for the long haul.

On the way to the cell, I got the broom and mop bucket. Eight minutes after I left her desk, the pod officer, Ms. Wards, stepped in the doorway while I was cleaning the toilet. "You want to help me and clean up the pod after lunch?" she asked me.

"Naw, I'm good, baby," I said smoothly, putting a feeler out there to see if she would accept me calling her baby. "I'ma be getting a visit soon, and I gotta make a few phone calls. I'm bonding out tomorrow. If you want to talk, you can have my number, and we'll talk then."

She looked at me as if I lied to her. "If you bonding out tomorrow, why you cleaning your cell?"

"First of all, this is not my cell. Secondly, ain't no telling who been in this motherfucker. I'm not gonna be here for long, but I do want to lay my head in a clean cell and shit on a clean toilet. You dig that, baby?"

"Yeah, I get it." She went quiet but still stood in the doorway, that indicating that she wanted to continue talking.

"I'll give you my number before you leave today, okay?"

"Okay."

I stopped cleaning to give my full attention to her, because I knew she wanted us to converse. I washed my hands, sat on the bunk, and then looked at her. "You look like a college girl. You in college?"

"Yeah, how did you know that?" she asked, surprised.

"You got a college girl vibe. Plus, I see you a smart girl." As fine as she was, I knew she received attention on the inside and outside of her job, so I had to throw a bullshit line out there appealing more to her brain than her looks. Plus, I figured since she's young, around 21, and mentioned something about paying bills, she had to be in school.

She smiled. "Thanks, Damion."

"You welcome. What's your first name?"

"Kimberly."

"Kimberly," I said to myself, making myself remember her name. "What you major in, Kimberly?"

"I'm majoring in communication journalism to be a radio personality," she said excitedly, which indicated that it was something she really wanted to do.

We talked for about 50 minutes about radio personality, about me knowing someone who owned a small radio station in East Texas that she could start at, and my singing career, until they called me for a visit. That whole conversation opened her up to me completely.

It was 9:34 A.M. when they called me out for visit. Rose and Syn were in the visitation booth looking good in their new outfits. "What's up y'all? Y'all looking good as a muthafucka right now."

They both smiled, spoke back, and thanked me. "I put $500 on your books. Here's the receipt," Rose told me and then put the thin piece of pink paper up to the glass so I could see it.

"Thanks, baby." This was the only place I thought I could talk to her about prostitution. I knew they were recording the collect calls and probably these visitation phones too, so I played it safe and asked, "Did you close down shop like you should have?"

"Yes," she answered back. "Uhh, Bre is back in Arlington. CeCe chose up with somebody in Miami. He served you three days ago."

"It's okay, baby. I'm not worried about it. Is there anything else I should know?"

"Uhh, yea, I was texting Jennifer a couple days ago, and I didn't quite understand her messages. She said something about Christie had her to set you up Monday. See." She put the phone screen eye level to my eyes where I could read the messages. "I still don't understand why would Christie want to set you up."

In the text, Jennifer said Christie told her in order to get the felony case in Austin dropped, she would have to set me up on a charge. That message was brief. As Rose scrolled down, I saw that Rose was talking shit to Jennifer, telling her how dumb she was for getting me locked up. I didn't know what to think about this information at the moment. I didn't quite understand why she would set me up this way, because I just talked to her a two days ago and it seemed like things were normal between us with a bit of tension from the night we were together at the hotel. But as I thought about it, she was acting kind of weird, acting like she didn't want to help me with this case. I thought I knew the reason for her setting me up. I guessed it was because of what happened the night I came over to her hotel room and on top of that, she blamed me for Tight game being in a coma. Since Christie wanted to play dirty, I'd play dirty. I'd play her close like I didn't know about the deal she had made with Jennifer. For the time being, while I kept her close, I'd have to think of something to get her off my back or come up with some ways to fuck over her worse than she did me. I wished Tight Game was awake, because she wouldn't have dared do no shit like that to me.

"Don't worry about it. I'll handle it when I get out." Since I knew I needed another lawyer, I told Rose, "Google this lawyer's name for me. His name is Bruce Lowes. Human trafficking lawyer in Dallas-Fort Worth."

It took her seconds to find his website. "Okay. I found it."

"Okay. When you call, tell him to come see me ASAP. Tell him my charge and to come see me so we can talk about a price. Tell him the money's good and you'll pay everything upfront after I talk to him. Matter of fact, just call him right now while you're here, see if he answers the phone."

She did what I told her to do. A couple minutes later, she said, "He didn't answer. Hold on, Daddy, let me call again." Seconds later, she asked someone on the other side of her phone, "Hello, how are you? May I speak with Bruce Lowes please?" Rose and Bruce Lowes' assistant had talked about Mr. Lowes not being in the office, my name, who Rose was to me, and gave his assistant her number to where Bruce Lowes could call her in a couple hours.

After Rose told me everything they talked about, I started talking to Syn, "Why you so quiet, Syn?"

"I'm worried about you getting out. I want you out, Daddy."

"Don't worry, I'll be out within two days, fo' sho. And we gon' do what I said we gonna do. I promise you that."

As Syn told me about my videos that she saw on YouTube, Rose and Syn both looked up at the clear window on the visitation door. "Why she looking in here like that?" Rose asked me.

"Like what?" I asked as I turned towards the locked door to see Kimberly looking at us. I smiled. "I'll tell y'all about her when I get out. She just curious. Y'all wave at her." They did.

She waved back while looking at my hoes. I told Kimberly that I'd talk to her later, and then I continued talking to my hoes.

After my visit, I chopped it up with Kimberly about some of her goals and dreams. I gave her some valuable information and insight on some of her plans until lunch came. "You really not gon' help me feed, are you?"

"No, I'm good. You gotta bunch of niggas in here that's willing to help you feed, anyway."

"But I want you to help me. Anyway, you still have to tell me more about that radio station."

"We got till 3 o'clock to talk. I'm getting out tomorrow, so we got plenty of time to talk."

"If you say so, Damion," she said with a little disappointment in her voice and curiosity in her eyes. I wanted to help her, but I didn't want to seem as if I was chasing her. I wanted her to chase me. And two, I really didn't feel like doing anything. I needed to be in the cell using this short time of incarceration to get my mind right.

To get her mind off me and back on her job, I told her, "Don't let me sidetrack you. Do your job. Cha need to be fed right now." The other pod next door had started feeding lunch four minutes ago. This pod hot box was still outside of the pod's door. "I promise I'll make time for you when I'm released, okay."

"Okay. Can you at least get the hot box for me and pull it inside?"

"Yeah, I can do that." As I got the hot box, she spoke on the intercom to the inmates to wake up and form a line if they wanted their tray. She called some yellow pretty boy along with two other dudes up to the front to help her feed. They were three of the five dudes I saw looking at me sitting at the two tables.

The commissary lady arrived on the pod 52 minutes after lunch. I bought a bunch of hygiene items and a bunch of food items to spread with, because I wasn't eating none of this jail food. I put my things up, took a shower, and then got on the phone to call my son's mother, Tiffany. "Hey, baby, what you doin'?"

"Don't baby me, Damion," she said with an attitude.

"Damn, what's up with all that? You okay?"

"Don't go there with me, Damion. You know what you haven't been doing. Now you want to call me when you get yourself locked up like it's all good."

"Tiffany, I apologize for the way I've been acting lately. I've been selfish. I ask can you forgive me. I'ma make it right with the family, Tiffany. I promise."

"Naw, Damion, uh uhh, I don't want to hear it. I can't do you no more. I'm sick of your shit. You can't have your cake and eat it too. I'm not about to kiss your ass anymore. I'm doing good in my life right now, and I'm not about to let nothing fuck that up."

"So what you saying, Tiffany?"

"Whatever we had left of our relationship is over, Damion. You fucked up for the last time."

"Oh yeah, it's over, huh?" I said as I nodded my head while I still held the phone.

"You the one that decided that with your actions, Damion. I'm just making it official. And I think you should know that I'm dating Kevin Rodgers now. He plays pro ball for the Atlanta Falcons, and he treats me better than you ever did, so you can stop calling me with that baby shit."

"Bitch, shut the fuck up with that bullshit. I don't wanna hear that shit," I said, reacting emotionally when instead I should have keep it player about the situation. I told her, "Bitch, you don't have to throw that shit in my face. I don't give a fuck about that. If anything, bitch, I'm happy you caught a baller." I wanted to get on some real live pimp shit with her, but I knew they were recording these phone calls.

"Oh, I'm a bitch now, huh Damion? After all I did was be good to you and love you unconditionally," she said, hurt and surprised. "But I'm a bitch, huh. Well, you don't deserve a good woman like me. Stick to them no-good, funky ass hoes you got. Me and mine gon' be good."

I hung up on her after she said that. I didn't want to hear that shit at all. Talking about I can't have my cake and eat it too. I'm a pimp with hoes. Ain't that what I was supposed to do, eat it too? She knew I was pimpin' when we first decided to be together. Now she wanted to part ways because she wasn't getting what she thought she deserves. She wasn't saying that when I got our family a house to live in, the shopping sprees, when I started her business for her, and when I put thousands of dollars toward my two step-kids and our son's college funds, all with my money. I felt like I'd gotten played.

But truth be told, I played myself. She would have stayed down with me if I had stayed down with her. I underestimated her. I thought she would be down with me damn near through no matter what. I guess she got fed up with waiting on me. I didn't see that coming. I admit I was wrong for calling her a bitch, though. And I agree, she didn't deserve the shit I was doing to her. She was a good woman. She deserved more than I could offer her in a relationship right now. That was my first time ever calling her a bitch, something I didn't mean at all. What made me mad was the tone of voice and the way she spoke what she said. I was wrong for the way I was doing her and our son. I guess she finally realized that she deserved better. She found her someone that could treat her better because she was fed up with what I was doing to her. I didn't think there was anything I could do about it. She was the type of woman when her mind was made up, she stuck to that. Maybe if I got completely out the game she would give me another chance, but we knew that wasn't happening. It was probably for the best, though. When it was all said and done, I was gonna marry Shae. That's where my heart was at. I ain't gon' lie to you, I was really in love with Shae. I owed her the world.

While walking back to the cell, I heard a nigga call out my pimp name. I continued to walk until he called me two more times, each being louder than before. Then I turned towards the voice with suspicion in my mind. When I looked at his face, I knew I didn't know him, but he looked familiar, like I'd seen him somewhere. He had a look on his face like he knew me and had a pimpish swag about himself. I walked over to where he was sitting in a chair in front of the flat 27-inch television screen. "Wuz up? Where you know me from?"

"I'm J-Mack. You knocked me for that ho Diamond at The McConnell Lodge Hotel two years ago."

I remembered that night. I played a little dirty that night. I got Diamond's information on an escort site my hoes were posted on. I saw on her ad that the ho was in the same area as me, so I called her up to set up a date, impersonating a trick. I showed up at her hotel door draped up in about $170,000 worth of jewelry, and dressed to kill. Once I was in the room, I started running my venom at the ho, that made her choose up. I called up J-Mack to inform him with the good news. We had our hoes at the same hotel in Arlington, but I didn't see him. The only way he knew how I looked was he must have seen me with her that night or the morning before I took her to another hotel in Dallas. That no-good ass ho only lasted three weeks until I blew the ho. She got out of pocket too much by trying to talk back when I checked her on something she had done wrong. I left that ho at the room while she slept to never return again. I never answered her calls nor called her again.

"Wuz up, P? It's a pleasure to meet you, pimp," I said while I extended my arm for a pimp handshake. "What, they got you on one of those pimp charges too, huh?"

"They tryna take pimpin' down, but a pimp gon' always find a way to stay up. Down is the hoes' place, ya dig." What he said made me smile. I liked the nigga already, but I was still cautious with him. I didn't know if he was an informant for the two detectives or not, trying to get me to tell on myself. If he got locked up in Arlington,

I knew he too had talked to the same detective who arrested me. Maybe I was tripping about him, but you never know with some niggas these days.

"I can dig it, pimp," I told him without saying anything else. I wanted him to continue talking.

"They got me on a trafficking of a persons charge."

"How long you been locked up?" I asked, trying to dig for more information from him.

"Forty-two days. I'm tryna get me a speedy trial. I heard the ho said she wasn't coming to court."

I got the impression that he wasn't an informant, so I sat down next to him in a chair. We rode for a little over an hour about the game, pimps, and hoes we both knew, until Kimberly called me over to the desk at 1 P.M. I found out he was my pimp partna Luxury P's partna. They were both from East Arlington. He was 22 years old and had been in the game for almost three years now. He had gotten caught up on a first-degree trafficking of a persons charge, taking a 17-year-old ho to an outcall that was a sting operation in Arlington. He could have been honest or he could have lied when he told me he didn't know her real age. He only had her for two days. Smart pimps knew how old a ho was because they would look at their hoes' identification card and do their research on the ho, which consisted of a background check and good screening before he accepted her in his stable.

Pimpin' on underaged girls was a desperate and impatient move to me, even if she was already hoing and willing to get down with you. Either he was trying to shake back from a fall in the game, or he wanted things to be easy and have more control, or he just didn't give a fuck about the consequences at that moment. I'd learned the only thing that came easy in this game was a case. I was glad I'd never gotten caught up with an underaged prostitute when I was 17 and I was fucking with a couple girls my age back then. Most young pimps that turned out in their mid and late teens fell into the trap of pimpin' young teenage girls, and some ended up getting caught up with them. I do admit though, some teenage girls I'd come across were far more advanced and Gamed up teenagers that had more game than some women in their twenties, but that didn't give a pimp the right to pimp them. There were boundaries, rules, and laws a pimp had to live by to really succeed in this game. If not, he would self-destruct and end up in prison.

I gave Kimberly my number on a request form like I was turning it in. "If you don't call, you fucked up a great opportunity. That number at the bottom is that white girl number you seen at my visit, just in case I don't answer."

"Believe me, I'ma call you. I want to fuck with you."

"I wanna fuck with yo' fine ass too. We gonna make some big shit happen together for us. Hit me up in two days or call Rose to see what's going on with me." We talked for an hour and a half until I saw the second-shift officer at the door.

A couple hours later, at 5:13 P.M., they called me for an attorney visit. It was Bruce Lowes. He was a tall, bald, beer belly, red-skinned, heavy-set white guy, but he looked clean in his dark-blue tailored suit. After we introduced ourselves, he told me, "Well, first off, I would like to say that I've worked on numerous federal and state cases dealing with trafficking and prostitution in Dallas and Fort Worth and surrounding counties. I specialize in human trafficking. I rank number one in Tarrant County and Dallas County when it comes to human trafficking cases. I'm 37/6 at winning cases at trial on your type of case, as well as gotten numerous cases dismissed. Now that we've gotten that out the way, I want to ask, do you want to go further with me?"

"Yes, I'd like to."

"Okay. Tell me what happened with the girl on your case."

I slid him the affidavit that Christie had given me and let him read it before I started telling him about the case. I told him the whole truth about what went down with Jennifer and me. I felt I had to since he was going to be my attorney. That's the only way he could help me, if he knew the truth about what I did. I also let him know what Jennifer texted Rose about the deal Christie made with Jennifer. Every so often, he would write down something I had said on a yellow writing tablet. From seeing that, I knew he was as good as he said he was.

"There's plenty of ways to attack this case than to use what Christie's doing. It's fucked up, but I know her personally, and I don't want to get into that dirty business with her. But if what you're telling me is the truth, we can beat this case no matter what. If we do end up going to trial, which I don't think we will because of the weak evidence, in these types of cases some of the girls involved statement won't be creditable in trial. Some of them have criminal history in these same situations and priors of prostitution charges. I saw that you have two federal prior convictions of pimping and human trafficking on your record."

"Yes, I do. That happened over five years ago."

"Well, that's nothing, there's ways around that."

"So how much will you charge me for taking my case?"

"Well, for your priors, the bond reduction, the bail, and your case, I will have to charge you $12,000. $15,000 if we go to trial, but I doubt that." I could see he was money hungry. I couldn't blame him, he was one of the best for my case. Anyway, I knew if you could pay a lawyer top dollar or boost their status up, they would fight hard on your behalf.

"Okay, that's not a problem. Get in contact with Rosemary and she'll give the you $15,000 tomorrow." I was giving him $15,000 to put in his head that I told him the truth about everything I said, and that I was prepared to go to trial if he couldn't get the charges dismissed. I wasn't signing for shit.

"That's good with me. I'll hop right on it. I have to talk to the judge first thing in the morning, but you should be out tomorrow sometime. I'll come back up here or call Rosemary to let you know I'm done with posting your bail. It all depends on how busy I am."

"Alright. That will do. Thanks, you have a good evening."

"You as well. And you're welcome. Oh yeah, Mr. Johnson, don't talk to anyone in here about your case."

I walked out the visitation booth feeling good. I had faith in Bruce Lowes that he would get this case dropped. I knew they couldn't pin this case on me anyway. I just hoped it didn't take too long to get dismissed.

I called Shae after I left the visit. "I just left the house. I'm on my way now," she said when she answered.

"Oh, okay. It's 6 o'clock. I was wondering why you hadn't come up here to see me yet."

"I was a little busy earlier, and I picked up Pinky a few hours ago."

"Oh yeah, where is she?" I asked excitedly, curious to know if she was really off drugs.

"Right here, she can hear you."

"Wuz up, Pinky?"

"Hey, Daddy, what's going on?" I could tell she was smiling while she talked to me.

"Just tryna get the fuck up outta here, everything good, tho'. Anyway, I can hear you smiling. How you feeling?"

"I feel good. I feel real good now. Thanks, Daddy." Her tone of voice expressed that she was telling the truth.

"You welcome. You know I missed your ass, right?"

"Yeah, I missed you too. I thought about you a lot."

"So, it's over, right? You done with that dope?"

"Yeah, it's over. I'm done with it all, Daddy. Thanks so much for getting me help."

"You welcome. You know it's my job to make sure you in the best of health. You in good hands, always remember that. Y'all almost here or what?"

"Yeah, we about to exit off 30," Shae said.

"Oh, okay. Well, I'ma let y'all go. I'll see y'all when y'all get here."

It was 6:37 P.M. when they finally called me out for a visit. They were both sitting in the two steel seats on the other side of the visitation thick glass. Seeing them smile made me smile big. I thought to myself, Damn, *I got two bad ass queens.*

From the moment I walked into the booth, I examined Pinky. It looked like she was off heroin. Her skin looked more clear, her face glowed with high spirits. I hoped she stayed that way, because she was more beautiful than ever.

In the middle of our visit, Shae told me, "You know I went to my doctor today for my checkup. He told me I'm pregnant, Tunke."

"Fo'real, Shae?" I asked, shocked.

"Damn, Tunke, why you say it like that? You don't sound like you happy about it."

"Come on, Shae. Don't do that shit, you know I'm happy. It's just that I'm surprised after all these years of nutting in you, you finally pregnant again. It's really amazing, because I really want to share a child with you." I was happy about Shae being pregnant. I also felt because of my lifestyle that I didn't need any more kids. I didn't spend the proper time with the kids I already had, and Shae knew that. I didn't know why she still wanted to have my baby. I guessed she really did love me, wanted my child, and believed her pregnancy would slow me down. To tell you the truth, it did make me want to change, because now I had a lot more responsibilities added onto my plate, and I didn't want any bad blood with none of my kids' mothers.

"I'm surprised too. You know I been wanting to have your baby for a long time now, ever since I lost the last baby three years ago."

"I know, things should go right this time. What you want us to have, a boy or girl?" I asked to make her feel better.

"A boy. I don't wanna deal with no girl," she said.

"Yea, me too. What about you, Pinky, what you wanna have?"

"I want a boy too."

I realized some things sitting here talking to my two pregnant queens, who I loved deeply. It made me think about the kids I already had and how I was affecting them by not being a father to them every step of the way in their lives. I made a promise to myself that I would make a better effort to be a full-time father. I loved my life, I loved myself, I loved my children's mothers, so there shouldn't be a reason why I neglected them like I did, especially when my children had my DNA. Being in jail now was affecting Shae and Pinky as well as my seed in their bellies. It was a must that I stepped up to be a better man, son, brother, uncle, and father. I owed them that.

# Smoove Dolla

## Chapter 15

The next day at 8:19 A.M., I was told to pack it up. I gave J-Mack my commissary, my phone number, and I got his information, because I was going to look out for him while he was inside since he didn't have a pimp buddy. Before walking out the pod's door, I called Shae to tell her to be on her way because I was getting release.

By the time I got released, Shae and Pinky were waiting outside the jail in her Chevy Impala. After talking with them for a couple minutes, Shae had told me that Tight Game had woken from the coma today. That was wonderful to hear, because I didn't want him passing away over my head, knowing I was the reason for us getting robbed and shot. He was my mentor, sponsor, father figure, and brother. I didn't want to lose him. It was only right that I gave him a call to check up on him to see how he was doing.

"Hello," he said when he answered the phone.

"What's up, Tight game, man?"

"Glad to be awake. What's going on with you?"

I kept it short, not saying too much. "Worried about you, man. I'm happy that you wake up from that coma."

"Yeaaa, P, I'm too strong for that, lil' brother. It ain't my time yet. I still got things to accomplish, shit to see, things to build and create. I still got many years ahead of me, P. You know what's fucked up tho'? I lost my sense of smell. Doc said slowly but surely it'll come back, but everything else is good."

"That's good. Tight Game, I want to apologize for what happened that night. If I would've knew that bitch was up to no good, she would've never been around."

"I know. Next time you get a ho, do your homework on the ho first before you allow her in your fold. And then you'll know," he said seriously.

"You right, you right." We talked for a little bit more until I heard some people come into the room and start talking to him. He told me he'd get back with me, and I told him I'd be up there soon to see him, and then we hung up.

They were out riding after they went shopping at The Parks

Mall when I called them to pick me up. When we got to Shae's crib, they had got the smaller bags and took them into the house while I grabbed the heavy ones. After I shut the truck, I heard a low noise behind me. It made me look back to see what it was, but as soon as I saw the black figure, it was too late. A pistol was coming down on my head.

\* \* \*

When I opened my eyes, all I could see was darkness. My eyes were covered with something. I was in pain on the top of my head. It felt like my wound was leaking blood.

After seconds of listening to my surroundings and moving around, I became aware of my whereabouts. I was in the back seat of a car with my hands and feet taped tightly together. A strong, funky smell of shit, piss, beer, and old trash all mixed in together invaded my nostrils. It had me gagging. I fought down the vomit going up my stomach into my throat, because if I would have vomited while this tape covered my mouth, I would've choked and died.

There were two questions that came to mind. "Who the fuck kidnapped me? And for what reason?

I couldn't think of anyone that I had beef with or had beef with me. I knew it couldn't have been my Mason brothers. Other than Jerry, it was all good between my brothers and me. That's what I wanted to believe anyway. Tight Game had woken up. Something told me that it wasn't my Mason brothers who did this. The next person popped up in my mind was Trick's and Rida's people getting back at me. The only way word could've leaked out that I killed Rida and his people at the club that night was through my hood niggas. If that was the case, that was a mistake on my part. That's why a nigga should do dirt one deep instead of with a group of niggas. I should have known that by now and lived by that code since a pimp's life was a lonely one. Really, I didn't think Trick's or Rida's people had anything to do with this either. I knew they would have left me and my two pregnant queens stanking where we stood in front of Shae's house. That's how niggas' thought process was. Only hood niggas and Mexicans murdered that way. This was on some professional shit.

I couldn't move my hands or legs because they were tied together with what felt like duct tape. Even my mouth was covered. To uncover my eyes, I rubbed my face up against the smooth edge of the leather seat. I managed to get my left eye uncovered after about twenty attempts. I was in the backseat of an old-model Town Car. My head was behind the driver's seat, so I couldn't see who was driving. There was no one in the passenger seat. It was completely silent in the car. The only sounds I could hear were small rocks hitting the front of the car and under it. I could tell we were driving through the country road because the road was bumpy, the dirt was coming up from the back of the car, and there were no street lights anywhere. Although, I still could see an abundance of trees because of the headlights from the car.

While trying to raise up and see who was driving, I heard the accelerator and felt the car speed up. My whole body started hopping up and down in the backseat on the floor. Out of nowhere, he slammed down on the brakes. My body went up against the back of the front seat, back down to the floor in between the front and backseat. Instantly, blood started leaking out from my forehead from hitting my head on the seat guide rail on the floor. "Sit your ass still back there," a black man with a strong country accent said. It sounded familiar, but I couldn't place the voice.

Blood was running down my face, and I couldn't wipe myself. I couldn't move. I couldn't fucking talk. My side and back hurt bad from it hitting the hump on the floor in the backseat. I did my best to calm myself down from getting mad and frustrated by taking deep breaths through my nose so I could come up with a plan to break free.

About two minutes later, we ended up stopping. I heard the driver's door open. Minutes later, the door slammed, and he started driving again for about four minutes. The driver's door opened again. Seconds later, the passenger back door opened. He grabbed a fist full of my shirt and the back of my pants, picked me up out of between the seats, and then threw me out the car into the dirt. I made sure not to look his way just yet. I didn't want him to see that I uncovered my eye. I knew there had to be a reason why he didn't kill me at Shae's house. I had a little time to borrow to think of an escape plan.

I heard footsteps walking away from me towards barking dogs. I put my wound on the side of my head and my forehead in the dirt to stop the bleeding. I blinked my eyelids a few times to get the dirt from around my eyelid until I could see clearly. I turned my head towards my abductor. I couldn't identify who he was just yet because of my view and his back being towards me, but I could tell he was a big, stocky dude, standing over six feet. He was built like a big, tall bodyguard or bouncer.

He walked up the porch stairs into the unlocked door at a big old, wooden, two-story house. As soon as he went inside without closing the door behind him and turning the lights on, I looked right to left, looking for anything I could use to free my hands. The car was the only thing I saw that could be some help. My body was sore, but I still had the strength to make it. I started rolling towards it until I made it to the car. I scooted back on the ground until my hands were up against the right back tire. I did my best to scrape and rip the duct tape from my wrist, but it felt like I was rubbing my skin off my arms.

I knew I was fucked when I saw him come back outside about two minutes later. He had a big bag of what looked like dog food in his left hand, and in his right, a 24-oz can of Budweiser. He downed the beer on the porch, then he dropped it. He kicked it to the side to the ground where a lot of cans were.

I still couldn't tell who he was because it was so dark, only the porch light was on, no street lights.

He walked up on me. "Oh, I see you tried to get loose. There's no way out of this but one way. There's nowhere to go out here anyway. You'll probably be eaten by wild hogs before you make it anywhere safe. You in the country," he said in a deep and strong country accent. He started dragging me by the pants a few yards away from the car. He dug his hand in a bag and pulled out a big piece of steak, and then put it in my shirt. Afterwards, he cut my belt in half with a sharp four-inch knife while it was still in the loops, and then put a piece of meat along with dog food on top of my buttocks inside my pants.

When he walked over to those dogs, letting them out their caged fence, I knew it was over for me. I felt hopeless. I felt defeated, because I knew there wasn't anything I could do to stop this torture I was receiving right now. I asked myself why he didn't just kill me already and get it over with. Letting dogs rip me apart would be too messy, right?

As he and the two pit bulls were coming towards me, I said a short silent prayer in my head to get me out this situation.

"Su, Su, get him!" he told them.

One dog bit the fuck out of my waist, making me roll to the left. He bit me two more times before he got to the steak, and the pain caused me to stop moving. At the same time, the other vicious dog went straight for the other piece of meat. He bit down a few times until it tore a hole in the back of my pants, pulling the cold steak out the hole. That shit hurt like a motherfucker. I yelled out loud as fuck every time I got bit.

Out the blue, I heard four gunshots, two quick shots and then another two shots a second later. I thought I had gotten shot until I heard the two dogs whining and didn't feel them biting on me anymore. I heard footsteps coming closer towards me. "If you move, I'ma shoot yo' ass like I did yo' fucking dogs," I heard a woman say. That voice could only came from one person, Shae. "Throw the knife to the ground!"

A couple of seconds later, the man said, "I'm not dying from anyone else's hand. If I die tonight, I'm dying from my own." Then I felt a body fall on top of my legs.

I heard a lot of footsteps from more than one person coming towards me and a bunch of female voices. They were all saying disgusted comments about seeing all the blood from his neck, to saying my name and asking was I okay. Shae slowly ripped the tape off from around my mouth and from my eyes. I was so happy to see Shae, Pinky, Syn, and Rose. I was glad I let Shae get a gun license a while back. Being good to and taking care of my hoes had paid off. I knew if I was gorilla pimpin' and treating them like shit, they wouldn't have ever come to my recue. Although I was glad they did, at the same time, I was embarrassed also because I was in distress. I was injured and ass out with dirt all in between my butt cheeks. I felt bad to be in the presence of them like this, but I would have rather been rescued than left for dead. I had no doubt that they cared and had some kind of love for me. I knew they did.

"Shae, get that knife out that guy's hand to cut the tape," Rose said.

"No, don't do that, Shae. He killed himself. You touch that knife, you might get charged. Just do this, find the line where the tape was tore at, take it off that way. After you do that, y'all help slide me from under him and leave him the way he is."

After they slid me from under him, Shae and Syn helped me to my feet. I limped hard until I walked off some of the pain. I heard Pinky laugh and then Rose joined in, doing the same. "Yeah, go ahead and get your laughs out. Because later, I bet not hear any laughing about it," I said, playing and serious at the same time. I would've been laughing at somebody too if they had the back of their pants bitten off to where most of their ass was exposed. I had to laugh from hurting bad. I couldn't wait to clean myself, change clothes, and go to the hospital.

I walked to my abductor. As soon as I got a good look at his face, I recognized him. It was Tight Game's hit man, Big Country. I had met him six years ago. Since then, I hadn't seen him. He had gained about 60 pounds since then. Damn, I couldn't believe Tight game put a hit out on me. We just talked to each other not even an hour ago. Nothing in his tone of voice suggested that he was angry and wanted to kill me over what happened. I got played again. SMFH.

I checked Big Country's blue-jean pockets, looking for his cell phone, but I didn't find anything. I stood up and said, "Shae and Rose, go inside the house and look for his phone. It should be near the door or in the kitchen somewhere. Mine should be right there too. Don't touch nothing. Just look for the phones and bring 'em back."

They both said okay and then made their way towards the house.

"Where is the car?" I asked Syn and Pinky.

"It's up the road. A big, long, wooden bar blocked the road leading here, so we walked up here," Syn said.

"Was it locked?"

"Yes," they both said in unison.

I didn't want to walk to the car, so I told her, "Syn get the car keys from Shae. Find a towel and handle his keys with the towel so you can open that bar and drive the car to me."

"Okay."

"Pinky, go with her so you can help her open it."

I laid on the ground on my side and waited on my hoes. Shae and Rose came out the house five minutes later. As soon as they walked up on me, Shae told me, "Tunke, you know that muthafucker has yo' momma's address, yo' sister, and my name and address. He even had pictures of all of us," she said angrily as she gave me a big manilla folder. I zoned out as Shae started talking shit about Big Country and about what was inside the envelope.

I pulled out two small photos of everyone she just named including me, and one old mugshot of me the first time I got locked up for pimping. The recent pictures were taken about a month ago. That shit had me hotter than a motherfucker.

Shae handed me his phone. I scrolled down his texts with Tight game. It'd been months since they last texted as well as called each other, and they weren't texting about me. The texts were all brief. When I saw that Christie was the last person to text him, I knew she was the reason for me being abducted and tortured. In the last month, there were texts where she told him to meet her at specific places and to call her. The messages had been going back and forth since the day I was in the hospital. The last text told him to take care of business.

I texted Christie from Big Country's phone. I studied some of his texts and made sure it sounded like Big Country.

Big Country
I took care of that. I ran across something
you should take a look at. Where can we meet?
9:43 P.M. Thursday 6/4/2012

Christie
K. Is it important?
9:45 P.M. Thursday 6/4/2012

Big Country
Yes, it is.
9:46 P.M. Thursday 6/4/2012

Christie
K. Come to the hospital. Text me when you get here.
9:48 P.M. Thursday 6/4/2012

Big Country
Will do.
9:49 P.M. Thursday 6/4/2012

Pinky and Syn arrived six minutes later. Shae and Rose helped me get into the car. I had to lay on the side in the passenger seat leaned back because my ass cheek hurt the most and I didn't want to sit on it. "How did y'all know where to find me?"

"I tracked your phone on trackaphone.com after fifteen minutes of calling and texting you. I knew something was wrong when I saw that our bags and your glasses were on the ground," Shae said.

"Good thinking, y'all. Thank y'all so much for coming to my rescue."

They all said 'you're welcome.' "So, where we heading now?" Shae asked while she drove out the country.

"Go to CVS first so we can get something for these wounds, and then head to your house."

Before heading to the hospital, I had showered, got bandaged up, put on clean clothes, and took three OxyContin pain pills. Even though I didn't do any drugs, I felt like I was forced to because of the pain I was feeling. It definitely killed a lot of the pain.

Shae and I left her house and headed to the hospital. We looked for Christie's white Benz she usually drove, but I didn't see it in the two outside parking lots nor the three-story parking garage. I knew she didn't expect anything to go wrong, because she trusted Big Country's skills. I could text her what I wanted to because she believed it really was Big Country.

Big Country
Are you still at the hospital?
10:51 P.M. Thursday 6/4/2012

Christie
Yea, why?
10:53 P.M. Thursday 6/4/2012

Big Country
I'm here. What car are you in?
10:54 P.M. Thursday 6/4/2012

Christie
A white Maserati. Give me some time, be down in a few.
10:54 P.M. Thursday 6/4/2012

We found her car in the parking garage on the second floor, which took a little over three minutes. Shae parked six cars away from her.

I got out the car and waited between a black Suburban driver's door and the passenger side door of Christie's Maserati while looking out for her. As soon as I saw her walking towards her car and looking at her surroundings, I kneeled down lower beside the passenger side of the car.

When she hit the alarm, unlocking all four doors and then opening the driver's door, I opened the passenger's door and rushed in with her. She screamed when she saw me. I put the gun to her head.

"Bitch, shut the fuck up and close that fuckin' do'!" She did what I told her to do. "What is this, Christie?" I asked as I shoved the manilla envelope in her face.

She didn't answer me.

"I know you hear me, bitch. I'ma ask you one more time, ho. Why is my information in this envelope?"

She continued to remain silent. After waiting five seconds for her to speak, I said, "Ok, we gon' see what you got to say when I go up there and tell Tight game what we did together and how you set me up. And what you paid Big Country to do to me." I moved, putting my weight on my left ass cheek.

"No, no, Tunke, please don't tell him. I'll pay you, don't tell him, please," she pleaded.

"Bitch, shut yo' bitch ass up, ho. That shit ain't gon' work. Yo' ass ain't no good and you need to be exposed, bitch." I forced the barrel of the Glock into her mouth while holding the back of her head. I started thinking about all the dirty shit she did, from getting me arrested to getting me kidnapped to being nearly killed. All that was because of what happened to Tight game. It made me want to kill her. What stopped me was the thought of me not getting away with it. Plus, Tight Game was awake now. I knew he had Christie handling a lot of things for him. I was already down bad for letting her suck my dick. I didn't want to get deeper in the hole with him by fucking up his money, so I let her make it on the strength of him.

"I should kill yo' no-good ass for what you did! You funky ass bitch! Bitch, all you had to do was wait, everything was gon' be alright. You so smart, you stupid. I want you to stay away from me and my people, bitch. I'm not gon' tell him what happened just yet, but I am. I want you to get my charges dropped, and if you don't, I got your fingerprints and some information that'll get yo' ass locked up too."

I forced the Glock deeper down her throat, trying to make her vomit on her pretty red dress. As she cried heavily, she tried to say something, but I couldn't understand what she was saying. Vomit filled her mouth. When I removed the gun, a lot of vomit splattered all over the steering wheel and red dress. She started coughing and then screaming loud while hitting the side of her fist on the driver's door. "My fucking dress! Get the fuck out my fucking car, motherfucker!"

I made her throw up on herself to force her to leave and lie to Tight Game on why she left. I wanted the thought to pop up in his head that something was going on with Christie. I knew he would catch on to her lie fast, because she would have canceled everything at the moment to be by Tight game's side. Especially for the first night of him being out of the coma.

I opened the door and told her, "And, bitch, Jennifer bet not come to court either, ho!" As I was getting out, she picked up two handfuls of vomit and threw it at me. If I wasn't quick, it would have landed on me. She was off by inches.

I went to Shae's Impala, gave the gun and envelope to her, and told her to take it back home I didn't need a gun to check in the hospital. I wanted to go see Tight Game, but I didn't want him to see me bandaged up since I wasn't going to tell him what went down between Christie and I nor with Big Country yet. I'ma wait for the appropriate time to tell him everything that went down, knowing he just woke from a coma. Plus, I was in too much of a bad shape to deal with the consequences if they came after telling Tight Game what happened.

\*\*\*

After checking into the emergency room and getting me a room, I laid in bed thinking about how being a pimp had affected my life and how it changed my life for the better. It had really been a blessing and a curse. I'd had some wonderful and amazing times as a pimp. At a time like this, it had been the worst I had ever experienced in the game. Never in my wildest dreams would I have thought some shit like this would come with the game. I had some real tightening up to do. I admit, I had slipped a couple of times, and I blamed it on my stupid decisions. Being in the hospital bed for the second time made a nigga think about giving up the game completely, but I knew I'd never do that, not now anyway. I knew a bunch of things would be changing now, on how I pimped and how I lived. I knew I possessed what it took to pimp on something bigger and better than the low level of the game. That's just what I would be working towards upon my release from the hospital.

I was switching it up and pimping on the legal side of the game.

To Be Continued...
Money Game 2
Coming Soon

## Submission Guideline

Submit the first three chapters of your completed manuscript to ldpsubmissions@gmail.com, subject line: Your book's title. The manuscript must be in a .doc file and sent as an attachment. Document should be in Times New Roman, double spaced and in size 12 font. Also, provide your synopsis and full contact information. If sending multiple submissions, they must each be in a separate email.

Have a story but no way to send it electronically? You can still submit to LDP/Ca$h Presents. Send in the first three chapters, written or typed, of your completed manuscript to:

**LDP: Submissions Dept**
**Po Box 944**
**Stockbridge, Ga 30281**

*DO NOT send original manuscript. Must be a duplicate.*

Provide your synopsis and a cover letter containing your full contact information.

Thanks for considering LDP and Ca$h Presents.

# Smoove Dolla

# Money Game

STREET KINGS III

PAID IN BLOOD III

CARTEL KILLAZ IV

DOPE GODS III

**Hood Rich**

SINS OF A HUSTLA II

**ASAD**

RICH $AVAGE II

**By Troublesome**

YAYO V

Bred In The Game 2

**S. Allen**

CREAM III

**By Yolanda Moore**

SON OF A DOPE FIEND III

HEAVEN GOT A GHETTO II

**By Renta**

LOYALTY AIN'T PROMISED III

**By Keith Williams**

I'M NOTHING WITHOUT HIS LOVE II

SINS OF A THUG II

TO THE THUG I LOVED BEFORE II

**By Monet Dragun**

QUIET MONEY IV

EXTENDED CLIP III

THUG LIFE IV

By **Trai'Quan**

THE STREETS MADE ME III

By **Larry D. Wright**

IF YOU CROSS ME ONCE II

# Smoove Dolla

By **Anthony Fields**
THE STREETS WILL NEVER CLOSE II
By **K'ajji**
HARD AND RUTHLESS III
**Von Diesel**
KILLA KOUNTY II
By **Khufu**
MOBBED UP III
By **King Rio**
MONEY GAME II
By **Smoove Dolla**

## Available Now

RESTRAINING ORDER **I & II**
By **CA$H & Coffee**
LOVE KNOWS NO BOUNDARIES **I II & III**
By **Coffee**
RAISED AS A GOON I, II, III & IV
BRED BY THE SLUMS I, II, III
BLAST FOR ME I & II
ROTTEN TO THE CORE I II III
A BRONX TALE I, II, III
DUFFLE BAG CARTEL I II III IV V VI
HEARTLESS GOON I II III IV V
A SAVAGE DOPEBOY I II

# Money Game

DRUG LORDS I II III

CUTTHROAT MAFIA I II

KING OF THE TRENCHES

By **Ghost**

LAY IT DOWN **I & II**

LAST OF A DYING BREED I II

BLOOD STAINS OF A SHOTTA I & II III

By **Jamaica**

LOYAL TO THE GAME I II III

LIFE OF SIN I, II III

By **TJ & Jelissa**

BLOODY COMMAS I & II

SKI MASK CARTEL I II & III

KING OF NEW YORK I II,III IV V

RISE TO POWER I II III

COKE KINGS I II III IV

BORN HEARTLESS I II III IV

KING OF THE TRAP I II

By **T.J. Edwards**

IF LOVING HIM IS WRONG…I & II

LOVE ME EVEN WHEN IT HURTS I II III

By **Jelissa**

WHEN THE STREETS CLAP BACK I & II III

THE HEART OF A SAVAGE I II III

By **Jibril Williams**

A DISTINGUISHED THUG STOLE MY HEART I II & III

LOVE SHOULDN'T HURT I II III IV

RENEGADE BOYS I II III IV

PAID IN KARMA I II III

SAVAGE STORMS I II

# Smoove Dolla

AN UNFORESEEN LOVE
By **Meesha**
A GANGSTER'S CODE I &, II III
A GANGSTER'S SYN I II III
THE SAVAGE LIFE I II III
CHAINED TO THE STREETS I II III
BLOOD ON THE MONEY I II III
**By J-Blunt**
PUSH IT TO THE LIMIT
By **Bre' Hayes**
BLOOD OF A BOSS **I, II, III, IV, V**
SHADOWS OF THE GAME
TRAP BASTARD
By **Askari**
THE STREETS BLEED MURDER **I, II & III**
THE HEART OF A GANGSTA I II& III
By **Jerry Jackson**
CUM FOR ME I II III IV V VI VII
An **LDP Erotica Collaboration**
BRIDE OF A HUSTLA **I  II & II**
THE FETTI GIRLS **I, II& III**
CORRUPTED BY A GANGSTA I, II III, IV
BLINDED BY HIS LOVE
THE PRICE YOU PAY FOR LOVE I, II ,III
DOPE GIRL MAGIC I II III
By **Destiny Skai**
WHEN A GOOD GIRL GOES BAD
By **Adrienne**
THE COST OF LOYALTY I II III
**By Kweli**

# Money Game

A GANGSTER'S REVENGE **I II III & IV**

THE BOSS MAN'S DAUGHTERS I II III IV V

A SAVAGE LOVE **I & II**

BAE BELONGS TO ME I II

A HUSTLER'S DECEIT I, II, III

WHAT BAD BITCHES DO I, II, III

SOUL OF A MONSTER I II III

KILL ZONE

A DOPE BOY'S QUEEN I II

By **Aryanna**

A KINGPIN'S AMBITON

A KINGPIN'S AMBITION **II**

I MURDER FOR THE DOUGH

By **Ambitious**

TRUE SAVAGE I II III IV V VI VII

DOPE BOY MAGIC I, II, III

MIDNIGHT CARTEL I II III

CITY OF KINGZ I II

By **Chris Green**

A DOPEBOY'S PRAYER

By **Eddie "Wolf" Lee**

THE KING CARTEL **I, II & III**

By **Frank Gresham**

THESE NIGGAS AIN'T LOYAL **I, II & III**

By **Nikki Tee**

GANGSTA SHYT **I II &III**

By **CATO**

THE ULTIMATE BETRAYAL

By **Phoenix**

BOSS'N UP **I , II & III**

# Smoove Dolla

By **Royal Nicole**
I LOVE YOU TO DEATH
By **Destiny J**
I RIDE FOR MY HITTA
I STILL RIDE FOR MY HITTA
By **Misty Holt**
LOVE & CHASIN' PAPER
By **Qay Crockett**
TO DIE IN VAIN
SINS OF A HUSTLA
By **ASAD**
BROOKLYN HUSTLAZ
By **Boogsy Morina**
BROOKLYN ON LOCK I & II
By **Sonovia**
GANGSTA CITY
By **Teddy Duke**
A DRUG KING AND HIS DIAMOND I & II III
A DOPEMAN'S RICHES
HER MAN, MINE'S TOO I, II
CASH MONEY HO'S
THE WIFEY I USED TO BE I II
**By Nicole Goosby**
TRAPHOUSE KING **I II & III**
KINGPIN KILLAZ I II III
STREET KINGS I II
PAID IN BLOOD **I II**
CARTEL KILLAZ I II III
DOPE GODS I II
By **Hood Rich**

# Money Game

LIPSTICK KILLAH **I, II, III**

CRIME OF PASSION I II & III

FRIEND OR FOE I II

By **Mimi**

STEADY MOBBN' **I, II, III**

THE STREETS STAINED MY SOUL I II

By **Marcellus Allen**

WHO SHOT YA **I, II, III**

SON OF A DOPE FIEND I II

HEAVEN GOT A GHETTO

**Renta**

GORILLAZ IN THE BAY **I II III IV**

TEARS OF A GANGSTA I II

3X KRAZY I II

**DE'KARI**

TRIGGADALE I II III

**Elijah R. Freeman**

GOD BLESS THE TRAPPERS I, II, III

THESE SCANDALOUS STREETS I, II, III

FEAR MY GANGSTA I, II, III IV, V

THESE STREETS DON'T LOVE NOBODY I, II

BURY ME A G I, II, III, IV, V

A GANGSTA'S EMPIRE I, II, III, IV

THE DOPEMAN'S BODYGAURD I II

THE REALEST KILLAZ I II III

THE LAST OF THE OGS I II III

**Tranay Adams**

THE STREETS ARE CALLING

**Duquie Wilson**

MARRIED TO A BOSS I II III

# Smoove Dolla

**By Destiny Skai & Chris Green**

KINGZ OF THE GAME I II III IV V

**Playa Ray**

SLAUGHTER GANG I II III

RUTHLESS HEART I II III

**By Willie Slaughter**

FUK SHYT

**By Blakk Diamond**

DON'T F#CK WITH MY HEART I II

**By Linnea**

ADDICTED TO THE DRAMA I II III

IN THE ARM OF HIS BOSS II

**By Jamila**

YAYO I II III IV

A SHOOTER'S AMBITION I II

BRED IN THE GAME

**By S. Allen**

TRAP GOD I II III

RICH $AVAGE

**By Troublesome**

FOREVER GANGSTA

GLOCKS ON SATIN SHEETS I II

**By Adrian Dulan**

TOE TAGZ I II III

LEVELS TO THIS SHYT I II

**By Ah'Million**

KINGPIN DREAMS I II III

**By Paper Boi Rari**

CONFESSIONS OF A GANGSTA I II III

**By Nicholas Lock**

# Money Game

I'M NOTHING WITHOUT HIS LOVE

SINS OF A THUG

TO THE THUG I LOVED BEFORE

**By Monet Dragun**

CAUGHT UP IN THE LIFE I II III

**By Robert Baptiste**

NEW TO THE GAME I II III

MONEY, MURDER & MEMORIES I II III

By **Malik D. Rice**

LIFE OF A SAVAGE I II III

A GANGSTA'S QUR'AN I II III

MURDA SEASON I II III

GANGLAND CARTEL I II III

CHI'RAQ GANGSTAS I II III

KILLERS ON ELM STREET I II III

JACK BOYZ N DA BRONX I II III

A DOPEBOY'S DREAM

By **Romell Tukes**

LOYALTY AIN'T PROMISED I II

**By Keith Williams**

QUIET MONEY I II III

THUG LIFE I II III

EXTENDED CLIP I II

By **Trai'Quan**

THE STREETS MADE ME I II

By **Larry D. Wright**

THE ULTIMATE SACRIFICE I, II, III, IV, V, VI

KHADIFI

IF YOU CROSS ME ONCE

# Smoove Dolla

ANGEL I II

IN THE BLINK OF AN EYE

By **Anthony Fields**

THE LIFE OF A HOOD STAR

**By Ca$h & Rashia Wilson**

THE STREETS WILL NEVER CLOSE

**By K'ajji**

CREAM I II

**By Yolanda Moore**

NIGHTMARES OF A HUSTLA I II III

**By King Dream**

CONCRETE KILLA I II

**By Kingpen**

HARD AND RUTHLESS I II

MOB TOWN 251

**By Von Diesel**

GHOST MOB

**Stilloan Robinson**

MOB TIES I II

**By SayNoMore**

BODYMORE MURDERLAND I II III

**By Delmont Player**

FOR THE LOVE OF A BOSS

**By C. D. Blue**

MOBBED UP I II

**By King Rio**

KILLA KOUNTY

**By Khufu**

MONEY GAME II

**By Smoove Dolla**

Money Game

**BOOKS BY LDP'S CEO, CA$H**

TRUST IN NO MAN

TRUST IN NO MAN 2

TRUST IN NO MAN 3

BONDED BY BLOOD

SHORTY GOT A THUG

THUGS CRY

THUGS CRY 2

THUGS CRY 3

TRUST NO BITCH

TRUST NO BITCH 2

TRUST NO BITCH 3

TIL MY CASKET DROPS

RESTRAINING ORDER

RESTRAINING ORDER 2

IN LOVE WITH A CONVICT

LIFE OF A HOOD STAR

Smoove Dolla

CPSIA information can be obtained
at www.ICGtesting.com
Printed in the USA
LVHW081734240222
711933LV00009B/857

9 781955 270403